Dead
But
Dreaming

Upcoming Releases from Miskatonic River Press

Dead But Dreaming II
edited by Kevin Ross & Keith Herber

For the Call of Cthulhu® Roleplaying Game

New Tales of the Miskatonic Valley
Edited by Keith Herber

Our Ladies of Sorrow
by Kevin Ross

The Outer Gods
edited by Keith Herber

and more...

www.miskatonicriverpress.com

Dead But Dreaming

edited by
Kevin Ross
&
Keith Herber

Miskatonic River Press

Westchester, New York • Lakeland, Florida
2008

DEAD BUT DREAMING edited by Kevin Ross and Keith Herber
Copyright © 2008 by Miskatonic River Press
All Rights Reserved.
For information contact Miskatonic River Press

Published in the United States by:

Miskatonic River Press
944 Reynolds Road, Suite 188
Lakeland, Florida 33801

ISBN 0-9821818-0-9

PRINTED IN THE UNITED STATES OF AMERICA

Copyrights

"Under an Invisible Shadow" by David Bain, copyright © 2002 by David Bainbridge

"Why We Do It" by Darrell Schweitzer, copyright © 2002 by Darrell Schweitzer

"The Disciple" by David Barr Kirtley, copyright © 2002 by David Barr Kirtley

"Fire Breathing" by Mehitobel Wilson, copyright © 2002 by Mehitobel Wilson

"The Thing Beyond the Stars" by Robin Morris, copyright © 2002 by Robin Reed

"The Call of Cthulhu: The Motion Picture" by Lisa Morton, copyright © 2002 by Lisa Morton

"Final Draft" by David Annandale, copyright © 2002 by David Annandale

"The Unseen Battle" by Brian Scott Hiebert, copyright © 2002 by Brian Scott Hiebert

"The Other Names" by Ramsey Campbell, copyright © 2002 by Ramsey Campbell

"Through the Cracks" by Walt Jarvis, copyright © 2002 by Walt Jarvis

"Epiphany: A Flying Tiger's Story" by Stephen Mark Rainey, copyright © 2002 by Stephen Mark Rainey

"The Aklo" by Loren MacLeod, copyright © 2002 by Loren MacLeod

"Bangkok Rules" by Patrick Lestewka, copyright © 2002 by Patrick Lestewka

"Salt Air" by Mike Minnis, copyright © 2002 by Mike Minnis

"Bayer's Tale" by Adam Niswander, copyright © 2002 by Adam Niswander

"Pay No Attention to the Man Behind the Curtain..."

Welcome to what I hope to be only the first in an ongoing series of Lovecraft inspired anthologies from Miskatonic River Press. The idea was first suggested to me by my formmer partners at DarkTales Publications, mostly because of my background with the *Call of Cthulhu* roleplaying game. I hemmed and hawed about it, unsure of what I would do, when I would find time, etc. Then I remembered Kevin Ross, my old buddy from *Call of Cthulhu* days. We always worked well together, and Kevin's taste in matters Mythos was fairly close to mine. I approached him about co–editing the project, and he was quick to agree.

But it was really a ruse. I would do the same thing to him with CoC projects, plan them together, then artfully dump the work load on Kev and go whistling off somewhere. He never seems to catch on…

So, off we go with it. This is pretty much Kevin's show so, love it or hate it, he's the guy you hold responsible. Unless, of course, this book turns out a monstrous hit. Then, like Joel Silver trying to take credit for *The Matrix*, I'll be whistling a different tune.

Keith Herber
Chicago, Illinois
March, 2002

Foreword: Into the Abyss

> "*The oldest and strongest emotion of mankind is fear, and the oldest and strongest kind of fear is fear of the unknown.*"

So wrote H.P. Lovecraft as the very first line of his seminal essay *Supernatural Horror in Literature*. Yes, it's familiar, and may even seem trite after all these years. But it points out *exactly* what's wrong with most Cthulhu Mythos fiction: the tangible elements that originally helped to make the Mythos new and strange and exciting (the books, monsters, gods, and so forth) have become hopelessly clichéd. And since they aren't unknown any more, they aren't scary any more. And in many cases the really frightening nihilistic philosophy behind it all has been neglected entirely.

One problem with most Cthulhu Mythos fiction is that the books, monsters, and such are not only over–used, but over–explained. Writers and editors who insist on endlessly quantifying and categorizing everything within the Mythos are sucking the life right out of it. If it's fully explained for us, it's not as scary anymore. In lamenting the too–pat wrap–up of the Laura Palmer murder in the *Twin Peaks* TV series, writer–director David Lynch once said something to the effect that he always feels disappointed when a mystery is completely solved. The same holds true for the horror story, and even more so for the Cthulhu Mythos story. Remember Lovecraft's words: "fear of the unknown."

It seems as if most modern writers who use the Cthulhu Mythos have forgotten that these are supposed to be *horror stories*. Many newer tales just aren't scary, they're predictable and tiresome. By simply reading a page or two of the average pastiche, you can just about guess how the story's going to end, right down to the phrasing of the final awful revelation *customarily rendered in italics for effect!* Some people find these pastiches entertaining, but for me, at least, they've sanded the disturbing philosophical edge off of them and made them bland and repetitive. Thanks to dozens and dozens of such anthologies, excessive familiarity with Cthulhu and company has bred contempt.

Another thing bothers me about how Cthulhu Mythos entities are portrayed: they aren't like us. They're aliens. So instilling them with human emotions and motivations trivializes them. They don't go around imprisoning each other with Elder Signs because some are "good" and some are "evil;" they don't make bargains for human souls, like some tentacle–festooned Satan; and they sure as hell don't stand around and prattle off their threats and plans like Fu Manchu or the villain in a James Bond flick. We are beneath them. Nyarlathotep seems to be the exception, but I think I've got him pegged: whereas humanity are just insects to the rest of Lovecraft's cosmic gods, and thus to be ignored, Nyarlathotep is that sick son of a bitch who delights in pulling the legs and wings off of us to see us twitch and crawl.

One of the things in particular that I think is lacking in most modern Cthulhoid fiction is the sudden realization—the "dark epiphany"—that not only is man not alone in the universe, he doesn't matter a damn within it. A lot of horror fiction deals with the discovery of monsters ("*Shriek!* There really *are* monsters!"), but in the end we're left with the comforting impression that mankind is still the dominant race in the universe. The best Lovecraftian fiction goes beyond that, revealing to its characters not only that "*Shriek!* There really *are* monsters!" but also "*Shriek!* Those monsters are as old as time, as vast as the ocean, and as powerful as the sun! Aaaaaah!" There is no God in Lovecraft's universe. Or at least, if there is, it's Nyarlathotep, and we're better off without him...

It's that dark epiphany that sets good Lovecraftian fiction apart from the mediocre (at best). Many horror stories deal with isolated, personal level horrors. Good Lovecraftian fiction can work on that level, but should also hint at the bigger picture, the grander canvas that encompasses all of space, time, history, evolution, and myth. Are we the most significant race in the universe? Are we important at all? Are we even who we think we are? Good Lovecraftian fiction is subversive enough to suggest—or brazenly declare—that the answers to those questions are No!, No, and No!?, respectively.

Perhaps the perfect example of what I mean by the dark epiphany occurs in Alex Proyas' film *Dark City*. Characters played by William Hurt and Rufus Sewell are searching for a place called Shell Beach, an elusive sunny haven that figures in the bizarre dark urban mystery they are desperately trying to unravel. They are hacking away at a city wall with pick axes, believing that Shell Beach lies just beyond. Instead, when their axes break through and the bricks fall away, they behold only a vast starry void, as far as the eye can see, in all directions. For the city in which they live is actually a spaceship, and they are captives subjected to experimentation by an alien race who are trying to figure out what makes humans tick, so that they can find a remedy for their own dreary doomed existence. It's a shattering moment, and you can see it on the faces of the protagonists.

And it's that type of thing that's missing from most post–Lovecraft Cthulhoid fiction, and thus why most of it fails. Again, some stories may scratch the surface of such dire philosophical moments, but many rely instead on none–too–cryptic passages from this or that fabled Mythos tome.

Which brings us, finally, to the book you now hold in your hands. When assembling this book, I wanted to set a specific tone, with a heavy emphasis on people being profoundly affected by contact with various Cthulhoid or Lovecraftian entities. Not just on a personal level, but in ways that would resonate not only within their perception of their world, but in the readers' perceptions as well. I sought stories that would challenge our knowledge of psychology, our perceptions of our own past, and question our place in the future. Here, among other things, you'll find star–spanning science fiction, a zombie holocaust, the horrors of two different wars, the psychology of cultists, voices from other dimensions and outer space, and frightening revelations about the origins of man. Needless to say, you'll find more than a few "dark epiphanies" here as well. I hope you'll find this book a little different from your typical Cthulhu Mythos anthology. Hopefully it'll give you a deeper look into the Lovecraftian universe, a look past the surface, into the abyss.

But remember what happens when you gaze into an abyss...

Special Thanks to: my old compadre Scott Aniolowski, for excellent contacts and good advice; Ramsey Campbell, Darrell Schweitzer, and Adam Niswander, for their generosity, patience, and understanding; and Doc Herber and Dave Nordhaus, for their trust.

Kevin Ross
eldritch gunslinger
Boone, Iowa
March, 2002

Table of Contents

A Foreword
by Keith Herber . . . . *vii*

More Foreword
by Kevin Ross . . . . *ix*

Epiphany: A Flying Tiger's Story
by Stephen Mark Rainey *3*

The Aklo
by Loren MacLeod *19*

Bangkok Rules
by Patrick Lestewka *31*

Why We Do It
by Darrell Schweitzer *47*

The Disciple
by David Barr Kirtley *51*

Salt Air
by Mike Minnis *59*

Through the Cracks
by Walt Jarvis *81*

The Unseen Battle
by Brian Scott Hiebert *97*

Bayer's Tale
by Adam Niswander *109*

The Call of Cthulhu: The Motion Picture
by Lisa Morton *125*

Under an Invisible Shadow
by David Bain *147*

The Thing Beyond the Stars
by Robin Morris *153*

Fire Breathing
by Mehitobel Wilson *163*

The Other Names
by Ramsey Campbell *179*

Final Draft
by David Annandale *193*

Dead But Dreaming

STEPHEN MARK RAINEY is author of numerous novels, including *Blue Devil Island*, *Dark Shadows: Dreams of the Dark* (with Elizabeth Massie), *The Lebo Coven*, and others. His short fiction has appeared in over ninety publications, including *Cemetery Dance, Shroud, Love in Vein II, Robert Bloch's Psychos*, and many more. For a decade, he edited the award–winning *Deathrealm* magazine, and has edited several anthologies. He currently lives in Greensboro, North Carolina, with his wife, Peggy. His entry in this anthology received an Honorable Mention in the 16th Edition of Datlow and Windling's *The Year's Best Fantasy and Horror*.

Epiphany: A Flying Tiger's Story

By Stephen Mark Rainey

I had just lit a cigarette and inhaled a deep lungful of smoke to celebrate my induction into the Hell's Angels' Aces Club when the staccato clatter of bullets across the back of my Tomahawk's fuselage rudely reminded me how quickly my own death could make an ace of some lucky Nip. A second later, I heard the distinctive *wham–clang* of a shell striking the armored plate just behind my head—the significance of which prompted me to scrunch down in my seat to present the fewest possible body parts to the gun barrels all–too–evidently aimed at my six. I bent the yoke to the right and kicked hard right rudder, rolling the plane inverted, and then yanked into a screaming split–S that sent me hurtling toward the earth at almost 400 miles per hour. Under the force of six G's, my vision went dim, and my body felt like it was going to burst through the floor of the cockpit. Another bullet shattered the rear glass of the canopy and smashed into my instrument panel, spraying crucial fragments of the gauges into my face like a little swarm of mosquitoes. I felt a warm rivulet of blood running down my forehead and over the bridge of my nose, but controlling the plane took both hands, and I could not release the stick long enough to wipe it away.

The P-40B could outdive anything the Japanese could throw at me, so I shoved the throttle up to war emergency power, hoping to put some distance between my pursuer and me. Another couple of heavy *thunks* behind my head let me know that I had not gained nearly enough lead. The enemy pilot had probably seen me shoot down one of the bombers he had been charged with protecting and was now out for blood. For all I knew, there might be a whole flight of the little yellow bastards glued to my tail, or swinging around for a scissors attack that would terminate my career as ignominiously as I had terminated five of theirs.

Chancing a look back, I saw a single, mottled green silhouette not 500 feet behind me. To my surprise, it was not one of the fixed–gear Nakajima I-97s we had engaged countless times over the skies of Burma, but a sleek, low–winged fighter with retractable landing gear. This must be one of their dreaded Type Zero fighters, I thought, which meant I was in big trouble. The Zero was faster and better armed than the I-97, but my Tomahawk could still outdive it—provided his bullets didn't kill me before I could make my escape. I saw tracers zipping past my canopy, so I banked left while forcing all my weight onto the right rudder pedal, sending the plane into a skid that I hoped would throw off the enemy's aim. The move cost me a little speed, but the enemy's tracers were now arcing wide to the left. Glancing back again, I saw the Nip suddenly cease firing and bank away to the right. He must have realized he would never be able to catch me and decided to rejoin his flight before I drew him too far from his wingmen and possibly into a waiting trap.

Trapping him, however, was the last thing I had in mind. Right now, the best I could hope for was to land my ace–making kill at Lashio and walk away unscathed. But the chances of accomplishing even that simple feat began to appear slim, for my engine suddenly stuttered and disgorged a thick gout of black smoke that washed over the windscreen, leaving a dark, almost opaque film of oil on the glass. Apparently, the Zero's guns had done more damage than I realized. Looking over my clocks, I discovered that I was as good as blind, for the shell had taken out the altimeter, vertical speed indicator, manifold pressure gauge, and compass. A disturbing silence over my headset, and a quick check of the transmitter, told me that the radio, too, was quite dead.

I had gotten separated from my wingman when I decided to go after a lone Ki-21 Sally bomber, which had ever–so–graciously exploded with only two bursts from my .50 calibers. Now, a thorough scan of the sky assured me that I was quite alone at something around 5,000 feet, heading roughly west. Assuming I survived the day, my flight leader, Charles Older, would surely have two fits over my flying off alone, and the Old Man—our reverent epithet for Gen. Chennault—might even ground me, despite my fairly spectacular aerial victory. That prospect was almost as depressing as the rough grinding sound that now came from my engine like the rattling cough of a dying emphysemic. I found that my engine temperature gauge still worked—somewhat to my chagrin—for it had gone into the red.

My best guess was that I was well over a hundred miles from Lashio. I could try coaxing the plane nearer to friendly territory, but getting all the way home was about as likely as bagging another kill.

The oil on the windscreen was now a solid sheet of black ink. I throttled back a little and cranked the canopy open so I could lean my head out to see where I was going. The improved visibility, however, only sent my spirits plunging further, for I now saw a trio of dark shapes, slightly above me at three o'clock, heading in my direction; a typical Japanese vic formation rather than an American four–plane section. As they closed in, I realized that these were Ki-43 Hayabusas—similar in design to the Zero, but underpowered and undergunned; not that this fact consoled me one whit under the circumstances. Even as I decided to go for broke and firewall the throttle, my engine choked a final time and died, spitting a few tentative streamers of flame from the exhaust pipes. Then the blaze began in earnest—a roiling firestorm that swept over the foresection of the fuselage toward the cockpit. I felt the heat as a few stray tongues of gold lapped in through the open canopy.

There was no way to ride this out. Praying the oncoming Japanese were poor marksmen—for they generally had no qualms about strafing a parachuting opponent—I unfastened my seat harnesses, made sure my chute was secure, and threw a leg over the rim of the cockpit. Then, pulling on the yoke with one hand to roll the plane on its side so I wouldn't be swept back into the tail, I kicked myself away from the firestorm that had been my trusty ride for the last three months, counted to five, and hit the silk.

As my chute billowed open, my back wrenched with the sudden deceleration. The roar in my ears became a gentle whisper, and the fierce, slapping wind in my face became a soft caress. I took a moment to evaluate the sensations in my body, noting that my hands and fingers tingled like I was clutching a handful of buzzing bees, and my feet felt like they had been immersed in flame. At least the pain in my back didn't seem serious; sometimes a chute opening can give you a case of whiplash. But at least until I hit the ground, I thought, it looked like I was going to live.

Or so I reckoned until I heard the low drone of engines drawing nearer. The three Japs were in formation above me, making an easy turn to the left—probably watching the plummeting fireball in the distance. I had intentionally waited until I had fallen a dangerous distance before pulling the rip cord, hoping they would either not see my chute open or at least decide against making a perilous strafing run at low altitude. As it was, looking down, I could see an endless expanse of dense rainforest no more than a thousand feet beneath my dangling legs. The thickly clustered trees did not bode well for a soft landing on mother earth; I was hardly out of the woods yet, so to speak.

A distant flare of light captured my attention, and I looked westward to see a ball of flame and smoke mushrooming into the air above the trees. My P-40 had met its end in the jungle, and I sincerely hoped my own fate would be less violent. It took several seconds for the thunder of the explosion to reach my ears.

The Japs continued on their course, and for a minute it looked like they, at least, would play no part in my possibly imminent demise. But before they disappeared into the distant clouds, the Hayabusas began to veer to the left, finally swinging back in my direction. As they descended rapidly and directly toward me, the sound of their engines rose angrily like an onrushing swarm of hornets.

"Jesus," I whispered to myself and reached for the Colt .45 secured snugly in my shoulder holster. Its solid weight reassured me, and I tried not to think about the effect that a stream of 12.7mm machine gun bullets would have on a human body. The lead plane looked like it had a flawless bead on me; its cowl–mounted guns virtually ensured that the pilot could not miss. As little more than a desperate gesture, I raised my .45, took as careful aim as I could, and tightened my finger on the trigger as the enemy fighter closed the distance between us at horrifying speed. When it was 300 yards away, I saw bright flashes above the engine cowling, and a stream of tracers slashed the air a mere yard to my right. I pulled the trigger, and the pistol jumped in my hands. I barely heard the report over the sound of the plane's engine. Again and again I fired, though I don't think a single bullet went anywhere near the cockpit. But somehow none of his shots came any closer than those first rounds, and in a second the fighter banked hard to the left and zoomed past me, catching me in its slipstream and spinning me like a top in my chute harness.

I expected the planes to come around again, but by now, I was drifting closer and closer to the treetops, and my first concern turned from my attackers to the thickly clustered branches below me. I could see no break in the foliage, no sign of solid earth beneath the verdant canopy. The harsh drone of engines grew louder again and, glancing eastward, I saw the three Japs turning toward me once again, evidently determined to make a last strafing run on me. I had expended all the ammo in the clip, so I could no longer even shoot back. The only comforting thought I had was that, by the time the fighters got back into firing range, I might already be hanging from a limb with a broken neck, spared the agony of having my body shredded by the enemy's bullets.

And then a curious thing happened. Between me and the approaching Hayabusas, a smoky, shimmering curtain seemed to suddenly rise from the jungle like a roiling heat–haze, only partially transparent, turning the fighters into distorted, birdlike silhouettes that appeared curiously two–dimensional. The sound of their engines became muffled, as if a solid mass had intervened itself between the planes and me. I was so surprised by this phenomenon that for a moment I forgot the fact that I was only seconds from striking the topmost branches of the trees below. And then, suddenly, the lead fighter seemed to slam into an invisible brick wall, for it exploded violently, hurling pieces of itself in all directions like a piñata full of liquid fire that had been smashed by a giant club. The other two Japs didn't even have time to react; a second later, both of them disappeared in fireballs like their leader, the sounds, if not the force, of the explosions also strangely muffled.

But my thoughts on this bizarre incident suddenly vaporized as my feet struck something hard. Looking down, I saw a giant hand of leaf–covered branches reaching for me, and I could not refrain from crying out in pain and terror as it first grabbed and then pummeled me mercilessly. Something jabbed me in the chest forcefully enough to knock the breath out of my lungs, and a flurry of stinging whips lashed my face, drawing blood. I had shut my eyes the moment I dropped into the branches, but even so, I had the impression of the light around me suddenly disappearing, as if I had fallen into a bottomless well. And then I felt myself jolted violently and painfully as my descent halted with shocking abruptness. Pain arced up my spine, and my body swung sideways as my chute tangled itself in the lattice of tree limbs. I struck the bole of a mammoth teak tree with terrific force, which drove the breath I had started to regain right back out of my lungs.

A minute or two passed while I hung dazed and incognizant, my mind unable to register the fact that I was no longer falling, that my feet were nowhere near the ground, or even that I was still alive. When realization finally began to dawn on me, the first thing that struck me was the utter silence of the surrounding darkness; a total, oppressive, and eerie lack of sound that made me wonder if I had been struck deaf. The second thing to become clear to me was that I was hanging a good hundred feet above the ground without so much as a nearby limb to grasp that might help me out of this predicament.

The darkness beneath the jungle canopy was almost as horrible as the silence. When I looked up, I could see multitudes of brilliant gold streamers fighting their way through minute breaks in the foliage, but none of them seemed to find their way to ground. Below, a shadowy pit leered at me like some sentient beast, daring me to unfasten my straps and drop into its eager maw. I might have risked it had there been a ghost of a chance I could survive the fall, even if it meant sustaining severe injuries. But the darkness could not hide the fact that such a drop would be indubitably fatal.

Reaching over my head—with some difficulty, as the harnesses restricted my arms' range of movement—I gave my lines a tentative tug, thinking I might somehow haul myself up to the limbs that had so rudely denied my passage to earth. I quickly found that this prospect offered little hope, for even that slight additional pressure sent me swaying precariously, and I heard the disturbing, unmistakable sound of fabric starting to rip above me. Even if I made my way into the branches of these tall teak trees, I would end up stranded in an only slightly less ticklish situation; shy of rappelling, or grappling my way with pitons, I could see no means of getting down the towering, limbless trunks. And as I had no means to do either, trying to unhang myself, at least for the moment, presented a graver threat to my health and well-being than remaining where I was.

I took a few deep breaths to steady my jangling nerves and tried to calmly assess the prospects for surviving the foreseeable future. It seemed that if I didn't move too violently, falling would not be an immediate danger. The survival kit fastened to my belt contained rations and water for three days, and some first aid supplies. I found that, at some point, I had shoved my Colt back into its holster. I still had two clips of ammo in my flight jacket, and a bowie knife sheathed at my waist. Other than a few bruises and minor lacerations, I didn't seem to have any injuries that would cause significant complications.

Aside from the small matter of being stuck at an unpleasant altitude without an obvious means of remedy, all in all, I was in pretty good shape.

Again, my brain began to register the fact that the darkness around me was uncharacteristically and uncomfortably silent. Ordinarily, the rainforest buzzed, chirped, whined, and yowled with the sounds of life. A couple of the airfields where I had been stationed had been built literally at the edge of the jungle, and even at a distance from the thick of the trees, one could always hear a cacophony of animal and insect sounds like a dismal orchestra. And now my thoughts returned to the bizarre phenomenon that had brought about the destruction of those three enemy fighters. Certainly, I felt no pity or sympathy for their plight; if I'd had my way, I would have dispatched them myself, had the condition of my airplane allowed it. However, the fact that something unknown and presumably still nearby could have accomplished such a thing gave me pause, for here I hung, a mere, mortal human in a desperate situation, subject to the whim of any natural—or unnatural—force that saw fit to have its way with me.

I could not help but believe that this uncanny silence was somehow related to the force that had destroyed the Hayabusas. I replayed the scene in my mind time after time—the vision of the strange, wavering haze that seemed to instantaneously emerge from thin air; the weirdly distorted silhouettes of the planes before they exploded, appearing almost as if through a convex, smoke–coated lens; the curious muffling of sound that inarguably corresponded to the manifestation of the thing I had witnessed. In all my experience as a fighter pilot, of walking hand in hand with death on a daily basis, I don't believe I had ever felt so thoroughly terrified by my condition as a solitary, fragile, and ultimately miniscule being as I did now.

I had bailed from my plane at approximately 14:20 hours; a glance at my watch told me that, a mere six minutes ago, I had been engaged in a heated battle in the sky. I desperately examined the trees around me, ever hopefully seeking some limb, some vine, anything that might offer a way out of this fix. But there was nothing. The nearest branches large enough to support my weight looked to be 15 to 20 feet away; too far to try swinging toward them, even if my chute didn't rip in the attempt. And again, even if I could reach them, I would never be able to make my way down the pillar–like trunks without falling.

I felt a pang of despair that I quickly forced behind the wall of discipline I had erected through months of training and exercise. I had to calmly consider the fact that, in a matter of moments, my whole perspective on the world had been profoundly altered. From the sky, the earth appears at once vast and minute; though the horizon stretches to limits that cannot be seen from any point on the ground, distances seem deceptively short. The river that meanders through an endless expanse of green forest may seem a scant few hundred feet away, while in reality it is many miles distant. The clouds that hover placidly nearby appear as soft, beckoning puffs of vapor, but if one flies into them, he may find himself caught in a blinding, swirling maelstrom that fiercely resists his plane's passage through it. From up there, one looks down and sees a small, mundane, peaceful planet that looks to be one thing, but that in reality may be something else entirely.

Here and now, beneath the dark jungle canopy, I had no idea what the world had become.

The one thing of which I could be certain was that no help was going to come. No one, save three dead Japanese pilots, knew where I had bailed out. I was still deep in enemy–occupied territory, where rescue attempts often failed even if the approximate whereabouts of a downed pilot were known. Scattered regiments of the Burma Rifles sometimes scouted behind the lines, but they would generally skirmish only briefly with the advancing Imperial Japanese Army, then retreat and regroup to fight again elsewhere. The chances of one of their patrols happening upon me were slim to none. No, if any human were likely to find me at all, he would almost certainly have a name like Fujiyama, or Takarada, or Yamamoto, or some such. In that event—truly a worst–case scenario—I would be better off releasing my straps and deliberately plummeting than allowing myself to be captured. The Nips were not known for the courteous and hospitable treatment of guests who did not have slanty eyes.

A sudden, nearby squawk startled me, sending my hand automatically flying for the pistol in my shoulder holster. My heart nearly burst two or three times before I realized that I had just heard the shrill call of a bird. A moment later, a distant chirp clawed its way through the silence, and after a few seconds, a reply came from somewhere yet farther away. And then the rainforest was alive again, with sounds of life exploding from every corner of the darkness: screeches, clicks, rustles, shrieks, grumbles, and grunts, all of which intimated a return of normalcy to the setting, for all that this did not reassure me. I knew that some of the creatures making those noises might not be much more congenial to visitors than the Japanese.

Before I consciously understood why my hand had reached into my jacket pocket, I had inserted a cigarette between my lips and was flicking my battered old butane lighter with trembling fingers. The smoke washing down my throat and into my lungs was an instant balm, a tiny little moment of routine that, beyond all proportion to the gesture, forced the alienness of my position to some far corner of my mind, allowing me to indulge for at least a scant few minutes in pure *joie de vivre*. I took a small measure of comfort in the fact that most of the pack was left.

I decided that, until I reached for my last cigarette, I would not even begin to contemplate how truly desperate a human being could become.

For a time, the cigarette satisfied me, permitted me to focus on something other than a hopeless outlook. But once I tossed the butt into the shadows below, I realized that I was uncomfortably hot. No, I was roasting. I was still wearing my heavy flight suit and jacket, and the temperature in the jungle was probably in the 90s. Up at 20,000 feet, in an unpressurized cockpit, with what is at the best of times an inadequate heater, the air is freezing. You can't wear enough layers up there, at least until the heat of combat begins to break the chill. The realization that I couldn't even maneuver myself to take off my jacket first depressed me, then infuriated me, for to me, the greatest anathema of all was to be forced to await death in utter discomfort. Unfortunately, nearly everything about my current situation pointed to just such an unhappy conclusion.

"Well, shit," I said out loud, my voice seeming to come from somewhere above the canopy, up in the free, blue sky.

I knew I was trying to think about anything and everything but the fact that something had destroyed those Japanese planes, had lurked in the darkness somewhere appallingly nearby, and had finally gone away, as the renewed voices of animal life clearly indicated. But my instincts screamed to me that, whatever it was, it had not gone for good. And while I might ordinarily wish to shake by the hand anyone or anything that could casually bat three enemy fighters cleanly out of the sky, I was fairly certain that I did not care to meet whatever nameless power hid in the depths of this rainforest.

I suppose that every fighter pilot constantly plots in his head all kinds of scenarios that might result in his ultimate demise, and I am no exception. Six months ago, I had resigned my commission in the Marines and joined the American Volunteer Group, commonly known as the Flying Tigers, mainly for the money and the chance to get away from routine duty stateside. And, at the time, it had simply seemed the right thing to do. Not that I had any grandiose ideas of glory or other such illusions. I knew I might die in combat, or be maimed for life, or get captured by a barbarian foe. I knew I might even be killed parachuting from a stricken aircraft. Yet I would never have counted on things working out quite like this. Of course, as yet, I was not entirely dead and therefore not quite ready to give up the ghost; however, I could scarcely afford to cling to any vain hope of rescue, or my final remaining moments, whenever they were destined to arrive, would be bitter indeed.

Sweat had begun to trickle down my forehead and into my eyes, and I was just about to remove my flight helmet when I felt a disconcertingly heavy thump right on top of my head. Something slithered onto my shoulder, and rolling my eyes downward, I saw a yellow and black centipede, some six inches long, with great stalk–like antennae and prodigious mandibles, deftly crawling toward my collar. With an involuntary cry of "yaaah!" I swept it away and watched it fall, wriggling, into the dark pit below.

So I resigned myself to suffering the heat and left my flight helmet on my head.

And smoked another cigarette.

Now and again, some brightly–colored winged beast would swoop past me, occasionally issuing an indignant squawk as if perturbed by the presence of an intruder in its territory—never minding the fact that the intruder was no less perturbed by his own inability to withdraw to better quarters. Once, I shifted restlessly, trying to make myself at least marginally comfortable, but a sharp ripping sound prompted me to freeze my muscles and hold my breath until I thought my lungs would burst. Finally, I exhaled deeply, now more angered than ever that I could barely even shift my position to keep my circulation from being cut off. My parched mouth and throat convinced me that what I really needed was a cold beer or several. This was a shame, since the knowledge that I would probably never be able to drink another only served to deepen my depression. I settled for carefully unhooking my canteen from my belt and taking a meager swig of water.

After a time, a light breeze came through, helping to relieve some of the heat and humidity, and a slight deepening of the darkness hinted that storm clouds might be gathering overhead. In this part of the world, dense cumulus clouds tended to pile up during the early part of the day and unleash furious torrents late in the afternoon. I welcomed the draft of cooler air, but I was now afraid that a storm would rock the trees enough to send me falling to the earth. But so far, the gentle wind had set me swaying only slightly, without dire effect. I took this as a good sign and lit another cigarette.

Soon, the rain began to fall, and low thunder rumbled menacingly in the distance. I expected a deluge at any moment, but the thick foliage seemed to be catching most of it. Only a few token droplets occasionally splashed onto my head and shoulders, and while I happily let any available water trickle into my mouth, I refused to lean my head back, open my mouth, and catch the rain, for fear that another centipede or kindred monster might drop in unexpectedly. The wind remained low and nudged me gently, but never buffeted me severely enough to dislodge me. And within a half–hour, the rain moved on, and I could feel the humid heat returning as the sun again reigned high above the jungle.

Now, though, as the afternoon began to wane, a dread of the coming night settled heavily upon me; every nerve in my body railed against the idea of hanging helplessly in this place once the sun had gone down. Something told me that the presence that had destroyed those Japanese fighters belonged to the night, and that I would be far better off simply perishing than coming face to face with whatever it was.

Indeed, as evening began to settle over the jungle, the sounds of the native creatures rose to an agitated cacophony, louder and more furious than anything I had heard in my experience. And as the last golden beams that filtered through the trees withered and died, thrusting me into a boundless ebony abyss, the shrieking chorus abruptly, spontaneously ceased. Like in those first moments after I dropped beneath the canopy, the silence screamed in my ears. I dreaded taking a breath for fear that the sound might be detected by something I fervently prayed did not exist.

It was too dark here. There should have been at least a single glimmer of moonlight breaking through the foliage. But there was not. Looking up, I tried to make out at least a single star, some reflection of light against a cloud.

Nothing.

For what seemed like hours, the loudest sound I heard was the accelerated, heavy thumping of my heart. The rational part of my mind tried to refute my perceptions, insisting that such a crushing silence amid a veritable ocean of life was simply not possible, that I was suffering some kind of delusion due to the trauma of being shot down and left in a position that almost certainly spelled death. Yes, it was much easier to wish that I had at least temporarily taken leave of my senses, that the source of this aberration lay within me, rather than out there. Because if it really were out there, then I hung on the verge of departing this existence with a world view so skewed from reality that my only choice in my last remaining moments was to despair.

Sound returned sometime later; minutes, hours…I have no idea. The sound was a low, whispering moan, drifting through the darkness from some vast distance like the wheels of a lonely train sighing on the rails. And then I heard—or rather felt—a deep, rumbling thud, not unlike the concussion of a howitzer from afar. I actually prayed that it was the sound of guns, if for no other reason than I could attribute it to human activity—a concept that had never been more important to me than it was now. But even that little hope was to be dashed; a few moments later, the sound came again…and again: a slow, rhythmic, bass beat like the living heart of an unimaginable giant. It did not seem to be moving closer or farther away. It *was just there*, and continued beating for an interminable period of time.

Then the nauseating feeling of being watched seized me like an iron fist.

Truly, I was being tortured or toyed with. I could feel my emotions being consumed, savored by the dark, malevolent presence that held dominion in this place. Though I could see nothing, I knew I could *be* seen; I wanted to cower, to hide, even to fall.

Or so I thought until I felt a subtle tug on my chute lines and I began to sway slowly back and forth.

I gasped in shock, for no wind had whisked through the trees to set me in motion. The deep thumping continued in the distance, but seemed to increase in fervor as I swung faster and faster. Unable to stop myself, I cried, "No!", only to hear my voice echo strangely through the trees, its supplicating tone becoming mocking, as if articulated by other lips. I was going to fall; I knew I was going to fall. Yet I could hear nothing of silk being shredded in the limbs above, and my perception that something had actually taken hold of the lines became more pronounced. The nightmarish ramifications of such a possibility froze my vocal cords so that I could not even cry out.

Then, in the limbs above, I heard the sharp snapping sound of limbs being broken. But I did not drop; if anything, I felt as if I were being lifted…and a moment later, a sudden brush of leaves and creepers over my head and shoulders confirmed this suspicion. I was being pulled out of the branches! But under the circumstances, rather than rejoicing, I could only wish to be right back where I had been for the whole of the afternoon. With this incredible development, I felt that my demise was no less certain, though perhaps more extravagant.

For a half-second, the idea of drawing my gun and firing blindly skyward had a certain morbid appeal, but the instinct for self-preservation prevailed, convincing me that I didn't really want to hasten my death or exacerbate any suffering my captor intended to inflict due to my annoying it. Now, in addition to a few branches, I felt the wind slapping my face, apparently from acceleration. The sheer helplessness I felt, the sense of being no more significant than an ant, very nearly reduced me to a mindless, cowering brute, no longer capable of reasoning or even coherent thought. A strange odor swelled on the wind, washing over me in thick and sticky waves—a stench something between roasted flesh and burning sulfur. It quickly became so cloying that I nearly retched.

But then, I beheld a wondrous sight: light! It was pale and ghostly and immeasurably distant, but it was light.

The moon. The gibbous moon looking down on the same expanse of jungle I had flown over earlier that afternoon. Though my present situation precluded anything like real jubilation, my heart nearly burst with excitement at the sight of something I had come to believe I would never see again. At least, I thought, if this were to be the moment of my death, I would feel less alone. The eye of the night itself would be my witness. The dispelling of that darkness did something to my soul, offered me a new hope that I could face whatever unfolded as something other than a paralyzed victim.

Peering all around me, I tried to determine what was happening to me—and *how* it was happening. The *what* was simple enough; I was flying through a moonlit, midnight-blue sky at an incredible velocity, being whipped by a frigid wind that—for the moment—felt like a refreshing draft after having sweltered in the ungodly tropical heat for so long. The jungle below appeared as an expanse of gray and black shadows, and far in the distance I could see a reflection of moonlight on water—undoubtedly the northern reaches of the Irrawaddy River. But even in the moonlight, I could no more see the thing that held me than I could in the pitch darkness. By all appearances, I was simply hurtling through the sky as if launched by a catapult. Looking up and back, I saw the remains of my chute trailing like the tail of a kite, and for a brief, hopeful moment I thought that, should my unknown means of suspension suddenly fail, my chute might actually open and lower me safely to the ground. But no; the lines had become hopelessly tangled, and I could see enough holes in the silk to confirm that the parachute was no longer a useful device.

All the time I was moving, I perceived a sense of climbing higher, and sure enough, I now realized the wispy clouds above no longer seemed so distant. Below, the earth had again become a black pit, disturbingly like the darkness of the jungle I had left behind. I knew I must have reached an incredible altitude, yet I could still breathe, and the fingers of the wind, though cold, did not claw painfully at me as I would have expected at this height and speed. I now began to consider the fact that I might actually be dreaming; certainly, it seemed the most logical possibility, although, in a curious way, the hard edge of reality had never seemed so profoundly clear to me. But perhaps the day's experience had proven too much for my mind, and it had simply vacated the fatally situated shell of my body. Might I not still be hanging from a tree in the Burmese jungle, suffering from hallucinations, or journeying into some dreamland whose vividness belied its fanciful origin?

Peering at the shadowed earth receding beneath me, and the ever-brightening crystal stars above, all I could think was, "Fuck, no."

Increasingly, I was coming to the chilling conclusion that I might already be dead.

I no longer had any idea whether I felt afraid, excited, sad, exhilarated, or any combination of these. As the seconds of forever ticked by, I looked down and saw only a faceless plane of pure black, while above and around me, the light of countless stars burned cold and unblinking, as if undistorted by any atmosphere. Their clarity, and their sheer number, convinced my last doubting sense that I had traveled somewhere far beyond the confines of my home planet; yet my body continued to function normally—if the term "normal" could any longer be applied.

With my perception of time completely ruined, I could not guess how long I remained in this state; it seemed a long time indeed. Eventually, though, I began to notice a subtle change in my environment, the vague suggestion that *something* was about to happen. I realized then that one of the stars ahead glowed more brightly than its neighbors, with a hot, greenish flame that blazed like a beacon. Soon, I could actually see it growing in size—or I should say looming larger, as my flight propelled me toward it. Something about this star unsettled me. Not the fact that I might fly into its heart and be instantaneously burned to a cinder, but that the thing was not actually a star at all. It was something else entirely.

Now, my mind shrieked that, surely, I *must* be dead, and that for my sins I had been condemned to some hellish domain more horrific than anything the Bible or other holy book could have elucidated. What I saw now was some kind of entity—sentient and malevolent—with a face of fiery plasma, surely thousands of miles across, watching and waiting for me. I could see a filmy, translucent sphere of many shifting shades of green enclosing what appeared to be a disembodied head, its features composed of pure jade flame and black shadow. Its eyes were hollow pits that opened to some distant dimension of outer space; ebony and impenetrable they were, yet undeniably cognizant. Though its face shone as bright as the sun, I could look upon it and see every detail all too clearly; in fact, try as I might, I could not avert my eyes.

The one undeniable reality of this nightmare was that the thing knew me, anticipated my arrival. I became aware of this as if a voice had told me so, though the silence through which I sailed was absolute, except for the frantic pounding of my own heart.

This awesome mien continued to expand in my field of vision, though I could tell it was yet hundreds or thousands of miles away. Within its globular, translucent casing, I could now see hundreds of spidery filaments of green light that formed intricate, weblike patterns woven through the space between the casing and the blazing face itself. Among the webs, I began to detect dark shapes that climbed and crawled along the strands, seemingly with purpose and deliberation, and when my mind began its inevitable conjecturing as to their intent, I could not keep from screaming loud and long into the void. I heard the sound in my ears, though whether anything actually escaped my lips, I cannot guess.

Gradually, I perceived a swirling black cloud forming in the center of the bright sphere, eventually growing larger and moving faster until it became a gargantuan, rapidly spinning vortex. But like the hollow eyes that peered at me, this aperture led to other spaces, for within it, I could make out indistinct shapes and colors as if through a warped lens, their forms suggestive but never quite defined. Above the pounding of my heart, I could now hear some kind of musical trilling and chirping—a shrill cacophony of unearthly woodwinds, like a threnody piped by insane flautists. For a moment it brought to mind the songs of the jungle insects I had left behind, and I felt a brief pang of longing to return to my own lost reality, where the only threat looming before me was a quick and possibly painless death.

The whirling maelstrom, limned by brilliant green highlights like a fiery corona, now dominated my entire field of vision. Still, around the edges of this yawning orifice, I could make out hundreds of those dark, spider–like things scuttling and skittering frenetically, as if laboring at some elaborate design. Deep within the depths of the chasm, something shifted and pulsated, like a half–seen black heart that beat rapidly and violently.

The sounds of piping rose to a fever pitch, and I rocketed into the chasm at unimaginable speed, surrounded on all sides by shades of ebony and onyx so intense they burned my eyes. How could my heart continue to beat while my body, my entire life essence, was consumed by this monstrous, infinitely–deep mouth that had opened in the void of outer space? Where was I going, and why? Try as I might, I could not will my heart to stop. I remained fully, horribly, and irrevocably alive and aware. The piping noises became a terrible, constantly rising shriek—not unlike the tortured wail of my old P-40's engine in its screaming, final dive.

Far away in the onrushing blackness, I saw a strange, distant glimmer; a greenish filament that wavered and swayed hypnotically, almost like the glowing tendril of some unimaginably huge sea creature. Then I saw more and more of these: a blossoming flower of glowing strands as wide as a galaxy. And the *things* were there, those black, crawling monstrosities, drawing nearer and growing larger with every second. Huge…ferocious…ravenous.

One of them, a scorpion–like thing, no smaller than the planet Earth itself, slowly rotated on an axis of arced, segmented appendages, its myriad eyes glowing red and green and focused on me. I saw a bristly array of jointed arms rise, and millions of barbed claws spreading wide as if to grasp an offered morsel.

Behind it, something even blacker, and infinitely larger, began to stir.

And I continued to hurtle toward it, screaming, as around me, the shrieking, piping music built to a crescendo—the sound of exquisite torment, simultaneously unleashed by every soul in God's own Hell.

✳   ✳   ✳

"Jack?"

The voice crept toward me through a black velvet veil, and at first I resisted reacting to it. I was warm and comfortable and somewhere far from the source of the sound.

"Jack, can you hear me?"

I thought perhaps the voice was calling my name. *Strange*.

I opened my eyes and saw light. It was vague, without form; but something in the light was moving. After some time, things began to crystallize and I saw figures—*human* figures—some shuffling around in a sunlit room, others leaning over me, their faces shadowed with concern.

One of them wore the long white coat of a military physician. Two other men in khaki stood next to my bed with searching, inquisitive faces.

"He's opened his eyes," the doctor said in a soft, baritone voice. "I think he's coming out of it."

With a concerted effort, I raised my hand, held it up before my eyes. It was my hand, yes. At least, it *looked* like my hand.

"Where am I?" I managed to whisper.

"Kunming," one of the khaki–clad figures said. After a time, I recognized him as my flight leader, Chuck Older. "We've pulled out of Lashio."

"How long have I been here?"

"Three days. You've been out for almost a week."

I struggled to remember what could have brought me to this point. The last thing I recalled was darkness...a terrible, green flame...a monstrous face...flying.

The other man leaned over me. It was Parker Dupouy, our vice squadron leader. "Thought we'd lost you, Wyndham. We'd about given up on you."

"How did I get here?"

Chuck Older gazed at me with concern. "A regiment of the Burma Rifles found you. Just a few more miles and you would have made Lashio."

I tried to remember, but something didn't seem right. "I was a long way from Lashio. I remember...I bailed out. Got hung in a tree."

"From what they told us, you must have been wandering around for days. Didn't know how you got there, where you came from. Doc says you've probably got a concussion, but otherwise, you're pretty sound. Could've been a lot worse."

"I made ace," I whispered.

Older and Dupouy chuckled. "You made ace," Chuck said.

I closed my eyes and took a deep breath. I could hear my heart beating in my chest. My back ached, but it was a dull, dimming pain that would go away soon.

"We'll leave you alone," Dupouy said. "Glad to have you back."

"Yeah," I said. "Me too."

*   *   *

The image in the mirror looked like the Jack Wyndham I had known forever. When I moved my arm, the image moved its arm. When I opened my mouth, the image opened its mouth. And the voice sounded like my voice. A tired, strained voice—as if my vocal cords had been worn out from screaming—but it *was* mine.

But there was something else I couldn't quite identify, something not right, both about the way I felt, and about the reflection in the mirror. I remembered hanging in a tree for what seemed like days; a terrible, complete darkness; the sounds of chirping and screeching; and then...that terrible music.

And sailing through the stars.

Yes...I had seen what I had seen; I knew this with the conviction of genuine faith. I had not dreamed it. I had not suffered any kind of hallucination due to extreme trauma. Where I had gone and why I had gone there, I did not know. The only thing I was certain of was that I *had* been there.

And I had brought something back with me.

When I gazed closely at the face in the mirror, the lines in the face, the shape of the nose, the jaw line, the stubble of beard, the narrow ears, all of these things were mine.

But before I had taken that last flight, my eyes had been violet blue, not jade green.

Yes, there was something out there, something *in* the jungle but *from* somewhere else. I don't know what it is, though I am sure it still holds sway in that dark, virtually untrodden corner of our planet. Or at least some aspect of it, some incomplete portion of a much greater whole. Part of it resides somewhere infinitely distant from this world, and I was, for a brief time, transported to its source.

I think it has come here to explore, to learn. Perhaps to judge. And now, another portion of it has left the jungle. Wherever I go, it is there. It is with me, and it sees through my eyes. It knows what I know, feels what I feel. I sometimes wonder if I am some kind of test subject, a laboratory animal meant to perform for its edification. I cannot forget that I was found wandering in a place far, far from where I bailed from my burning plane. I could never have escaped from that terrible plight on my own.

I am reasonably certain that, at that time, I did, in fact, die, but was sent back here for a purpose. *It* had a reason for taking my body and soul and then returning me to an environment where, through me, it may move among us, study us, determine our nature and methods; to simply learn what it means to be a member of the dominant species of this planet.

As for me, I will go back to my duty. To fly and fight, and very likely to kill or be killed.

As for the *other*, I do not believe that it is going to like what it finds here. And I very much doubt that we, as a people, are going to like the way that it shall one day reveal itself to all.

LOREN MACLEOD's "The Aklo" sprouted from a number of disparate sources, mainly H. P. Lovecraft, Michael Ondaatje's *The English Patient*, the movie *The Wizard of Oz*, and an article in *National Geographic* about the Sahara desert and its history, sunken volcanoes, abandoned oases, and mysterious stone circles. Loren herself has been writing edgy fiction since 1997, with stories published in a range of magazines, from *Harpur Palate* to *Flesh & Blood*. She was nominated for the British Fantasy Award and received honorable mention in *This Year's Best Fantasy and Horror*.

The Aklo

by Loren Macleod

From the papers of Nigel Moresby (b. 1902), reproduced courtesy of the Winthrop Museum of Archaeology and Ethnology, Boston, Massachusetts. Annotations by Louisa Curwen, Curator of Manuscripts:

September 24, 192–
Never kept a journal before, but Harry [Farallon–Jones] said it wouldn't be cricket not to, especially now that the two of us are embarking upon what is sure to be a terrific adventure. The muse of archaeology beckons irresistibly in the distance! Even to such bumbling amateurs as ourselves, it seems. Already put the screws to the EDSD [Egyptian Desert Surveys Department] for what half–baked charts they've made so far of the Great Desert, and persuaded the Egyptian Ministry of Defense to part with a map of the wartime petrol dumps left behind by the 18th and 214th Squadrons of the RFC [Royal Flying Corps]. Arrangements with Cairo Aerodrome for two decommissioned Gypsy Moths with long–range tanks and "air wheels," large balloon tyres specially adapted for taking off and landing on sand. In two days' time we fly down to Aïn Ballas, an oasis three hundred miles west of Thebes.

    Dinner and drinks with Harry, [Sir Geoffrey] Brokenborough, et al. at the Opera Casino.

September 25, 192–
Packed pocket compass, .318 rifle, tinned foods, medicines, and a bottle of brandy to ward off the chill of the 30° desert nights. Paid another visit to rooms in the Cairo Museum given over to the temporary storage of the artifacts recently recovered from the tomb of a pre–dynastic ruler in the Valley of the Kings. Among these is a painted wooden war chariot whose elevated front panel continues to baffle the experts. The two side panels illustrate the ruler's subjugation of black Nubian warriors from the lands south of the First Cataract (the historical Mazoi, Sethu, etc.), and of brown–skinned Libyan tribesmen, ancestors of the present–day Touareg and Reguibat. The ruler himself is depicted

with the dark reddish complexion of the ancient Egyptians. The front panel, however, shows a tall, sharp–featured man with pale orange eyes and snow–white hair and skin. Birdlike white wings sprout from his shoulders, but a cartouche of proto–hieroglyphics identifies him not as a deity, but as a prince of the "Aklo," a mysterious people whose history and origins remain completely unknown, although Harry says he remembers a passage from a 13th century mystical Arab text, the Kitab al Kanuz [Book of Hidden Treasures], which talks about some sort of forbidden harem–city with "walls of jet and women of ivory" located at the foot of a mountain deep within "the trackless wastes of the Sahara [desert]."

A clever fellow, Harry. Always ran rings around our tutors at Eton.

Brokenborough threw us a splendid bon–voyage party at the Pasha Hotel. Everyone believes we've gone mad, and expects we won't make it further than Aïn Ballas.

[*break*]

Can't sleep, and it's not because of the champagne. Reread year–old news dispatch regarding discovery in northern Abyssinia of hominid skull at least twice as old as Piltdown Man, which would date it to circa 100,000 B.C. That is very old, indeed. [Dr. Eustace] Starkweather, the leader of the Abyssinian expedition, is a colleague of Charles] Dawson, who unearthed Piltdown Man in Sussex in 1911. Starkweather's skull manifests an evolutionary stage between Piltdown and an ape, and he has outraged the scientific community by declaring it the common ancestor of both the Negro and Caucasoid races. However, I can't help thinking that if he is at least correct in locating the dawn of all mankind on the African continent, then this Aklo chap could be a forefather of the Stone–Age Europeans (i.e. Piltdown) and, if so, must belong to an entirely separate branch of early homo sapiens. Harry enthusiastically agrees my theory's worth looking into, hence our own ambitious little expedition.

September 26, 192–
Departed Aerodrome at ten o'clock and climbed to 1,500 feet above the white-washed roofs and minarets of Cairo, the glittering green ribbon of the Nile, a suburb of adobe mud huts, and then the Pyramids at Ghizeh. What an attestation of engineering and imaginative genius they are! Three geometric monoliths towering above a rocky plateau strewn with the mastaba [tombs] of lesser nobles. And beyond them the illimitable emptiness of the Great Desert and its thousands of miles of barren, roadless terrain. According to Harry, the Arab name for it is bahr belà mà, "sea without water," an appellation clearly inspired by the ripples of sand sheets and waves of smooth–sided dunes. The sky was azure blue and the sun glared off the fuselage like the very eye of Ra. For hours there was nothing except the roar of the propeller, the shadows of the Moths gliding over

The Aklo

the soft yellow dunes, and the gusts of the hamattan, a perennial wind.

England seems very far away and dreamlike, a mirage of damp gardens and drizzly weather. (Note to self: write Mummy upon return to Cairo.)

Smelled Aïn Ballas, the sudden liquid in the air, before a line of darkness broke the horizon and resolved into an oasis with palm trees, adobe dwellings, and murky pools where water had bubbled up through a fissure in the earth's crust. As soon as we landed a horde of ragged urchins descended upon the aeroplanes, and I disbursed as many coins as I had in my pockets. We asked our way to the hut of Abu Kabar, a retired caravan–guide of the semi–nomadic Touareg, from whom Brokenborough heard an intriguing anecdote (he passed through Aïn Ballas during a survey funded by the RGS [Royal Geographic Society] in 1924.) Abu Kabar wore the traditional, indigo–dyed robes of his tribe, and his eyes had gone milky with cataracts from decades of staring across the sun–blasted reaches of sand. He and Harry began a lively conversation while I stood dumbly by like the village idiot (my Arabic's only adequate for haggling over Greek amphorae in the Khan el Khalili bazaar). Abu discussed a cluster of three peaks to the southwest, "several days' journey by camel," where there were caves full of paintings by "the first infidels," including one, we deduced from his description, of the Aklo. Then he warned us that now was the season for the dreaded simoom, a rare but tremendously powerful storm first described in Herodotus' The Histories [ca. 425 B.C.] as being capable of moving mountains of sand and engulfing entire armies and cities which are never seen again.

Travelling in the desert is a risky and unending lottery of perpetual uncertainty. It reminded me of the tragic story of the Basingstokes, who took their six–month–old son on an impromptu jaunt in an A–type Ford. The hamattan stirred up a dust–cloud and they lost their bearings and drove into a field of stone splinters that punctured the tyres. As their situation grew desperate, they cut themselves and gave the child their own blood to drink. The baby died first, his lordship a few days later, leaving his wife alone in the vast desert. But as she lay slowly dying of thirst, she wrote in her journal about the beatific silences and swarms of stars in the night sky.

September 28, 192–

Thousands of years ago the Great Desert was a fertile environment with lakes and seas; there are pinnacles eroded by rainfall, mineral–lined depressions, cracked dry wadis [riverbeds], and water–carved canyons and ravines.

Stopped to refuel at a petrol dump cached near a mushroom–shaped mass of pebbly sandstone. Amusing to think how these relics of the Great War are now being put to peaceful use.

Flew due west until three granite massifs rose out of the plain: the Jebels Khassou, Al–Qarat, and Ouweynath, first sighted by Prince Kamal el Din's ground expedition in 1919. The wadi is shut in by these jebels [mountains], which rise above it in wind–scored tiers and fall in 1,000–foot precipices to the crocodile-infested pools below. We landed and were hailed by a solitary camel-herd with the prognathous features and elaborate facial scarification of the Nubian–descended Senussi (archaic: Sethu) tribe. We were wary of him at first, Harry having mistaken his black robes for those often worn by the nefarious Reguibat, pirates of the desert who descend upon caravans to steal precious supplies of salt and firewood. But his name was Toubou and, like Abu, he was a jolly, good–tempered fellow and wasn't a bit cowed by the aeroplanes, having seen plenty of [Sopwith] Camels and [Martinsyde] Elephants dogfighting with the Germans over the desert during the War. He lit an extremely primitive lamp, a wick of braided reeds stuck in a lump of camel fat, and guided us through the cave–galleries tucked under the cliffs narrowly overhanging the wadi. These were extraordinary: prehistoric rock engravings of sabre–toothed tigers and other long–extinct animals; paintings of lakes populated by turtles and hippopotami; ochre–skinned people swimming and catching fish with their bare hands; pregnant goddesses; deities of both sexes with the heads of animals (jackals, ibis, etc.) which must precede the ancient Nilotic pantheon. And then, on the wall of one chamber: the Aklo. Unmistakably. White–skinned and –haired. The artist had drawn about two dozen men, then surrounded the lot with a large, arrow–spiked circle. All of the Aklo sported ochre–coloured, geometrical wings with spans far exceeding the height of the figures themselves. Harry referred these appendages to Toubou, who launched into an animated discourse on djinns, which even I know means "genies."

Harry took snap–shots of everything with his Kodak box camera and the additional light of a portable carbide lamp.

Ate a raw–tasting mix of ground grains, goat cheese, and local water for dinner. Toubou offered it with the timeless hospitality of his people and it would have been churlish to refuse. So I obliged, grimacing. Then Toubou showed us a suppurating lesion on his leg, begged us to cure it, and also asked to try on our leather helmets and goggles.

September 29, 192–
Despite Harry's objections I gave Toubou some boracic powder for his sore, and then we took off to the south. After 100 miles or so we passed over the object Toubou had told us about, a stark circle of stone he astutely identified with that drawn about the Aklo. This at approximately 20° –' N, 25° –' E. About a half–mile away in each of the four cardinal directions are four arrows of similar construction pointing away from the circle. An uncanny thing. We landed and estimated the circle to be 75 feet in diameter. Harry took several photographs of it. We have no theories about its age or origin, only that it was meant to be seen from the sky, although it doesn't appear on any of the EDSD or Defense Ministry maps. But then very little is indicated in the region west of the Jebels and south of the Tropic of Cancer.

Took a 200–mile detour to the northeast to refuel at the petrol dump in

The Aklo

Ouarza, a ghost–oasis the tribes refuse to visit because of its former career as a station along the slave route. We explored a series of collapsed adobe buildings of relatively recent vintage, and an ancient cave partially blocked at the mouth by a tumbled–down wall of rough, unmortared stones that was at least ten feet thick. The entrance was equipped with an immense boulder that could be rolled sideways to seal the cave from the inside. Nothing in there now except scorpions and snakes. Stepped on and crushed a pale rock which turned out to be a human jawbone with teeth still attached. Decided to leave at once; the atmosphere was distinctly creepy, even in broad daylight.

Camped next to the circle and endured a dinner of digestive biscuits and tinned beef washed down with wadi–water from one of the two goatskins Toubou kindly provided us with. Dreadful stuff, desert water: warm and thick and dirty with sand and sludge. Had a bit of fun with the goatskins, though; these are poorly cured and sewn together in a way that retains the animal's shape, with the legs comically serving as drinking spouts. We laughed and told jokes and Harry called me Niggle."

I hate it when he does that.

[*no date*]

I cannot, I simply cannot, I cannot describe the events that have befallen us since we encountered that abominable compass of stone[.]

October 2, 192–

Finished the brandy to steady my nerves, although this will only result in greater thirst. Harry had a theory about the circle's south–pointing arrow, which is larger than the rest. Followed its lead and, after about 100 miles, an isolated, steep-sided jebel reared abruptly on the horizon. Ascended to about 2,000 feet and found ourselves over an extinct volcano whose sunken caldera held a number of dark objects that did not immediately suggest a natural origin. We overshot the caldera, then banked sharply to the right and turned around for another look. To my astonishment, these objects were rectangular solids with pyramidal roofs reminiscent of Egyptian architecture. We circled the caldera repeatedly, gradually losing altitude until we had dropped inside the rim. The city was laid out along a grid of minor and major thoroughfares, including one grand avenue which bisected the whole on an east–west axis and was long and wide enough to accommodate the aeroplanes. Landing on it seemed an implicitly better idea than attempting to scale the old volcano on foot and trying to make our way down into the caldera, as the only apparent means of negotiating the precipitous inner slope was a rock staircase with great pieces fallen out of it and terminating in a cracked stone platform at the top of the rim. The city was comprised of scores of towers, row upon row of austere, obelisk–shaped buildings of uniform height whose proportions became terrifying and oppressive once allowances were made for the fact that the city was at least half–buried in sand. I should not have been able to explore it but for the presence of Harry. We quit the Moths and walked dazedly down the avenue past the upper floors of these towers, which had been built from fitted blocks of black volcanic basalt and were now significantly eroded by the elements. There must also have been one or more catastrophic geological upheavals in the past, for mighty fissures ran up the walls of some, while others had been reduced to mountainous piles of rubble. The bright–yellow blanket of sand contrasted starkly with the pitch–black masonry. Sunlight glittered on shattered panes of flawlessly transparent mica set into large, square windows which gaped open like the entrances to tombs. Harry clutched his camera and I my rifle, although who or what we expected to encounter at that point is impossible to say. It is difficult even now to communicate a coherent idea of our thoughts and feelings while we proceeded awestruck along that dust–smothered avenue; the sheer appalling antiquity and monotony of the architecture rendered us mute as we continued bewilderedly, almost unconsciously, toward the colossal structure at its eastern extremity, which we arrived at after climbing the upper portion of a Cyclopean flight of steps to the floor of an unadorned, vaguely Graeco–Roman portico upheld by massive pylons. From there we were able to turn around and survey the city from a suitably elevated vantage point, and were impressed all over again by the odd, repetitive geometry of the towers. Harry took more photographs.

The atmosphere was one of millennia–long abandonment and silence. There was no movement or sound in any quarter of the city, only the faint howling of the hamattan as it blew over the top of the caldera. Then we noticed a rank odour issuing from the thirty–foot entrance to the structure, which we assumed to be a temple or seat of municipal authority. It cut through the clean air of the desert like a knife. We wondered at its source, then determined to investigate the interior.

[*break*]

Am exhausted. The sun was very bad today. Whenever I crawled out from under the shade of the fuselage it stabbed me through my head and neck. Plenty of water left in my goatskin, at least.

October 3, 192–
Words fail to adequately describe the psychic cataclysm precipitated by our exploration of the picture gallery, a vast, rectangular hall only minimally drifted in with sand and pierced by high–set windows that spilled light onto floors and walls of polished obsidian. Here were thousands of intricate bas–reliefs carved with all the fiendish talent of the Aklo. These detailed pictures demonstrated their mastery of the principles of flight, how they fashioned one–man gliders

from the wood of extinct tree ferns and the thick, hairy skins they flayed off the living backs of the prehistoric cave–dwellers. They also devised a lightweight, portable catapult of sorts that could be reassembled on the ground to launch missiles composed of a burning substance deep into the caves to flush out the doomed inhabitants. That apparatus was far surpassed in terms of sheer diabolism by yet another, an implement shaped like a violin bow, but with the string wrapped around a crystal–pointed stake and used by the Aklo to drill holes into the cranium via a rapid, forceful, side–to–side motion. After subduing their victims with apparently preternatural strength, they would bore the holes and insert a handle of sorts into each hole to transport their flailing, screaming captives in mid–air back to the caldera. Many expired from hemorrhage during the gruesome skull–drilling operation, while others succumbed in transit. With a shock, I remembered Ouarza and the walled–in cave designed, I realise now, to repulse the Aklo. It is also clear now why that pre–dynastic ruler chose to emblazon his war chariot with a white, winged image. Why else, indeed, but to try to instill terror in those he desired to conquer? Although by his time the Aklo must have been extinct for centuries, and even their legends grown faint, for there are no depictions of these lethal beings in later Egyptian art, and written history is completely ignorant of them except for the cartouche and the one ambiguous reference in the Kitab al Kanuz, whose authorship besides is suspect and obscure.

But I digress. According to the bas–reliefs, those who died of their wounds were the lucky ones. The fate of the survivors is nearly unutterable. Buoyed by the hamattan, and guided by the crude stone compasses they had installed on the desert floor, the Aklo were able to navigate home post–raid, and then their loathsome metropolis became the scene of atrocities to render those of the Inquisition friendly by comparison. The captive cavemen were worked to death quarrying volcanic rock, carving it into prodigious blocks, and laboriously hauling them up temporary earthen ramps to construct the towers. The Aklo laughed as the women were violated with grisly implements designed to slash their insides to ribbons and then thrown into vats of boiling water.

[*break*]

Oh, the torments endured by our wretched, ape–like ancestors! The agonies visited upon them for as long as they could stand for the entertainment of the Aklo. There were vivisections of babies, children, and pregnant women. They were imprisoned in tiny wicker–work oubliettes until they went mad from immobility and mutilated themselves with stone knives gleefully supplied by their jailers. The Aklo devised tortures so hideous that the poor sufferers chewed off their own hands and feet in the attempt to distract themselves from the pain [...] activities culminating in the eating of human flesh and the drinking of their fermented blood.

Who could have created these infernal creatures? Or have allowed them to flourish as they did? As we staggered silently from one ghoulish scene to the next I was overcome not only by their nightmarish deeds, but also by a spiritual dislocation born from the realisation that the myth of a merciful God, spoon–fed to us from infancy along with the pudding and trifle, is just so much sugar–coated nonsense.

[*break*]

I must put these blasphemous thoughts aside, must look up at the night sky and feel the presence of a benevolent Creator. I remember the serene words of Lady Basingstoke, but the stars are like cold eyes peering down at me.

No Aklo females. An utter absence of them in the reliefs. The males begat offspring off the women they stole, then killed the mothers and any hybrid daughters thus produced. Not keen on the ladies, I'm afraid. A sector of the city was reserved for the rearing of the male issue, who mostly resembled their fathers in appearance and always took after them in terms of later behaviour.

October 4, 192–
I continue [...] distracted by the bas–reliefs, Harry and I completely forgot about that odour. Now, as we approached the end of the hall and another thirty–foot doorway, it occurred to us that we were surrounded by a putrid stench suggesting a subterranean charnel pit. This stench was tempered by blasts of sulphur and bitumen apparently emanating from the gulfs below the floor of the caldera. When we stepped into the next chamber, which was windowless and had a vaulted ceiling as high as a cathedral's, we looked down at our feet and found ourselves teetering on the edge of an abyss with an orange spot of live magma glowing many fathoms down at the bottom. Narrow ledges of rock jutted out from the black walls of the abyss, and these were thickly covered with a pale, calcareous powder. Suddenly, I understood. "Harry," I croaked. My throat was parched. I turned to the strangely radiant face of my friend. "This is where they threw all of the bodies. The bodies of their own dead and what was left of those aboriginals." Harry smiled and nodded and coughed. The igneous emissions were noxious and the volcanic heat billowing up from the depths of the abyss was almost unbearable. "It's how they got to the surface, too," I added.

I believe this monstrous race sprang, like Evil itself, from a primordial hole in the centre of the earth.

October 5, 192–
We were only halfway back to Ouarza for refueling when we crossed paths with a simoom. Below us the desert began to boil, and then the sand leapt up to

form titanic columns at least three thousand feet high. The storm advanced in our wake at a speed that overtook both planes within moments, and I saw flashes of lightning within its furious yellow ramparts. The storm roared and arched over us like a tidal wave. It seized Harry first in its mighty paws, buffeted his plane about in an almost playful manner, and then swallowed him whole. Scant seconds later it caught up with me and drove my plane down and into the crest of a petrified dune, clipping both the wheels and mangling the wings. I woke up with a bloody face blistered after hours of roasting unconscious in the sun. Some of my ribs are broken, too, I think.

[*break*]

My brain is a many–chambered horror. It moves into realms of fantastic conjectures, manufacturing links between the modern world and this lost world of the Aklo. Is it really lost? I do not think so. I see in my mind's eye a mass migration, a winged exodus from the city. I see the Aklo ascending the stone staircase and gathering for the last time on the cracked stone platform. I see them abandoning their ancestral aerie and flying north, guided by the great compasses to the unknown territories lying across the Mediterranean. I see them dispersing northeast and northwest, then discarding their gliders to melt anonymously into the Stone Age populations of Europe and Eurasia. Yet what caused this airborne diaspora, this abrupt dissolution of such a perversely insular society?

I know, and the certainty of the answer hums in the marrow of my bones, causing vivid pictures to leap up and caper against the hot, blue sky [...] albino bats descending upon me like a flock of harpies.

With precise, daemonic intuition, the Aklo foresaw a catastrophic climatic revolution: the coming desertification of their lush and amply populated hunting grounds. More importantly, they were able to divine the eventuality of mankind's technological advancement in the latter's domestication of fire and, later, the construction of impregnable cave–fortresses, such as that at Ouarza. They knew this would be followed by the taming of the horse and the development of weapons that could launch sharp wooden or stone projectiles with superior force and accuracy. Their predictions [...] the emergence of powerful, warlike civilisations after the Bronze and Iron Ages. Dynastic Egypt and Sumeria. Babylon and Assyria. Greece and Rome.

But what remains of their malign legacy? The interbreeding with the Neolithic tribes in the northlands must have resulted in [...] tell you, their blood runs in ours. Germany and Russia. England and France. America. The Moth that shelters me today will get bigger, nastier. It will grow a carapace of steel and drop titanic explosives, sophisticated bombs that murder millions on impact and poison the land and water for hundreds of miles in every direction!

Our proximity to the city must have stimulated this hereditary clairvoyance coursing through my veins, this damned latent [...]

[*break*]

Only a little wadi–water left in my goatbag. There is an oasis called Zer on one of the maps, near the First Cataract. I have abandoned the Moth, not merely to improve my own chances of survival, but because I must live to deliver this warning to all mankind [...] to avoid future apocalypses and atrocities [.] In a shameful fit of cowardice I had thought to escape southwest, toward Abyssinia, and then into the dark, impenetrable jungles of the African interior, deep into the blessed realms of the Negro, to fabled Mgolo and G'aa and Ib, where I would never behold nor fear another white face again [...] merciful God, the ice in my dear Harry's eyes when I gave the medicine to Toubou and money to those urchins and [...] the look on his ecstatic face, enchanted by those horrible pictures [...] the blood–taint of those creatures [...] I see the letters AH and a second and then a third Great War [...] oh, their hatred of other people and races [...] astronomical mushroom clouds [...] and breeding fatal diseases in secret underground laboratories to exterminate [...] Confound it! Harry's pictures are lost [...] walking due east now [...] Ak in Aklo = auc in Caucasus? [...] hence Caucasian? I think [...] now about the hole in the cranium of Starkweather's sk[ull.]

[*Curator's postscript: The body of Henry (Harry) Farallon–Jones was never recovered. This journal and the corpse of Nigel Moresby were found by nomads a mere two hundred yards from the tiny, then–uncharted oasis of Akhailah in what is now northeastern Sudan. A team of British and Egyptian investigators led by Sir Brokenborough was dispatched to the area and verified the existence of the stone circle and volcano–city. A planned excavation of the latter was permanently derailed when quakes along the Sidi Ahmet fault–line caused the floor of the caldera to collapse in 192–.*]

PATRICK LESTEWKA is the author of *The Preserve* as well as *Rust and Bone* and *The Fighter* written under the name of Craig Davidson. His nonfiction has appeared in *Esquire, The Washington Post, Nerve, The London Observer,* and others.

Bangkok Rules

by Patrick Lestewka

My name is Junior Covington. I kill folks.

Heeeeyy...chill *out*, man. I'm not on some Manson–Bundy–Dahmer kick, all right? Check my pad: no decomposing bodies, no lamp shades made out of skin, no fingers floating in the pickle jar. For me it's always been a means to an end. Found out a long time ago that I was good at making people go away, and fell in with some folks who paid me up front to do the one thing I seem preternaturally predisposed to do. Probably could do something else but what the hell; never did go to school, too much pride to flip burgers.

Always was a punk. I can be honest with myself now. My shrink tells me it's healthy to confront my latent feelings of inferiority; says it's the only way I'll be able to reconcile myself with the essential duality of my nature. Sometimes I think that bitch is full of shit, but I can see the degrees on the wall same as anyone. Besides, she's got this whole Erica–Jung–sister–confessor–whore thing going on; I'd pay her fee just to be able to stare at those legs for an hour. Funny how things work, huh? Here she went to school for ten years to headshrink a guy who jacks people for a living and spends his session gawking at her thighs while all of her hard–learned analysis drifts in one ear and out the other. She might as well be a stripper in a champagne room—wouldn't need a degree for *that*. Besides, I think my inner child was stillborn, so none of it's going to do me any good anyhow. But I like telling people I'm in therapy. So I go.

"Front desk, Elliot speaking."

"Yeah, it's Covington. Be down in a minute."

"Very well, Mr. Covington. Shall I have the car brought around?"

"Yeah, do that, but get somebody other than that Indian. Last time he brought it around the upholstery smelled like ragged ass for a week."

"Certainly. If you'd like we could have him fired. I'm sure management would be more than willing."

"Ah, Jesus, Elliot. I don't need that. Fucking bad Karma, man. Just keep him away from the car, that's all I'm asking."

We evolved from a society of hunters and gatherers, you know that? If you were a gatherer, you spent your days rooting around in the dirt, digging for tubers or picking berries and nuts in the forest—that was your job, what you did to merit inclusion in the tribe. If you were a hunter you spent the day out in the woods with a bow and arrow, shooting at buffalo and elk and birds. Your job was harder—it's a lot easier to pick a berry than to bag a deer, right?—but your position in the tribe was higher than the gatherers because your contribution of flesh was prized over theirs. But if you couldn't catch anything, or if you went long without bringing back meat, you were demoted. And if you didn't accept your demotion you were exiled, or killed.

Some people think we've evolved, and in a lot of ways we have. But underneath it all we're the same: hunters and gatherers. Most of us wander through our lives meekly rooting around—in offices, stores, banks, bureaucracies, wherever—looking for those little nuts and roots and berries that will get them through to the next day. There are still hunters stalking through the urban jungle, though. We're marking prey—the corpulent, the weak, the targeted—and taking it down. For a shitty hunter the penalties are basically the same: you go into federal exile for a couple years if you're lucky, or *you* get jacked. For the few of us who are good at what we do, selectively thinning the herd can be rather lucrative.

And I'm good. A rep is a hard-won thing in this business. You don't earn one without establishing a decent track record. Major thing is not to leave the mark breathing. Go ahead and leave a body, that's fine unless the contract stipulates otherwise, but *don't* leave the scene until you know the mark is coffin meat.

You might think that's a silly rule—*of course* the guy's gotta be *dead*, right? I mean, that's what you guys get *paid* to do—that what you're thinking? Yeah, well, you'd be surprised how many greenhorns and even a few vets will charge into a room, pop a few slugs into a target and hit the bricks. Guys who do that don't really understand the resiliency of the human body at all. Sure, you drill a guy twice in the melon and you're golden; you tag him with a couple well-placed chest shots and you're probably on easy street, too. But if you fire off a few rounds, see the guy go down, assume he's toast and head for the open road, you're making a big mistake. I heard about a mark who took six shots—two in the thigh, one through the cheek, one in the stomach, one in the shoulder and a cheap plug in the crotch—still managed to get up, grab a gun off the night table, stagger to the window and blow the hitter's head off as he climbed down the fire escape.

No shit.

I got a sixty-second rule. Drop the hammer and then observe for a minute. If you're *sure* the guy's fit for a toe tag, leave. I time it; I don't care if I hear sirens, I make sure the guy is *dead*—not unconscious, not playing possum—but stone dead. It's the little things that give a hitter longevity; attention to detail helps build a strong rep. I sleep better at night without the spectre of some pissed-off mark that I didn't rub properly sitting in a hotel room, nursing his wounds and biding his time. I got enough other shit on my mind. Like this meeting I've gotta get to.

"Good afternoon, Mr. Covington."

"Afternoon, Elliot. Car ready?"

"Yes, sir. Joshua should be waiting outside."

"Thanks. Messages?"

"None today. Were you expecting something?"

"Nothing particular, no. I have a meeting with Mr. Hariyoshi."

"Very well. Would you like me to make any callers aware of your location?"

"No."

Elliot's a good shit—doesn't bother me with shit I don't need to know. Few years back he hired me to dispose of some guys who had almost killed his kid brother. Guess his bro is a bit of a fancy lad, spends his nights with a mouthful of pillow and whatnot. Never been an issue with me. So. Couple of rednecks gang-beat him outside an after hours club, lay his face out over a curb and kick the back of his head till they'd bust all his teeth out, split his skull down the middle.

"See you in a bit, Elliot."

"Have a good meeting, Mr. Covington."

I tracked them down by staking out the club for a few nights, figuring the fear of their own latent homosexuality would draw them back. Crept up on them in an alley where they were stomping a skinny kid in a Hawaiian shirt. Dropped one guy by gapping him twice with a phillips–head screwdriver, once in the neck and once in the ear. I held him by the hair, eased him down to the pavement, leaving the screwdriver jutting out of his head. Other guy hadn't seen me yet; he was laying the kid's arm over a sewer grate, probably so he could stomp 'til it went snap. I slit his throat with an eight-inch box cutter (a hitter doesn't need a lot of fancy weapons: spend forty bucks at a hardware store and you'll be set for a career). He flowed hot and fast, so I leaned his body over an open dumpster and let him bleed out over the trash. Counted backward from sixty. Left.

Christ, it's hot as a bitch outside.

"Real nice car, sir."

"Yeah, thanks."

The carhop looks all right. Clean cut, no visible piercings or tats. Doesn't seem to smell. Hell, I don't even see any pit stains, and it's the middle of the goddamn summer. Okay. Tell Elliot to let this kid deal with my ride from now on.

"What's your name, kid?"

"Joshua, sir."

"Hmm…okay."

Just got the car back. Always drove nice, but I wanted the AC tuned up before the heat wave hit. Kid must've turned it on when he started the car—sitting down is like stepping out of a sauna into a meat locker. New freon's a bit *too* powerful. *Franken*–freon, for fuck's sake.

Hariyoshi's place is halfway across town. Freeway is usually best but I know it's packed this time of the day, so I'll snake my way through the uptown grid.

"*Whooo–eeey kids, it's a scorcher out there! Lather up with the sunscreen, boys and girls, this could get ugly; just got a report that tourists are melting on the boardwalk! You could fry an egg on the pavement, I mean it's that hot...*"

Goddamn glib weathermen. Just give me the temperature and shut the fuck up, will you? People get edgy enough in this heat without listening to some shithead patronize them. Christ.

Haryoshi's from Japan, someplace up north. Does business out of a sushi restaurant. I was referred to him four years ago. Work for him exclusively now. He's got enough work to keep me busy year–round, swallows all expenses, and pays better than a drunk businessman at a titty bar.

Traffic's heavy through the core. I'm going to be late. Better call.

"Moshi moshi. *Kitenzushi*–domo."

"Hai, moshi. Covington–kun wa. Haryoshi–san wa?"

"Hai, hai. Chotto dake, sumimasen."

I don't know what kind of business he runs, and the work I do for him doesn't bring me any closer to an answer. Honestly, I don't really care, and curiosity has killed too many dumb–ass cats for me to make an issue of it. Guess I've done maybe ninety jobs over the years, no two of them the same. Before this gig, the marks I clipped all fit the same general MO: deadbeat junkies, mid–level muscle, faux–flash dealers who overextended themselves, petty thieves, pimps, lowlife dirtbags who said the wrong things to the wrong guys—basically, punks who had nothing to redeem themselves, no semblance of social worth, nobody to mourn them.

The jobs Haryoshi sends me out on are different, though.

"This is Haryoshi."

"Afternoon. Listen, traffic's thick. I'm running late."

"When can you be here?"

"Give me fifteen."

"Fine. I am waiting with someone."

"Thought this was a private call."

"Things have changed. I'll explain when you arrive."

Somebody else? What the fuck is he talking about?

"Okay. Be there soon."

When we first met, Haryoshi asked me about my moral code. I told him to be more specific. He asked me who I'd be willing to kill. I told him nobody'd ever asked, but I supposed it would depend on the price. He seemed pleased with my answer.

I use the term "guy" when I talk about a mark. I suppose maybe it's the socially acceptable thing to say, right? It isn't always a guy. The idea of a hitter's "code" is a creation of the media. No women, no kids? Bullshit. You've got to cut down the chaff with the wheat; for anyone whose morality condones killing another man for money, it's a relatively short ethical leap to extend the umbrella and the almighty dollar breaks through any moral dilemmas.

Not that I have any.

I don't know what these people have done to Haryoshi, why he wants them dead. The price is ten grand a head—his price, not mine—and I usually do a couple jobs a month. He's had me tramping under overpass bridges, jacking bums. He's had me sneaking into residential homes, topping yuppie families. He's had me breaking into dorm rooms, strangling drunk freshmen. It's always a specific person—not just *any* bum, specifically Jack Clemton; not *any* student, only Colleen Ainsworth. He tells me where to find them. I do the rest. He prescribes a specific method and where to leave the body. The rest he leaves to my discretion. As I said, the money's good and work's steady so I hold my tongue. I know better than to bite the yellow hand that feeds me.

Parking lot's almost empty. Two o'clock, lunch rush passed.

There's a decorative glass cabinet next to the restaurant's front door. It's three tiers high and displays plastic reproductions of the food served inside. Haryoshi tells me all the restaurants in Japan have similar showcases. It's eerie, the models frozen in stasis—chopsticks standing upright in a glassy bowl of drab soba noodles, a glass filled with eternal polyethylene ice-cubes and brightly colored lacquer, a moth-eaten cocktail umbrella bobbing on its hardened surface. Mannequin food. Looks like it's been awhile since anyone's cleaned up: a thick layer of dust and the stiff corpses of several large bluebottles litter the glass shelves.

Mashahiro, the old *maitre-de* from Osaka, meets me at the reservation podium.

"Konbanwa, Covington-san."

"Konbanwa, Mashahiro-san. Hariyoshi-san wa, domo?"

"Hai."

He leads me to the back room, banking around the network of slowly rotating conveyor belts. He stops in front of the door, bowing low.

"Arrigotto goziamasu, Mashahiro-san."

"Hai, hai."

Hariyoshi is sitting in his usual position behind a huge oval table set in a raised alcove. I've never seen him move from the spot, even to take a piss. An overstuffed red leather bench rings the table in a tight semicircle; the table surface is draped with a pleated crimson tablecloth, trailing to the ground. Everything is the same as always, except for the man sitting to Haryoshi's left.

"Mr. Covington, welcome. I was beginning to become concerned."

"You should know me by now, Mr. Haryoshi."

"Yes, yes. Come. Sit."

I climb three steps and sit down. I keep my eyes on Haryoshi, but take in the other guy on the periphery. I haven't seen him before. Looks Italian, maybe Greek. Swarthy bastard. He's staring—I feel his eyes scouring me.

"Congratulations on your latest job," Haryoshi says. "Very well done."

"Have I ever let you down?"

He chuckles softly. "No, Mr. Covington, you've been nothing if not consistent."

There's a couple stories floating around about Haryoshi, nothing concrete. He just showed up on the scene one day about ten years back, looking like a Jap but talking like a toffee–nosed Brit. Started farming out jobs to just about anyone who'd take them. There was a rumor that he has a brother and a mother: brother's apparently crazy as shithouse rat; a severe, homicidal kind of crazy. He's shut away somewhere. Nobody knows anything about the mother, but no doubt he shut her away, too, cooping her up in one of those executive geriatric complexes so he doesn't have to watch her rot away.

I was working out of Tampa at the time so I wasn't in on the ground floor, as it were. Anyway, Haryoshi eventually settled on a guy named Kinglake, made him the designated golden boy. I knew of the guy. Solid hitter, good rep. Big guy, with a face you couldn't place—couldn't pick out of a lineup, maybe. Wore one of those full–length trench coats, black leather. Heard he used to carry a double–barreled shotgun hooked to a swivel–holster mounted at waist–level. Rumor has it he'd drill a mark at close range, cut the poor fucker in half at the navel. He took his name out of the general assignment pool because Haryoshi gave him as much work as he'd take.

"Would you like something to eat, Mr. Covington? We just received a shipment of sea urchin from Sapporo. I'll have the chef crack a few for you."

"Sea urchin?"

"That's right."

"That's fine, I'm not a fan."

"Pity. They must be eaten quickly; urchin has a tendency to sour when aged."

About four years ago, Kinglake disappeared. Hitters are a private bunch, but word spreads through the circuits; if another hitman goes underground—metaphorically or literally—we usually got wind. Not this time, though: one day he was leading the good life, popping Haryoshi's cushy marks every couple weeks, and the next he's a whisper.

I heard a story a couple years ago from a guy named Grundle, a two–bit shill and needle freak, an easy pump for street dirt. Way he told it, he was taking a piss in the alley next to some crackhouse. Said he heard noise coming from the back, in the shadowy eddies just beyond the point where the streetlight's glow stretched. He couldn't make out what it was, perhaps due to the fact that he had a skinful of low–end crank ricocheting between his synapses. Said it was big. He squinted into the gloom, straining his eyes trying to distinguish what was moving.

Grundle said that the thing started moving toward him, fast. Said it seemed to billow out as it advanced, becoming twice as big. He screamed and fell backwards as it charged, but the thing stopped at the point where the light would have illuminated it clearly. Grundle said it was making noises that he had never heard before, a mixture of clogged gurgling and shrill, girlish laughter. He was trying to stand and run when the thing took a small step forward, and for one brief second made itself visible.

That's where the story drops off the edge of reality and descends into drug–fueled paranoia.

Grundle said it was Kinglake, or it kind of looked like Kinglake. His face was dead white and his skin deeply wrinkled. *Like he fell asleep in the tub for a few days*, Grundle said. He was bald, skull lacerated with ragged, bloodless slashes running from forehead to neck. Grundle told me that Kinglake looked so big because he'd held up his tattered trench coat, flapping it like a bat. His eyes were black, *oil–slick black*.

Kinglake opened his mouth but didn't talk. Grundle said insects started flying out of the black pit in the middle of his face: fat, sluggish, albino bugs, things he'd never seen before with white bodies and bulging red eyes. One landed on his arm and its body was scorching hot, and bubbling blisters formed and burst where it landed. Grundle said it started to tear into his flesh, wiggling around, trying to get under his skin. He showed me his arm. There was a puffy, pustular weal amidst the network of track marks.

Before he could make out anything else, Kinglake stepped back into the shadows. *Or was pulled, I dunno*, Grundle said. *I could see his heels dragging along the pavement like something big that I couldn't see was pulling him back. No fooling, man. Anyway, I got up off my ass and ran until I couldn't run no more, and I wouldn't never go back to that house, even if they start givin' the juice away.*

I told him he was full of shit. He said I could think whatever I wanted to. Didn't see much of Grundle after that; he disappeared like a lot of those pinheads tend to. No big loss.

And now I have to deal with this big pile of shit sitting next to Haryoshi.

"Perhaps I should perform the introductions, since you both seem reticent," Haryoshi says. "Mr. Covington, meet Mr. Sorbetti; Mr. Sorbetti, this is Mr. Covington."

I reach over the table and shake. As I expected, the big jackass tries to crush my hand. His forearms bulge as he squashes my fingers together: trying to prove he's the alpha–male with a bigger dick. I'm relieved. Anyone who knows their business would know that brute force rarely has a place in our game, and someone who displays any kind of aggression without need is probably a rank amateur. I settle back into my seat and sneak a few looks at the guy, size him up. For his part, he tries to stare daggers through my head: more dick swinging.

He's a big fucker, anyway. Wears one of those chest–hugger shirts designed to highlight a decent physique, which he has—pecs like twin slabs of lead, upper arms corded with bunched muscle. Looks like a health club, nautilus–machine body rather than one that's seen much real abuse. No scars or muscle knots. Maybe a 'roid freak. Another point in my favor. I know I can take this guy down. He might get in a few shots, but I feel confident I could bottle him up and snap an arm or a leg or his neck if need be. It's one of the rituals of the hitman trade: constantly sizing everybody else, determining whether or not you could jack the goon sitting across from you if need be. I know he's looking at me thinking he could pop my head off in the crook of his arm. He'd be wrong, but I'm not going to give him any reason to doubt his assumption.

"Although you don't know one another, you are both valued employees," Haryoshi says. "Perhaps each of you assumed that you were the only one working for me, and I felt no compulsion to tell you differently. It's just that I have so much work needing to be done that I felt it unwise to overtax either one of you with an unnecessary burden of work."

The two of us been working for him? This is a new development.

"Excuse me, Mr. Haryoshi: how long've you had both of us in your employ?"

The big Italian glares at me.

"What's it matter to you how long I been workin' for Mistu Hay–oshi? If he'd a wanted to tell ya, he woulda."

"Oh, geez. Sorry." I say. I'll pretend I'm scared of him, like his tough guy act is working. He leans back smugly. What a stupid fucking mouk.

"To answer your question, Mr. Covington, Mr. Sorbetti has been in my employ for about a year an a half."

At least I'm the veteran. I don't know how much more work Haryoshi could have: I mean, I'm tagging twenty–five bodies a year, steady. How many enemies does the guy have?

Mashahiro comes through the doors with a large wheeled cart laden with food: tuna rolls, crab soup, bowls of soba noodles in duck broth, roasted lobster dumplings wrapped in bamboo leaves, a plate of horse–meat sashimi, a heaping bowl of short grain rice. While we eat there is little conversation. I wait for some explanation from Haryoshi but none is forthcoming, so I just savor the food.

"Did you enjoy?" Haryoshi asks when we're finished.

I nod. Sorbetti belches, pats his belly.

"Good, good. Well, I must get down to brass tacks, as you say. I have two jobs that need tending to. One is relatively easy and the pay is standard. The other one will require more work, and the price will be doubled."

Honestly, I don't care which one I get. Ten grand for a walk in the park or twenty for a ball–twister—the work's steady, I can live on five grand a week. Sorbetti stares at me. I know which contract he wants.

"I can't decide who I want to do these jobs, since you are both reliable operators. I thought we'd have some fun. We'll play a game, and the winner can decide which job they would prefer. Does this sound fair, gentlemen?"

We nod.

"Splendid. The game's a pastime invented by the Thais. Although they are a filthy, backward race, they do enjoy their diversions. I believe they call it *Bangkok rules*."

He reaches under the table and I sense movement. My muscles tense.

"It's okay, Mr. Covington. All part of the game," he smiles, teeth a butter-yellow smear. "Before either of you arrived, I secured a young lady and asked her to sit quietly under the table until I gave her a signal."

"You're shitting me!" Sorbetti says.

He tries to lift the tablecloth.

"*Do not do that!*" Haryoshi screams, face reddening, "It...it would take away from the mystery, would it not?" Regaining his usual composure. "The rules are clear. The woman must not be revealed until the game has reached a conclusion. I assure you she is there. Katsuko, please say hello to the gentlemen."

A supple yellow hand, fingernails painted pale gold, appears from underneath the tablecloth for a moment before disappearing.

"Good shit!" Sorbetti says, "I love Asian broads."

"The rules of the game are simple: Ms. Katsuko will rotate amongst the three of us under the table and out of sight, administering...*stimulation*. The first man to unleash his passion loses, and relinquishes the right to choose his preferred job. If I lose...well, that is doubtful," he looks as us archly, "but we will determine an appropriate course of action should it occur. Does this seem fair?"

Well, be damned if anyone can accuse me of an unwillingness to try something new. I figure I'm as globally-minded as the next fellow—hell, took a stroll through Chinatown, bought some firecrackers. Just have to clear my mind of impure thoughts, block that psychiatrist of mine out. Think of baseball, maybe.

I think she's over with Sorbetti. I can see his face tense and relax. His hands go down to his lap as he helps the woman under the table remove his pants. I can hear deep sucking sounds, and he's making a dopey, cross-eyed face. Christ, I hope I don't look that stupid when my turn comes.

"Mr. Sorbetti," Haryoshi says, "Did you achieve release *already*? If so, you've certainly made for a short game."

Fat beads of sweat dapple the big Italian's brow. "I'm still capped," he pants, "Just getting warmed up."

There is sly movement beneath us. I sense the girl move away from the far side of the table, crawling toward me. Hands—soft small hands—on my trouser leg. She is lifting my pants up, massaging my calves and thighs, raking the skin with long nails. She breathes on my cock through my pants, grinds her face into my crotch. She pulls me forward with more force than I expect, trying to engulf me. I can't see her face; it's hidden under the thick material. Haryoshi watches me intently, his face an inscrutable Asian mask.

My pants are down. I hear seams ripping, wonder how I'm going to make a dignified exit with in a pair of torn, drool-flecked trousers. Then I'm in her mouth, and everything else is forgotten.

Of course I've had hummers before. Most have been downright shitty: slobbering, listless experiences I'd rather forget. Best oral I ever got was from a coked-up whore I'd been hired to snuff. She thought she could escape the scythe by blowing me, and I felt no compulsion to dissuade her. The fear was

Dead But Dreaming

what made it so fine—her looking up at me, tears streaking cheap mascara down her sallow face, snot coursing from her smashed–up nose, mixing with the saliva, lubing me up. I jacked her in the throat with a sharpened leather punch as I came, half worried I'd stab my cock.

The treatment I'm currently receiving puts everything before to shame. I've heard about Asian women—geisha girls, Roppongi's famous "soapland" brothels, Kabukicho theatre—a society where women are subservient and the system patriarchal. Desirable women are those who know how to service their men.

This one's learned her lessons well.

She bobs up and down until I feel like the top of my head is going to blow off. She stops abruptly, and I breathe a sigh of relief.

Haryoshi now. His expression doesn't change at all. I can see she's manipulating him, hear the surreptitious sucking sounds. If anything, his countenance expresses a barely contained revulsion; he breathes sharply, gritting his teeth. Then again, perhaps he's deep in some Zen trance, trying to divorce mind from body. Thinking about Japanese baseball?

Haryoshi's a rock. She moves back to Sorbetti, whose fat cock pokes above the lip of the table. Obscene. It's dragged underneath and subjected to further treatment. Sorbetti tries to act casual but I know he's on the verge: a thick, pulsing vein bisects his forehead, his hands clutch handfuls of the tablecloth. The liquid noises intensify. The Italian squints his eyes and looks to Heaven, mouth wide. The girl makes soft, encouraging coos.

"Oh…oh, God…I'm gonna bust a nut." Sorbetti moans.

He groans and starts to unload, big body collapsing. Haryoshi shakes his head.

Then Sorbetti starts to scream, a high, wheedling squeal like a scared animal.

What the fuck is going on here?

The table bucks and quakes; Sorbetti's screams intensify as he stares down into his lap, eyes livid. Haryoshi remains calm. Loud noises, the sound of flesh being torn and rent with incredible force.

I part my coat, moving for the Glock 9mm I keep in a cheater holster at my hip.

The Italian's face is ashen. He pushes feebly at his crotch, bull arms quaking. When he pulls them up most of his fingers are gone. The ragged stumps are severed at different lengths and pulpy tatters of flesh hang from them. It's as if they've been *chewed* off. Blood gouts from each truncated digit, thick scarlet arcs. I see a ring of puncture marks on his palms.

Christ, they look like *bite* marks.

I locate the gun, flick the restraining strap.

Blood and substantial bits of gore are shooting up from Sorbetti's lap in erratic pulses, splashing his body with his own shredded guts. He isn't screaming anymore: his mouth hangs slack. The sounds emanating from the other side of the table are vicious, horrific: meat and gristle sucked through a wide straw into a greedy maw.

I unsheathe the Glock, stand. The table tips over, crashing down the carpeted steps...

...and I see it all.

Haryoshi has no legs; nothing exists beyond upper–thigh. The stumps are glistening and raw, looking like uncured ham hocks. The shards of his naked thighbones jut from the mass of quivering meat, leaking marrow. A sticky pool beneath him, oozing blood dripping from the shredded mess, pattering down to add to the puddle.

"Please calm down, Mr. Covington. I'm sure this all must seem rather alarming, but allow me to explain."

A long, twisting strand of greasy flesh, thick around as a pop can, protrudes from Haryoshi's fishbelly–white body, where his groin should be. The flesh cord is festering and boil–ridden, striated with long curving runnels; the meat seems to drip and run like tallow from a burning candle. It's translucent, resembling a filmy catheter or the exoskeleton of an insect. I watch as viscous fluid courses through, into Haryoshi.

The oversized umbilical strand flows from Haryoshi, drooping down to brush the carpet, and ascends, attaching to the back of the skull of the monstrous thing that has been quietly waiting under the table all this time.

I snap the safety off. Can't stop my hands shaking.

"I assure you, there's no need for that. Calm yourself."

Sorbetti is worse off than Haryoshi; his body's been devoured up to the navel. The creature that ate him—*the thing that had its lips wrapped around me a minute ago*—is buried in Sorbetti's body cavity to the neck. Blood and limp chunks of offal fall from the massive entrance wound; the body bucks and shimmies like a rag doll as the thing inside gorges. I see its delicate fingers, painted fingernails gouging deep into warm, quivering flesh.

"I must apologize for my brother's manners. I do my best to keep him under control but his appetite is insatiable and there is only so much I can do. He's little better than an animal, but sly like one too. I've had to slowly sacrifice my own legs to his incessant hunger, as you can see."

He jerks the fleshy rope that binds them, snapping the thing's head back as if it were a dog.

"Say hello to Mr. Covington, brother." He looks at me apologetically, "Again, I must beg pardon for my sibling's behavior, but he did wait so patiently while we were eating. It's all so very taxing on him."

I draw a bead on the blood–slicked monster that directs its gaze on me. It has a flat, simian face and an elongated, hairless skull. The mouth is cavernous; double rows of tiny yellow teeth are bared at me. A long, hemisected tongue, a snake's tongue, darts out briefly. I feel bile rising in my throat: that subhuman thing had *my dick in there!* It scrabbles across the carpet on all fours, coming toward me.

My finger tightens on the trigger.

"Stop! Both of you!"

The thing halts its progress, pads over to his brother like a tamed animal coming to heel. It rubs up against one of Haryoshi's legs, takes a surreptitious nip. Haryoshi punches it in the face, snapping its bulbous head back.

"Bad. Very, very bad. Haven't you had enough?"

The thing mewls and starts edging towards Sorbetti's body.

Gotta get the hell out of here. Question is, do I kill this freak before I jet or let it go? Money is money, and this...thing has the cash to keep me in the pink. Other hand, maybe a little blackmail's in order—pay me to zip my lip or I make a call to the folks at Ripley's.

"He is a terrible burden, as you can see," Haryoshi's saying. "Keeps me pent up here like *I'm* the animal. You don't know how many times I've looked at this shackle," he says, caressing the freakish umbilical tube, "And thought about cutting it in half, permanently severing us. Many reasons have prevented me, though. I'm not sure if I'd survive, and I'm half afraid that something new might grow in place of my brother—the devil you know is better than the devil you don't, hmm? Then, there's always the thought of how mother'd react."

While he's talking I take a few steps back. I've got them sized: old legless Jap and his bastard Siamese half–breed brother who can only move in a short radius without dragging his gimpo bro behind him—a radius I've since cleared. I've got thirty–two bullets on me, more than enough to drop them both, plus any kitchen help who want to play the martyr.

"My brother and I are simply links in a bigger chain, just as you are...and Mr. Sorbetti was. Now that you know our family secret, you may no longer wish to work for us. That would be unfortunate. Or you may think you can leverage us in some way. Extort our weakness, as it were. This would be a terrible mistake on your part, let me assure you."

I've had enough of this shit. I thought Sorbetti was a punkass grinder and the sight of his hollow corpse doesn't register at all. But what if I had shot *my* load *first?* I think I have to drill the thing that ate Sorbetti, if only as an act of self–cleansing atonement.

Yeah, that's a must.

"I'll keep on, Haryoshi, but I've got to do a bit of housekeeping first."

I raise the gun and jack a deuce into the creature's head. It's a big target and my shakes are gone. The bullets are crosshatched dum dums, maximum spread. The thing's head explodes in a red spray and the body slumps to the carpet.

Haryoshi looks at the jetting stump of his brother's neck, and back at me. His face is pale and quivering. He looks terrified.

"Oh, Mr. Covington, that was a terrible mistake."

The restaurant begins to shake as if in the grip of a Richter–busting earthquake. I hear dishes tumbling and crashing on the ground in the main dining room. The floor seems to flow and roil as if liquid: something massive moves underneath. Haryoshi is in an apoplexy of fear. He holds onto the leather bench, trying to remain seated. His brother's corpse twitches bonelessly on the floor, a fleshy anchor. The man is babbling insensibly, in an unrecognizable language, neither English nor Japanese.

"Yoggsothoth, hie! Forosog–naa! Ka–paan–tu sed piu, nasee, nasee!"

Size it up, size it up...

The far door bursts open. I see Mashahiro stumble by, screaming. The white–faced *maitre de* has no arms: something's torn them off at the shoulder joint. His white suit is heavy with blood. As I watch, something darts past the doorway, moving so quickly I can barely register it. Mashahiro's headless body crumples to the floor and is dragged away.

Christ. Back into a corner, cover all flanks. The remains of Sorbetti slump down the steps, looking like the torso of some horror house mannequin.

"Hiyem con gossoh! Nasee, nasee con giaor, Yoggsothoth!"

Haryoshi starts to move. Upward.

Oh sweet fuck. Oh dear Jesus, what the fuck is going on?

Bugs. There are bugs all around the room. Huge white bugs with fat red heads. The are birthing themselves from the thick shag, wall cracks, ceiling tiles. All around me.

Sweet Christ.

"Covington," Haryoshi's head hangs forward, eyes jet–black. "Meet mother."

He's pushed up on a thick pedestal of knotted gray flesh, like elephant skin. It flows out of a slime–slicked hole in the bench in a smooth, sinuous wave, carrying Haryoshi to the ceiling. I see his body is melded to this horrific appendage, a marionette impaled on the fist an obscured puppet master. He's propelled upwards as if weighing nothing, trailing the swinging corpse of his brother behind. He rushes towards me, propelled by some monstrous force.

Dear God, what have I done...

I crouch in the corner, trying to cover up, to become invisible. There is no way to size up such a thing: it's an incomprehensible force from another place, another time. I am nothing before it. Nobody is. I think of Grundle's story, of the Kinglake–thing.

Haryoshi hovers directly above me. The blood from his brother's neck drips onto my face. The smell is unspeakable—flyblown garbage rotting on a hot day. Haryoshi's mouth is open. Bugs crawl in and out, busying themselves in the septic wounds on his legs. The floor buckles and creaks. The jaw of the thing that I knew as Haryoshi falls open. I stare into the shifting blackness within.

"*You...will...be...mine.*"

It is a voice no human or animal could mimic: a cold, ageless voice from beyond the nether stars, a region where time and space and the insignificant works and toil of man hold no weight. Soft and malignant and seductive, it drills into my ears, slicing into my brain like a million razor blades, a sonic drill.

"Yes, yes, yes..."

In the calm eye of terror, I can see that Haryoshi is borne up on a thick tentacle. There is a neat grid of suckers on the underside of the mucous–coated skin. I look closer, mesmerized…

Each sucker is a face. A tiny, twisted, screaming face. They stare back into my eyes. I think I see the faces of past marks—the middle-aged waitress, the studious history professor, the young boy who came home from little league after dark. They twist and strain, coiling around one another in agonized double-helixes, moaning and gibbering and snapping at each other in madness, staring at me with reproachful eyes before starting to scream again, each of them imprisoned in stasis to the creature that lives and feeds in the darkness below. I cower prostrate at the foot of some ancient, unblinking evil. My body is a chalice of blood and tissue, an insignificant offering to its immortal, ceaseless, insatiable appetites. A creature that has sat idly by as solar systems burnt and faded, something hideous and unspeakable, an eater of stars, devourer of galaxies, an infinite being of endless desires and awful hatreds. My fevered mind wonders how far it might stretch under the earth, how many other appendages dwelled above ground, how many subservient puppets it had at heel—how far might it stretch under the city, the country, the world…where did it range, gathering meat, gathering strength, gathering souls?

"*Go…now.*"

I run.

*   *   *

I still work for Haryoshi. I say I work for him, but I know I work for someone…something else. I say "Haryoshi" to put some kind of human identity on my employer.

It doesn't work.

I stopped seeing my shrink.

I don't go out much.

I got my first new assignment a month ago. Middle of the night; maybe three, four o'clock. Knock at the door. Didn't want to answer. Knew I had to. The lights in the hall were out. I could hear noises in the darkness. Sounds I knew too well.

It was Sorbetti.

He was in a wheelchair. His wounds looked fresh, still…still *dripping*.

He didn't speak, at least in his own voice. None of them do. His arm raised stiffly, like a robot. He held an envelope full of cash. In his other hand, a picture and an address.

"*Do…this…tomorrow.*"

His mouth open, head tilted up at me. I could see a massive eye staring at me from the red flesh at the back of his throat.

His other eyes were gone.

"Okay."

Bugs flitted in and out of the gaping cavity in his body, wiggling contentedly in soft pulp.

    I try not to think much. Thinking is bad for business. Mostly I think about life after death. I used to be an atheist, like most in the business. Now I can't be. Wish I could.

    Sometimes, at night, I hear noises in the apartment. Sly, surreptitious noises, like something is trying to be stealthy.

    But not too stealthy.

    In the morning, outside my bedroom door, there are two envelopes, coated with a thin layer of warm ichor than burns when I touch it.

    My name is Junior Covington. I kill people for money.

    My soul is forfeit.

    I knew that long ago.

    Maybe there are things worse than hell.

    We'll see.

DARRELL SCHWEITZER is the author of three published novels, *The White Isle*, *The Shattered Goddess* and *The Mask of the Sorceror*, and has recently completed *The Dragon House*, a Young Adult fantasy with Lovecraftian elements. His nearly 300 short stories have appeared in the usual venues, such as *Twilight Zone*, *Interzone*, *The Horror Show*, *Cemetery Dance*, *Night Cry*, *Fantastic Whispers*, etc. but ranging as far as *Analog* and *Alfred Hitchcock's Mystery Magazine*. Some of them are collected in *Refugees from an Imaginary Country*, *Transients and Other Disquieting Stories*, *Nightscapes*, etc. He has been four times nominated for the World Fantasy Award, twice for best collection, once for best novella, and once as co-editor of *Weird Tales* (which he won). He co-edited *Weird Tales* for 19 years, and has recently turned to anthologies, such as *The Secret History of Vampires* (DAW, 2007, with Martin H. Greenberg) and the forthcoming *Urban Werewolves* (Pocket Books). He even edited an anthology in the form of a "reprint" of an imaginary pulp magazine, *Weird Trails, the Magazine of Supernatural Cowboy Stories* (January 1933 issue) for Wildside Press. In the Lovecraftian field he is respected as the editor of *Discovering H.P. Lovecraft*, but secretly fears that he will most remembered for rhyming "Cthulhu" in a limerick.

Why We Do It

by Darrell Schweitzer

The point was never *what* happened, of course, but *why.* As in classical tragedy, there were uncertainties, little, subtle turnings of free will and action which lead to the seemingly inevitable, unsurprising conclusion, but could possibly have led elsewhere.

Things were certainly *not* certain, *not* set in stone as I drove the car and said to Kimberley, "For the second time I have to ask you, do you really want to go through with this?"

She got out her notebook.

"Ooh. Sounds ominous. Is that a ritual question?"

"Uh, yeah."

She wrote slowly. "There's gonna be three of them, right?"

"Right."

Already we were far enough north of Philadelphia that the prosperous suburbs were far behind, and we began to see signs for towns with biblical names: Nazareth, Bethlehem, Emmaus. I took the wrong fork on the road to Emmaus, and we passed deserted farms and bare hills, brown beneath a steely December sky.

I tried to sort out my feelings in silence.

I was eighteen, a college freshman. For just four months I had been away from home for the first time in my life. Now I was returning. The road sign said: CHORAZIN, 12 MILES.

Almost there. The precise middle of nowhere. Chorazin PA is about as isolated as you can get in this part of the country. We don't have cable. You can't buy *Playboy.* The Amish shun us and there's nothing for the tourists. And here was this gorgeous girl two years older than me condescending to accompany dumb hick Howard back to his village so that she could witness his people's barbaric rituals and write them up for anthropology class.

That was insulting. But whenever I was around her, I somehow felt as if my shoes were on the wrong feet and my underwear was outside my pants. I felt stupid, all wrong, but somehow I hoped she liked me. I wanted to believe in the possibility of love.

Yet I had been selected by Elder Abraham himself, sent forth and bidden to return, for a far different purpose.

My heart was in my throat all the way.

"What's so special about December 17th?" Kimberley asked, dropping her notebook in her lap.

"It's just the day we do it. Always has been."

"Let me guess. You dance naked on a hilltop—"

"December would be a bit cold for that."

We crossed the mill stream. I saw the grove where I used to play Hanged Man and Ghost as a kid.

I parked the car. Kimberley stared at the tumble-down houses, the empty windows.

She was about to say something, but then people started to emerge, surrounding us.

"Come on," I said. "Meet my folks."

"I see we're expected."

I got out and opened the car door for her. "Um, I have to ask—"

"The third question, right?"

"Yes."

"I'm here of my own free will. Will that do?"

"Yes."

How-do-you-do's followed. Kimberley whispered to me, "They all seem so *normal.*"

"You were expecting maybe chanting cultists in hoods?"

Inside, before we sat down at the big table, Elder Abraham took me aside and said, "Howard, you did fine. I know it's hard. We're all proud of you."

I felt like Judas with the thirty pieces of silver before him.

Over dinner, the talk was of college, and TV shows, and Kimberley's recent Broadway excursion, although it was soon obvious even to her that no one here could even imagine New York. There were awkward moments of silence.

She whispered to me, "That old guy . . . he must be almost a hundred."

"More like a thousand."

She giggled and jabbed me with her elbow under the table. But then she reached over and took hold of my hand, which confused and amazed and uplifted me all at once. Now I was the one who had to make an effort not to cry out or run away from the table, who couldn't figure out what to do or say or think from one instant to the next, while Kimberley, of course, maintained perfect poise.

She explained what she was here for, and the Elder answered her questions politely, but he was also speaking to all of us, the Chorazinites, reaffirming our commitment in this decadent age. He spoke of the place at the edge of the universe to be prepared for the elect once the Earth is cleared off, and how our rituals must be observed, painful though they might be.

Kimberley nudged me. "And you actually *believe* this shit?"

"It's not a matter of *belief.*"

Then dinner was over and I took her upstairs to my room, just to show her where I'd lived and grown up, and I was babbling, sure, about my childhood, and about the countryside. At one point I was suggesting that we go up to the ridge above the Old Dark Hollow—

"That's what they call it," I said, trying to joke, imitating a TV hillbilly accent, "The Old Dark Holler... It's a great place for picnics."

She rolled her eyes toward the ceiling and imitated something I'd said previously, getting the slightly irritated, I've-been-patronized tone down perfectly. "December would be a bit cold for that."

And I tried to make conversation, showing her this and that: the college banner on the wall, the model airplanes dangling from the ceiling, the poems I'd published in my high school newspaper. But I am sure it was just a boy's room to her, all kid's stuff. I was getting nowhere. Then I took the plunge, like someone who's jumped off a cliff into water that might or might not have sharp rocks just below the surface. I put my hands on her shoulders and tried to give her a kiss and ask her if she might possibly love me, at which point we'd obviously have to run away together—

For just a second I thought I saw something in her eyes, and for just that same second I dared to hope that what we were doing *wouldn't* reach its unsurprising conclusion, but whatever it was in her eyes faded like a lamp going out, and her glittering, amused contempt returned.

"Howard," she said. "Sometimes I think you're kind of cute. But sometimes I think you're a dork."

She broke away, and it was over, definitively, like a door being slammed shut.

But instead, someone knocked, and the door to the room swung open, and Elder Abraham stepped in.

"Oh, there you are," he said. "We're ready now." Our eyes met. "Are you?"

"Yes," I said. "I am."

✳   ✳   ✳

Only Kimberley could have been surprised.

She watched us with growing horror as we gathered atop the stone-crowned hill and slashed ourselves with knives of unearthly metal and smeared the altar with our blood.

"You're all crazy!" she screamed. "Why are you doing this?"

Of course it was too late for me to explain, though I think she understood at the very end that it wasn't a matter of *why* at all. Elder Abraham really *is* a thousand years old, and he *can* call down the Ancient Ones from the stars, and they *do* lust after young flesh such as hers so they may devour her soul and fill the husk of her body with their holy, black fire.

But I don't think she ever knew that I wept for her as I stood there with all the others, shivering and naked, as the sky opened up.

DAVID BARR KIRTLEY'S short fiction appears in magazines such as *Realms of Fantasy* and *Weird Tales*, and in various anthologies. His story "Save Me Plz" was selected by editor Rich Horton for the 2008 edition of the anthology series *Fantasy: The Best of the Year*. A screenplay adaptation David wrote of his story "Lest We Forget" was shot as a short film and shown at the New York Independent Film and Video Festival. David has been profiled as part of "Speculative Fiction: The Next Generation" by *Novel & Short Story Writer's Market*. He was the second-youngest writer selected for the anthology *New Voices in Science Fiction*. As a freshman, he won first prize in the Dell Magazines Award for undergraduate science fiction, given by *Asimov's* magazine. He grew up in Katonah, New York and majored in Government at Colby College. He has studied writing with many well-known figures, including T.C. Boyle (*The Road to Wellville*), Orson Scott Card (*Ender's Game*), Karen Joy Fowler (*The Jane Austen Book Club*), Irvin Kershner (*Star Wars: The Empire Strikes Back*), and Janet Fitch (*White Oleander*). David is the son of Buckley prize-winning physicist John R. Kirtley. David's website features illustrations, interviews, and free fiction: www.davidbarrkirtley.com

The Disciple

by David Barr Kirtley

Professor Carlton Brose was evil, and I adored him as only a freshman can. I spent the first miserable semester at college watching him, studying the way he would flick away a cigarette butt, or how he would arch his eyebrow when he made a point. I mimicked these small things compulsively. I don't know why, because it wasn't the small things that drew me to him at all. It was the big things, the stories people told as far away as dear old Carolina.

You heard the name Brose if you ran with any cults, and I ran with a few. Society rejected us, so we rejected them. The more things you give up, the less there is to bind your will. There's power there. We were sure of it. But that power was damned elusive.

I used to shop at an occult bookstore where a friend of mine worked. One day while he was shelving books he told me, "These guys you hang with, them I'm not so sure about. But Brose, he's the real deal."

I said, "You believe that?"

My friend stopped what he was doing and got a slightly crazed look in his eyes. "I've seen it, man, personally seen it. Flies buzz up out of the rot and swirl in formation around him. He can make your eyes bleed just from looking at him. The guy's tapped into something huge."

I was skeptical. "And he teaches a class?"

"Not just a class, all right? It's this special program. Only a dozen or so are admitted, and they get power. I've seen that too. Then they go away. Every spring."

"Go where?"

My friend shook his head. "Damned if I know. Places not of this world. That's what some people say."

"I don't buy it," I said. "If he's got so much going for him, why's he working a job at all? And what kind of school would let him teach it?"

My friend just shrugged. "I don't know about that. All I know is that Brose is for real."

"Then why aren't you in his class?"

My friend scowled, and went back to shelving. "Brose wouldn't take me. Said I had no talent, no potential. It hurt like hell, but that's another reason you

know he's legit — what kind of fraud would turn people away like that?"
I had no answer, and I'd known a lot of frauds.

I traveled to Massachusetts, to the university where Brose taught. I sought out his office in a secluded corner of the Anthropology building, then waited on a bench in the hallway and pretended to read.

Finally, the office door opened. Brose emerged, closed the door behind him, and walked in my direction. I glanced up, as if accidentally, as if his movement had caught my eye.

Brose stared back with eyes the color of a tombstone. The shadows seemed to lengthen and darken as he passed. He smiled knowingly. I shuddered, because I was sure just from that look that it was all true. Brose radiated power. On that day my initial skepticism transformed into the most helpless adoration. I enrolled in the school.

In the winter, I met with Brose for the first time. The inside of his office was like some terrible jungle. Loose papers drooped from the shelves. A filth-choked and apparently unused fish tank cast a pallid green light. From my seat, I could look out the window and see the lonely stretch of gray-green woods that was called the Arboretum.

Brose sat behind his desk, in those shadows of his own making. "So you want to join the program?"

"Yes," I whispered.

"Why should I accept you?"

"I'll do anything," I said. "No hesitation. No regret."

His lips curled into that now familiar smile. "And what will you be bringing to the program?"

I knew he meant power. "Nothing. Not yet. But you can—"

He shook his head. "If nothing's what you have, then nothing's what you get from me. Go back to literature. It's really—"

"No!" I broke in. "I don't have much, that's true. I've lost things in my life. So many things, but I've gained something too. I've gained this rotting emptiness inside me, and I can use it. I swear I can use it. All the loss, it can't have been for nothing." I added softly, "I won't let it be."

Brose watched me for a long time. Finally, he nodded. "All right. You'll do. I'll get the form."

I leaned back in my chair and let out a long sigh of relief. Brose disappeared into another room.

Something on the bookshelf caught my eye. A black statue. Like Brose it seemed wrapped in strange shadows. I rose from my seat.

The statue was a foot tall and depicted a creature resembling the head of a man, but with a beard of tentacles. The creature's eyes were utterly empty, and it had no body, only more tentacles.

I went to pick up the statue and study it closer, but when I lifted it I gasped. The thing was unearthly heavy — heavier than anything that size could possibly be, heavier than I could hold in one hand. The statue tore itself from my fingers and plunged to the floor, where it thudded and lay still.

From behind me came Brose's voice, "Don't touch that." I started.

Brose placed a shoebox on his desk, then lifted the statue with two hands and returned it to its place on the shelf.

I said, "I'm sorry. I..."

My voice died in my throat as Brose reached into the shoebox and lifted out a small white mouse, which squirmed and flailed and sniffed.

I said, "What's that?"

"This is the form. The application form." Brose paced over to that gruesomely overgrown fish tank and removed the lid. He offered me the mouse, and I took it.

Brose nodded at the tank. "Fill out your application."

I stepped forward and held the mouse over the foul water. The mouse nibbled gently at my fingers.

Brose eyed me. This was a test. Of what? My willingness? My resolve? I let the mouse go. It fell into the water and began to thrash and scream. It clawed at the filthy sides of the tank. Water soaked its fur and garbled its cries. Then it died and floated there, spinning slowly, its four pink legs hanging down, its tail trailing after.

Brose said, "Your application's been accepted. Congratulations."

※　　　※　　　※

There were thirteen students in the special program. Most were male. All had sallow flesh and haunted eyes. We moved into a sprawling colonial house on the edge of campus. My room was small, with hardwood floors and peeling white paint. I hadn't yet met my roommate.

Class convened in the house's dim cement cellar. The walls and floors bore eerie dark stains. The students sat in a circle, and Brose stood beside a desk. He spoke for hours about mystery and power.

Finally, he said, "The most important thing you must learn is to bind yourself to another, to attach yourself to its will."

He crucified a cat. Right on his desk, in front of us. The cat howled and squirmed, but the nails driven through its outstretched limbs held it fast. Blood trickled from its paws. Brose stanched the flow with a cloth.

Then he turned to me. "Make it bleed again."

I was filled with an aching desire to prove myself. I wanted him to think I was his most talented, most dedicated, most favored student. I would have done anything, endured anything, to make him adore me, the way I adored him.

I whispered desperately, "I don't know how."

Brose paced back and forth. "To control the body, you must feel the mind. Pain is conspicuous, it'll point the way, but don't depend on it. There are greater things than cats you must connect to, greater things than you, and they have never felt pain."

He turned to another student, a broad-shouldered guy with dark, scornful eyes. Brose said, "Make it bleed."

The student never even glanced at the cat, but instantly the cat's paws began to bubble and ooze and spurt.

"Good." Brose nodded. "Very good."

At the end of class, Brose admonished us, "Tell no one what you learn here."

I returned to my room. When my new roommate entered, I recognized him immediately. I said, "You're—"

"Adrian," he replied.

I finished, "—the one who can make the cat bleed."

He stared at me. "I can do a lot of things. I'm the best in the class, and Brose knows it."

"We'll see," I said. I was jolted by the way Adrian seemed to have figured me out. I couldn't believe it was an accident, the way his words seemed calculated to tear at my greatest longing: to be favored, to be adored.

I added, "It was only a cat."

He tensed. "You think I should've used something bigger?"

Before I could answer, I felt a wetness on my upper lip. I hurried to the mirror. Blood leaked from my nostrils and coated my mouth and chin.

I gasped, and seized a nearby towel. I leaned my head back and mopped my face.

Adrian ordered, "Don't lean back. Keep pressure on your nose. The bleeding will stop."

* * *

With each passing week, I lagged further behind Adrian in absorbing the macabre lessons we received. Adrian was right. He was the best. Adored by the class. Brose's favorite.

If I could not be favored by Brose, I would have preferred to be disfavored, to be his enemy. In reality, he was indifferent to me. I was not important enough for him even to despise.

As I walked the shaded pathways of the college, I pondered the strange role that Brose played here. It was obvious that the other faculty suspected the dark nature of our program. They kept their distance, and shot us looks full of fear and hostility. But they made no effort to disrupt us. Were they simply afraid of Brose? I couldn't decide.

As the semester wore on, Brose grew more and more agitated, and his lectures became increasingly frenzied and mad. He raved of nothing but the binding.

"You must learn faster!" He pounded on his desk. "The hour is near. It has all led up to this." He took a deep breath. "You must bind yourselves to the impossible mind of the Traveler on Oceans of Night, the Stepper Across the Stars. If you

The Disciple

ingratiate yourselves, you will earn a place as His favored disciples and journey with him forever to those places only He can make by his dreaming."

I glanced at Adrian, but he kept his eyes fixed straight ahead. So now we knew our fate. We would gain the ultimate power we sought by pledging ourselves to this ultimate being.

Brose reached into his briefcase and pulled out the black statue — the tentacled man-thing with its empty eyes. The statue was darker than any earthly object could ever be. Then I saw something I'd never noticed before. Among the creature's many limbs clung tiny human figures. That almost made me dizzy, for it meant that the creature must tower to unimaginable heights.

The Traveler on Oceans of Night. The Stepper Across the Stars.

It was Him.

That week I dreamed murky dreams of upside down cities built from granite and slime. One night I awoke to find Adrian lying on the floor and whimpering. He stared upward in terror, as if something horrid hung from the ceiling.

I asked, "What is it?"

"Oh God," he wailed. His usual swagger had vanished. "Can't you feel it? Are you blind and deaf and numb to everything? His boundlessness reaches across the void to poison our dreams."

I pressed, "What?"

Then I knew that he wasn't staring at the ceiling, but at the sky and the stars and the dark emptiness beyond.

Adrian whispered, "The Traveler on Oceans of Night. He's coming."

*   *   *

I had failed to win the adoration of Brose, but who was Brose, compared to all this? Compared to this great Traveler? Brose was nothing. He was a small man who lived a small life, pointing others along an exalted path that he himself dared not follow. I had found an object far more worthy of veneration. To be a disciple to such power, to be favored by the Traveler!

I wouldn't fail this time.

The night of the binding arrived. The Traveler was near, his imminence palpable. The air crackled with magic. I looked out over the forest, and the trees themselves seemed to tremble.

My classmates and I donned black robes, and Brose led us into the Arboretum. We passed beneath withered branches, and trod faint trails that wound between mossy boulders. Brose held the dark statue before him, and we didn't need light to see because the statue seemed to suck the shadows from beneath our feet and pull them into itself.

In the deepest corner of the woods, within a grotto of gray stone, there sprawled an ancient shrine overgrown with rotting ferns. Brose set the statue on the ground, and we settled down to wait.

I don't know how many hours we lay there. Then a breeze came. It snatched up damp leaves and flung them about and raised them into columns in the sky. The wind blew faster and louder until it seemed to shriek in pain.

I was suddenly struck by a maddening sense of dislocation, a nightmare cacophony of unbearable sensations. The shadows leapt from beneath the trees to block out the starlight and wrap themselves around my throat and sink behind my eyes.

The Traveler on Oceans of Night was there, his form stretching upward to infinity. All of him was far away yet somehow pressing close all around us. He was so enormous, so horrible, and so magnificent that we collapsed and wept helplessly and without shame to behold Him.

Through the confusion came the voice of Brose screaming, "Bind yourselves! Do it now!"

Adrian was first. He rose off the ground with his arms outstretched and his robe whipping about him. His face was full of ecstasy. One by one my classmates lifted from the earth until they circled around that great being. They were like flies, I realized suddenly. Like flies rising out of the rot to swirl around Professor Carlton Brose.

I looked at Brose, and his expression was one that I had come to know too well. Indifference. Something was horribly wrong. I imagined I saw the same indifference mirrored on the incomprehensible otherworldly face of the Traveler.

I would not bind to Him. I crawled until I found a rock to hide behind, then I screamed to my whirling classmates, "We're the flies! Oh God, we're like the flies."

The Traveler made one ponderous motion with a million of His slimy tentacles, and He stepped away toward another star, another dimension, another world He had dreamed. Then the night was silent and empty.

Brose strode toward me. He said darkly, "You failed the binding."

I lunged at him, startling him. I grabbed his throat and forced him down against a stone. I growled, "You lied. You said you'd make us His disciples."

Brose eyed me uneasily. "The Traveler on Oceans of Night is a great vessel. I would put you aboard."

"As what?" I said. "A rat in the hold? Or rather, a flea on a rat."

I imagined I saw the dozen bodies of my classmates, sucked away into the bitter black void between worlds. I imagined their frozen forms twirling slowly in an endless dance among the stars.

Then Brose seized my temples with his muddy fingers and made me look down into his cold, tombstone eyes. My own eyes began to bleed. I knew he meant to kill me.

As I flailed, my fingers fell upon the dark statue. I lifted it with two arms and brought it down on Brose's forehead. The statue sank without resistance until it reached the ground. When I pulled the statue away, there was a gaping hole where the face of Professor Carlton Brose had been.

The Disciple

The empty eyes of the Traveler could see things that humans never dreamt of, but He was blind to the pain of this sad world.

*   *   *

You were the best, Adrian. You were better than me, better at a lie. Are you proud?

Today a student came to beg admission to my special program. He stood at the fish tank and clenched a mouse in his fist. Then he held the mouse underwater until it drowned.

"Congratulations," I said. "You've been accepted."

He smiled.

I do this initiation — as I'm sure Brose did — to ease my conscience, to reassure myself that my students are evil and deserve their fate.

The college hates the program, but they know it's necessary, and after Brose died I was the only one who could replace him. New England has some dangerous people — ones who've latched onto darkness, or might — and they need to be dealt with. The harmless ones I turn away.

I've learned the truth that Brose knew: It's best to be a big fish in a small pond. Fish can't live outside the pond, and being a fish isn't so bad. Every spring, before I send them off to die, a new class studies with me. They are enthralled by my meager powers. They long for my briefest attention.

They adore me.

MICHAEL MINNIS was born in Saginaw, Michigan, Oct. 20, 1969. His current publishing credits include *Dead But Dreaming* (obviously), *Eldritch Blue, Arkham Tales, Horrors Beyond, Reves d'Ulthar, Anencephalous and Other Poisoned Dreams, Rehearsals for Oblivion,* and *Lost Worlds of Space and Time.* "Salt Air" was chosen for Honorable Mention in Datlow and Windling's 16th Edition of *The Year's Best Fantasy and Horror.*

Salt Air

by Mike Minnis

I'm glad for your company tonight.

My wife Mary retires early, you see—social gatherings drain her, much as she enjoys them. More so than myself, I should say.

Hmmm? Oh yes...the window. I thought I heard something. Tapping. A branch, perhaps. Or my imagination.

Melancholy?

If I am, it's nothing. I was thinking of the other guests, is all...what they said...how they are faring on their way home this night. Windy, isn't it? And Thompson drank too much, as usual.

He'll lose his post at the university yet...the poor oaf.

And another position will remain untenanted until spring, what with the influenza and all.

Sorry, you don't like talking about that, do you? No one does.

Speaking of empty positions, however...a few did remark on Gammell's absence. I'm not surprised. Miskatonic University seems to have lost one of its more eminent professors, and now everyone comes to me in search of answers.

And I tell them what I know: Gammell is gone. And I don't think he will be back.

At least I pray he won't...

Well, yes, it is a terrible thing to say.

But I don't say it out of spite or malice.

If you'd seen what I have seen...and was forced to endure what I have endured, you, too, would sit quietly by your window night after night and wish the same.

More wine?

In vino veritas. There is truth in wine.

And perhaps it's time I told the truth as well.

I'm afraid, you see. Afraid that Gammell will return some night, when the fire burns low and I am at last too weary to keep vigil, and sleep in this chair...

Please...stay. Keep me company, if only for a little while.

And understand that it was all for Professor Gammell's own good...

Gammell was in poor health.

He had never entirely recovered from the particularly virulent strain of influenza abroad last year. Indeed, the man lost his wife and only son to it—she while in Boston, as a volunteer nurse for the Red Cross, he while in France during the last days of the War.

Their names?

Anne and Joshua.

The son had been quite a strapping package, the model of young manhood. All sunburned flesh and sound limbs and even white teeth—the American antidote to the Kaisers and Crown Princes of the Old World.

The dark-eyed wife, meanwhile, never failed to offer me coffee, and exuded a faint perpetual scent of powder and almonds. Mild worry was etched lightly into her good-natured oval face—the strain of volunteer nursing, compounded by her only child's departure in 1918 for Europe.

The boy promised her and his father that he would return.

But September came and with it, the influenza.

Boston was first, and from there the disease spread like flames—to Arkham, to Salem, to the countryside and the states, to the world beyond.

Almost no one speaks of those terrible days now. The gauze surgical masks; the cheap unvarnished pine coffins stacked high as a tall man; the death carts; the crepe ribbons in so many windows, denoting the age of the deceased by shade: white, gray, or black; the blood-flecked froth and choking of victims drowning in their own fluids. Proclamations. Quarantines. The university was closed. Military police walked the streets.

My Mary and I shuttered the windows of our home, locked ourselves away. Not a knock was heard at the door for nearly a month.

Against my better judgement, I reread my entire collection of Poe. Lives ended, the leaves fell, the moon gazed upon empty streets and dark doorways, and all the while Mary and I lived like Prince Prospero's favored—exchanging timid pleasantries, indulging in small comforts grown cold, awaiting the arrival of that last horrid guest...but we were spared.

The War ended in November, 1918, and with it the epidemic. Winter came and snow buried the dead again.

No one knows how many died in those few awful autumn weeks, but hardly a family remained untouched. Mary's Aunt Sandra died during the first stages of the outbreak. I lost two of my students and my grandfather in October—the latter being an unusual case, the doctors tell me, since the disease preferred the young and vigorous rather than the old and infirm.

It was nearly December before we learned that Gammell had lost his wife and son. Gammell himself had barely survived. The apparition that greeted me at his door was both a horror and a pity. Every third sentence was seemingly punctuated with his harsh, hectic coughing. He disconcerted me still further by asking after his students. Were they all right? I honestly didn't know. I would not say that any of them had feared for Gammell's life, however. They had never liked him very much.

Not that it matters anymore.

Godfrey Gammell is with his wife and son now.

I wish that I could say this brings me peace.

Salt air.

That was what the university officials said: *salt air is the cure.*

Should I close my eyes, I am again in that paneled, polished, and yet somehow still dusty and dreary college office, with its fantastic Oriental rug, its thick curtains, its huge antique globe, its bookcases and framed diplomas and oil paintings of scholars past. Thin winter afternoon light filtered through the high Gothic windows. Behind a massive mahogany desk, like a modern Medici, sat the Dean, and beside him stood the owlish and uninspired vice–president.

The Dean had spoke at length, his tone as cultured and proper and depressing as his surroundings. Winter should have such a voice; it spoke of leaden skies and deep sleep, of hibernation.

I was Professor Gammell's best friend, he noted.

I nodded.

He filled a pipe, struck a match—a brief flicker of light within that shadowed cubicle—and then well–bred gloom again. He puffed strenuously. The tang of tobacco was as sharp as ammonia in that narrow space.

Things had been most…well…difficult for Professor Gammell lately, hadn't they? First his wife, then his son. A terrible tragedy. Reminded him of the typhoid epidemic of 1905. Thank heavens this recent…unpleasantness…was over now.

The vice–president cleaned his spectacles, nodded silent assent.

The Dean was concerned that Gammell's health had shown no real improvement.

Again, the vice–president nodded. A solemn bald owl—that's what he resembled.

The Dean tented his fingers. It was warm and close in that office—too warm, as a matter of fact. It made one drowsy, words slow and awkward, silences lengthy. I was of half a mind to open a window, to welcome in clean cutting air.

The winter semester will be over soon, the Dean noted. Spring will be here.

The firm set of his jowls was mirrored in the temple of his hands, a countenance that said, *I am a reasonable man, but I am in no mood for arguments today.*

I nodded, wondering what the man might possibly have planned.

The Dean recommended that Gammell take a leave of unspecified duration for reasons of health. He was well aware of the Gammell's love for his work and that in the midst of this…crisis…it was his most likely salvation. But, as said, there had been no real improvement in the man's condition.

I asked what they recommended.

Salt air, the Dean said, and the vice–president nodded emphatically. Meaning?

The vice–president finally spoke, his boyish voice at odds with his appearance. Salt air. It was a well–known cure for respiratory ailments. The man's own physician recommended it. Now it was the turn of the Dean to nod. Salt air and a change of scenery would do Gammell good. He needed to be away from Arkham for a time, away from his troubles.

The virtues of salt air—an utterly absurd solution, I thought. But they did mean well, and they were concerned. I myself had seen Gammell hardly able to get through his classes, he coughed so badly—the deep, tearing, vital sounds of a tubercular patient.

I asked what they might recommend. Boston was of course out of the question. As was Innsmouth. Cape Cod? Nantucket? Providence? At each name the vice–president slowly shook his baby–pink head. The Dean waited patiently. Where, then?

The vice–president folded his arms behind his back, smiled and informed me that since Gammell was Arkham University's Professor of Antiquities, that perhaps Kingsport would be most to his liking.

Kingsport?

Yes, Kingsport. The vice–president and his wife had been there last summer. Both had loved it. It was a fishing village hardly five miles from Arkham, dating back to colonial days. Surely I had at least heard of Kingsport? Wasn't I interested in old things, like Professor Gammell?

I replied that, Yes, I had heard of Kingsport—had been there once as a boy—but my field of expertise was military history, not antiquities. And as for antiquity, Kingsport was old but hardly ancient.

That's beside the point, Mr. Dandridge, the Dean informed me, with just the slightest edge of irritation in his voice. The matter concerned Professor Gammell's health, not his interests. And if the Dean was not mistaken, didn't the old fellow have family in Kingsport? Or ancestors, at least?

I could not answer that...he was a private man.

Well, he was from there, wasn't he?

I believed so, from what I had heard.

Several uncomfortable moments passed, and the Dean finally spoke, in a tone that suggested the matter was already resolved. Gammell would take leave. Kingsport seemed to offer the best of worlds for a troubled, sick man.

And since I was a friend of Mr. Gammell...would it trouble me terribly to perhaps visit on occasion, to see how he was getting along? The university would even go so far as to make provisions for necessary absences, should they arise.

The Dean watched me closely through his wire–rimmed glasses. Curious eyes. Wary, and gray, like sea foam. He was one to recall the most minor of slights and disagreements, long after they had ceased to matter. He had the mind of a scholar but the soul of a petty clerk.

It would be no trouble at all. We rose and shook hands.

The vice-president escorted me out of his office. In a fit of bonhomie, he clapped me on the shoulder. Kingsport was a fine town, he told me. An excellent choice on the part of the Dean. Why, had his own work not required him to remain in Arkham, he would be there this very moment, beside the sea. A fisherman, perhaps, or a carver of sea shells...

He laughed at his small joke, and I smiled politely.

So I had been there as a boy, then?

Yes, I had.

And?

It...it was difficult to describe. I had been quite young at the time, and it had been quite some time ago. Much of it was unclear now, like a dream.

It had been his turn to smile, then.

Childhood...

Yes, indeed. Childhood.

It was as a boy that I first knew Kingsport, in a summer long past, a summer evening at the other end of the world.

I came with family—stolid, imperturbable father with waistcoat and ruff of whiskers from the last century; small, freckled mother, self-conscious, smiling nervously, all but lost beneath a great white sunbonnet; two older, noisy brothers whose heels I dogged desperately, a stranger to their plots and games.

Summer tourists, is what we were. Weekend visitors.

Try as I might I could not keep pace with my brothers. It was an old torment, one disapproved of by my mother and father, but they had ceased trying to stop it years ago.

Let's see if little Edward can catch us!

And I did try to catch them.

Through crooked, cobblestone streets we darted, the excited maddening laughter of my brothers always ahead of me. Past moss-crusted, slate-roofed houses centuries old we ran, and our voices seemed much too loud in those silent sun-speckled spaces. Indeed, there were those that looked at us in askance—numerous cats, atop roofs, sitting upon crumbling fieldstone walls and colonial tombs, tucked away like precious stones within small comfortable niches and odd corners. Cats slender as willow-wands and shy. Cats with the air of Puritan elders. Cats the shade of sea-spray and cats the shade of storm clouds. Cats black as untold secrets and flights of nightmare.

Strange that not one should flee our riotous approach. They were merely content to watch us from all sides, their paws tucked under themselves, their thoughts their own.

But for one, who walked on two and not four feet.

My laughing brothers were upon him before they knew he was there—a man, well within that indefinable country between the middle years and old age, archaic in dress. Henry plunged headlong into him, but the man caught Henry by the shoulders with his powerful, snake-veined hands.

The three of us were stunned into silence. The face before us was of stone: unmoving, unforgiving, angular, hard, and framed by a white flame of beard. His brow jutted like a cliff, his mouth was a severe slash, a lipless wound. His sleeves were rolled to the elbow—a tradesman of some sort, perhaps a blacksmith, judging by the knotty toughness of his forearms.

Of life there was little suggestion, but for the gossamer halo of hair drifting about the eclipse of his darkish wizened skull, and in the small sharp flecks of flint that were his eyes.

Henry pulled away from the old man, who made no effort to recapture him. Staring fearfully, my two brothers rounded him and fled up the street.

The old man turned his attention to me. His expression was quite strange— one of intense curiosity and marked disapproval.

I muttered an apology, turned and hurried back the way I had come. The old man did not follow, nor did he leave. His hair trailed in the breeze like the train of an uneasy phantom.

Mark and Henry! Where could they be?

I heard them, calling for me, their voices made small by distance. They seemed very far away.

Although unnerved by my recent encounter, I was not yet afraid. I told myself that I must be brave. We would find each soon enough.

But the undecided streets and winding alleys of Kingsport proved my undoing. One does not chose his own path in Kingsport. The city leads one where it wishes one to be.

Ever fainter grew the voices of my siblings.

Soon I no longer heard them, heard nothing but the vital rush and pound of my own blood, of the sea. Not far away lay the ancient barnacle-studded wharves and rotting groynes of Kingsport Harbor, somewhere beyond the attic clutter of iron weather vanes and black chimney pots, beyond the faded colonial signs and small-windowed cottages.

I wandered aimlessly for a time, alone. The hour, already late, grew later.

I wondered what had become of my brothers. Perhaps they were back with my parents. They would concoct a story for mother: *We told him to stay with us, but he wandered off! He never listens!* They would then relish whatever punishment I received.

I called for them. *Mark! Henry!*

There was no answer, and I did not persist. The nature of the place did not invite such unruliness, and I heard nothing but the rhythmic crash of the sea, the thin wail of the wind in secret unseen places. At times the force of the latter rose to such a shriek it rattled the tiny bulls-eye windows in their frames.

(As a boy it had hurried me along with a wayward glance over my shoulder.

Salt Air

As a man, I know now what it was: a voice, desolate and railing, the sound of time and loss and darkness unfolding.)

And darkness was unfolding.

In the west fantastic clouds had crested like waves, a brilliant, flaring sunset of improbable shades: deep violet, heliotrope, orange and scarlet. It touched and made alive the dark windows of the houses and taverns, ringed the steeples and gambrel roofs in soft flame. To the north, where rose the steep, impossibly sheer cliffs and crags of Kingsport Harbor, it turned the ageless stone rose and gold. High above, gulls cried vespers.

I stood transfixed.

The cliffs spurred into the evening sky.

Beyond the bleak gnarled houses a pale stretch of sand beckoned. Thin scrub grass echoed the motions of the shadowed sea.

I passed between the oldest and most seaward of dwellings, rough and salt-crusted as the cliffs themselves. But for driftwood and wind, the narrow strip of beach was empty.

I chanced upon no one, yet I saw in the sand footprints other than my own.

Strange that they should emerge from the water. I looked about, saw no trail leading into the surf. Had a lone swimmer come impossibly far? Perhaps a boat had capsized or sunk!

I followed the line of prints, careful to avoid the water as it lapped against the shore—wet shoes were certain punishment. Father was very particular concerning the upkeep of things. *A good boy is a model of deportment*, he always told us.

The trail kept to the beach, close to the water. The sea had already erased some of the prints—those that were left made for the rocks further ahead.

The ground rose as I neared the cliffs, broken by all manner and size of stones and pitted boulders. Some were large as houses, their outlines softened by gray-green moss and wind and rains innumerable. Others were smaller, jumbled and piled atop one another, slimed here and there by weeds where the tide rose. Water boiled about the stones some yards away, a drawn-out sigh of sound, yet powerful, full of purpose. Occasionally a particularly strong wave struck this barrier with a crash and spume of foam. The air tasted faintly of salt. Fine, fine mist tickled my skin.

The water was loud here, among the stones, near the cliffs. It echoed within my skull. Beyond lay the harbor, the blue-black infinity of outer sea and darkening horizon. In the distance a bell buoy clanged, a slow funeral sound that made me uneasy.

My task was growing more and more difficult, given the broken ground—here and there I might spy a lone print or two. But my nerve was likewise beginning to slip away.

My father occasionally told my brothers and I stories of Kingsport, of white-sailed clipper ships taller than trees and whalers stinking of the kill. He told us of shipwrecks, of rough sailors full of uncouth words and old superstitions, of thirty grog-swilling Redcoats all poisoned one autumn night by an innkeeper with a curious, waxen face. And, when the fire burned low in the hearth, talk turned to ghosts, to shades, to the deeds of the Terrible Old Man and the odd hours at which strange things might be heard or seen.

The light was fading, and the wind had risen. Now and then it gusted about the stones with great force.

I grew uneasy, told myself I should be going.

I heard a sound. It was inconsequential, really—the clatter and crack of a small, dislodged rock, bounding down into darkness, loosened perhaps by the wind—but here it was more than that. I rose, licked my lips nervously. My mouth was suddenly dry, my throat full of dust and rusted gears.

I called to my brothers, to see if it was yet another trick. That would be just like them. There was no reply. The wind crooned in my ears. I offered yet another challenge to Mark and Henry. Nothing.

No, something…something near me, among the rocks.

Though I hardly realized it, I had begun to back away, slowly. Wonder and mystery had given way to dread. Behind me lay the clustered, worm-eaten remains of a village where the cottages were like faces old beyond reckoning, stark against the red sky. Before me was the muttering implacable sea and advancing night, clouds edged in ivory and silver. In the blue vault above cold stars emerged and soon only the great spire remained in the fading red-gold light.

There! Another sly scrape, suggestion of slow deliberate movement…

I warned whatever it was to stay away. My voice was very small and afraid. Reluctantly, I turned my back on it. Heart hard in my throat, I made my way back to the beach.

Headlong flight was out of the question. The ground was too uneven, the light too dim, slick in places with seaweed like the hair of drowned women. I would fall, twist my ankle, perhaps even break a leg. Forced to grope like a blind man, I wound my way through like a needle. The wind pulled at me. My panic eased slightly when, at last, my feet touched the beach, with its quiet foam-flecked surf, its swaying grass.

Out of breath, I stopped, glanced behind me. Nothing. The stones sat blind and dumb.

I would be in terrible trouble when I returned to the Inn.—if I found my way back—but the idea of knocking on one of those decaying, unlit doors to ask for aid was too repellent to consider. God only knew who or *what* might answer. Perhaps—

Something gripped my wrist. Fingers like old tree roots sank hard into the flesh.

With a gasp I pulled, but was held fast.

It was the old man. A dark disciplined lunacy lit his stern ferocious face, a flickering candle within a veiled lamp. His eyes were the color of old blood, rimmed bone-white. The thin mouth, pressed tight, trembled ever so slightly, ever so righteously.

I cried out and tore away. I stumbled, rose, waved my hands wildly about my head as if beset by unseen demons. I ran—I ran for all I was worth. Like a madman I ran through the empty winding streets of Kingsport. No longer did I wish to find my brothers. No longer did I fear the wrath of my father. I was desperate to escape the old man who had emerged as if from the very stones themselves.

And no one saw me, alone in my terror, but for the stars and the yellow–eyed cats, and I am sure they keep their own counsel.

I told Gammell none of this, of course.

Toward the weary end of winter he was prepared to leave Arkham. The Victorian town house he had lived in—formerly the abode of some obscure logging baron—would soon be left untenanted, in a state of stasis but for the tick and chime of the wall–clock. The neighbors had agreed to look after the place. Ownership of the family bulldog—a cream–colored good–natured brute named Orville with a face folded and seamed as a November jack–o–lantern—would pass to a distant relative in Philadelphia. The dog had been Anne's more than his, Gammell explained, and the emptiness of their home had worn greatly on the poor old thing, perhaps even more so than Gammell himself.

I didn't mention it at the time, but Gammell's health seemed somewhat improved. He still coughed, and was rarely without a cup of hot tea, but some of his old color and vigor had returned.

He had resumed teaching some of his classes. The students were as indifferent as ever—the country's sullen future assembled before him, enamored of booze, adultery, the home team, and little else. Countless glassy eyes mesmerized by that tiny executioner of souls, the minute hand.

Gammell's exams proved unusually difficult that year.

We spent one final, bleak March night in the study of Gammell's old home. The wind was strong and pressed hard against the elegant French doors. The embers of a fire flickered in the grate. Occasionally Gammell prodded at the charred logs with a poker, stirring a flight of sparks. At our disposal were two comfortable leather sitting chairs, padded footstools, and snifters of good brandy.

Gammell had a rather extensive library. Bookshelves lined the walls and flanked the fireplace to either side. I do not recall the many titles they held, but more than a few were of a nature rather different than Gammell's narrow pre-occupied life suggested. Among the dry archaeological treatises, the collected writings of Plato and Virgil and Homer and the studies of Classical architecture were books strangely out of place.

I read the titles silently to myself: Swedenborg's *Heaven and Hell*. *The Divine Comedy* of Dante. Mathieu Giraldo's *Histoire curieuse et pittoresque des sorcier*. Baron Guldenstubbe's *Pneumatologie positive et experimentale*. Frazier's

The Golden Bough. Barrett's *The Magus*. A hoary old tome titled *Le Petit Albert* sat next to Crowley's disreputable *Liber AL vel Legis* and the even more suspect and suppressed *The King in Yellow*.

I joked that all Gammell needed now was the pallid bust of Pallas above his chamber door.

He scowled briefly—drink usually did nothing for his humor—and returned to his fire–lit brooding. He had never held his liquor very well, and lately, slowly, steadily his drinking had increased. So far it had not impinged upon his professional life, but I was nevertheless glad he would soon be away from Arkham, this house and its ghosts.

Gammell waved a dismissive hand when I asked after the stranger books. Most of them had belonged to his father's father, and most, in his opinion, were dross. Metaphysics. Alchemy. Sorcery.

And why should I be interested in such things, he wondered. Wasn't Wellington's use of the reverse slope at Waterloo more my cup of tea?

I retrieved Guldenstubbe's book from the shelf and returned to my chair. My French is a little rusty, I admit, but I was able to translate some of the text—an astounding and improbable work concerning the phenomena of "spirit writing."

Gammell sniffed when he saw the book I had chosen. It was nothing but various scribbling and scrawling that claimed to be the words and signatures of such long dead notables as Pierre Abelard, Heloise, the mistress of Louis XIV...even emperor Augustus and Julius Caesar had left their mark.

I leafed carefully through the brittle pages. Some of the spirit messages were so illegible Guldenstubbe had been forced to appraise them himself. I read two or three to Gammell. He snorted and shook his head. One of the passages gave me pause.

L'amour qui nous reunit a fait tout notre bonheur, I read quietly—Heloise's thoughtful words, framed by the soft hushed sounds of the dying fire and the March wind outside. *The love that reunites us was all our happiness.*

Gammell sat silent, features etched in stark relief by the glowing embers, head resting upon hand, thoughtful finger to his temple. His appearance frankly disturbed me. His hair and nails had been allowed to grow improperly, almost decadently long. From his chin sprouted an affected satyr tuft of goatee he had lately cultivated. There was some color to his thin lips—but it was the false hue of the mortician's art, and spoke nothing of vigor or life. His pallid flesh was made even paler by the darkening of the folds under his eyes, which were as curious as ever: stern, fierce and yet dreaming, black as the March tempest outside.

I had seen such eyes before, but I pushed that thought away...

He rose and stood before the French doors, gazing out into darkness, his back to me. The wind moaned about the gables and eaves of the house, trying all windows. Occasionally it rose to a thin frustrated scream. It was a fitful, restless night hardly ameliorated by hearth or company, and I cast about the shifting shadows for the familiar homely face of the ormolu clock. A hundred excuses threaded through my uneasy thoughts as I did: the lateness of the hour, the preparation of lessons, a worried wife, the savagery of March...

But Gammell, detached, bemused, was first to speak:

Along the shore the cloud waves break,
The twin suns behind the lake,
The shadows lengthen
In Carcosa

He turned to me and offered a slight, sardonic smile. Cassilda's Song, Act One, Scene One, *The King in Yellow*. Had I ever read it?

Yes. Parts of it. Had not the French government seized nearly all the known copies and destroyed them?

Gammell did not reply. Instead he returned to the fire to provoke more sparks with the iron poker. Up the flue they ascended, a multitude of orange and yellow fireflies. He returned to his seat. The hidden clock announced the hour. The wind persisted at the French doors.

Would I be visiting him in Kingsport?

Yes, of course.

This seemed to ease him somewhat.

I asked him if he had family there.

Yes, but not in the true sense of the word. 'Ancestors' was a better term. He did have distant familial ties. Cousins older and several times removed. Perhaps even a long lost great–grandsire or two, but no true family or blood–ties.

But I would visit, yes?

Yes. I reassured him that I would be seeing him, soon.

Very soon.

My wife had always thought Gammell strange and fey, and did not accompany me on my sojourn to Kingsport.

Nor did she approve of my going; she was from a proper, God–fearing family, and Kingsport was, in their eyes to say the least, suspect. Tale and rumor had shadowed the ancient seaport for generations, and her ancestors had been familiar with the old legends.

My going was the subject of several terse, sharp arguments that proceeded more often in silence than in words. I myself was reluctant to depart—memories do not die easily—but in the end she relented.

I had debated the wisdom of bringing with me a companion. There was Unsworth, a fellow antiquarian in my department, but he was entirely too jovial, entirely too fearless. Ask what good had come of the War, and he would tell you that democracy had finally been given its chance. The influenza epidemic? The nation is better prepared for just such calamities in the future, sir.

Indeed, if I had mentioned that I thought Kingsport might be haunted, he would probably reply, A few restless spirits always add character to any setting, my good fellow.

I can only imagine what he is like at a funeral.

Ellerbee, for perhaps an hour, was a second possibility—Ellerbee from the university's own Holy Roman Empire, the vast, unwieldy, glacial English Department. He was a good friend, but where Unsworth was the soul of optimism, Ellerbee was ponderously gloomy and terribly imaginative—a gothic protagonist. A few hours in Kingsport could very well send him screaming into the countryside.

As it had me, once...

And so I went alone.

Though the snow had departed, leaden muffled winter still lay over the landscape. I made my way on foot to Kingsport beneath a vault of gray clouds so low I could all but spear them with the end of my walking stick. Errant snowflakes pirouetted in strange designs before my face.

(Some might think me daft not to drive a motorcar, or ride a bicycle. I have no use for such mad contraptions or mechanical toys. Besides, I have always been a vigorous man for my age, and Kingsport is at most two to three miles away.)

Of company there was none. The road to Kingsport is never well traveled, even in warmer months. During winter it is deserted. The countryside is likewise empty. I hardly heard a noise other than the crunch of dirt and gravel beneath my boots, the small evil creak of denuded branches in the wind, the sudden raucous uproar of crows as they burst forth from a bank of dead weeds.

Before long the bleak loneliness of the land began to tell upon me. I pulled the brim of my hat lower, clutched tighter my valise. The crows followed me for a time, croaking to one another—the sound of rough, vulgar laughter. I was grateful when they finally tired of me and departed, black tatters carried away with their dire pronouncements by the wind.

Mossy, crumbling stone walls and posts flanked my route. From bramble-choked culverts came the scratch and scatter of old leaves. I angled my head against the bitter air, retreated even further into my scarf and heavy coat.

The rhythm of the sea was within me before I ever saw it—the distant primordial rush and pound of waves. The road rose, continued to rise, wound up a willow-crowned hill, wound through the enormous, scored willow trunks. I marveled to think how beautiful a crown for the village below in better times, summer-green giving way to the gold of autumn, but now twisted, blackened, belonging more to winter, to some god of the underworld.

There below lay the city, beyond it the sea.

Salt air.

Kingsport.

The toadstool cluster of steep roofs clinging to the rocks like a living thing. The distant gray white-flecked sea. The crazy, cemetery tangle of weather vanes and chimneys. The tiny lattice windows and empty round portals. The streets that wound through it all like thick vines through a dismal long–overgrown garden. And thirty years later, it was all here, unchallenged, unchanged. At any moment three boys should come pounding up the street. And I am sure even the cats would be in their appointed places, awaiting me.

I began my descent.

Prior to my visit Gammell had sent me a letter. In it he spoke of many things: his first impression of Kingsport; the quaint appearance and reticent nature of its people; the salutary effects of sea air, rest and good plain food.

He had been especially taken with the sheer *age* of Kingsport. Unlike cities such as New York and Chicago, and to a lesser extent Arkham, Kingsport was in no hurry to cast down everything in the name of modernism. Motorcars were still very rare here. Electricity went largely unused. Talk of radio, of telephones and phonographs did little more than raise eyebrows. The War, influenza, President Wilson, Henry Ford, gangsters, Bolshevism—it was all far, all very removed from these folk, descendants of colonial fishermen, smiths, and whalers.

Many inns would be closed for the winter season, according to Gammell. But there was an inn open he could recommend, the Pipe and Pint. Look for the huge old oak out front. Marvelous place. Smoke–stained wainscot walls. Stained glass windows bearing ancient armorial standards. Carved corbels and cornices. Pewter plates and mugs stamped with the mark of their creator: SQUIRE WILLIAMS 1796; ELIAS YOUNG 1814.

The Pipe and Pint was said to have been a favorite of the Massachusetts Bay Governors. Later it had billeted the soldiers of King George the III. Gammell, in fact, had billeted in the same room as SARJENT JOHN FITZPATRIK—the bluff innkeeper had shown him the small rude one hundred and fifty year–old strokes cut into a ceiling beam. A commanding if gloomy view of the harbor, and the great bare oak, lay outside the large bay window.

Gammell, meanwhile, was quartered at a house on Back Street. Distant relatives, an old man and his wife. Some research and a chance meeting had facilitated matters. They lived much as their forebears had, by sun and moon, rain and candlelight. Gammell rented a sparsely furnished garret above them. He found the house a wonder of colonial preservation, but I still thought it odd that he should comment at some length on the depth, make, and dimensions of their ice cellar.

I did as Gammell had suggested, and the room SARJENT JOHN FITZPATRIK once claimed became mine. But for the view, there was really little to enjoy about the place. The bed was small, the chair and stool antique and uncomfortable. Across the room, directly opposite the bed, was a formidable armoire of dusky exotic wood, while in a corner stood an old dressing screen of some sort. A pair of candle stubs sat on a nearby table. Everywhere, heavy beams and solid planking. It was like being deep in the hold of an old ship, and I was glad that I should not be staying long.

Nevertheless, I unpacked and made use of the armoire. Gammell expected me the next day. Tonight I would try to sleep.

I lit the candles, and read, but I found it difficult to concentrate.

Occasionally I glanced out the bay window to see if the day's demeanor had improved, but it only grew darker and darker, and Kingsport fell into shadow. A curious unease giving way to dislike came over me. For something to be so *unchanged*, so *ageless* after three hundred years, let alone thirty, struck me as unnatural. I saw nothing new, nothing of the mark of time; not rot, not decay, not dust. Nothing. I belong more to the conqueror worm than did the village outside.

Toward eleven o'clock I decided to retire.

Sleep was another matter. The bed was as hard as ill luck. Outside the wind rustled, a sheet on a clothesline. The clouds had cleared and a small cold rime of moon sat high in the corner of the bay window.

I thought it very much like the eye of a cat.

I had slept perhaps an hour or two—I am not sure when exhaustion finally overcame me—when I was awakened by a gentle insistent tapping on the window.

Absurdly, at first, I thought it was a branch, and then realized the oak was too far for such things. Irritation gave way to fear. Scarcely daring to breathe, I strained to listen, the blankets pulled up tight to my chin. *Tap–tap. Tap–tap.* Slowly I sat up in bed. Yes, there—a shape outside the window. I swallowed dust and croaked, Who's there?

The shape did not reply. *Tap–tap.*

Heart pounding painfully, I steeled my nerves and repeated my question.

A muffled, eager voice told me that it was Godfrey Gammell.

Relieved, astonished, mystified, I fumbled for one of the candle stubs and lit it. Unsteady yellow light suffused the room.

Yes, it was Gammell outside my window at this odd, ominous hour, peering in, but I was hardly comforted.

He was strangely dressed, for one thing, in a wide–brimmed hat and heavy coat, collar upturned. It was bitterly cold out that night, I realize, but his manner of dress spoke as much of subterfuge as necessity.

He wanted me to open the window. I did, with a bit of a struggle.

I was about to ask him why he was here, but he quickly put a finger to his lips. I was told to dress and come with him.

Through the window? Why not summon the innkeeper to unlock the door? And just what in God's name was this all about?

He would explain, soon enough. Now would I be getting dressed, or was this all going nowhere?

I chewed on my lower lip, a moment's hesitation spinning outward into eternity.

Salt Air

Finally I said, All right, then. Wait here.

To this day I don't quite know why I agreed to go with Gammell. Was I still half-asleep? Did I fancy myself within the internal logic and wild terrain of a dream? Or had Kingsport itself—at once awesomely old, dimly aware, and terribly vital—cast a spell upon me?

Dreams, divinations, whispers, there were no answers, only night and the wind. The air was bitter with the promise of snow.

A horse and cart awaited us. I gave a start at the sight, had not seen such a thing since the epidemic. A hooded lantern sat upon the seat.

Gammell placed his hand on my back. Come along, Dandridge. They're waiting for us.

Who?

I would see when we arrived.

Reluctantly I climbed onto the cart. Gammell took the reins of the horse.

Still curiously languid, still strangely enervated, I turned in my seat to see what, if anything, lay inside the cart.

Something was there, dimly luminous in the lantern's faint glow. Two objects, side by side, oblong, roughly cut. Coffins, cheaply made, of pine. And old—the sharp resinous scent long gone now, the smell much more of black earth, of decay, of worms.

My wife and son, Gammell said simply of the coffins.

How—

Others helped me with the task, he replied. But it is not yet complete.

Perhaps this in itself should have been shock enough, but what finally did pierce my stunned reverie with cold horror was, to the untrained eye, quite innocuous.

In the unvarnished wooden lids new, rude, shallow cuts had been made. Markings, near the head of each coffin. They were the size of a man's palm, and of very unpracticed workmanship. They were symbols of some sort—evocative, enigmatic, dark and yet suggestive of some even greater darkness. It was not until Gammell raised the lantern, peering into the gloom ahead, that their outline became clear, and I gasped aloud.

Each coffin bore the mark of the Yellow Sign.

Perhaps I should not recall what followed. The hour is late. The fire is dying. Are the curtains drawn?

Good.

And are you certain you wish to know what became of us? Dawn is still far away and a long, lonely walk lies ahead of you.

Very well...

Gammell and I rode in silence through empty streets to the harbor. All there was to hear was the febrile whine of the space-borne wind, the dream-like toll of a far–off buoy. Or *was* it a funeral bell? I do not know. All I knew was the thin squeal and clatter of that death–cart, the unsteady hollow misstep of the gaunt horse, the crawling horror of the Yellow Sign.

Gammell finally spoke. There were others, he said, who would be waiting for us, by the water. His relatives would be among them, as would be those who had aided him in *recovering* his wife and son, and he was anxious to make a good impression. Now, if I would kindly lay aside the fixed notions and prejudices of *this* world—

Of the rest I don't remember much. It was politely mad, I assure you. Talk of returning the bodies to the sea…of possession…of ruined Carcosa gazing upon itself in the black lake of Hali where dwells something nameless.

Madness.

Before long, we reached our destination. Horse and cart came to a halt. In a narrow alley shadows peeled away from shadows, became figures.

There were several of them, and not one did I like.

First were two sailors or longshoremen; one broad–shouldered, crudely built, with a great waxed mustache and slender clay pipe; the other taller, thinner, of East Indian or Caribbean blood, wearing a high beaver hat. Both had the air of men with an unwelcome task before them.

An oily young priest, or some approximation thereof, shook our hands, offered a name I choose to forget and a smile utterly insincere. His robes and clothing were of a curiously luxurious cut, the sleeves rimmed with fine fur.

I saw no collar, no crucifix—only a threadbare heretic's miter. Embossed upon it, the Yellow Sign.

Present, too, was a young woman. Despite the bitterness of the night, she wore only a loose flowing pale yellow dress. Her feet were bare—as was the top of her head, her auburn hair cut in the tonsure worn by medieval monks. Curled locks trailed down her cheeks. She bore an instrument. It resembled most closely a cornet, exceedingly long and not of metal, flaring dramatically at the mouth.

They fell in behind the death–cart, but for the priest, who went ahead bearing the lantern.

The squat longshoreman muttered something unintelligible, and the East Indian laughed, a low chuckle from deep within him that rose to the pitiless stars above.

The alley was narrow, the ground uneven. The cart nearly scraped the fungus–blighted walls to either side. Ahead walked the priest, lantern bobbing like a nacreous corpse–light.

The beach was as I remembered it, but now I saw a small black knot of mourners gathered, not far away. At least I think they had come to pay grievance. They made not a sound, shed not a tear. I nervously attributed this to stern Puritanism.

Land, sea and sky seemed to exist in a void. I could not tell where one began and the other ended.

Again, we halted.

From behind us came a series of long notes. It was the young woman, cornet held aloft, blowing. Solemn, dreary, monotonous music, the sound of the abyss, of the titanic gulfs of space and time. Darkness had come to devour whatever remained of the light, while at the periphery of the senses, hidden things crept and moved.

The priest raised high his arms and said:

Behold He Who is Not to be Named! We stand at the Lip of the Void and await Your Sign!

The mournful cornet ceased. The wind rose and the waves in their eternal appointed task muttered darkly.

From the gathered mourners came a lone figure, slow and sure of step. As he drew closer, fear rose within me, became terror.

Despite the grim formality of his dress, I recognized him—the white penumbra of spidery hair and beard, the hard planes and deep shadows of the face, the stern, silently wild eyes.

A powerful hand took my own—the same hand that had seized a terrified boy a summer evening thirty years ago. I dared not pull away.

An indefinable smile creased the man's weathered features, which had hardly been affected by the passage of time.

Gammell introduced the man as being his granduncle.

The sea was to receive a great gift this night, Gammell's granduncle said. His voice was as strong as his grip, not loud, but carrying, compelling.

And upon me he had likewise bestowed a great honor.

I was to be a pallbearer.

Songs of my soul, my voice is dead,
Die though, unsung, as tears unshed
Shall dry and die in
Lost Carcosa.

Really quite beautiful, isn't it? It is a beautiful play.

Beautiful and cruel.

We returned to my room at the Pipe and Pint, Gammell and I, silent, the cart empty.

Night was growing old. A frosted sickle of moon hung low on the horizon. Despite my fear, despite my ill ease, I was even more exhausted than before. Gammell, however, was honed and alert, restless, almost sniffing the wind.

Flakes of snow were falling, drifting through the air. Somewhere a steeple chimed the hour—two in the morning. Had it all really only taken an hour or so? The coffins adrift in the blackness of the sea, each branded with that eldritch mark, each condemned to the depths or eternity or Hell or God knows what…

The very ordinariness of my room was a comfort to me—but I locked the window behind us, nonetheless, and closed the curtains.

Gammell sat in the antique chair. I lay full length upon the bed, utterly weary.

After sometime Gammell spoke, commenting idly on the signature carved into ceiling beam. Quite astonishing, the lack of literacy in the eighteenth century...

I told him that he must return to Arkham.

Why?

...because Kingsport was more terrible than I had ever suspected. It was an evil place. He must come away.

He chuckled quietly at this and replied, No. Kingsport was not terrible. Only those who brought evil with them suffered evil. Why, old witch–haunted Arkham was no less an evil place than Kingsport; probably more so. Perhaps *I* would be safer *here*.

Frustrated, I fell silent. Sleet ticked against the windowpanes. In the candlelight Gammell seemed impossibly old, somehow ageless, and wise beyond reckoning.

I told him that what he had done that night was terrible beyond words. What he had done was of offense to God.

It was no more terrible than what he had suffered, he replied. He was alone in the world. Forgotten. But it mattered no longer. It was out of our hands. It was out of God's hands.

Now was the time to sit and await judgement.

The judgement of whom?

He would not answer.

Toward dawn I was awakened, not by Gammell, but by cold—bitter March cold.

I was at a loss to explain the snow drifting about the floor, or the snow that dusted the tabletop and chair where Gammell had sat, until I realized that the bay window was open. The curtains fluttered in the wind. I drew them back to reveal a world gone white as myself.

Morning in Kingsport brings with it a sea–borne mist of fantastic character. It wends its way inland, creeping, filling culverts and gullies, rising all the while like water, so that each cottage is soon like an island, and then submerged. Distant sounds become uncannily clear, while those close by are strangely muffled.

Along the shore the cloud waves break...

Beneath the mist, new fallen snow lay on the ground like a shroud.

I called out the window, *Gammell! Godfrey Gammell!*

There was no reply. Somewhere a dog began to bark faintly, furiously.

Daybreak was not far off; the mist was slowly burning away, fading like a ghost at cockcrow. And as the light grew, I saw at the bottom of the bay window footprints—obscured somewhat by fallen snow. Three rows of footprints, trailing off into the mist, one row approaching...two leaving.

At first I was afraid, but suddenly I laughed.

Of course! The old man!
Gammell's granduncle had come for him during the night!
It was all a trick.
Yes...a trick.
Gammell had been more affected by recent events than I had ever imagined.

I resolved at that moment to bring him away from Kingsport—by force, if necessary. I would go to the house on Back Street and demand to see him. I would then return to Arkham, go to the Dean and inform him, frankly, that his judgement left much to be desired. As for the uninspired vice–president, well...if he wished to live by the sea, carve seashells and sing chanteys, I would personally pack his belongings for him.

The mysteries about me were insubstantial as the mist.
Dreams did not intrude upon the waking world.
But I was wrong.

I heard a small sound, outside, to my right—chillingly similar to the one I had heard as a boy among the rocks of Kingsport thirty years ago. But now it came from above me, from the great oak.

Something was there that I had not noticed before, upon one of the thick boughs, made obscure by the mist, but not for long.

It was a figure, sitting so that I could not quite see its face, its legs drawn up, hands clasped about its ankles, and I saw that it was a woman, clad in little more than diaphanous rags and tatters. The skin was bluish and slick, but that was not all what was wrong. In places it was seemingly *corrupted*—scales, like that of a serpent...

And the hair! Long, dark and rimed with ice, trailing like seaweed down the bare back.

Hair disturbingly familiar...
Anne?

It did not hear me at first—and I will never know why, in God's name, I uttered its name again.

It heard me then—the death mask head swiveled slowly, lifelessly about, and I winced to hear the delicate crack and crinkle of bone and breaking frost. The eyes—half-hidden by black hair, rolled so far back into their sockets as to be dead white orbs—found my own.

My voice died in my throat.

A cock, unmindful of either terror or the dead, crowed the hour.

But what I saw in the ancient tree in the yard of the Pipe and Pint was not the worst of it. No, not even the clotted black froth of pestilence gathered at that thing's nostrils and upon its chin—even that was not the worst.

For as the light grew it began to fade, like the mist. Before long the bough was empty. And soon only the footprints remained, winding through the mist, through the snow, through the streets, back to the sea.

I do appreciate your company tonight.
But it is getting late, and I suppose you should be on your way.
What of me?
I will be awake for sometime yet—keeping the embers company, you know. Sleep doesn't come easily these days and the night is a lonely universe.

It is those footprints that trouble my dreams. And the Yellow Sign.

It was Joshua, you see...Joshua had returned for his father, as he had promised. *The love that reunites us was all our happiness.*

Though I doubt there was anything of the sort in this case, as dear Heloise says...

Perhaps Kingsport will sleep once more, dreamless, now that Gammell is with them for eternity. I know that I shall never return there.

But I believe the dead are restless, and love company as much as the living. And I am left to wonder, will Godfrey someday return for me?

WALT JARVIS grew up in Central Texas, attended college in Tennessee and was a combat photographer in the Vietnam war.. He now lives in Los Angeles. He is married with two sons and two grandchildren. He discovered H.P. Lovecraft through "The Lamp of Alhazred," an August Derleth pastiche, and has been an avid Lovecraft reader ever since.

Through the Cracks

by Walt Jarvis

"Someone's going through the garbage again."

Stefan, his back to Margot, pretended to be asleep. He could hear it himself, over the twittering of the birds in the bougainvillaea: a rooting, sloughing sound, punctuated now and again by the counterpoint of aluminum cans being emptied from plastic bags. A homeless person picking his way through the dumpster.

"Stefan, I know you're awake," Margot said. "Aren't you going to do something?"

"Our apartment complex probably doesn't reflect a high enough level of conspicuous consumption to keep him occupied long," Stefan murmured, drawing his knees toward his chest.

"Remember the last time? You spent half the morning picking up trash that the guy had tossed out trying to get to the bottom of the dumpster."

Stefan remembered. "Right," he said, springing out of bed. He grabbed his wallet, and, dressed only in his boxers, leaned out the window.

He looked down on a broad back hunched over the garbage. Flies buzzed angrily around the transient. The man wore a shapeless gray top coat, even though the morning was unseasonably warm. His hands, pawing methodically through the plastic bags and emptying them one by one, were caked with grime. Stefan thought he could smell him from the second story, a different, higher stench than the general rankness from the now open dumpster.

"Uh, sir," Stefan called out, "how about accepting a cash donation and moving on?"

The man's head snapped up. Deep–set, hollow eyes glared emptily at him. Stefan's own eyes widened in astonishment. He recognized that face, as incredible as it seemed.

"Professor Strickland, is that really you?" he asked.

The man growled and angrily shook his head, but in that instant, Stefan saw a flicker of acknowledgment in those blood–shot eyes. Raymond Strickland, his old psychology professor, his favorite teacher in college? No, it couldn't be.

"Don't you remember me, Professor Strickland?" he asked. "Stefan. Stefan

Minassian. I was in one of your classes."

The grotesque figure pressed his finger to his lips in an exaggerated call to secrecy and said in a voice hoarse from disuse: "Don't say that name. Never say it. *They* will hear you and know where I am." His eyes shifted from the right to the left, as if he expected an ambush. Then with a snarl, he pulled himself over the side of the dumpster and hobbled crab–like down the alley between the apartment buildings

"Wait a minute," Stefan called out. "I want to talk with you."

Margot had joined him at the window. "You know a homeless person?" she asked incredulously.

"I'm afraid I do," Stefan said, watching the figure lumber around the corner and disappear from sight.

The head of the university's psychology department was housed in a suite of offices that Sigmund Freud would have felt comfortable in: walls paneled in dark cherry, overstuffed leather chairs, thick, plush Persian rugs, a massive hand–carved mantel over an artificial fireplace, a painting of a ruined castle that took its artistic cues from the 19th century. The only concession to the modern world was a computer and cell phone placed discreetly on Dr. Pinckus' desk.

Stefan had difficulty in getting in to see him. Being an alumni didn't seem to carry much weight. It was not until he told Pinckus' secretary that he was a freelance writer working on an article on America's top psychologists that he got an appointment.

"I've been interviewed before, but only by academic magazines," Dr. Pinckus said, leaning back in his leather chair and giving Stefan a faintly condescending smile. "Some general media exposure would be appreciated. Where exactly are you planning to publish this article?"

"Well, the *L.A. Times Magazine* is interested," Stefan said. A small lie, but what difference would it make once he got the information he had come for?

"Local exposure. So much the better. I suppose you're interviewing Drs. Croft and Rosenbaum?"

"Uh, both of them," Stefan, who had never heard of either, answered cautiously.

"A word of advice: take anything that Rosenbaum says with a grain of salt. The man is a notorious self–promoter."

"I'll remember that. Before we begin, there's something I'd like to ask you first. It's about a professor I had here as an undergraduate. Dr. Strickland. Is he still with the university?"

"We have no Strickland on the faculty," Dr. Pinckus said, his smile fading.

"I'm sure that was his name. It doesn't ring a bell?"

"There *was* a Dr. Strickland when I took over as head of the department. Unfortunately, he suffered a mental breakdown and had to resign."

"Oh, that's too bad. I hope he's better now. Do you know how I can reach him?"

"I'm afraid I don't. I hope you don't want to contact him for the article. He was espousing a very questionable theory on the causes of schizophrenia at the end of his career."

"What theory was that?"

"That a certain form of schizophrenia has a supernatural cause," Dr. Pinckus said with a dismissive smile. "Completely preposterous, of course. Now, shall we start on that interview? My time is limited, Mr. Minassian."

Stefan went through the motions—turning on his tape recorder, nodding as Pinckus elaborated on his own pet theories of psychology—but all the time he was wondering what had transformed Dr. Strickland from the beloved teacher he remembered into that grotesque shambling creature in the dumpster. What had led to a breakdown so complete that it had destroyed not only his career but his life?

After the interview was over, Pinckus' secretary caught Stefan's eye as he was walking through the outer office and signaled him to approach her desk.

"You need to talk to Dr. Strickland's daughter," she said in a low voice. "He was a wonderful man, a great teacher. He deserved better than what he got from the school, but you didn't hear that from me."

She handed him a number scribbled on a Post–It note. "He may have been wrong," she whispered, "but he was always nice to the staff, unlike some other people."

Her name was now Jennifer Morrision. Her husband was in the MBA program at Pepperdine. There was no way they could afford to live in Malibu, so they had rented a place in Oxnard. They lived in a high crime area, where the palm lined streets and cookie–cutter apartments were peaceful by day but sometimes a war zone at night. She was more afraid here, Jennifer said, than she had ever been in Los Angeles.

She was a plain–faced girl with rosy cheeks who looked as if she had just stepped off an Iowa farm; he could see the shadow of her father in her good–natured smile. There was a permanent sadness in her eyes, though, an unspoken reminder of why Stefan was here. She carried a stocky toddler in her arms.

"Do you mind if we go out in the backyard to talk, Mr. Minassian?" she asked. "My son has just learned to walk, and he's into everything. It's a warm afternoon. If I put him in his play pen, maybe he'll fall asleep."

The sun beat down on the back of Stefan's neck and he began to feel sleepy himself.

Jennifer came back with two lemonades and sat down across from him. "I don't know how much help I'm going to be where my father's concerned," she said. "I haven't had any contact with him for a number of years. Not by choice, either. I just don't know where he is anymore, although I've tried to find him."

"I saw him recently."

"You did?" she asked, leaning forward. "Where?"

"On the street. I hate to be the one to tell you this, but he's a homeless person now. I'm not sure he recognized me."

"Where did you see him?" she asked. "I'll start looking for him right away."

"It was near where I live, actually." He didn't add that he had found Strickland in a dumpster next to his apartment. "I don't understand what happened to him. He was such a great teacher...and now this."

"Do you want the official story or my version?"

"I'd like both," Stefan said. "Let's start with the official one."

Raymond Strickland suffered a mental breakdown due to stress. Partly this was because he was passed over as head of the psychology department (Dr. Pinckus' contribution to the legend), partly it was because of the controversy arising from his work. His "Theory on the Paranormal Origins of Selected Forms of Schizophrenia" was considered unpublishable; what little was circulated about it through the academic grapevine made the department and others on the faculty extremely nervous. It was as if Strickland had promulgated a theory that the Holocaust had never happened, or the world, after all, was flat.

Finally Dr. Pinckus requested that he resign, for the good of the university. Strickland had tenure, however; there would be no dislodging him if he really wanted to stay. And it appeared he intended to fight it, when something happened.

"He interviewed a patient whom he was sure would provide corroborative evidence for his theory," Jennifer said. "Someone who had been very ill, but then had been miraculously cured. This patient, Edgar Valgrens, was under the care of a woman who at first refused to allow my father to talk to him. Then she had a change of heart and let Dad set up an interview, as long as she was present as well. The three of them were together for several hours. When he returned home, he was strangely silent and preoccupied. Both my mother and I noticed it right away. There was a look in his eye that we had never seen before, a kind of dread that never seemed to leave him after that. "

It was shortly thereafter that the first symptoms of schizophrenia appeared in her father. They caught him again and again in an attitude of listening. He complained that objects had taken on bizarre shapes and colors were brighter and more varied than they should have been. Strickland became morose and irritable, a temperament that was completely unlike him. He would explode at the slightest provocation, get into shouting matches with his colleagues, berate his students over relatively minor mistakes. He seemed to be in a constant state of mental anguish; they heard him whispering to himself when he thought he was alone, arguing even, or pleading.

"He didn't respond to treatment?"

Jennifer shook her head. "That's the sad thing. He wouldn't allow himself to be treated. As far as he was concerned, there was nothing wrong with him. He was being tormented by forces from outside, he insisted, a typical symptom of schizophrenia. We tried to get him to seek help, once we realized how serious his condition was. He refused. It broke my mother's heart. Two years ago she suffered a heart attack and died."

Without warning he submitted his resignation to Dr. Pinckus. The very next day, he vanished. "It was as if he slipped through a crack and disappeared forever," his daughter said.

"That's one version, Jennifer," Stefan said. "What's the other?"

She had gone through his notes, written in a crabbed hand on yellow legal sheets, and, of course, the rough draft of his book, which grew more and more disjointed as it progressed, reflecting his deteriorating mental condition.

"My father came to believe that not all schizophrenia had a physiological root," Jennifer said. She drew a deep breath and looked down at her lap. "I know this is going to sound crazy, but Dad thought that there were, uh, spirits, invisible beings, that existed only to torment mankind. Most people were oblivious of their existence, and the very few that did become aware of them were driven mad by the knowledge. A madness that exhibited all the signs of classic schizophrenia."

"How did your father come up with this theory?"

"Over the years he interviewed thousands of schizophrenics or their caretakers. In all but a handful of patients, the traditional diagnosis applied. You know, schizophrenia is one of the most tragic forms of mental illness. Someone once called it a sentence as well as a disease. Already there was a lot of misunderstanding and baggage about the disease. Then Dad comes along and says that some of the victims would be well if it weren't for these invisible creatures who torment them.

"Once he made his views known, my father was completely discredited in the academic community, but he held to them steadfastly. Dad always said that the Invisibles were like selfish children, always clamoring for our attention, fighting to make themselves noticed, but most people weren't sensitive enough to be aware of their existence. They weren't dangerous until they entered our consciousness." She raised her eyes and looked at Stefan. "That's one explanation of what happened to him, isn't it? He became aware himself, and it drove him mad."

"Do you still have your father's notes?" he asked quietly.

"Yes, I've kept them. Why?"

"Would they contain Edgar Valgrens' address?"

She nodded. "You won't learn anything from him, though. Now that's he's cured, my father doesn't exist for him anymore."

"I want to talk to him anyway. It can't hurt."

Among the professor's journals, which Jennifer gave him for background, Stefan found the following entries, jotted down in Strickland's crabbed, hurried handwriting:

July 19, 1996
Ever since my terrible interview with V., I've noticed that all noises are louder to me than before. Background noises in particular seem to be more audible. The worst is that I now seem to hear voices behind the background static: occasionally they seem to be calling my name, although I know this is an impossibility.

This affliction makes it extremely difficult for me to concentrate on my manuscript. I don't understand how this could come on so suddenly, unless A. actually has some link to Them. Is that even possible? She struck me as a scam artist, hiding behind a false New Age sensibility. She tempted me with actual contact with them, but I spurned her offer. Is this her retribution? Or is it simply a result of a hyperkinetic imagination, fueled by stress over P.'s Machiavellian maneuverings. No matter what, I know I'm not crazy.

August 3, 1996
The voices continue to become more strident. I'm exhibiting all the classic symptoms of schizophrenia, the acute auditory sensitivity, hearing voices that no one else can hear (but they're so damnably real!), the paranoiac sensation that I'm being observed by invisible eyes, yet I know I'm not going mad.

These voices are real—I understand them though they are not speaking English. How dangerously seductive they are; yet all they promise is a kind of slavery.

September 24, 1996
God in heaven, make them stop! They refuse to give me a second's rest. I hear them quarreling in my head even when I want to sleep. I can't teach, I can't carry on the normal functions the workaday world demands, I'm being driven mad by their incessant whisperings. But I won't let them have me, even if madness is the only way out…

The man stared at Stefan with an almost clinical detachment that made the latter's skin creep. Valgrens was a short, compact man in his late fifties, unremarkable in appearance except for piercing blue eyes. His sister was a tall, elegant looking woman dressed in a dark pantsuit that set off the almost albino whiteness of bleached hair.

"Edgar, this is Mr. Minassian," Barbara Valgrens said. "He's helping Dr. Strickland, the man who interviewed you when you were sick a number of years ago. You do remember Dr. Strickland, don't you?" She spoke slowly and carefully, almost as if she were addressing a young child.

"Yes, I remember him. Strickland should come back and talk to me now that I'm well," Valgrens said in a level voice, never taking his eyes off of Stefan. "To complete his research. But then he's no longer being published these days, is he?"

"No, I'm afraid he's not," Stefan said, thinking that it was hard to do research from the bottom of a dumpster. "It's Dr. Strickland who needs our help now. He suffers from schizophrenia himself, unfortunately"

"How awful," Barbara said, her shock genuine. "Professor Strickland was such a wonderful man. He immediately struck up a rapport with my brother. And that was when Edgar was quite ill, and having trouble relating to anyone."

"I'm much better now," Valgrens said.

"Of course you are, dear," Barbara nodded. "Much, much better. Thanks to the help you got from people like Dr. Strickland and Miss Arbuser."

Stefan found he had to look away from Valgrens, whose weirdness his sister seemed so completely oblivious to, and let his eyes roam quickly around the room. Then he noticed something else. This, the main room in a separate guest house, a sunny little bungalow surrounded by birds of paradise and bougainvillaea, was the center of Edgar's life. Yet it was as devoid of personality as if it were a room in a vacant house. A generic-looking sofa, a boring wooden coffee table and a few cast-off chairs were the only furniture. The walls were blank, unadorned by paintings or anything else. If it reflects its owner, Stefan thought, then Edgar must be little more than a cipher.

"Dr. Strickland considered Edgar one of his more unique cases," Barbara said in a voice directed only at Stefan, as if her brother was not in the room. "The first time he saw him, Edgar was in an institution, dangerous to himself as well as others."

"The restraining devices bit into my flesh," Edgar said. "I couldn't even turn my head."

"The last time he saw my brother, Edgar was as you see him now," Barbara said, patting him lightly on the knee. "Cured. Well, almost cured," she hastened to add.

"How were you cured, Edgar?"

He leaned forward and looked at Stefan with his cold, dead eyes. "Dorothy Arbuser," he answered.

"He started talking about the Invisibles when I was a freshman in high school," Barbara said. "At first we thought it was just a phase he was going through. You know, a child's invisible companion thing. When he saw that we didn't believe him, that we thought it was a kind of joke, he tried to hide it from us. That was when we became concerned."

As Edgar grew older, it became worse, not better. The Valgrens arranged for Edgar to undergo psychiatric treatment. it was then that he was diagnosed as being schizophrenic, suffering from delusions that he was shadowed by powerful, invisible beings that were everywhere.

"But Edgar," his psychiatrist had asked gently, "if you can hear these beings, than why can't the rest of us?"

"You're the lucky ones," he had replied, as if that were all the answer that was needed.

Eventually he had to be institutionalized; that seemed to be the only way to keep him from hurting himself or others. The hospital—Stefan recognized it as one of the most prestigious private clinics in Southern California—kept Edgar heavily sedated so that he was more dead than alive. When he was not drugged, his arms and legs were restrained and, toward the end, he was even forced to wear a mouth device to keep from swallowing his tongue. When he was conscious, he babbled incessantly about the invisible beings all around him, carrying on screaming, one-sided arguments with them, or alternatively, begging them to leave him alone.

"Edgar's condition continued to deteriorate," Barbara said. "It was a soul-wrenching thing to watch, and the worse thing was the sense of helplessness all of us felt. Then, amazingly, from one day to the other, he began to get better. It was a true miracle, Mr. Minassian."

"What happened?" Stefan asked.

"We were lucky enough to find Dorothy Arbuser," she said.

Arbuser was seen by the Valgrens as a last resort. The woman had received no formal training in psychiatry or psychology. In fact, she was held in disrepute in by many in the mental health field. She presented herself as something of a mystic, promulgating a union between man and nature, a return to a more animistic world view. Despite her lack of academic credentials, she nonetheless had a word-of-mouth reputation for enacting some remarkable cures. They were desperate to try anything.

"Of course, the clinic fought our efforts to remove Edgar," Barbara said. "Why not? We were paying them a small fortune for my brother's care, but all he did was continue to get worse. I had a chorus of people tell me that it was futile, even dangerous, to contact this woman, but I honestly believe I have her to thank for Edgar's cure."

He didn't look completely cured, Stefan thought critically. Functioning, yes, a model citizen compared to the hollow-eyed grotesque that was Dr. Strickland. He was clean-shaven, his hair neatly combed, his sports shirt freshly starched. Yet there was something that belied this aura of normalcy. It was the eyes, Stefan decided. Yes, that look in his eyes. There was a coldness there, an alienness, that was chilling. Stefan wondered that his sister Barbara did not see it.

"Miss Valgrens, I'd like to talk to Dorothy Arbuser," he said. "Is there any way you could put me in touch with her?"

"No!" Edgar said suddenly, sitting bolt upright in his chair. "Dorothy doesn't see outsiders."

"I thought perhaps she could help Dr. Strickland," Stefan said.

"Ah, that's altogether different," Edgar said, visibly seeming to relax. "She always wants to find new patients—to cure them if she can."

Barbara went to get the woman's phone number, leaving the two men alone in the room. Stefan sat silently with his hands resting on his knees; normally he would want to make small talk with an interviewee, to try get him or her to open up; but he had no desire, strangely enough, to interact with Edgar Valgrens.

Edgar started, as if awakening from a dream. "You can see them, you know," he said with a sly look at Stefan.

"See what, Edgar?"

"They're not invisible all the time When they are ready, they'll let you see them—a glimpse, anyway. I know that first-hand."

"What did you see?"

"A magnificent sight. Eyes that burn with all the knowledge of the universe, yet filled with the longing of a little child. The longing to be in the world instead of always outside of it." He shivered uncontrollably. "It was only for an instant, but I'll never forget it."

"How did Dorothy Arbuser cure you, exactly?"

Before Valgrens could answer, his sister bustled into the room. "Here it is, Mr. Minassian," Barbara said. "I hope the number is still good. I'm sorry we can't spend any more time with you, but Edgar and I have tickets to the Long Beach Symphony and we're already running late. Edgar, will you show Mr. Minassian out?"

"Thanks for everything," Stefan said. "I'll let you know what happens with Dr. Strickland."

"Yes, please do. I hope Miss Arbuser is able to help him."

Jerkily Edgar rose to his feet and motioned silently for Stefan to follow him. At the door Stefan glanced over his shoulder and saw Barbara Valgrens smiling proudly at them from the sofa. Perhaps it was a small victory for Edgar to relate with someone else, even if it were something as mundane as walking a guest to the door.

It was not easy to contact the Arbuser woman. The telephone number led to an answering service; patiently Stefan kept leaving messages, with no call backs. It wasn't until his fourth message, when he mentioned Dr. Strickland, that she deigned to return his call.

"What's your relationship with Dr. Strickland, exactly?" she asked. "Is he a relative? A co-worker? Or just a friend?"

"He was an old professor of mine," Stefan said. "I'd like to help him recover if I can."

"If you could bring him to me, perhaps I could do something for him."

"Could I talk to you first, face-to-face? I have some questions."

"I don't do interviews, Mr. Minassian." He did not remember telling her he was a journalist.

"Look, he's a street person. He's going to be impossible to find."

"If you really want to help him, you'll find him. When you do—and I'm sure you will, Mr. Minassian, you sound like a very resourceful person—then I'll drop whatever I'm doing to talk to him. To the both of you. Fair enough?"

Stefan began his search without much optimism. If Jennifer Morrison hadn't been able to find her father, what made Stefan think that he could? Fortunately he was between assignments, so he had time to look.

He started downtown. He found the homeless asleep on city bus benches within blocks of the ocean, black stains in the bright sunlight, or staring up at him with mad–dog eyes from the narrow alleyways between the gentrified boutiques. When he found one of them shambling down a palm–lined street, pushing a shopping cart filled with the detritus of their daily existence, often talking a mile a minute to no one at all, Stefan drew close enough to make sure that it was not Professor Strickland before allowing the transient to continue on his or her meaningless journey.

Until he began his search, Stefan had no idea that there were so many of them. Surely they had always been there and he had just conveniently ignored them in the past. Some of them he saw over and over again, like the white–haired woman whose cheek was split by a vivid scar, whom he always glimpsed on Ocean Avenue pushing what looked to be the same rusted Costco cart, or the man in the Army fatigues who stalked up and down Lincoln Boulevard, shaking his fist and shouting angrily at some invisible adversary. How many of them were actual schizophrenics like Raymond Strickland, he wondered, and how many of them were the victims of drug abuse, the Vietnam war, or neglected childhoods?

He found Strickland finally in a place where he had never thought to look. Stefan had returned to the university to pick up biographical information for a future feature on the college's most famous living alumni, who was about to receive a White House appointment. He was walking back to his car when he spied a lumpy figure sitting on a bench across from the fountain that marked the center of the campus, a figure that looked vaguely familiar. Stefan veered away from the parking lot and walked over to the bench.

It was Strickland, wearing the same greasy overcoat that he had had on in the dumpster, and a pair of work gloves that were positively blackened with dirt. With his red–rimmed eyes he was staring across the campus at the psychology building.

Carefully Stefan sat down beside him, leaving enough personal space so, he hoped, that Strickland would not feel threatened.

"Dr. Strickland," Stefan said softly.

"I used to teach here," the other said in a low voice

"I know. I was one of your students."

Strickland looked in his direction without recognition.

"I was the one who had trouble understanding difference between the ego and the id. Looking back, a little studying would have helped."

Strickland nodded slowly and a faint smile touched his cracked, sunburn lips. "I do remember you now. My memory was good then, before *they* began to prey on me."

They were silent for a few moments, Strickland clutching his knees and rocking slowly back and forth, as if the mental effort to hold himself together had a physical manifestation.

"Your daughter Jennifer would like to see you again," Stefan said at last.

"When you're ready."

"Jennifer?" Strickland looked up with a little start. "Jennifer is lost to me as long as *they* won't leave me alone. They're everywhere, you know. I imagine there's one of them listening to us now."

"Dr. Strickland," Stefan said, "I think I know someone who can help you. Someone who can make the voices go away." He saw a spark of hope flicker faintly in Strickland's blood–shot eyes and pressed on: "Will you come with me to see her?"

Dorothy Arbuser lived in a 1930s style stucco Spanish mansion on a hillside in Altadena, set so far back from the road that only the roof was visible. The very remoteness of the Arbuser place hinted at mysteries and secrets. Stefan had taken time to bone up a little on the family name: it was old Hollywood money, transported to the San Gabriel Valley, of which Miss Arbuser, an only child, would be the last direct recipient.

A maid silently admitted them into a dusty courtyard where a fountain tinkled. Her face remained stone–blank, she made no eye contact, and if she smelled Strickland's unwashed sourness, she gave no sign of it.

"Miss Arbuser will be with you in just a few minutes," she mumbled, and vanished.

Stefan thought it would be as difficult to see the woman as it had been to get her on the phone the first time, but, surprisingly enough, she had agreed to meet them right away, standing by her original promise. When she appeared out of the shadowy coolness of the house, Stefan found her older than he had expected; too old to be so darkly tanned. She swept across the tiles in a flowing jebella, bone–white except for a faintly Arabic motif in red over her right breast. Her sandy colored hair fell loosely around her shoulders. She wore no makeup, and her face was gaunt and leathery from too much sun.

"Mr. Minassian, I'm Dorothy Arbuser," she said, offering her hand. Then she turned to Dr. Strickland and Stefan had the sensation that he had been quickly dismissed. "Dr. Strickland, it's been a long, long time. Won't you come with me into the house, please?"

She ushered them down a cool, wide hallway whose white walls were broken with Oriental tapestries and into a high–ceilinged room which, surprisingly enough, was devoid of furniture. Stefan was reminded unpleasantly for a moment of Valgrens' living room in the bungalow. Full length mirrors on all four walls reflected their images but nothing else. In the distance Stefan heard the front door slamming. The maid leaving for the day?

Arbuser turned to face them. "I had hoped you'd come back before now, Dr. Strickland, but I'm glad to see you nonetheless. It's been a long time since you came to see me about Edgar.

"At that time you wanted to find out all there was to know about the Invisibles. Your intellectual curiosity was admirable, but I warned you then that you might learn more than you bargained for."

"I thought I was safe," Strickland groaned. "I thought my rationality would protect me."

"Your dread in their presence is nothing to be ashamed of. They've been here forever, you know," she said, glancing at Stefan. "Primitive man knew them better than we do, because our ancestors were more closely attuned to Nature. Their presence has waxed and waned through the ages. We are living in an epoch where they have very little influence, but that, too, will change. Even so, some of us are lucky enough to sense their presence glimpsed through the hairline cracks in what we mistakenly call reality."

Stefan was appalled by what he was hearing.

"Miss Arbuser, I thought you were going to help Dr. Strickland," he said angrily, "not confuse him further."

"Be quiet, young man," she snapped. "I am going to help him attain enlightenment and self–understanding. If you don't want to be a part of that, please leave the room."

Angrily Stefan folded his arms across his chest but fell silent. Surely the Arbuser woman knew what she was doing. After all, hadn't she helped cure Edgar Valgrens, or at least returned him to society?

"Dr. Strickland," she went on in a soft voice, "the Invisibles have tormented you because you've resisted instead of embracing them. How much grief and suffering you could have saved yourself and your family if you would have simply accepted them from the beginning."

"I don't want to accept them," Strickland said, violently shaking his head. "I just want them to leave me alone."

Stefan felt a faint draft stir in the room, making the candle flames flicker and the curtains tremble. He wondered where it was coming from, since the windows were closed.

"They only want a small part of you, professor. That's all they want of anyone. Can you blame them, really? To be so powerful and yet to be as ephemeral as a spider web must be supremely frustrating."

"Who are you, to know so much about them?" Strickland whispered.

"I am one of their servants on earth," Dorothy Arbuser said proudly. "I opened myself completely to them early on; but instead of taking me, they instructed me to help others become their vessels. I can help you as well, Dr. Strickland, if you'll let me."

"Yes!" Strickland said suddenly in an agonized voice, stumbling to his feet. "I know who you are now; I remember. Yes, do with me as you wish. I can't stand the pain anymore. Anything is better than this!"

Before Stefan could intercede, Dorothy grabbed Strickland and pushed him against one of the mirrors. She held him there against the glass as if she were trying to push him through it. Stefan saw his mouth twist grotesquely as if he were racked with pain. In a moment his face went slack and it was over. It appeared he would have fallen to the ground if she had not held him up.

It was only when Stefan looked away that he caught a movement in the mirror behind her. It was so faint, and so quick, that had his eyes been focused anywhere else, he would missed it. Something was floating there in the glass, a wavering, indistinct shape that was not just a reflection behind the surface itself, as if the mirror had three dimensions instead of two.

"You saw it!" Dorothy Arbuser cried triumphantly, catching the horror in his eyes. "I suspected you might. You're a lucky man to receive the gift, Mr. Minassian, even if it has come late in life to you!"

Terrified, Stefan turned and fled the room, banging against the door as he stumbled into the hall . He raced through the courtyard, the pounding of blood in his ears drowning out the noise of the fountain and the soft music of the wind chimes hanging in the trees.

A week passed, a week in which Stefan lived in a state of perpetual anxiety. He could not sleep or eat, and every moment was consumed by the memory of what he had seen—or thought he saw—in the mirror. He tried to convince himself he had imagined it. Dorothy Arbuser had wanted him to see one of the creatures, and his imagination, heightened by circumstances, had obliged her.

He was also stricken by having abandoned Professor Strickland to a woman who in retrospect seemed more dangerous than anyone the man could have encountered on the streets. He was afraid to find out what had happened to the professor. He couldn't even bring himself to call Strickland's daughter for news of her father.

The experience had affected him so much that it had intruded on his own sense of reality. Now he began to hear voices, whisperings that were unintelligible but constantly audible, like faint static on a radio. They seemed to follow him everywhere he went, and he caught himself looking wildly around, trying to find their source.

Concerned, Margot suggested that he see a doctor and then, as his condition worsened, insisted on it. The physicians could find nothing physically wrong with him, however, even after running a battery of exhaustive tests. They recommended psychiatric evaluation.

One afternoon, after listlessly wandering downtown, hoping that the noises of the city would drown out the constant sussuration, he came home to find Margot packing her bags.

"I'm moving out," she said, her mouth twisted set in a hard line. "I can't live like this anymore, Stefan, I just can't. I have a healthy frame of mind, and intend to keep it that way. I've asked you again and again to get professional help, and, since you won't, I'm forced to cut my losses. Here's the number where I'll be staying. Give me a call when you've done something about your condition."

The doorbell had rung at least four times before Stefan became conscious of it. Slowly he rose from the table, where he had been staring listlessly into the sun–dappled garden, his hand covering momentarily the eviction notice lying on top of the stack of unopened mail. Stefan had learned some time ago that if he did not think of anything, the voices could be kept at bay, at least some of the time. That knowledge had come at the price of his career, his girlfriend, and his family; but it was worth it for the periods of respite it brought him.

He blinked in surprise to find Dr. Strickland and his daughter standing on the front porch. Strickland was barely recognizable as the homeless creature that had shuffled into Dorothy Arbuser's lair. He was well–groomed and wearing a blue blazer and a pair of khaki slacks.

"Mr. Minassian," Jennifer said, "excuse us for coming to see you unannounced. I did try to call, but there seems to be something wrong with your phone." She was polite enough not to mention that it had been cut off for non–payment. "Are you all right?" she asked hesitantly. "You don't look very well."

"I'm fine," he managed to say. "I've been ill, but I'm feeling better."

He did not invite them to come inside.

"My father has made a complete recovery, thanks to you and Dorothy Arbuser," she gushed. "He staying with us now and talking about teaching again. Oh, it may not happen any time soon, but it would have been impossible even a month ago. It's a miracle what the two of you have done for him."

Strickland took a step closer and offered his hand. "I want to thank you in person, Stefan," he said. "Yes, it's true. I'm recovered and I have you and Dorothy to thank for it."

Jennifer looked at the door, as if still expecting they would be invited in. "Well, I think we should go now, Dad," she said uncertainly when they were not. "It looks like Mr. Minassian needs his rest."

"You go on to the car," Strickland said. "I want to talk to Stefan alone for a moment. "

"Yes. Well, good–bye Mr. Minassian." She turned and hurried down the path that led to the street.

"My thanks *is* sincere," Strickland said when they were alone. He fixed Stefan with a cold, sardonic look. "You really did help me find an inner peace. So what if I've had to give up a little of myself? Part of my soul, some might say. The trade–off makes it worth it. I'm a temporal host for them now, and they have expanded the boundaries of my world infinitely. You have an inquisitive mind, Mr. Minassian. I know you've heard them calling you. I can see it in your eyes. Why don't you open yourself to them, as I eventually did? They only want to share a small part of you. They'll give you so much in return."

He paused and gave Stefan a knowing smile. "And the voices will stop, I promise you. That alone will make it worth while. But if you refuse, they'll continue to grow louder and more insistent. And the Invisibles always get what they want. Time means nothing to them."

"I—I don't want to become like Valgrens," Stefan whispered. "Or you."

"Suit yourself. Someday then I'll see you on the street, carrying on angry conversations with things that no one else can see, stumbling away from approaching footsteps that only you can hear. Take the easy way, young man, while you still have time. Think about it."

Gently he closed the door, a smile of both cruelty and pity never leaving his face.

"No," Stefan moaned. "No, I won't." Then he covered his face with his hands and sank to the floor as the angry, relentless alien voices rose all around him like a tide that would eventually drown him in madness and despair.

BRIAN SCOTT HIEBERT lives in his native Grand Junction, Colorado with his wife, Cheryl. He works at his local church and a bookstore. He is a 2005 graduate of the Odyssey writing program and has additional stories published in *Talebones*.

The Unseen Battle

by Brian Scott Hiebert

The year I was fourteen, a man came into my life. His name was Carstens. I overheard the doctors who brought him to the hut near our village say he must recuperate. I didn't then know the meaning of the word "recuperate" so I ran to Mama, who washed clothes in the creek.

"It means he must get better," she said, wiping sweat off her forehead. Her skin glowed in the late afternoon sun dappling through the palms and ferns. She was beautiful in a way that made men of our village turn their heads as she passed. I hoped one day to become as pretty.

"I don't see anything wrong with him," I said, helping her wring the clothes and lay them across rocks to dry.

"Did you see his eyes?" she asked. She had a scarlet Bougainvillaea tucked behind her ear. It made her look young, though five children had aged her beyond her years.

I nodded. The doctors brought Carstens to the hut from the hospital in a cart behind a donkey. The hospital stood on a hill overlooking the village, white and pristine, surrounded by green lawns and a black wrought–iron fence covered in vines. The patients, in white gowns, wandered or sat on wooden benches underneath casuarina trees.

Carstens wore a gray woolen suit with white shirt and thin black tie. He walked straight, as if he had a pole tied to his back, eyes staring. They were the emptiest eyes I had ever seen, other than Papa's when he died. Carstens' eyes were emerald, like the plumage on a bird, yet as flat as a stone.

"Sometimes," Mama said, "a man dies inside. It takes a little while for the body to catch up."

"Will he be all right?" I asked, hands already tired from wringing. Mama did at least one load a day and she never got weary.

"If he wants," Mama said. "But the war was a horrible thing. It's in God's hands."

I nodded, though I didn't understand. Mama and I took the clothes back to our *fare*. We then cooked rice, fish, and mango for my older brothers, who came in from working in the pineapple fields.

The next morning, Mama had us dress in our best and we went to church. The path took us by Carstens' hut. He sat on the veranda, still dressed in his gray suit, watching waves roll in from the lagoon. No, watching is not right. His eyes looked beyond the horizon, as if he stared at a distant place. They did not move.

"Probably thinking about France," Hiro, my eldest brother said. He nudged Ponui, the youngest, with his elbow. France was a distant place. The French controlled this island and because of that we heard about the Germans, the stalemate, and the Western Front. But it was all so far away that I paid no attention when it happened.

"Quiet," Mama said. Papa was French, a sailor who had met Mama in Papeete. I thought of myself as a French maiden, strolling the streets of Paris, imagining places Papa told us about. Papa promised to take me to Paris one day, but never did.

When we returned late in the afternoon from Mass, the only thing different about Carstens was he had taken off his jacket and tie. The sun beat mercilessly. Sweat poured off his head and I thought it looked like he was drowning. There was a pitcher of ice water on the bamboo stand next to him.

As I turned to watch, a nurse emerged from inside the hut, poured a glass, and then put it to his lips. He drank, but his eyes never wavered from the lagoon.

The next morning I passed by Carstens' hut on the way to school. He sat on the veranda. Someone had changed his clothing to a loose white cotton shirt and navy blue shorts. I knew he could not dress himself.

I snuck glances as I walked, books clutched to my chest. I felt sorry for him, but wondered what could be so terrible that it could damage a man on the inside?

The war grazed us. Once a German plane flew over the village and the pilot shouted crudities. Two German cruisers came into Papeete harbor and sunk a French ship. Bombs exploded in our lagoon, sending up great spouts of water which killed thousands of fish. We feasted for a week.

The closest the war came was something Papa called a "patrol boat." It beached beyond the lagoon and disgorged a bunch of sailors as the captain went to the hospital. The sailors threw off their clothes to their underwear, swam in the surf, and climbed trees for coconuts. They were white, hairy, and loud. I thought of them as chattering monkeys, like the group which plays in the trees in the jungle next to the mountains. A couple of the women who sell themselves came down, and many soldiers disappeared into the *fares* with them. The grunts and groans encouraged my thoughts of monkeys.

"Who were they?" I asked Papa the next morning when the boat was gone. This was before the sickness came and took him.

"Australians, I think," he said. "Never mind them. They just needed to let off some steam. It's the war."

"Oh," I said. I was sorry I had thought of them as monkeys, then asked God for forgiveness. That's what the priest said I must do if I did something I felt was wrong.

The Unseen Battle

Walking back from school, Carstens mumbled words. I turned toward him. His eyes locked on the ocean, didn't even look at me, but he said, clearly, "Where are the other girls?"

I knew what he meant. There were some tiny baby girls, and lots of women, but no one my age.

"They died of the sickness. The flu," I said. My school, run by Catholic nuns, was filled with boys. There were several younger girls, but all my friends were dead.

"I'm sorry," he added. I didn't look at him, because his eyes were frozen on the lagoon. Perhaps he is blind. That would explain why his eyes never moved. "What's your name?"

I hesitated. Sometimes people from the hospital escaped, and because they were sick in the head, Mama warned me not to talk to them, or tempt them. However, she knew Carstens. Plus, the doctors wouldn't have let him out if he was dangerous. Would they?

"Michele."

"That's not a native name," he replied.

"My father was French. My mother is from the islands. As a compromise they decided native names for the boys, French names for the girls. I was the only girl."

"It is a pretty name. Good afternoon."

"Good afternoon," I said, then walked away, feeling odd about talking with Carstens. Was that his last name or his first name? Where did he fight in the war? What did he see when he looked out across the lagoon? What had hurt him so bad? Should I talk to him again?

When I reached home, I did not tell Mama. I don't know why. Anyway, she was busy cooking. She handed me a broom as soon as I walked in and told me to sweep.

"What about my homework?" I asked. Usually she made me go to my hammock and finish whatever work the nuns had given me. Most of the time it was reading, which I didn't like as much as the arithmetic. I liked numbers and working with them.

"We have a visitor," Mama said. "Now do as you are told."

A visitor wasn't unusual. Mama had many suitors among the single men on the island. After the sickness killed women and girls there were who would have given almost anything to have Mama. But I don't think Mama was interested, because she was busy keeping my brothers fed. When suitors came Mama always cooked a fine meal, but she never cleaned.

As I dragged the broom across the wooden floor, I knew cleaning meant only one thing. Father Tomas.

Not that I didn't like Father Tomas. He was a fine priest, and he made sermons interesting, but Mama always made us confess our sins after dinner. I hated confessing sins in front of my brothers.

Father Tomas came just as Mama and I finished setting the table. The table was one of the finest on the island. Papa had it shipped from his family's home outside Paris. We had a few other nice things, but Mama had to sell most of them to get us through the hard times after Papa died. She wouldn't sell the table.

As we sat down, Father Tomas said a prayer. And at the end he said, "And let us not forget poor Mister Carstens who has lost his soul. Amen."

As I crossed myself, my body tingled. I found myself thinking of Carstens at odd times of the day, when walking along the beach looking for shells, or sitting in class and staring out the window at the trees. I knew such thoughts were unclean, but I couldn't help myself.

I think it was because his eyes were empty that I liked him. The men and boys looked at me with hungry eyes, as if I was a piece of meat, or a juicy mango, rather than a girl. I knew soon I'd have to choose one as a husband—that was the way of the village. Though I knew I would probably marry and have many children, I secretly wished someone would take me to Paris like Papa had promised. Carstens was the first stranger to come into my life who could take me away.

"What's wrong with him?" Ponui asked.

"It's not polite to talk about other people," Mama said. "That is gossip."

Father Tomas raised a hand. "No, that's fine. Knowing the facts about his situation is not gossip."

"Then what's wrong?" I blurted, way too loud. I felt my face blush and I looked down at my plate, studying the skeletal remains of my fish.

Father Tomas smiled, then steepled his hands in front of him. "It's called shell shock. Mister Carstens' case is one of the worst ever seen. He hasn't spoken a word in over three years, since the end of the war. They found him wandering in a particularly bad place, not far from Ypres. That's in a country called Belgium."

That Carstens had chosen me to be the first one he had spoken to in three years made me feel special. Though I was the only available girl on the island, I never felt special.

"So he was hit by a shell," Hiro said. "He doesn't look hurt."

"He had superficial wounds, the doctor said, but nothing to cause him permanent damage. Except on the inside. It's an emotional wound. It runs so deep in Mister Carstens that I'm afraid it has destroyed his soul. You can see it in is eyes."

"Then there is no hope?" Mama asked.

Father Tomas smiled gently. "There is always hope when God is concerned. That's the wonderful power of grace."

Though I kept my head down, still ashamed from speaking out of turn, I jumped for joy inside. Carstens was getting better! I knew it! Perhaps he would talk to me again and we could become friends. Then I would ask him to take me to Paris.

After dinner I wanted to run to Carstens. But we cleared the table, then Mama had us confess our sins to Father Tomas.

"It has been seven days since my last confession," I said. "I have taken the

The Unseen Battle

Lord's name in vain and have had lust in my heart."

"You will not see him ever again," Father Tomas said, voice deep with anger.

"Who?" I asked.

"Carstens. You've been seen talking with him. Do not talk with him. If I hear you have been I shall report it to your mother," he replied.

"You can't."

"I will make certain she finds out," he said. I shivered under his threat, but said nothing more. After all, he was the priest.

After confessions, the boys went out to fish while I helped Mama finish cleaning.

"It's not fair," I said, grumbling. Rarely did I say what was in my heart, but this time felt it needed to be said.

"Life is not fair," Mama said. "Your Papa dies and I'm stuck here on this island until you are grown or married. After that I'll probably be taking care of grandchildren, then who knows? I'll probably die of exhaustion before I'm forty. Don't tell me about unfair."

I clenched my teeth. I knew Mama worked hard, but didn't know she had dreams. She had listened to Papa's stories. She probably wanted to go to Paris. Did I dare tell her about my dream of Carstens taking me? Because of what Father Tomas said I decided not to share my secret until Carstens got better. I didn't want to get her hopes up.

The next morning I left for school early. The sun had barely peaked over the lagoon. The air was cool and fresh, like after a storm. It was my favorite time of day because it held promise.

"You're up early, Michele," Carstens said as I approached. I felt warm inside because he remembered my name, then guilty because Father Tomas told me not to talk with him.

"I'm not supposed to talk to you," I said.

"That silly old priest is just jealous."

"I like the morning," I replied, trying to be a proper lady. I had to impress Carstens that I could be civilized once we got to Paris.

"I don't like the night."

"You shouldn't be frightened of the dark," I replied. "Only small children are afraid of shadows."

Carstens laughed, but there was no humor in the sound. I shivered and clutched the books tighter to my bosom. A chill had settled where moments before there had been warmth.

"Oh, to be young and innocent again," Carstens replied. "You don't know much about the real world, do you?"

"I don't know as much as you," I said, defiant. What right did he have to tell me I wasn't grown up? Or what I did or did not know?

"There are some things one should never know."

I felt cold. His words went against everything I was taught. The nuns said learning was the most important thing in life. Never stop learning was Sister Francis' motto. She made us repeat it every day, and Mother Superior had it engraved on a plaque on her desk.

"What's your name?" I asked.

"Carstens, Richard P., second leftenant, British Royal Army," he said. My mind grappled with the words because he said them so quickly. Then I realized that Carstens was his last name, Richard his first.

"Have a nice day, Richard," I said, then continued toward school. Though his eyes never wavered, I did learn more about him. Not all of it good, but some of those bad things were probably because he was sick.

While walking home from school past the hut, I heard Carstens mutter the words, "Night Lands." I turned toward him, but he seemed more lost than usual. Drool slithered from the right corner of his mouth, and his left arm twitched like a palm frond in the wind.

Though I was defying Father Tomas, I stopped and turned back toward him. "What did you say?"

"Watch out for the night!" he shouted, standing up and pointing across the lagoon. I stumbled backward, dropped my books, then looked where he pointed. There was nothing there but the waves, the lagoon, and two fishing boats out near the reef. I couldn't see anything.

The nurse appeared out of the darkened doorway like a ghost. "What did you say to him?"

Her voice was shrill, like a mynah. Her accusing stare raked over me and I turned to hide from its gaze, gathering books and sand. I ran away, breathing hard by the time I came to our *fare*.

"Why did you run?" Mama asked, chopping onions.

"Something scared me," I mumbled, which was the truth. There was something wrong with a man who would shout like that. Our village had an old man whose mind went rotten, like an orange left in the sun too long. He wandered, shouting and screaming at nothing in particular. Any movement would set him off. The monkeys learned to tease him. He finally died.

"Well, there's nothing to be afraid of." Mama wiped her brow, then smiled at me. "There are no monsters to take you."

I nodded, but I didn't believe her.

The next morning I went wide around the hut, which added to my walk to the school, and in the afternoon I was going to take a different path back home, but a couple of the other children whispered that the hut was again empty. Curiosity drove me back along my normal path. Like they said, the hut's door was closed, the windows shuttered as if against a storm. I was happy Carstens had gone away.

Yet, disappointed. I would be on the island forever and never get to see Paris.

The hut remained shut all week. The next Monday I was happy again and had forgotten Carstens. I turned the corner expecting the empty hut, but

The Unseen Battle

instead he sat out in front.

"I'm sorry," he said as soon as he saw me. He still stared out at the lagoon, but his face had changed. It was softer, without the deep lines I had seen before.

"You shouldn't yell at people," I scolded. I hadn't seen Father Tomas other than at Mass the last couple of weeks, so I figured I could tell Carstens I was upset with him.

"I know. I'm sorry, Michele. I just don't want them to get you," he replied.

"Who?" I asked, curious. "Mama said there were no monsters to hurt me."

"But there are," he said. "Bad ones. I don't want to scare you. But they will come for me. Sometime. I don't know when. They have to find me first."

"I'd better get going," I said, then walked away. I almost laughed. Monsters. Only little children believed in monsters.

I still didn't tell Mama about talking to Carstens. I don't know why. He was my secret, but it was more than that. Perhaps it was time that I found my way out of Mama's shadow, to explore the world on my own. Most girls did that by marrying and having babies. I didn't want that. I wanted Paris.

The next morning Carstens sat out on the veranda like before, though I could tell something was different. He wore dark glasses and faced the lagoon, but turned to watch me come up the path between the rocks. He had never looked at me before and it made me feel uncomfortable.

"Good morning," he said in a cheerful voice. It did not fit him.

"Good morning," I said, cautious. This was not the same Carstens. Perhaps his immortal soul had returned and God had forgiven him for any sins he committed during the war.

"Stay a moment. The nurse has gone to Papeete for smokes," he said. "I hope you accept my apology. I did not mean to frighten you the other day."

"Accepted," I said, slowing my walk. He was friendlier than he had been in the past. "Are you feeling better?"

"Much. Thanks to you, I might add," he said.

"Me?" I pointed at my chest, then stared at the sand. I did not like attention drawn to myself, though sometimes I enjoyed the stares of boys.

"Yes. You were a bright ray of sunshine into the dreariness where I had fallen. It took a shock to my system, when I realized that I had terrified you, to make me understand that the war was over. I am now cured."

"Is that why you wear dark glasses?" I asked.

He touched the rims. "No. I asked for them because the sun is so bright off the sand and water. It hurts my eyes."

"It didn't hurt them before," I replied.

"I wasn't seeing the sun. Only darkness."

I nodded, as if I understood. I did not trust this new Carstens. He sounded as if he were making up everything, just to make it look like he was better. Or maybe I was just imagining his continued hurt? Can someone get better that fast?

"The night lands?" I asked, remembering what he had muttered just before he began shouting.

"Yes," he said in a harsh whisper. "The night lands."

"What are the night lands?" I asked, moving closer.

He stood up abruptly, back snapping straight again. He held a cane in his right hand. He walked down the steps off the veranda to the sand in front of me. Using the cane's tip, he drew two parallel lines in the sand.

"Imagine, this is Belgium. The French and British forces have stopped German aggression in the midst of farmer's fields and small villages. They have dug holes in the ground, and shoot guns back and forth at each other. There are small guns and large guns. You can't imagine what the shells sound like."

When he said shells he shuddered and crouched down. I understood he only heard and saw the shells in his mind. Perhaps this is what Father Tomas had meant by shell shock.

"What kind of noise do they make?" I asked. A few of the men have guns to hunt birds, and for protection. They are small, but very loud.

"As if the earth is ripping itself apart," he said in a voice so cold that I shivered.

"I have never heard such a sound."

"Pray that you don't," he replied, then tapped the cane tip between the two lines. "These are the night lands. Some called them No Man's Land."

"Why?" I asked.

"No man lived there. They all died. We called this place the night lands because the sun never shone there. I mean, the sun should have risen, but it never did. Not the entire time I was there."

"And how long was that?" I asked.

"More than two years. Felt like twenty," he said with great sadness.

"That's not possible," I said, suspicious. How could the sun not shine for two years?

"I know. But it happened. Our watches stopped, but the bullets and shells did not. I imagined God so sick of the war that he took our little piece and put it aside. Or else, something else hid it from God's eyes. If I was God I would have hated looking at that horrible place."

Carstens shuddered, as if cold, though the sun was hot enough to bake bread.

"It must have been awful," I said.

"So many bones. They crunched when you walked on them, like shells on a beach. But that wasn't the worst thing."

"What could be worse?" I said. I often went without my sandals on the beach, and sometimes I stepped on a shell. It hurt a lot. One time I stepped on a dead jellyfish. What would it be like to step on dead people's bones, or their dead bodies? Suddenly I knew why Carstens was cold.

"There were things in the night lands."

"What sort of things?"

"They crawled like crabs, slithered like snakes, and roared like lions. Sometimes they would scream. We never saw them. But if you went on a patrol, or a wire party, you would find slime trails. Like those snails leave behind. Have you seen snails?"

I nodded. Deep in the jungle there would be snails in the shadows. My brothers would hunt them, then dip them into boiling water to eat. I never ate them because they were slimy.

"Something similar, but it smelled like sulfur, gun powder, and blood. I shall never forget that smell. This place smells of nice flowers."

Carstens got that far away look again, staring across the lagoon. I shook my head, still not believing, and went to school.

On the return home, Carstens was not on the veranda, and the shutters were closed again. I helped Mama with dinner, did my homework, then stayed up reading by lamp light.

That night I couldn't sleep. The *hupe*, the cool wind coming down the mountains, was my companion as I thought about Carstens and his night which never ended. If I never saw the sun I would go crazy, just like Carstens. Papa said in Paris sometimes it rained for days on end. It was so cold and wet. But on spring days, when the sun was out, it was a beautiful city. But he still liked Tahiti better because the sun shone almost every day. He said it made him feel better.

I slept late, but woke to commotion outside the *fare*. My brothers were shouting. They should have been at work in the cane fields, but instead ran around yelling for people to come out of their *fares* and help them.

"What's wrong?" I asked Mama, rubbing sleep out of my eyes.

"An old man went fishing last night because it was a full moon. When he didn't return, his wife asked some men to go look for him," Mama said.

"Have they found him?"

Mama shook her head. "No. But they found his boat smashed on the reef. It is in such tiny pieces that they think a great fish, or a shark, came after him."

Though groggy, I shuddered. A giant thing rising from the ocean, towering over the man in his small boat, then crashing its tail down. I had not heard anything in the night, though I was awake most of the time.

"You're late for school. Now hurry up," Mama said.

I hurriedly dressed, washed my face, then grabbed my pack and lunch on the way out the door. As I rushed by Carstens' hut I noticed he wasn't sitting outside, though there was a pitcher of water and a glass on the table outside. When I got to the school, the children were all so excited about the smashed boat that the nuns couldn't control us. There was also word that the leper colony had been attacked two nights ago, two huts crushed, the bodies of the lepers missing.

The nuns let us go home early because of all the excitement. I ate my lunch, then strolled home.

"The night has come," Carstens said. I turned, but did not see him.

"What?" I asked, peering into the darkness beyond the hut's door. Carstens sat inside, in the shadows. "Why are you hiding?"

"They've come. They search for me, but they cannot find me. Not yet. Ask the villagers. Ask your brothers. Did they find slime? Like with a snail? If they did, they must light torches at night. As many as they can. They love the darkness, the shadows. Only light drives them away."

"You're scaring me," I said.

"I want to frighten you, Michele. The world is a horrid place, filled with monsters. Not only the kind which come out of the night lands. But human monsters as well. What kind of man devises a gas which eats eyes, a bomb which shreds flesh, a war which takes so many lives? Sometimes I don't know which is worse. The human monsters, or the ones out of the blasted ground."

"I think I'm going to be sick," I said, turning away. He filled my mind with so many awful images I knew I wouldn't be able to sleep.

"Find out. Then warn them about the night land monsters. Go!"

He barked the last word like a command. I scuttled away, like a crab retreating before the onrushing tide. Brothers Hiro and Ponui were at home, discussing the missing fisherman.

"It must have been a whale," Ponui said. He sat outside out family hut carving a fetish. He was good with the knife.

"Squid," Hiro said, gazing out to the lagoon with curiosity.

"What are you talking about?" I asked.

"The fisherman's boat. No shark could do what was done to that boat. Something much larger. Huge. And it left a sticky mess behind," Ponui replied.

"Oh," I said, then went inside to help Mama with dinner.

As we cut pineapple and coconut, I told Mama that the villagers must light torches to keep the thing away.

"Which thing?" Mama asked.

"The thing which killed the fisherman," I said.

Mama laughed. "Who has been telling you these stories? They will give you nightmares."

I struggled for a moment. If I told Mama I'd been talking with Carstens, then all hope of going to Paris would be gone. But if I didn't tell her, then the village would be dark.

"Carstens," I said, barely above a whisper.

Mama grabbed me by the shoulders, then spun me to face her. Rage filled her face. "You have been talking with that person?"

I began to cry. "Yes. Mama, he's not that bad."

"He has lost his soul. Do you understand that?" she said, shaking me. My teeth rattled against each other, and my shoulders hurt from where she grabbed me.

"Yes," I said between gasps.

"He might take your soul, or worse, corrupt you. Do not go near him again. Promise me!"

"I promise," I said, then ran to my hammock, where I cried. I knew there was no way I'd see Paris now.

The Unseen Battle

I must have fallen asleep, because when I woke and it was dark. What caused me to wake? Usually, once I fell asleep, it took a lot to wake me up. I laid in the blackness waiting for something. Then cold fear radiated from my stomach. The night lands.

Then I heard it. A soft, squishing sound, like when I poked dead jellyfish with a stick. Then more sounds. Men shouting for torches, a scream, wood breaking. I trembled, too afraid to move, muscles clenched against the possibility that they came for me. Yet, deep in my heart I knew different. They had come for someone else.

I waited, eyes open, until the room lightened with the coming dawn. I didn't go outside until the sun was fully above the horizon, its light revealing what the darkness had concealed.

There were several bodies on the beach, crushed beyond recognition, but I knew that none of them were Carstens. Village men with unlit torches clenched in cold hands. They laid in wide depressions across the sand, all leading up the beach toward their true quarry. I stepped around puddles of greenish goo, walking in a daze, following the destruction.

Carstens' hut was a collection of sticks and goo. As I poked around, looking for some sign, dark clouds gathered above the island. A couple strokes of lightning were followed by thunder, then a tremendous downpour unlike any other I'd seen on Tahiti. By the time the shower was finished I was soaked to the bone and most evidence of the monsters had been washed away by God's tears.

Most said Carstens destroyed his hut, then walked into the sea. I knew different, but I didn't say anything. What could I say? That unmentionable creatures, stirred by a far away war, had swum thousands of miles to seek one who had escaped? Later I came to understand that Carstens never escaped. Though he had traveled beyond the night lands, the horrors still lived in his mind. Maybe he was the one who had summoned them.

Later I made it to Paris. During World War II I fell in love with an American soldier, who took me to France for a honeymoon. I insisted on a side trip to Belgium. It was a gray, cold day when I got to Ypres. The locals said the sun hardly ever shone. We went to the war memorials with evidence of the most recent war to end all wars around us. Shattered buildings, bomb craters, and torn ground. There are places where nothing grows. It's as if evil had touched the place and it would never be the same.

I truly believed that the artillery pounded the ground and awakened a great evil. That evil infected everything in Europe, caused men to do terrible things to their fellow human beings.

Standing in the rain, I closed my eyes, thought about the look in Carstens' eyes, and could almost see the horror. Almost.

I now live in Arizona. Tahiti is a distant memory, yet I always sleep with a light on.

ADAM NISWANDER is the author of The Shaman Cycle novels—*The Charm, The Serpent Slayers, The Hound Hunters, The War of the Whisperers,* and the *Nemesis of Night*. His other works include *The Sand Dwellers, The Repository, Golden Dreams,* and a short story collection titled *Blurring the Edges of Dream.* When not actually engaged in battling weird monsters, he collects books and beer steins, brews his own beer, and lives in Phoenix, Arizona, with a couple of cats named Fafhrd and The Gray Mouser. As Brian Lumley once observed, "Adam inhabits deep, dark places . . . and drinks there."

Bayer's Tale

by Adam Niswander

Clutching the pylon as the waves battered me, I felt the grinding of my flesh where it rubbed against the barnacles, but dared not loosen my grasp even to seek a firmer hold. The moon hung in the deceptively clear sky, a mere sliver—a strange, grinning crescent that leered down at me bereft of compassion. Cloudless and innocent, that black canopy of velvet, sequined with winking stars, ignored the howling winds and the froth of roiled ocean.

Exhaustion threatened to loosen my grip and pry my knees away from the thorny wooden pillar that rose so stolidly out of the angry water and reached up to the tantalizing safety of the remaining pier ten feet above. Dulled by pain and the frigid sea, my senses hovered in that no–man's land of unthinking single–pointedness. I hugged the remnants of life with the superhuman strength of mindlessness.

But my mind was screaming.

I do not know what kept me affixed to that huge wooden trunk. I simply clung, despite the constant thunder of the waves which sought to wrench me away and deliver me to death—or worse than death.

I knew I could not simply let go and wash up on shore. The raging currents led away from the solidity of earth and out into the Stygian deeps. And the rocks of the coast more closely resembled shark's teeth than stepping stones. Somehow aware of the lashing seas and the undertow, my rational mind had accepted the hopelessness of my position and long ago despaired. Yet there is something in a man that cannot and will not accept the end when even the smallest vestige of hope remains.

And even in desperation, that screaming part of my mind knew that, out there, just beyond my range of vision—mindless terror waited.

Fear—a four–letter "F–word" so disarming in its short simplicity.

Eyes closed, muscles straining, my brain ached with the pressure of seeking solutions. Synapses firing like machine guns, plans for escape materialized, met with the harsh and unforgiving test of reality, and fell shattered into that abyss of despair.

And, as the possibilities were exhausted, my traitorous mind began the next

Dead But Dreaming

stage of decline and hurled recriminations at a conscience already overburdened. And, finally, I surrendered to the terror.

I am not an imaginative man. My world—the realm of police crime detection—is overwhelmed daily by the banal absurdities of human ignorance and cruelty.

For twenty-seven years, I have started each day with the disheartening knowledge that some of my fellow human beings have exercised their option to sink well below the standards of acceptable behavior and commit some horrible act which I and my fellow law enforcement colleagues will have to clean up, catalogue, solve, and prevent from reoccurring. There is no joy in it, but the task is necessary if we humans are to remain civilized and continue to strive for something better.

As a result, it was no shock to arrive at the Precinct on the morning of February 27th and find that I had been assigned to investigate the discovery of bodies in the woods of the coastal area of Massachusetts, in Winthrop Park.

At 0503, during a routine patrol of the park environs, Officer Wesley R. Smith, badge number 0443529, had come upon a scene of carnage that brought a frantic call to the department. Though details were sketchy as yet, Officer Smith had suggested that the bodies were victims of some kind of occult ritual ceremony, perhaps a sacrifice. The possibility of a mass suicide had not been entirely discounted.

As a result, my partner and I were en route to Winthrop Park by 0810, and I read Smith's initial report as we drove.

The report (transcribed from his radio call) stated that the crime scene had been quiet—unusually so—and that the smell of cooked meat had permeated the area. Though the sky had just begun lightening at the time of the initial discovery, Officer Smith had not observed the pile of bodies right away. They had been stacked and burned in a small, circular area surrounded by trees, and thus hidden from sight until he entered the clearing.

Smith seemed to have been on the ball, as he had gone through the basic drill without missing a beat. The coroner had been called, the crime scene cordoned off, the park closed.

It took a while to work our way through the rush hour traffic, but we soon pulled up at the scene and saw the usual crowd of busy investigators. This was a big one. The press was being held back in a separate area. I noticed remotes from all the local stations and some national feeds as well.

Leaving the car and ducking under the tape, I could see that everyone else was already there—everyone, from Will Bates, the Arson Investigator to Doc Corelli, the Medical Examiner. The crime scene artist sketched, the still–photographer snapped away, District Attorney Bernard Hughes was huddled with a gray–looking Officer Smith and several other officers.

"Well, well, well. Look who decided to drop by. Lieutenant George Bayer, the shining light of Homicide. Good of you to drop by, Lieutenant Bayer," said Hughes.

"Sorry, Bernie. I was assigned at 0800 when I reported in. What do we know so far?"

Hughes shook his head. "Not much, George. But, as you can see, the press is all over this."

My partner, Dan Norman, asked, "Do we know who the victims are?"

"Not a glimmer, Dan," replied the DA. The bodies are pretty badly burned. And the initial report of eighteen may be a low estimate. The pile is fused together in places."

I had not really looked at the…site of the fire. The too–sweet aroma of cooked meat still hung on the air.

"Witnesses?" I asked.

Hughes shrugged. "No one. The people of Winthrop were, apparently, safely at home during the night. This park entrance is normally closed at dusk. To get in or out by road you have to use the North end, up by the cemetery."

I sent Dan to talk to the forensics team, then tuned to Officer Smith. "Why don't you walk me through it, Officer, from the moment you pulled in."

Smith glanced at Hughs, received a nod, and tried to smile. His attempt didn't work well. His eyes looked haunted. "Whatever you want, Lieutenant Bayer."

Together, we walked to where a lone cruiser was parked some distance away, besides the gated entrance. Smith was silent, and I could see that his face was still pasty white from shock.

"Are you all right?"

He shuddered, and then seemed to straighten up, becoming resolute. "No, but I can give you my report."

I put a hand on his shoulder. "Take your time."

"It had been a quiet night. This was the last scheduled stop of my shift. I've been on this route for three months now and it's always been just routine. I pulled up here, and checked the gates for signs of tampering. There were none. Like now, there wasn't much of a breeze."

"You saw no one?"

He gestured at the well–trimmed grounds. "No one. The sun hadn't risen yet, but the sky had lightened some. I wouldn't have missed seeing anyone out here."

I nodded.

"I'd just turned away from the gates when I smelled it." He reached out and put a hand on the open window of the cruiser, steadying himself. "You know, I served in the Gulf, and I've seen some stuff, but…" his voice trailed off.

"So you smelled something, and went to investigate," I prompted.

"I thought it was just some kids having a barbecue," he said quietly. "Maybe some highschoolers doing a little late night partying."

He led me toward the trees. "I crossed this way, not being particularly careful to avoid being seen. A lot of times, the kids see a cop and that's all it takes to send them scurrying home."

I followed him as we made our way around a small clump of bushes and between two of the trees.

"As I came through here," said Smith, "I saw a kind of mound up ahead. I don't know what I thought it was, maybe illegal dumping, a pile of discarded furniture."

I followed his pointing finger and saw the heap about twenty yards away. Even in daylight, I couldn't tell what it was.

"The smell has gotten a lot stronger," he said, his voice a little strained.

We moved toward the scene, and I tried to ignore the crowd of specialists bustling about it. I tried to see what Smith had seen at 0503 this morning.

About a dozen feet away from the focal point of all the activity, Smith stopped.

He cleared his throat before continuing. "I was just here when I realized it was a pile of bodies."

I stopped with him, and looked, for the first time, really, at the mound.

Atop a seemingly unidentifiable mass, a human form lay on its back, flesh charred and mouth open in a silent scream. The back was bent in an unnatural position, following the contours of what lay below. The sickly-sweet smell was overpowering.

My eyes followed the outlines of its shape, attempting to convince my mind that it had once been human, and were drawn to the pair of bodies on which it lay, then to the next, and so on. I turned away for a moment, swallowing hard.

Smith let out a gasping sigh. "You did better than I did, Lieutenant," he said at last. "I lost my morning doughnuts right here."

Had the clearing been marked with compass points, we stood in approximately the center, on the South side of the pile of bodies. I let my eyes scan the full circle of the trees, turning slowly counter-clockwise. My gaze had made it three quarters of the way around when I stopped. On the Eastern edge, the side closest to the nearby ocean, the space between the trees had been crushed and pushed aside.

Smith followed me as I walked over. "Yeah, it looks like someone drove a tank through there, but there are no visible tire-tracks at all."

The ground was covered by grass, so, other than looking flattened, there was no indicator of what had passed through. A large shrub had also been leveled. I walked over and knelt by it, reaching out to touch one of the crushed branches. My hand came away slightly wet.

"Do you have a sample bag?" I asked Smith.

Wordlessly he drew one from a uniform pocket and offered it. I took a pen out and scraped one of the leaves. It came away looking slick. Smith, leaning in, said, "Looks like some kind of mucus or slime."

I carefully put the sample, pen and all, into the bag and sealed it, handing it to the officer. "See that this gets to the lab and that the report is marked for my attention."

"Yes, sir," said Smith, turning and crossing toward the crime lab truck.

I stayed crouched there, and looked carefully around. I had started feeling edgy. None of this made any sense. After more than four hours since Officer Smith stumbled across the crime scene, we still had zilch. An indeterminate number of bodies burned in a heap. No witnesses. No suspects. No motive. No clue. And the best I had come up with was a little slime from a crushed bush, which would likely turn out to be spit.

I was pulled out of my ruminations by the sound of vehicles being started. Apparently, the photographers, sketch artist, and coroner were finished with the scene and the ambulances were being brought up.

I rose and began to walk between the trees, but stumbled. When I had regained my balance, I looked down and could see nothing which might have caused it. Bending, I ran my hands over the ground. Beneath the grass, there was a deep indentation, long and recessed.

I beckoned to one of the lab boys and he rushed over.

"Yes, Lieutenant?"

"This area has been crushed down, as if someone brought a heavy vehicle through here. The grass is too thick to see any imprint, but I can feel the ridge under it. Keep people out of here and see if you can get this grass cut away. Maybe we can get a cast of a tire track or something."

He nodded. "Right away, Lieutenant," and then hustled over to get the necessary men and equipment.

I waited in the spot, shooing people away until he returned, then went back to watch them bag the remains and load them into the ambulances.

By the time Dan and I had returned to the Detective's Division Office at the precinct, things looked no more promising. The first thing I had done on arrival was look up missing persons reports. You can't have eighteen bodies show up in a public park without having someone missing in the area, but that appeared to be exactly the way things stood. No one, aside from the usual teenager dealing with angst, and a single Alzheimer's sufferer, had been reported missing.

Where could eighteen (or so) dead human beings come from?

Calls to the airports, bus terminals, taxicab companies, and rail stations indicated nothing out of the ordinary.

Then, on a hunch, I called the port.

It took a while to reach the Port Authority, but the call was worthwhile.

It seemed that one Captain Alonzo Cruz, master of a medium–sized container vessel called *Rosita* and flagged in the South Pacific, had reported his crew missing without leave at 0800 this morning.

I left Dan to wait for something...hell, anything...from the coroner's office, took the car, and drove to the Port of Boston.

Main Gate Security directed me to the Moran Container Terminal, and one of the patrols sent me to the Eastern side, space 17, where I would find the *Rosita*.

The container ship was the only vessel berthed on the East side, and space 17 lay at the farthest extent of the docks. Not another single living soul was visible to me.

The ship served as a reminder that appearances can be deceiving. She looked to be in top shape, at least from the docks. Two–hundred feet from stem to stern, recently painted an almost military–looking battleship gray, she rode high in the water. She was a container ship, all right, but she hadn't started as one. Her age predated even the idea of containers. I had plenty of time to study her, for it took long minutes to walk the length of that pier.

No one hailed me when I started up the gangway, and not even sea birds came near her, The lines creaked and groaned while she shifted on the gentle swells of the harbor.

The Port of Boston is a busy, noisy, congested place, but, once on the *Rosita's* gangway, it seemed as if I had walked into a sound–proof booth. The cacophonous bustle of the surrounding port became muted. The very air felt heavy, and moved like invisible oil. I stopped when I reached the deck.

I called out in my best nautical manner. "Ahoy! Is anyone aboard? Captain Cruz? Are you aboard, Sir?"

I felt as if I were shouting into cotton. Nothing moved. The vessel appeared to be deserted.

I crossed to the staircase leading up the superstructure to the ship's bridge and climbed. I figured the Captain's cabin had to be near the bridge in case of emergencies at sea.

When I reached the bridge, I stepped in through the open Fidley hatch and called out again. "Captain Cruz? Are you here, Sir?"

The enclosed bridge didn't even echo with my voice.

I stepped back out and moved to the forward railing. She didn't look as shipshape from above. There was debris on the deck. Uncoiled lines, equipment, bits and pieces of clothing, even a tub of what looked like kitchenware dumped and scattered about.

Moving aft, I looked back toward the fantail. The same general clutter littered her afterdecks.

"They deserted."

The gravelly voice came from behind my left shoulder and I spun to find a swarthy little man in an immaculate white officer's uniform standing in the hatchway.

Trying not to look as startled as I felt, I asked, "Am I correct in assuming you are Captain Cruz?"

He nodded. "I am he. Are you from the Port Authority?"

I shook my head. "No, I'm Bayer from Boston P.D. I understand you are missing some men."

"I am," he replied with a gesture at the ship. "Nineteen, to be exact." He shrugged. "I told the owners that a crew of islanders would never work out, but they work cheap, you see, and showed up with all the proper documents."

"When did you last see them aboard, Captain?"

"Last night when I retired at 2200. I awakened this morning to find they had all deserted and that the ship's launch is missing."

"Describe the launch, Captain."

"White hulled, looks like an old whaling dingy. Clapboard construction. Fourteen feet from bow to transom."

I took out my cell phone. "I'm going to call that in, Captain."

He nodded, turned, and moved to the rail facing the bow.

I dialed and Dan answered on the second ring.

"There's a launch missing from a ship at the port. Did anyone check the nearest beach?"

Dan sounded surprised. "That's one of the reasons I hoped you'd call," he said. They found a fourteen–foot wooden job on the beach in almost a straight eastern line from the park."

"Then I think we know where the nineteen bodies came from," I said quietly.

"No, eighteen. Coroner's office just called to confirm it. Smith was better at counting than he knew."

"Hold on a second." I called to the Captain. "Are you sure there were nineteen, not eighteen?"

He glared at me. "I know how many men serve in my crew, officer."

I spoke into the phone again. "Dan, do we have anything other than the corpses that someone could identify?"

"Yeah, the sketch artist spent the middle of the day there. He made likenesses of the faces...at least what he could see of them."

"Great. Make multiple copies of them. I think we've got identities, and maybe even a suspect. I'll see you within the hour."

After I had hung up, I told Cruz, "I'd like you to come downtown with me. I think we may have located your crew, but it is not good news. We found eighteen bodies in Winthrop, a little coastal suburb outside the city this morning. We've had sketches done of their faces. Maybe you can tell me who's missing."

The Captain looked shocked. "Bodies? You mean they're dead?"

"I'm afraid that may be the case, Captain. You'll need to identify them and, if it is your crew as I suspect, help us figure out where the remains should be sent after this is all over."

Cruz still couldn't believe it. He had lost half his color. "Dead? Eighteen?"

Two hours later, I had narrowed my suspects down to two. The unfortunate condition of the bodies had made it difficult for the sketch artist, but the Captain had been able to tentatively identify seventeen of the victims. On one, he had been uncertain. Since the crew had shared a regional background, the diversity of their appearances was marginal, and the sketches emphasized bone structure. Also, the crew had been, as the Captain stated, islanders previously unfamiliar to him. But there had been two men of European descent among them, and only one sketch demonstrated clearly Caucasian features. This meant that one of the two Europeans must be the missing crewman amongst the bodies.

Reggie Batts had been Second–in–command aboard the *Rosita*, and Anthony Hippolito had been First Mate. One of them was not among the bodies.

The Crime Lab took additional samples from the caucasian body while we made inquiries about the individuals through international channels. One of the advantages of the computer age is the rapidity with which law enforcement agencies can now exchange information.

Within hours, we had been faxed medical records on Batts, who had been born in England and living as an expatriate in a port city in Madagascar. The tissue and blood samples matched.

By process of elimination, then, we knew that Hippolito was our missing crewman, and he became the primary suspect in the mysterious mass conflagration.

I arranged for Captain Cruz to pack up Hippolito's remaining personal effects and sent a squad car to pick them up at the port. My hope was that items among the man's personal belongings would tell us something about our missing person.

Two hours later, the patrolmen brought Hippolito's effects to my office. They consisted of an oversized duffel and a small, strange, carved, wooden chest.

Enlisting the aid of the officers, I pushed the furniture toward the walls, creating an open area in the center of the room. Dismissing the men, I summoned Dan and, together, we laid out the personal effects of First Mate Anthony Hippolito.

The duffel contained clothing and a toiletry kit, some embroidered pillows portraying dancing native girls, sneakers and boots, and other similar but unremarkable items. With the clothing laid out in neat piles according to categories, I had Dan record an inventory while I turned my attention to the wooden chest.

It did not look particularly old. I have seen similar chests made of rosewood or some other reddish colored lumber in curio and import shops. It was just under three and a half feet long, a foot and a half wide, and a foot and a half tall. It stood on attached wooden feet with brass fittings to protect the wood. The carvings which covered the entire surface were of sea creatures, from whales to seahorses, squids to fish. It had a high–gloss finish and looked sturdily built. The lid curved in a quarter circle to meet the sides, and a heavy brass hasp was secured with a large metal lock. I saw no evidence of a key.

I went out to the equipment locker and grabbed a big bolt cutter, then returned to the office where Dan had just finished writing up the inventory of clothing. Crossing to the chest, I asked him to witness as I cut the lock and removed it.

Opening the lid, which moved easily on brass hinges, I found that the entire top was covered by a well organized tray with various compartments. My eyes were drawn to one containing papers, where I found Hippolito's passport, inoculation record, shipping orders, maritime papers, mate's designation and a packet of letters, apparently written at sea. Whatever else the man might be, he was neat and precise. The chest tray held everything in well-organized groups, from stamps to pencils, writing paper and envelopes, two wristwatches, a pair of glasses, and various personal items like a key chain, a pair of dice, and a change purse. The passport photo showed a burly, stubbled, Spanish face with dark eyes and an interesting crescent-shaped scar on one cheek. In the picture, he wore a knit watch cap squarely on his head. I had an officer take it out to have copies made. Our suspect now had a face.

I lifted out the tray and placed it on the floor beside the chest, then turned and peered in to see what lay below.

First, I saw a machete. It lay on its side, the blade almost gleaming in its cleanliness. The grip was a simple tape-wrapped wooden oval, but it had been well cared for. Next to the machete was a rather modern looking snub-nosed automatic handgun, a Browning, accompanied by several boxes of ammunition. A velvet-lined tray lay under the weapons, but it was empty. I lifted it out, but there was nothing below but the floor of the chest. Examining the empty tray, I could see that the velvet had been permanently crushed in places by whatever it had held, indicating that it must have been something heavy. From the shape of the tray and the impressions, one could conclude that the object was rectangular, almost square, measuring just under a foot wide and perhaps just a touch over a foot long.

After Dan had recorded all the contents on his inventory sheets, I had him take the chest and duffel to the property room where they were logged in and secured.

I moved my desk out from the wall and rearranged the furniture, then sat down and tried to puzzle out what—if anything—could be learned from Hippolito's stuff.

He had left the ship with the others sometime after 2200. He had not been expecting trouble, because he left his weapons behind. Something had occupied that tray for a long time, but it wasn't there now, so it seemed logical the man had taken it with him. The paperwork would not have been left behind had the man not expected to return. The maritime papers, passport and personal items were not the sort of things a seaman would abandon.

So what would take an entire crew clandestinely off a ship late at night without the Captain's knowledge? How could they end up miles away at a seaside park near a quiet residential community, stacked like cordwood in a smoldering heap? Why would just one man out of nineteen be missing?

The answers, if they existed, were all within the mind of Hippolito, if he remained alive. I knew I had to find the man.

Later, as evening began, I received a small package by courier. It had been sent by Captain Cruz. The note said, "I found this taped under the First Mate's bunk. After seeing what it was, I called for a courier immediately. Can such things be?"

I had been about to call it a day, but was intrigued. Removing the plain brown wrapper, I found myself looking at a small, worn, leather–covered book. It was Hippolito's diary.

I immediately turned to the last entry. It was dated the day before the discovery of the bodies.

I tremble in anticipation. The stars are right. The acolytes are subdued but compliant, resigned to the great part they will play in opening the door. I have the object which is the key. It is the 26th. He will return at last. Tonight will be the beginning of the new glory.

The handwriting was extremely precise, almost calligraphy. It was maddening, because this entry and a dozen previous entries made no specific reference to what the ultimate result of this "opening the door" might mean. It was clear from the tone of anticipation, that Hippolito was excited, almost fanatic, but the diary seemed to have been written with all the essential facts already understood, and, thus, there was no clear picture of what it all meant. As I worked backward to the beginning, my sense of frustration only grew. There were no names, no clear delineation of events.

But, inside the front cover, carefully drawn with a steady hand, was a sketch. It showed a strange bear–like creature with wings, with a bulbous head bearing tentacles. Next to it was a small stick figure, with a half–dozen strange wiggly lines coming from its head. The larger drawing was at least five times the size of the stick figure. There was no writing on the page, and a careful rereading of the entire text made no reference to the drawings. The larger creature was exquisitely drawn, complex in it's detail. The eyes were piercing and a feeling of cold dread crept up my spine. The Mate had artistic talent, that was a certainty. Then why was the stick figure so crudely rendered?

What could they mean? Just doodles? It was, after all, a diary. Despite the careful calligraphic writing, the book was a collection of non–specific personal memos and data.

I put it aside and sat back to think.

I was still wrestling with possibilities when the phone rang.

"Lieutenant George Bayer?"

The voice possessed a slight accent, but I couldn't identify it at first. "Yes, this is Bayer. Who's this?"

"I think you know who this is, Lieutenant?" came the reply. The accent was Spanish, though very cultured. The English was precise.

"No, I don't kn…wait! Hippolito? Is this Anthony Hippolito?"

"You are very quick, Lieutenant," said the voice with a chuckle. "I merely called to tell you that you are too late."

I was almost speechless. "What? What do you mean?"

Bayer's Tale

"Last night, at midnight, as it became the 27th of February, Jupiter and Venus were aligned. From February 20th through February 27th, Venus and Jupiter were in a dance that culminated in the two planets being less than a quarter of a degree from each other. It is this alignment that took place in 2 BC which astronomers believe may have been the star of Bethlehem! The two planets were so close they appeared as one to the naked eye. And since there were no telescopes, perhaps the ancients believed a new star had been born. Of course, the sky was overcast all this week so most people here would not have seen it."

Belatedly, I realized I should be tracing the call. I stabbed at the button that would automatically initiate the trace. Meanwhile, I said, "You should come in to the office, Mr. Hippolito. There are a lot of questions you need to answer."

The deep voice fairly roared with laughter. "I think not, Bayer. I am not worried about answering to you. I must now face a higher authority, and I hold out no hope of mercy from that quarter."

"What do you mean?" I asked, almost shouting. "Stop talking in riddles."

"Not riddles," he answered without mirth. "I was to have been one of them last night, and my courage failed me. It has made things...inconvenient...for the one I serve."

"What are you talking about?"

"You are a fool, Bayer. Just listen."

His voice fell in volume, forcing me to listen intently.

"The alignment happened as foretold, but nineteen were needed to open the door fully, and I failed at the last minute. As a result, the door opened momentarily, but not long enough. My master, the Great One, came through, but the opening snapped shut before the others could follow. Now He must wait more thousands of years for such a celestial event to reoccur. And, He must wait alone. His displeasure with me cannot be described."

I thought I understood. "You mean you were just a hired hand? That someone else is responsible for the deaths of your crewmates?"

He laughed again, but without humor. "My crewmates were better servants than I, Lieutenant. The requirement was for willing sacrifice. They went singing. I failed."

Officer Smith came rushing in the door and I shushed him with a gesture. He approached, leaned over, and said, "He's at a pay phone at the port."

"You're at the port, Hippolito. We'll be there in minutes to arrest you."

There was no laughter in his reply. "As I said, Lieutenant, you are too late. Even now, He rises from the waves. Come if you think it will do any good, but you may wish otherwise."

And then the connection was broken.

Grabbing my hat and calling to Dan to follow with backup to the port, at the Moran Container Terminal, East Side, Space 17, I rushed from the office.

With siren blaring and lights flashing, I bucked late evening traffic and raced to the port. The sky had remained deceptively clear. The sea swell had risen as I drove right out onto the docks and headed for the *Rosita*, my headlights showing the way.

I had just reached the base of the gangway and come to a screeching halt, throwing open the door and drawing my revolver, when the world seemed to tilt.

With a tremendous groaning and cracking, the front of the pier simply collapsed below me, even as I saw the ship rock violently. I fell into the freezing water and grabbed frantically at a remaining pylon.

Then I saw two things I shall never forget.

One was a human figure who had fallen not far from me. He was not far away, perhaps only fifty yards or so, but I could not have reached him. It was Hippolito, his swarthy face pale in the scant moonlight. He clung to a bit of timber which was drawing him away from the shore and the ruined pier. He saw me, but uttered no sound. I have never seen such hopelessness on a human face. But, worst of all, his watch cap had been lost to the waves, and I could clearly see his shaven skull bobbing on the surface. From the top of his head, a half-dozen wriggling, worm-like, appendages moved like snakes in the wind.

And then something rose out of the water and, with a tremendous splash, the man was gone without uttering so much as a single cry.

What I saw cannot be described. It was vast, huge…a giant…something. It was dark and scaled, and the water roiled. I thought I saw tentacles for an instant, but the larger…something…was…a limb? An arm? It was dark, remember. The moon only a crescent. I do know that, for some reason I cannot explain, my entire body went numb. I saw, just for a split second, two huge red eyes glaring at me from the raucous sea, and then it was gone. I screamed like a young girl. I'm afraid I was no longer in control of my faculties.

I'm told I was still screaming and clinging desperately to the pylon when Dan found me. Within minutes, divers had rescued me and I lay shivering and babbling at the end of the remaining pier. I honestly have no memory of this. My senses had fled.

Two days later, I was back at the precinct, still a bit shaky, but determined to get back to my work. I had made my statement for the record. I said I had seen something, but had not been specific. I didn't want to get committed to a padded cell. No trace of Hippolito had been found, so there were no other witnesses. The case of the *Rosita's* crew went down officially as "unsolved."

I had not been injured aside from bruises and scrapes. I was sore, but perfectly fit for duty, and I was determined to get back up on the horse, to continue my career.

Then the phone rang and it was Ed Cryer from the lab. He seemed a little shaken. He wouldn't talk with me about it on the phone, but urged me to come immediately to the lab.

I left the building and walked the two blocks to the lab. Cryer was waiting in his office. When I started to ask him about what he'd found, he shushed me and gestured for me to follow him. We passed through the outer laboratory area and into the secure section in silence. Coming to a halt beside a guarded door, Cryer sent the guard down the hall, took out a key, and unlocked the door, gesturing for me to precede him in. He closed and bolted the door behind us. Once inside, he explained that the grass had been trimmed around those depressions I found on the sea–side of the park, and plaster impressions had been made. Honestly, I had forgotten all about them.

"Aren't you being a little dramatic, Ed?" I asked. "I mean how risky is it to let the guards and lab workers see plaster casts of tire tracks?"

"Tire tracks?" He looked at me accusingly. "No, I don't think I'm being a little anything," he replied with a shaky voice. "And if I find out you're pulling some sort of a hoax on us, I swear I'll have you up on charges, George."

I was taken aback by Cryer's obvious anger. "What's going on, Ed? I don't have the faintest idea what you're talking about."

Still glaring at me, he moved to the rear of the room where there was a pile of cloth. It looked like there must be twenty or thirty sheets in a pile. He reached over with a trembling hand and grabbed one end, pulling the material back toward the center of the room.

My eyes widened as I finally realized that the cloth was a large single sheet, like a painter's drop cloth, covering a single object.

"What the hell . . .?" I started to ask, but then memory came flooding back.

I know I was pale as a ghost as Cryer said, "That's what was under the grass, George. That is what has nearly frightened me to death. It can't be real. But it is not alone." He added in a trembling voice, "There are multiple tracks, and we've made casts of all we could find. They came up from the sea and then went back to it."

The scale was immense, and the off–white plaster had been propped at an angle. What the cast duplicated was a single gigantic print—not even remotely human. The details were lacking, probably because of the grass and the soil covering the depression, but the overall shape was unmistakably a large four taloned hand or foot, perhaps more a claw, some nine feet long and six feet wide.

I am leaving the force, taking early retirement. I've decided to live in Arizona, outside a small town in the middle of the desert. I hope never to see the ocean again.

I do not understand it all, but I think I have an idea of what happened. I think Hippolito and his fellows performed some rite on that February night that brought something into the world, perhaps, if the diary entry was correct, something *back* into the world.

My nights are troubled and I plan to undergo therapy as soon as possible. I have terrible nightmares. And, it is not only the progressive interruption of sleep that troubles me. Nightly, I swear I see two glowing, malevolent red orbs fixed on me even after I realize I have awakened myself screaming.

And, hidden, in a wooden box at the back of my closet is one other thing. After my rescue, Dan had been checking the collapsed pier and found it wedged between a pylon and the retaining wall. He showed it to me and I said I would log it into the property room, but I did not.

It is a statue made from a strange green kind of stone. It depicts a creature like the sketch in the diary...and...what I think I saw in the ocean when Hippolito disappeared. The base of the sculpture exactly matches the velvet tray in the bottom of the First Mate's chest.

I do not take it out of the box. Looking at it gives me the shakes. But I am unable to give it up. I feel tied to it somehow. But, mostly, as long as it lies in the back of my closet, it cannot be used as a key.

LISA MORTON is a screenwriter, reviewer and the author of three nonfiction books, including *The Halloween Encyclopedia*. Her short fiction has appeared in several dozen books and magazines, most recently *Unspeakable Horror: From the Shadows of the Closet*, *Winter Frights*, *Horror Library Volume 3*, *Terrible Beauty: Fearful Symmetry* and *Dark Passions: Hot Blood XIII*. She won the 2006 Bram Stoker Award for Short Fiction and is a two-time winner of the Horror Writers Association's Richard Laymon Award. Her first novella, *The Lucid Dreaming*, will be published by Bad Moon Books in 2009. She lives in North Hollywood, and can be found online at www.lisamorton.com .

The Call of Cthulhu: The Motion Picture
(Posted online by Gene Chan, of Los Angeles)

by Lisa Morton

"*The most merciful thing in the world, I think, is the inability of the human mind to correlate all its contents...some day the piecing together of dissociated knowledge will open up such terrifying vistas of reality, and our frightful position therein, that we shall either go mad from the revelation or flee from the deadly light into the peace and safety of a new dark age.*"
—H. P. Lovecraft

I. The Horror in Clay

The most merciful thing in the world, I think, is *not* the inability of the human mind to correlate all its contents. Correlation is a rational process, and rationality turns back the dark tides of mystery and madness. Even the darkest mysteries revealed lose their dimness, and under the light shed they can become everyday fact.

No, the most merciful thing in the world, I know, is the inability of the human mind to perceive eternity. If we could perceive eternity, the infinity of the cosmos around us, then we would also perceive the limitless forms of horror. I have seen our frightful position in the terrifying vistas of reality, and I now retain the most tenuous of holds on my consciousness; to perceive the fullness of endless terror would utterly annihilate even the strongest of minds.

I wish that, like the protagonist in the typical terror tale of old, I could fear approaching death, either from some primeval terror or from its frenzied worshippers; but, as you'll see from this narrative, I can't look forward to death to escape the glimpse of infinity I've had. I will live, bearing this hideous knowledge, and the even worse responsibility. Granted, I didn't begin the horror; but I did nothing to stop it. My only consolation is that it is probably insurmountable, and my attempts, had I made them, would have proven fruitless.

I first became aware of the nightmare's existence in the summer of the new millennium, 2001. That's when the sculpture was given to me, a model made

Dead But Dreaming

from clay that would soon enough acquire different substance. That model became part of my dreams and so, I suppose, part of my soul.

But this narrative really begins the day before I first saw the sculpture.

I was an unemployed screenwriter (a redundant phrase, I know), on the verge of seeking employment in Southern California's always-burgeoning food service industry when the call came.

My agent had called two weeks earlier to tell me that she had submitted me for a job developing a horror script based on a story by H. P. Lovecraft. My screenplay *Absolute Zero* was one of those legendary unsold scripts that had been read by every producer in Hollywood (and several in Europe), optioned a half-dozen times, and always returned to me at the end of the option period. It gave readers nightmares—which was exactly why it remained unfilmed. Apparently no one in this town wanted to touch a script that was genuinely frightening.

But it still made for a great writing sample, and had opened doors for me before. So far those doors had led to nothing but meetings, no actual work. This latest interest expressed showed every promise of likewise leading nowhere, but the producer was someone I wanted to meet anyway; his earlier adaptation of Lovecraft's "The Rats in the Walls" (you'd know the film under its release title *Rats!*) was an infamous cult classic that had found its way into the *Guinness Book of World Records* for the most real animal parts ever used in a film.

His name was Benjamin Azenay; he was an ex-investment broker who had forsaken a lucrative career to pursue his passion for horror movies. He'd lucked out with his first production, but had produced nothing to equal *Rats!* in the five years since its release. Now he had new sources of capital and was looking to make the biggest film of his career. He wanted to adapt Lovecraft's "The Call of Cthulhu."

Our first meeting took place at his San Fernando valley production offices. It was summer in Los Angeles, and the mercury had climbed into the three-digit range. There was a smog alert on, and the air in the valley was oppressive and draining, like the stinking breath exhaled by some huge parasite. Withering palm trees dropped long, desiccated fronds, leaving the tree-dwelling rats and possums to burn. Streets were sticky with tar, and buildings were shut tight to seal in the precious cool air, leaving the sidewalks strangely abandoned. A homeless man asleep on the bus bench might have been dead, and left there as a kind of warning.

I found the office building at the corner of Magnolia and Cohen, a two-story structure with crumbling pink stucco and graffiti on one wall that looked like alien hieroglyphics. Azenay's production company was on the second floor, situated above an ancient pizza parlor. The pizza parlor's doors were wide open, a telltale sign of a life of struggle that hadn't led to enough profit to afford an air conditioner. I caught a glimpse of a man in his fifties slumped over the front counter; his eyes were filled with what I could only describe as apathetic desperation.

The Call of Cthulhu: The Motion Picture

I was relieved to find Azenay's offices cool and modern (the 100-foot walk from my car had left my forehead slick and with pounding temples). It was a suite of four or five rooms, maybe more; a friendly, efficient young assistant greeted me, and introduced me to my prospective employer.

That first meeting was brief. Azenay was younger than I'd expected, in his late thirties; he was cordial but cool, with a slight air of anxiety. He spent the fifteen minutes of our meeting nervously shredding a small slip of paper; but he never took his eyes off me as he told me of his intention to make the truest filmic adaptation of Lovecraft yet. I confessed that my knowledge of Lovecraft was limited to what I'd read in school—"The Outsider," that favorite of basic literature textbooks everywhere; and, inspired by a viewing of the Boris Karloff-starrer *Die, Monster, Die*, I'd sampled "The Colour Out of Space." We talked about *Absolute Zero*; we talked about *Rats!*; we talked about why one previous draft of *The Call of Cthulhu* hadn't worked. I stole glimpses at the various foreign posters for *Rats!* that lined his office, and felt a tinge of jealousy. I'd had my cult hit as well—the black comedy *Meet the Weirdos*—but it had enjoyed nothing like the notoriety of *Rats!*

I left, convinced the meeting had been uneventful, that I wouldn't get the job. I had it by the end of the day.

The offer my agent outlined was an average medium-budget step deal. I'd get so much for each draft I delivered, more if the film went into production, and a bonus if it was produced solely from my draft. There was money up front; there was even a pair of percentage points. I would start tomorrow.

I went out that night and celebrated by heading to L.A.'s best used and rare bookstore, and buying every Lovecraft book they had. I bought collections, I bought biographies, I bought chapbooks, I even bought one rare paperback edition of *The Shadow Over Innsmouth*. I read "The Call of Cthulhu" twice in one sitting.

That night the nightmares were—not worse, but stronger. Stranger.

I'd had them for over a month now. It made sense—I was anxious over money, and the sputtering wall-mounted air conditioner didn't reach my single bedroom, with temperatures in the 90's at night.

But that didn't explain the content of these dreams. Or the regularity; night after night, they varied little. Always the same huge, half-glimpsed form, an almost human form, but with something else where a head should have been. Always with me running, locked in the slow-motion sickness of a dream, feeling the thing at my back, bearing down on me, breathing its stinking air on me...That night before I signed my figurative soul away to Benjamin Azenay, I stopped and turned to face my pursuer, but all I could see was a thick smog, an infinitely impenetrable and vile miasma.

The next day I spent an hour with Azenay, and told him of my plan: I wanted to know Lovecraft, *really* know him. I felt that if I could understand exactly how the man had worked and cut to the core of his work, I could figure out how to best translate it to screen. Azenay explained that previous adaptations had failed because they'd tried to rely on the surface elements of Lovecraft's work; thus, "The Dunwich Horror" was reduced to a psychotic obsessed with otherworldly creatures (and women, coincidentally enough), or "The Lurking Fear" became a fourth-rate thriller about underground demons that could burrow at astonishing speed. Even *Rats!* had succeeded not because of its reliance on Lovecraft, but rather because of the sheer spectacle of its gore. No one had yet captured Lovecraft's milieu of cosmic fear, his New England backwoods and mistrustful farmers, his dread of otherness.

And no one had yet dealt with Lovecraft's supreme creation, the elder god Cthulhu, and his pantheon of "Great Old Ones." Azenay wanted to be the first to capture Cthulhu, Lovecraft's tendril–headed, winged corporealization of ultimate evil, on film. He gave me three things that he thought would assist me in finding the essence of Lovecraft: a contract, a check, and the clay sculpture.

When Azenay first brought the sculpture into his office and set it on his oak desk before me, I gaped in eerie recognition. It absolutely was the clay model which formed the basis for the first third of "The Call of Cthulhu," the one recreated from his dreams by the disturbed young artist Wilcox. Upon closer examination, I realized it was bigger than the five-by-six inch bas–relief Lovecraft described, a change no doubt necessitated by the need for the piece to read well on film. Otherwise it was utterly accurate, down to the Cyclopean architecture behind the foreground figure—the tentacle–headed monster god Cthulhu.

Azenay told me the piece had been sculpted by his usual makeup effects artist, "Red Boy" Hidalgo; he had commissioned the sculpture to impress his investors and help secure financing for the film. I already knew Red Boy by reputation—he was a talented, flamboyant young wizard who had not only provided the effects for *Rats!* and all of Azenay's other films, but who also had a local cult following for his wildly perverse artwork. Azenay told me that Red Boy was already at work on the other designs for the film, and he even suggested that we meet, to share ideas and enthusiasm. When I started out of the office, he called me back and gave me the bas–relief; he thought I should keep it next to my computer for inspiration while writing the script.

I spent that night studying the sculpture, not working on the script. The detail on it was striking, and I realized Lovecraft had been wrong about the size—the amount of information and the sheer otherworldliness could not possibly have been conveyed by a piece as small as what he had described. And the realism…even though the piece was in unpainted, grey–green clay, and lightly fired, it felt more like a window than a flat opaque slab. Depending on time of day and angle of lighting, the figure of Cthulhu even seemed to take on slightly different postures, although the expression of arrogant malevolence never changed.

The rest of that first week was devoted to studying Lovecraft. I read the biographies; I discovered a brilliant but bigoted eccentric whose life and work were ruled by his fear of any *otherness*. It became clear to me that his most famous creation—the Great Old Ones, who once ruled the cosmos and waited dreaming in their sunken city R'lyeh—were in fact extensions of his own paranoia, his sense that outside his small New England realm there existed a world full of degenerate monsters that lived only for the day when they would claim the earth back for themselves and their hideous purposes.

Truthfully I began to dislike Lovecraft; certainly he would have loathed me, since my heritage was Hokken Chinese. I tried to focus on Lovecraft the writer, the master craftsman of the macabre; but something kept intruding at the edge of my consciousness, some hint that there was more to Lovecraft than either supremacist or pensman. A notion of an extraordinary direct path to his subconscious, a super fast connection to his own personal demons.

Even as I disliked the man, I envied the writer's ability to tap his own bleakest, blackest regions. I would need that ability, to recreate him in screenplay format. While I prided myself on my own imagination and creative abilities, I would have to look deeper, into places I'd never thought to explore. And I felt quite sure that Red Boy, the twenty–something young cinematic artist, was ahead of me there.

I called Red's number, and set up an appointment to meet him. His "studio" turned out to be a three–car garage in a large suburban tract home, in a newer development near the northeast rim of the Valley. Although temperatures had dropped (to the mid–nineties) on the day I drove there, the streets were deserted, the residents having sensibly fled the heat. In fact from the time I entered Red's development ("Paradise Hills!") until I pulled up before his dull tan house, I didn't pass a single human being. The houses perched on the edge of a high–desert canyon, and I thought I saw a tarantula on one sidewalk, rendered more sluggish than usual by the weather. Two doors down from Red's, a child's scooter lay on its side in a gutter, one wheel twisted at an impossible angle.

Loud metal music roared at me when Red opened the front door. He was a painful clash of crimson (hair), pitch black (clothes), and dark earth brown (skin). As he waved me into the house and offered me a beer, he seemed distracted, but I soon realized he was simply exhausted. He led me down a dark hallway to the garage, and his studio.

The studio was as out–of–place in this suburban ghost town as Red was. Two walls were lined with workbenches and shelves; the third held a large industrial sink and cabinets. On the shelves were models of monsters I recognized, and head casts of actors from Benjamin Azenay films; the benches were littered with drawings, slabs of clay, easels, sculpting tools, huge injection guns and special ovens.

Without even offering me a stool, Red immediately returned to his current project: creating the small three–dimensional sculpture of Cthulhu found by Inspector Legrasse in the second section of "The Call of Cthulhu." Even though the model was still only about two–thirds complete, it was already unmistakable. It would be astonishing when completed.

Red never stopped working while we talked; for sixty minutes he bent slavishly over the sculpture, delicately turning each fold of clay with a small metal tool, sometimes brushing the surface with an alcohol–soaked brush. His words were slightly slurred, but more from concentration than drunkenness.

From what he told me, he had every right to be drunk. Very drunk, and for a very long time.

When I asked how the bas–relief piece had come about, he began by telling me that when he was first hired for the project—this was when another screenwriter was attached—he had done exactly what I was doing now: exhaustively researched Lovecraft and his gruesome pantheon. That had been six months ago; Azenay had told him he wanted several pieces of concept art and the bas–relief to woo potential investors and distributors.

Within a month of receiving the assignment, he'd handed Azenay three color conceptual paintings and the bas–relief, but they'd both known the art was lacking. While technically polished and more than suitable to Azenay's purpose, it felt too much like an artist's rendition of the weird, and not the weird itself. Azenay kept the three paintings, but sent Red home to start over on the bas–relief, which would also serve as the actual prop in the film.

That night Red had the first dream. Although he didn't remember it clearly, when he woke the next morning he'd proceeded to work for the next forty hours straight, and saw something very different taking shape beneath his fingers. He finally collapsed, too exhausted to go on, but slept only a few hours before waking, startled and uneasy, from another dream.

Red soon began to remember parts of the dreams, and when he told me what he could recall I actually laughed. He described voices whispering strange words to him, glimpses of Cyclopean vistas—he described, in other words, almost exactly what the fictitious artist Henry Anthony Wilcox related in the story of "The Call of Cthulhu."

I, of course, thought he was joking, but he completely ignored my laughter and continued on in a way that swiftly convinced me he wasn't. In the dreams, he was shown the bas–relief piece in great detail; he held it in his dream hands, turned it over and over, scrutinizing every millimeter of it. When he woke, he simply sculpted what he had been shown.

The dreams hadn't ended, and so after Red had finished the bas–relief he had begun to paint. Without turning away, he waved one hand over a shoulder and told me to check out the canvases leaning against a wall near the doorway leading into the house.

The paintings were half–hidden under the sink, carelessly stacked there as if they were toys abandoned by a thoughtless child. There were five, all roughly three by four or five feet.

My breath froze in my throat as I held the first one up to the bleak overhead light. It showed one of Lovecraft's dripping, monolithic cities, in almost photorealistic detail. Each chip in a granite block, each tendril of moss, each oily ground puddle—all captured in perfection. The sky overhead was neither night nor day, looking more like a greenish, toxic foam than earthly cloud formations.

The first four were variations, as if Red was a camera panning the length of the same hideous avenue. But the fifth… The largest canvas offered a gigantic, gaping doorway in one of the block–built structures, an opening into complete blackness—but with something just starting to emerge from the blackness. A hint of eyes—too many eyes—glowing from the dark interior, something like a limb or tentacle the color of absinthe emerging.

As unnerving as the paintings were, worst of all was Red's answer when I asked him if Azenay had seen these yet. He told me no, because they weren't finished.

When I left that deceptively suburban workshop, I firmly believed that Red's dreams were the result of an artist immersing himself in his work, that his careful study of Lovecraft and "The Call of Cthulhu" had paid off in ways even he could not have foreseen; but there was one important difference between Red Boy Hidalgo and the fictitious sculptor Henry Anthony Wilcox, upon whom he may have unconsciously been modeling himself: Wilcox's dreams had stopped after a time.

I doubted that Red's would cease any time soon. At least not until he was finished with *The Call of Cthulhu: The Motion Picture*.

II. The Tale of rfurman@swmailboxes.com

The day after my meeting with Red, I decided to sit down with the screenplay in earnest. Now I realize, of course, that the I shouldn't have been so quick to dismiss Red's dreams as simply the specters of a fanciful mind; after all, I was having my own share of unfamiliar nightmares, and even Lovecraft had originally written "The Call of Cthulhu" after a strange but very precise dream.

But instead I was wrestling with the dilemma of the script. The original story provided any conscientious adapter with a considerable challenge: The protagonist, one Francis Wayland Thurston, didn't actually *experience* any of the remarkable things that happened; instead, he remained aloof from the action, merely reporting what others had said. I actually thought it was questionable that this worked in the story; for it to work in a movie was unthinkable. Although Azenay wanted to retain the period setting, there were certain contemporary elements—a romance, a female lead—that would need to be introduced into Lovecraft's sterile, masculine world.

Certain answers were obvious: Thurston would accompany Inspector LeGrasse when the New Orleans policeman led a bayou raid that uncovered a horrible sacrificial ritual; and Thurston would be the one in the finale—not the Norwegian sailor Johansen—who would witness mighty Cthulhu's rising from his tomb in R'lyeh. But how could I introduce a female lead and still reflect the essence of Lovecraft? The old writer himself obviously felt far less comfortable with women than he did with spaghetti-headed cosmic monsters, since his entire body of fiction featured very few characters of the feminine gender.

I began to wonder more and more why the first screenplay—the one by another writer—had failed, and so I called Azenay's office, to ask if I could see a copy of that draft. Azenay was out, but an assistant corrected me when I mentioned the draft that hadn't worked; she told me that in actuality it had never been completed. The writer had spent several weeks on the project, then returned his advance and left.

Returned his advance? That bespoke either more honor than I'd ever heard of in a Hollywood writer, or absolute terror. I asked who the writer was, and the assistant gave me the name Gerome Furman. The assistant claimed no knowledge of the earlier uncompleted draft, and said she didn't think the writer had ever delivered one to the office.

After I hung up, I logged online and ran the name Gerome Furman through several databases. What came back was not especially surprising—Furman had written *Rats!*, as well as more low-budget horror films, for both Azenay and others—but it was disturbing. Furman and Azenay obviously had a good working relationship, so why would Furman have left *The Call of Cthulhu* so decisively? Especially when it promised to be the biggest film of his career?

I found an e-mail address for Furman, and after a brief debate, decided to send him a note. My message was simple: I was the current writer on *The Call of Cthulhu* for Benjamin Azenay, I was wrestling with certain aspects of the script. I had already seen Red Boy, and now wondered if he, Furman, could offer any advice.

I received a reply twelve hours later. It was long enough to take nearly a minute of downloading time. I'd half-expected Furman to be irritated or at least terse; I certainly could never have expected the cautionary (and ultimately unnerving) tale his e-mail contained.

He began by telling me he knew how good the money was, and how hard it was to turn down a job—but he had done it. And it was important that I know exactly why.

Not long after accepting the work, Azenay had told him that he had an "expert" who could provide valuable insight into the script. Furman thought he'd be meeting a Lovecraft scholar, a student of the horror genre, a fan with an extraordinary collection...but the woman he met was none of these things.

Her name was Maria Block; they met in Azenay's office. When Furman had asked if she was any relation to Lovecraft's famed correspondent Robert, she'd stared at him blankly, and Azenay had hastened to add that the spelling was different. Later, she'd told him that the name had been shortened when her family had come to America; she told him the original name, and he'd laughed and told her it did indeed sound quite unpronounceable by the American tongue. She was a small woman with dark hair, pale skin, black eyes, and a sharp nose; younger, she might have been possessed of an exotic charisma, but there were lines around those ebon eyes and grey streaking the long hair. Even after he'd heard the original family name, Furman couldn't guess at her real ethnicity.

Furman asked her what exactly she was expert in, and she told him simply that the investors had asked her to assist him. Furman later asked Azenay who was providing the backing for the film, and Azenay had anxiously muttered that they were a group of "venture capitalists" who actually had come to him, based on the success of *Rats!* Furman knew better than to ask for names.

Maria Block told Furman she'd like to introduce him to a circle of friends whom she thought would provide him with a great deal of inspiration. She wanted to pick him up late Wednesday night, the 19th, at 11 p.m. Furman asked why so late; she only inquired if it was a problem. He told her no, he was a night owl anyways, and the arrangements were made.

Wednesday came, and Maria appeared out in front of Furman's apartment at exactly the appointed time. It was December, and he'd dressed warmly, but Maria told him he'd need a stronger jacket; they had about an hour's drive, because her friends would be found on the coast.

They took the 101 Freeway, heading west; at the late hour on a weeknight the freeway was quiet, and nearly deserted once they left the confines of the San Fernando Valley. The drive took them through the western suburbs—Thousand Oaks, Agoura, Westlake Village—all marked only by one or two off ramps and overlit convenience stores, whose brightness seemed to stand in defiance against the desolation just beyond the asphalt.

They turned off before Santa Barbara, and wound through coastal foothills for a short time. Once their headlights caught a glimpse of an impoverished raccoon at the side of the road, limping, dragging a badly mangled leg. Furman wondered what had hit it; they hadn't seen another car since the freeway.

At last the winding road crested a rise, and the Pacific Ocean lay spread below them, a vague scintillant mass. Within minutes they were pulling into a small, sand–strewn parking lot. Furman counted three other cars, including an ancient, battered VW van that would have looked at home in the Summer of Love. He didn't see anyone else around; she told him they'd be on foot from here.

They climbed from the warmth of Maria's SUV and Furman was hit by the cold, a hard stinging slap to his lulled senses. He pulled his jacket tighter and followed Maria onto the beach, wondering why she didn't seem to notice the ocean chill when she wore only a light dress and shawl.

They plodded through the sand for some time, until Furman's ankles were beginning to protest. As they trudged on, a fog crept in, dulling whatever light there had been, making it almost impossible to tell where water ended and land began. He was only dimly aware that they had rounded a rock point, and were now in a small cove, sheltered by seaweed–covered outcroppings on either end. The tide was low, and the beach strewn with what the departing waves had deposited there; the fog smelled of rotting sewage. Furman guessed a crunch under his heel to be a used hypodermic, and realized this beach, as hidden as it might be, was as subject to the filthy whims of pollution as every other beach in Southern California.

He heard their goal before he saw it—a low rhythm, carrying through the saline fog. At first he took it for recorded music; then, as they drew nearer, he realized it was live, the sound of at least four or five drums, like congas or bongos. Finally he saw a glow in the fog, which formed itself into flames. A large fire pit had been constructed, and there were maybe a dozen figures surrounding it, some seated, some upright and moving. No, not moving—*dancing*. Dancing to the beaten drums with an abandon that could only be called primitive.

At first Furman had the ridiculous thought that she'd dragged him to some sort of holiday celebration—Christmas was less than a week away, and he knew just enough about the day's origins to know that there were some who still celebrated it as a pagan holiday. He began to hope he wouldn't be asked to participate; he could just see himself laughing as they asked him to chant or drink the sacred wine. Perhaps, he smiled to himself, they could resurrect the great beach god Moondoggie.

They walked closer, until Furman could make out the faces of the revelers; they were as mixed a group as the rest of the population of Los Angeles—Hispanic, Asian, African-American, caucasian, male, female. One girl—she couldn't have been older than 18—was beautiful, with features that looked Mediterranean. She was also pregnant, Furman guessed at least six months along.

He was wondering if they'd been seen yet when his guide abruptly dropped her shawl and walked into the celebration, her body already swaying to the demanding rhythm. She exchanged kisses with the three men who were dancing; they all completely ignored Furman.

Furman shivered in the cold fog, then glanced at his watch; it was after 1 a.m. He wondered how long this would go on, what was expected of him. He opted to wait and find out. For a while he was interested in the drum beats and the dancing, then even that became dull in its endless repetition. He thought about going for a walk, but didn't want to run the risk of becoming separated in the fog, finding himself lost, freezing in the foul, thick air. He considered making a scene, barging in, demanding to be taken home; like the writer he was, he played the scene in his head, even watching it from different angles.

He was about to act on this last fantasy when something changed in what he had begun to think of as the ritual. The drum beats quickened, and the gorgeous youthful mother-to-be danced alone into the center of the ring, nearest the fire. All the other dancers moved back away from her, all but one—an older man with a pitted, craggy face, a man whom Furman somehow knew to be the leader.

Suddenly there was a long, glinting knife in this man's hand. Furman had missed how it had gotten there, but his eyes couldn't leave it now, not even when it slit the exquisite girl's throat.

She fell immediately to the sand, and Furman saw it redden around her head. He staggered back a step, and caught himself on the verge of running; he had the irrational fear that if he ran, they would come after him. So he stayed, shivering violently, listening to someone moan and then understanding that it was himself.

But the drums hadn't lessened, and Furman watched now as the man bent over the dying girl. For a moment he seemed to study her throes, in something like compassion; then Furman saw him raise the knife again, and he jerked his head away just as the blade came down. Down into the extended abdomen.

Furman turned his back, desperate to block out the scene behind him. Still, it was somehow shocking when the drums stopped, all together, on some sort of cue. All Furman heard now were a dozen breaths panting in fevered exhaustion, and horrible wet gurgling sounds. Then there was a cry, a shout in a voice rich with exaltation and frenzy; the voice he was sure belonged to the knife wielder, but the words were unrecognizable. Strange guttural sounds, belonging to no language he knew; the only part that sounded even remotely familiar was a final string of syllables that sounded like "*Kloo–lu.*"

And then, in the sudden taut silence, something answered. Something out in the fog, in the direction that Furman guessed was the sea. Something had uttered a high, wavering cry out there, a cry unlike anything Furman had ever heard.

The ritual participants were noticeably excited by the sound. The drummers dropped their instruments and leapt to their feet; those already standing turned as one and tried to peer past the fog.

Something could now be heard moving in the water; whatever it was, it was obviously big, and coming this way. It uttered that cry again, and was distressingly close. Furman heard something wet slapping sand, telling him the thing was out of the water, on the oil–slicked shore now…

And that was when he turned and ran. He only knew he ran in the direction away from that hideous approach. When he ran into the cliff walls that encircled the cove, he didn't bother to work his way around to the points; he scrabbled up the cliff in darkness, unheeding of the pain in his scraped fingers and knees. He got lucky and found a small ravine that cut through the cliff wall; he ran up the ravine and finally emerged at the top of the cliff. Then he regained himself enough to walk slowly, careful not to get turned around in the damp lightless air and find himself tumbling down the cliff. When he thought the cliff was well behind him, he quickened his pace until he found a road; just before sunup he stumbled into a twenty–four–hour minimart, where the sullen teenaged attendant provided him with the address and change for the pay phone. He knew the taxi ride home would cost him a fortune, but he didn't care; if he could pay extra for the cab to arrive even sooner and whisk him away to sanity again, he would.

He was afraid to go home that day; after all, Maria of the unpronounceable last name had picked him up there. He checked into a hotel and tried to sleep, but his one successful attempt was interrupted by a nightmare of shambling seaweed–covered shapes. What finally convinced him to go home was a combination of his own weariness, his need to return to his life, and what he'd heard as he'd clambered up that cliff wall on the beach: the screams of the revelers as something tore through their midst, something that made slapping sounds on the sand...

A day later—after he'd finally taken enough scalding baths to warm himself again—he called Azenay and asked if he'd heard from Maria Block in the last day or so. Azenay admitted that he had not, and confessed he also knew very little about her, only that her knowledge of the Cthulhu mythos had "come highly recommended." In that same conversation Furman told Azenay he was leaving the project; when Azenay reminded him that he'd received an advance, Furman had promised to return it. He did, that afternoon. Then he began making arrangements to move.

He'd moved three times since; he'd realized he couldn't stand the idea of living somewhere with a close shoreline, and so he'd fled to the southwest desert. His few remaining Los Angeles friends knew him now only as I did, through an anonymous e–mail address.

Furman ended his missive with a strange—and troubling—question: Had I dreamt of Lovecraft yet? The last line lingered with me long after I shut off the glowing screen:

"Don't listen to the Old Gentleman—he's lying even to himself."

III. The Madness from the Sky

I made no attempt to reply to Gerome Furman. I thought about an incident two years ago, when a well–known screenwriter had inexplicably driven his SUV through the wall of a bar and killed two of the patrons, and I thought it was fortunate that Furman's pressure–induced psychoses hadn't injured anyone else yet. I certainly knew firsthand what a difficult business we shared, but I was sure at that point that I could cope with whatever had unhinged my predecessor.

And then I had the first Lovecraft dream.

I'd gone to bed late, after working on the script. I'd just completed the first of the scenes with Wilcox the demented sculptor, but the scene was still rough, missing something. I fell asleep with it foremost in my mind, and so it was no surprise that the spectre of the scene's originator should visit my subconscious.

But this dream was still startling in its casual realism. I was at the computer, pondering, when I heard a voice behind me:

"These machines are remarkable, but can they, I wonder, make a better writer of a mediocre one?"

I turned and, with the calmness that only a dream could provide, beheld Howard Phillips Lovecraft.

He stood behind me, in semi–darkness, but I could see that he was dressed in one of the twenties–era suits he'd worn in photographs. He wore small glasses, and peered at me disdainfully. I knew I disgusted him. I was, after all, not of his beloved master race. Indeed, he told me I was not worthy of the task before me, but he would assist me to protect his work.

I answered that he was worth less than I, since he was dead. He barked a single, dry laugh, and told me that I was seriously in error. Then he began to speak.

I awoke to frustration; there was nothing else of the dream I could remember, only his Rhode Island drawl, the awkward lilt of it without the sense of the words. I was sure he had revealed hidden knowledge, great secrets; all gone now.

Then I walked from the bedroom to the computer, and what I saw on the screen turned the sweat on my body to clammy chill. Everything he'd told me in the dream was there on the screen.

As my numb legs dropped me into my desk chair, I had a vague dream memory of Lovecraft telling me to write down what he said. Apparently I had; now I began to read. The monologue in twelve–point font started with a seventeen–year–old Lovecraft, poised to leave high school and enter Brown University, but beset by such monstrous and intense nightmares that he instead became a recluse, nearly an invalid, for the next six years. In 1914 the night terrors revivified, but this time the older Lovecraft was prepared, and started writing in earnest to assuage the anxiety brought on by the dreams. Two months after Lovecraft began a frantic period of authoring amateur journalism, the Archduke Ferdinand was assassinated, and the 20th century was set firmly on its war–torn path. These two events—Lovecraft's rebirth as a writer and the start of World War I—were directly related. Both were the result of a troubled sleep not their own.

The ancient forces Lovecraft dubbed "The Great Old Ones" had slept, undisturbed and undisturbing, for many centuries, forgotten since before the birth of the Roman Empire. But something had begun to nudge at the archaic evil, some karmic itch. Lovecraft suggested it might have been the terror cultivated by the gruesome work of Jack the Ripper; if anything, I would have blamed the Industrial Revolution. Perhaps the thundering of steam–driven turbines had pulsed all the way through the earth to the ancients' resting place.

Whatever had caused it, the psychic stirring had struck sensitives all over the world. Lovecraft, a delicate child from a family whose history was rife with mental illness, had felt the vibrations and first withdrawn, then begun to write; on the other side of the globe, a small band of Serbians had been similarly touched, and had committed perhaps the most portentous act of assassination in history.

While the century's first great war raged, Lovecraft finally grew past his scribbled non–fiction and began to transcribe what the dreams told him. In 1920, the battles had ended, but Lovecraft still saw eldritch horrors at night. He transcribed one dream which eventually became "The Call of Cthulhu." However, his journal was incomplete, since it mentioned only a museum, an ancient relic, and some cryptic dialogue. In truth, the dream had included a vision of Cthulhu rising from his watery tomb and promising Lovecraft immortality. Lovecraft had used the tableau of the dank resurrection in the short story;

the promise he kept to himself.

The notes ended there. I tried to remember coming to the keyboard in the middle of the night, typing this with the same coherence I possessed when awake. Yet, upon reading it over again, I realized another disturbing fact about it: It was unmistakably Lovecraft's voice. It employed some of his idiosyncratic vocabulary (surely I would never have come up with "eldritch"), his often–florid style. But there was a bitterness there as well, something new, something I hadn't seen greatly expressed in the old Lovecraft's work.

I spent the rest of that day in decision: Did I continue with this project, or follow Furman's lead? So far I hadn't myself experienced anything worse than dreams; were dreams enough to base a bad business decision on? There was Furman's terror at winter solstice (I had recognized the date—the early morning hours of December 20, a few days before Christmas—in his story), but that was nothing but pixels, tiny bits of electronic information which lacked even the tangibility of paper. And if Furman was telling the truth, where had leaving the project taken him? Down a road of real or imagined pursuit; either way, that road would have been easier to travel with the money earned by delivering a completed screenplay.

So I continued with my work. It became easier the longer I worked on it; some nights I was even able to sleep. Other nights Lovecraft haunted me, always dressed in the same suit, always addressing me in that dismissive, arrogant tone. Some times he'd tell me about how Cthulhu had drifted slowly up through consciousness throughout the 20th century, how each new level of wakefulness achieved had brought about a great calamity—World War II, the Cold War, the Jonestown massacre. Other times he rambled on about his immortality, and I came to realize that he didn't mean the lasting fame secured from his writings, he referred to actual physical immortality. I would wake from these episodes feeling perplexed and even betrayed by my own mind, for creating these unwelcome visitations.

Finally I handed in the first draft of *The Call of Cthulhu*. When I drove to Azenay's office and passed the script and diskettes over, he looked more haggard, drained. He told me the investors would need to see the script, and when I asked about the director he revealed for the first time that he would be handling that position as well. The investors, he said, had specified that as part of the deal.

I left the office with a strange mixture of relief and dread. Relief that the first draft was completed, dread at what changes would be ordered—or, more specifically, dread at the prospect of what changes "the investors" would demand.

A month passed. I lived comfortably enough off the money I'd earned from the first draft, and the dreams faded; while they didn't completely pass, they at least receded enough to allow me to sleep again. My days were spent in a kind of air–conditioned haze; I often used up over half the day in bed, avoided leaving the apartment, watched late–night movies hosted by insipid car salesmen. Two months. I thought about writing again. I didn't. Three months. No calls from Azenay, no changes yet.

It was four months after when I received the phone call. It came very early in the morning, just before sunrise. I was awake, having spent the night drinking cheap beer and watching infomercials, which I found reassuring in their mundanity. The ringing phone was startling enough to cut through my alcohol drift like a chill wind through summer. I had been letting my machine answer for me, but I was confused enough to find myself picking it up and answering before I could decide not to.

The voice on the other end was husky, soft, more slurred than my own. It asked for me by name, and I demanded its owner's in return. It was Red Boy. He asked me if I'd seen the shooting schedule. When I stupidly asked what schedule, he told me, the one for *The Call of Cthulhu*, of course. It was now in its fourth week of shooting.

Before I could respond, Red continued: Tonight was the "big scene". He didn't elaborate. He told me only that I should be there. It was a location shoot. He gave me directions, to a spot in the desert northeast of Los Angeles. It was about an hour and a half away. He informed me they would be there shooting all night. I told him I'd try to make it, and he hung up, apparently satisfied.

I wasn't. I was furious—I was now owed a considerable amount of money—and baffled—why were there no changes? Had they even used my draft? And why did Red care? Why should I be there tonight, of all nights, for "the big scene?"

I considered calling Azenay that day, or my agent, but decided that I would follow Red's directions and instead confront Azenay on the set. Provided I could get on, of course.

I set off late that night, to make sure traffic had died. North on the 5, then east on the 14 until it ended, deep into the desert on dusty surface roads. Jagged Joshua trees pierced my headlights on either side of the narrow roads; once I had to swerve to avoid a tumbleweed that was nearly as large as my car. On one particularly pot–holed road, I slowed to 15 miles per hour and saw a coyote pacing the car. I caught one glint of its hungry gold eyes before it veered off into the desert's black night again.

Soon I saw the lights. I knew they were still some distance off, and I knew that they could only be the heavy klieg lights of a movie crew. For the first time, I wondered what scene they could possibly be filming out here; nothing in my script had called for a desert location. Then, even while still a half–mile away, I saw what it was, and pleasure coursed through me, despite my ire:

It was R'lyeh, Cthulhu's sunken city.

They'd built it out here in the desert, around a natural rock formation that leant its own baroque shapes easily to the monolithic slabs (of foam) placed around it. Here was a vista of that Cyclopean city which Lovecraft (and I) had described. It had been artfully dressed with moss, sprayed with glycerine and lit by green–gelled lights to suggest an effulgent waterside necropolis. I even recognized the portal that would open to admit Cthulhu into our world, which bore an immense version of Wilcox's/Red's bas–relief sculpture. I had to admit that my admiration for Benjamin Azenay had just gone up several measures.

I saw a small group of cars parked near the generator and lighting trucks, and pulled up. Two things surprised me: There was no security, and only the merest skeleton of a crew. I saw Azenay, apparently operating his own camera with only one assistant; I saw two grips, a handful of actors, two set dressers, Red Boy—and that was it. No sound crew—apparently they were planning on looping the dialogue in post, no special effects men other than Red. Not even a craft service person.

Perhaps I was too early. But no, they were filming even as I approached. Some instinct prompted me to stay back, in the shadows of one of the trucks. I watched as the four actors—including the star of *Rats!*, playing Thurston, the protagonist—made their way slowly around the great half–sunken doorway. Even though no sound was being recorded, they read the lines so they could match later in looping. Or should I say, they read *my* lines.

Because I felt the absolute thrill of recognition at my work. This was my draft. I had added the mysterious deaths of two men in R'lyeh before they found the portal, and now the lead made mention of one of those men. I felt my lips moving in the darkness, reciting the words as the actors did.

The take finished, Azenay called cut and print, and then told his small crew that the doors would be removed for the next shot; apparently the actual opening would be a CGI effect, added later.

As the set dressers worked at removing the doors, I felt my throat tighten with irrational fear: In the script, the doors opened—and Cthulhu, the polyp–headed nightmarish eldritch horror, emerged and ravaged.

But when the doors had been hauled to the side of the set, what appeared behind them was nothing more than a cone draped in black duvateen cloth, a meaningless and empty funnel. I felt a surprising disappointment as my fear evaporated; obviously any elder gods appearing in this film would be a product of wire frames and light points on a computer.

Red, who had set up a small work bench, was obviously there to provide only Cthulhu's crimes, not the Great Old One himself. As I watched, he was working on a severed arm, filling it with blood tubes that would pump furiously on cue.

Azenay was filming close–ups of the actors as they peered over the edge of the vast doorway. In quick succession and with only minor lighting changes, he popped off four shots, then called for a break.

Now seemed the time to confront him. His assistant was changing the mag on the camera, and Azenay was going through his script—*my* script. I took a few steps forward, then stopped. I hadn't noticed the stretch limousine, parked on the far edge of the line of cars and trucks. Now the back door opened, and two figures emerged, a man and a woman, walking toward Azenay. They moved with a regal ease that bespoke wealth and power; they were obviously the investors.

I held back as they reached Azenay, and the three engaged in a conversation too quiet for me to hear. As the exchange progressed, Azenay looked plainly more disturbed. He glanced skyward at one point, shook his head at another. As I watched this odd and uncomfortable tableau, I began to wonder if I'd seen the woman before. She looked vaguely familiar to me...and then I knew why. She looked exactly the way I'd pictured Maria Block, when I'd read Gerome Furman's e-mail.

It must be coincidence. But then again, why not? Perhaps Furman really had met the woman he had described; that didn't mean the rest of his preposterous (if frightening) tale was true. Maybe he really had been driven by Block to a secluded beach, and had let a fog-shrouded night and unfamiliar customs lead his active imagination to absurd conclusions.

After a short time, Azenay seemed to slump in some sort of acceptance, although a shrewder judge would probably have called it defeat. The elegant pair returned to their limo, which started up, and drove off—perhaps a thousand feet. I saw the motion of the car cease the moment before the headlights went out. They had simply moved the car away from the set.

Why? Had they argued with Azenay, and were now mulling over strategies? Were they perversely unimpressed by the set, and considering pulling out?

Azenay was standing, staring out into the desert night. A cigarette smoldered in the fingers of his right hand, and I realized I hadn't known that he smoked. The fingers were trembling, sending small sparks of ash swirling down to the sand.

He must have heard the sound before I did. I saw his head tilt up, and then he had dropped the cigarette. He didn't even bother to grind it out, just left it forgotten, its tiny fire dying. He was rushing to his assistant, urging him to hurry with loading the new mag.

The rest of us heard it then: A distant thrumming from the black sky, the sound of wings scooping air—but it was too distant. Nothing could have wings that big...

I saw the others all looking up, and the actors began, unconsciously, to back away from the portal. Azenay suddenly directed Thurston, or the actor playing Thurston, to clear the shot and return to his trailer. When the man was slow, Azenay actually shrieked at him. This time the hapless performer nearly tripped over his own feet in his haste to leave the set. The other three actors looked to Azenay, who told them to react to the sound, and then he called for action.

This was nothing I had written. Cthulhu was supposed to emerge from the portal in the slope, and yet Azenay was filming three supporting actors now who were peering uncertainly heavenward, as that ghastly sound grew louder, nearer, descending...and suddenly stopped.

The only sound was the soft purr of Azenay's unblimped, shoulder-mounted camera. The three actors were ad-libbing now, and at least one had completely forgotten he was supposed to be acting; he called his director by name and demanded to know what the hell was going on. Azenay urged them all to hold places, keep talking.

There was a shriek from somewhere off to my left. Red was gone from his work table. Another, more muffled and agonized cry issued from the darkness now, behind where Red had been. I thought I saw a flash of light glinting off a green eye, but an eye the size of spinning saw blade. One of the actors bolted and ran. Azenay was, perversely, still filming, and he pushed in on the faces of the two terrified men who remained.

And then something gelatinous and writhing came down from the rocks. One of the actors screamed as the log–sized appendage wrapped around him, lifting him. His screams were drowned by the sounds of the thing that had him—an over–amplified, high–pitched piping, full of mad glee and release. There was a sickening snapping/gushing sound as the captured actor was constricted until he literally burst, at which point his mangled corpse was rudely flung aside.

Now the monster strode into the center of the set, a star entering to find his spotlight. The set was plainly too small to contain the towering monstrosity that loomed over us all, a mass of coiling tentacles and scaled, slimed skin. A smell like the burial pit from a death camp assaulted me, knocking me back with its force. The remaining actor fell to his knees, sobbing; the assistant and the set dressers ran. One of them didn't make it. The thing—who I couldn't bring myself to call by its proper name yet—leaned forward and picked up the prey with the pseudopods sprouting from its horrid, misshapen head. I saw a glimpse of an open, waiting maw, then the victim disappeared.

I was in a small area of shadow right now; if I ran, surely the thing would see me. But I couldn't stay, and so I began to edge out towards the rim of dangerous light. Finally I was exposed, away from the safety of shadow, and I began backing away slowly, my eyes—like Azenay's camera—never leaving the vast horror before me.

Then it happened: I felt those immense glowing eyes fix on me. I had been seen. My legs turned to disobedient stone, my heart hammered until I thought surely my shirt would split. It occurred to me that this might be my last thought; my last thought would be about my last thought, a meaningless mobius strip that finally unravelled in death.

But the abominable thing didn't move. It didn't move towards me or reach out for me. Instead, it tilted its dripping head back, and hurled a staccato screech into the night.

It was laughing at me.

I found my senses again, now part terror and part sheer indignation. Azenay was looking at me, shocked and angry. And now I did turn and leave. I didn't even run. I walked back to my car, shaking but mostly under control. I don't remember what else happened. Somehow I climbed into my car, started the engine, and drove away from the scene of created and genuine horror.

I woke up—or, at least, found consciousness again—the next day in my bedroom, still dressed from the night before. I walked to the corner liquor store and bought a paper. On the front page was a store of an accident that had occurred on the set of a local horror movie, one that had resulted in the deaths of five people, including renowned effects wizard Red "Red Boy" Hidalgo. They were blaming it on faulty wiring in the generator, which had apparently exploded, also destroying most of the set. The director/producer, Benjamin Azenay, was unavailable for comment.

I wondered what would happen to the survivors. I was sorry about Red, and about the fact that I would never find out now why he had called me. In a way the ones who hadn't made it were the lucky ones; they didn't have to endure the nightmares, the threats that would probably ensue, the guilt…

Of course I'm the only one enduring guilt. Because, you see, *The Call of Cthulhu: The Motion Picture* opens nationwide tomorrow. The film was completed. I was even paid, and with an added bonus I hadn't contracted for. I can live well for a very long time now.

For some reason, they haven't tried to contact me. Azenay knows I was there that night, but there have been no midnight phone calls or appearances on my doorstep, no requests to visit the beach on a solstice night, or pick up missing shots in the desert. I moved only because I bought a house, a spacious hillside four-bedroom that I haven't bothered to furnish. Somehow I like the blank rooms.

And I understand now what Furman meant when he told me that the Old Gentleman—Lovecraft—was deceiving even himself:

A month after the incident in the desert, I had the last of the Lovecraft dreams. He was reluctantly congratulating me on the script, which apparently had pleased the investors and Lovecraft. He also, of course, congratulated himself on the source material, which had first brought Cthulhu to life. I did something it had taken me far too long to do: I told him I thought he was a fool, a bigoted, obsolete fool. His prejudices had kept him from seeing that Cthulhu's acolytes weren't "degenerate races;" the adoration of evil transcended all racial lines, even those of gender. At first he looked startled, then he uttered a dry chuckle, one that sounded like paper scraping over a blade. For some reason—a dream reason—I suddenly understood that he was a delusion. I walked up to him, reached up to his long-jawed face…

…and tore away what was little more than a paper mask. A cry of horrified discovery sounded, and I tore into his torso, parting the 1920's suit, then tearing away handfuls of protective batting, like fibrous cotton. And underneath that I found him, the real Lovecraft, in the immortality they had gifted him with: He was a grey mass in some sort of translucent jar, floating in a thick liquid, with wires and tubes distending from the enclosure itself. With sudden understanding, I saw that he hated himself now, and would remain that way forever.

When I woke from the dream, I knew that I would never see him again, and I was glad. Glad partly because of how much he hated me, but glad as well because seeing him reminded me of too many things we shared, things I wanted desperately to forget.

I began to wonder what other deceptions he had committed. I found out when the first preview screening of *The Call of Cthulhu* was held.

It was a test screening, in a multiplex in a small Los Angeles suburb. I was surprised that I was invited; I received the invitation in the mail, no return address. I sat in the back away from Azenay, the investors, and the rest of the VIP's. They knew I was there, but didn't speak to me.

I didn't need to read the audience comment cards to know that the screening was successful. Immensely successful. The audience gasped and screamed at the right places. The scene when Cthulhu ascended from his dank tunnel—a Cthulhu plainly generated by computer, and considerably less terrifying than the reality—even inspired several episodes of fainting. My script was a triumph. I received sole credit as screenwriter.

But when the lights came up was when I had the answer, to the question of Lovecraft's biggest deceit. As the audience poured from the theater, a typical crowd of posturing suburban teens, I heard the name "Cthulhu" pulse through them like a mantra. They weren't afraid of him; they adored him. They idolized him. They wanted more. And, in a corner of the theater lobby, the investors nodded, very pleased.

And so I understood that Lovecraft had lied when he had told me that Cthulhu's slow awakening throughout the last century had been the cause of many of its disasters. Certainly Cthulhu's sleep–borne emanations had reached out and touched many, as they had Lovecraft, but the truth was the other way around. The evil acts we'd committed as a race had been entirely our own doing. We had awakened Cthulhu. Cthulhu, like any god, needed worshippers to survive. As the century's sins had built, so had the number of His flock.

And tomorrow a film will open, a film bearing His name, which will grant Him millions of fresh worshippers all over the world. His awakening will finally end. He will rise again, to be celebrated by all those who already believe they know Him, because of a motion picture. A motion picture that I scripted, unwittingly or not.

Perhaps I could have carried this guilt, gone on living in my too–large and empty house in the hills, had it not been for that night in the desert. As it is, what I see over and over is not the eldritch terror committing unthinkable crimes, but rather when it laughed at me. It recognized me, and laughed at my ignorance and my future.

So I leave this, hoping to at least to avoid Lovecraft's malicious deceit. I don't know how long I can continue like this, knowing what I've done; but then again, if you've survived long enough to read this, perhaps you can offer me some small measure of absolution, and pray to any other god that I haven't received the same final gift they bestowed upon Lovecraft.

DAVID BAIN's fiction, nonfiction and poetry have appeared in many publications including *Weird Tales, Strange Horizons, City Slab, Doorways* and *Withersin*, with honorable mentions in The Year's Best Fantasy and Horror. He has an M.F.A. in Fiction Writing from Columbia College Chicago and is currently on the adjunct English faculty at Ivy Tech Community College in Fort Wayne, Indiana. He is the editor of *Whispering Worlds*, a large, free e–book of speculative poetry which received an 'Internet Hot Spot' nod from Ellen Datlow and was named the most impressive such online collection by *Black Gate* magazine.

Under an Invisible Shadow

by David Bain

Know this: Humanity was still hanging on when I wrote this. But that may not be the case for long.

✳   ✳   ✳

Only a few dozen of us have made it this far. Most are Russian, Scandinavian, Canadian or Eskimo.

Me and Janie, we made it all the way from Florida.

Janie was my guide. I can't see the zombie souls, but she can, and it was primarily her vision that led us here, somewhere deep in the wilds of northern Canada.

I used to say I didn't believe in anything I couldn't see, and that I'd seen nothing I couldn't explain.

But these days I surely believe in ghosts—or rather, I believe in souls, or whatever the hell the spirits of the zombies and the thing we've dubbed The Invisible Lovecraftian Terror are.

Since I've been deemed the most accomplished scribe of the dozen or so English–speaking persons to arrive here at Ground Zero, it's to be my words that are put to paper. See, I once thought of myself as something of a poet. Yes, once upon a time I thought I was above my culture, that I was an aloof observer, sort of floating over it all. Now I realize I was—and am—but a disposable product of it. The zombies have humbled me that much at least.

All of this is simply to say that I will write this document in my true, common voice—my human voice—rather than the elitist one to which I sometimes aspired.

Here goes:

✳   ✳   ✳

The dead started rising from their graves about thirteen years ago.

Before we reached Ground Zero, we had our theories. God released his wrath. Scientists released a bug. Something passed by the Earth. Whatever the cause, things went down quickly.

The dead arose *en masse.*

Zombies lurched, swarmed, reigned.

Humanity hid, fought or was eaten.

All too quickly: Political chaos. Military collapse. Anarchy. Mass hysteria. Total communications breakdown—even my beloved Internet was quickly useless.

I was a University of Florida grad student, majoring in biology and working in the field for the summer, deep within the Everglades. Until Z Day, I spent my spare time writing dippy nature poems and faithfully sending them off to the types of magazines that paid in contributor's copies and were only read by other contributors, if that.

I saw it all go down on the satellite dish until every last station was either overrun or went off the air.

Antisocial bastard that I am, I decided to stay while everyone else in my group went back to help. They said they'd send someone for me when humanity won the battle against the zombie legions. Victory was inevitable, they said.

No one ever came back.

For me it was actually pretty idyllic. I knew how to get along in the 'glades indefinitely, eating everything from gator to the indigenous breed of miniature deer that had been on the verge of extinction until the zombies cleared out its greatest enemy—man.

Plus, for all practical purposes, I was a million miles away from the zombies—I only ever saw three of them in the 'glades, and one looked an awful lot like Jimmy Hoffa. (That's a joke.)

After a while, I found a few stations back up, usually run by a staff of no more than two or three. The ones that seemed relatively serious about serving humanity were from Mexico City, Denver and Berlin. They would play reruns of whatever they felt like—the guys in Berlin were PBS types, the guys in Mexico City liked Mexican soaps and variety shows, and the guys in Denver showed mostly B movies rescued from nearby video stores. Occasionally the people running these stations would do things like offer survival tips, food-gathering advice, and updates on the zombie situation outside the station walls.

Long story short: zombies ruled the Earth for just over a dozen years, destroying and wandering and devouring the brains and guts of any living thing they could get their claws on.

Then a curious thing started happening.

The dead started dying.

Denver reported it first—the dead were suddenly dropping like flies, and the ones that didn't die right off were no longer a threat. I remember one of the Denver guys finally ventured out live on the air and kicked a zombie in the butt just to see what would happen. It barely even paid him any attention. The creep just turned, then looked at its claw–like hand as if it knew it was supposed to rip the living guy's head off and dig out the juicy filling, but it had forgotten how. These slow zombies reminded me of late autumn wasps in my native Michigan—drunkenly ambulatory but hardly dangerous.

I remember distinctly that I sighed when I heard the news. Then I held my head in my hands and cried. Then I swore a blue streak and gave in. It was time to cast myself out of Eden and search out other survivors.

I went to the obvious meeting place. The victory had been gained by forfeit, but no matter. Humanity had won the Armageddon Super Bowl, and we were going to Disneyworld.

* * *

It's a Small World, the countries of Epcot and Main Street, U.S.A. were a shambles. The cleanup of the stinking dead zombies was still going on when I arrived. Most of the survivors were camped around Cinderella's castle.

I'll spare you the tedious, predictable details—the territorial squabbles, the bickering, the stealing, the fights over food, all the dumbass alpha males strutting around, campaigning and contending for leadership.

What matters is Janie, who arrived shortly after me. Janie, and what she saw.

The zombies were dying all right, she said. But souls—or spirits or whatever—were leaving their bodies. The souls were leaving the zombie bodies as they died, and they were flying off in a north by northwesterly direction.

Furthermore, she said, souls which were apparently from other zombie bodies which had dropped in parts of the world south of us were consistently flying by overhead.

Even after the world had been overrun and destroyed by the living dead, Janie had a hard time convincing people of what she was seeing.

Until, that is, this former supermodel who had done Tarot card infomercials back in the old days suddenly said she saw the souls too—interesting that she hadn't said anything until now, despite the fact that she'd been among the first to arrive.

Then, and only then, it was decided something had to be done. We had to see where these things were going and why. The alpha males advised they were needed to lead the group, and the Tarot woman said she had to remain as spiritual advisor.

I volunteered because I didn't like people, and especially not this desperate, self-pitying and quarrelsome bunch. Janie went because, first of all, someone had to see the zombie souls, and second because she was as good as I was with a gun.

Although we hadn't met prior to Cinderella's castle, I think we saw something in each other from the start, an independent spirit we mutually admired. We have since become soul mates. The lady's no supermodel, but she warms me body and soul, and that is all that matters.

Without many supplies, we left the next morning, given the precious gift of a Harley–Davidson motorcycle.

I don't think anyone ever really expected to hear back from us. We recently dispatched a crew to try to reach the Denver station to tell the world about The Invisible Lovecraftian Terror, but, as I said before, from here on in, we don't know what will happen.

✱ ✱ ✱

I'm going to skip a lot here.

We had several "adventures" between Florida and Ground Zero up here in the Canadian hinterlands. If there's time, maybe I'll write them down in detail, but if there was ever a time for the *Reader's Digest* version, this is it.

As we expected, we encountered occasional pockets of humanity. Some were mighty peculiar and some were mighty interesting, but we could never stay; Janie kept seeing zombie souls coursing by overhead.

In what was once known as The Deep South, we ran into a forlorn cult that had given up rattlesnakes and had turned to worshipping the very zombies that tried to eat them—I didn't pay much attention, but it had something to do with the fact that zombies could take a dozen rattler bites with no ill effects. Now a divided church, one offshoot was predicting a blissful Second Coming as we left, while another was preaching Doomsday. The main group was ignoring the splinter factions and was trying to make amends with the snakes.

In Missouri we met a former AMA scientist who was near to proving, he said, that some sort of virus had animated the corpses—a virus which was now dying off. "Damn lot of good your hypothesis does twelve years after the fact," I told him as I kick-started the Harley. He muttered something about the scientific method and shuffled back to his makeshift lab.

In the Dakota badlands we met an old Native American who had managed to actually tame a few of the dead buggers. He'd taught them rudimentary skills, like farming his land, which he showed us videotapes of. Pretty resourceful, considering all the horses and cattle had been eaten—but now that all the zombies were dead or dying, the chief was back to scavenging, like everyone else. The scientist had told us the zombies had possessed a very limited sort of intelligence, but I think even he would have been surprised by how far the injun had come.

Somewhere in there we switched from motorbike to mountain bike and hooked up with a steadily growing number of crusaders, some of whom, like Janie, had The Sight.

Later we gave up the mountain bikes for snowshoes and found ourselves sitting on dog sleds.

✱ ✱ ✱

We crested a rise, seemingly in the middle of nowhere, and suddenly everyone who had The Sight gasped. Correction—one or two of the more sensitive ones actually screamed.

Several without The Sight gasped too, for there below, about two miles distant, were dark dots in the middle of all the white. Surrounded by a hundred miles of nowhere, we were approaching an encampment of maybe a dozen or so people.

* * *

Some believe the crater by our encampment was the result of a meteor which probably carried the virus which caused the dead to rise.

But it hardly matters. What matters is what's above the crater.

Janie and all the other visionaries say the zombie souls are flocking to the air there like homing pigeons. They are flying here from all directions, the visionaries say, zombie soul after zombie soul joining into a single giant being, The Invisible Lovecraftian Terror, floating about a thousand feet above our heads. This central being is said to have a huge, ever-growing amorphous central globe as its main body, with mile-long tentacles flailing out in all directions.

Those with The Sight say The Invisible Lovecraftian Terror appears to be in some sort of stasis, content to simply float and wait, collecting thousands upon thousands of zombie souls unto itself, growing slightly larger with each one.

* * *

We do not know what is going to happen.

The souls of the creatures that once threatened to destroy humanity—that once were, in fact, *us*—might morph into a solid creature and attack. Or the creature might simply rise off into the heavens. Or it might sink into the Earth and poison it forever.

We don't know.

We only know that we've resolved to make a stand here in this cold valley, in the invisible shadow of this horrible presence.

We only know that we can, for now, keep trying to communicate this monstrosity to the rest of humanity.

We know only that we'll continue to fight in the one way we know how—by living within this invisible shadow as human beings, as survivors, raging against it from deep within our hearts.

ROBIN MORRIS lives in Los Angeles, where the Old Gods are all movie executives and have beach houses in Malibu. Robin has been published in anthologies from *Twilight Tales*, *Dark Tales*, and Britain's *Rainfall* Books. She was seen among the pixels on the lost and lamented webzines *Feral Fiction* and *The Deepening*. Robin has the obligatory writer's cats, and lives in a garret, or as they call it in L.A., a "single."

The Thing Beyond the Stars

by Robin Morris

The truth drove humanity mad. There on the planet named Earth, cradle of our species, man evolved to the point where he could discover his origin. Theories of heavenly creation, mythologies of titans and gods, stories of arising from under the Earth, while they still had their adherents, clearly had little relation to known facts. With reason and scientific inquiry humanity discovered its evolutionary relationship to all the other life on the planet.

This ability to learn the most basic biological truth gave man a feeling of superiority at the same time it reduced him to just another animal species. It was the brain of man that made him different, able to understand himself. It was man's feeling of superiority, his assumption that he was master of his world, that led to chaos.

In exploring their world, humans of that time began to venture into the ice shrouded southernmost continent, called Antarctica, a place frozen since long before humans stood on two feet. Several expeditions were carried out that saw nothing but ice and snow. Then a small group of explorers made a discovery that would change everything.

The account we have of that expedition, part of the scant record we have of those times, was so ill received by the scientific community that it ended up being published in a journal of popular fiction, and was regarded as fantasy. This is the only reason that we still have it to read, because it was reprinted many times in collections of fiction, and some of those books survived.

The author of that account warned against any further exploration in the mountains of the Antarctic. Even so, a larger, second expedition was mounted. That group of explorers completely disappeared and were not heard of again.

Man went on for another century, ignorant of the truth. Technology accelerated. The world became united by a network of computing machines. Medicine learned to cure most diseases. The science of genetics allowed humans to change their own cellular structure. The same science proved once and for all that we are animals, closely related to the rest of the Earth's life. No gods or creation myths could stand before this knowledge, though many still clung to those antiquated ideas.

In a laboratory the beginnings of faster than light star travel took shape. This technology would be delayed for some years.

Then the truth erupted out of the frozen past of the planet Earth. Antarctica was in the process of being mapped, centimeter by centimeter, with satellite cameras and explorers on the ground working to ferret out every last secret of the icy continent.

They stumbled on the ancient city described by the author of the earlier account. It was a place clearly not built by or for humans. It was older than humanity, older than our relatives the apes, older than the earliest life form that had ever been known to exist. The explorers learned a lot about the residents of that city from the sculptured history they had left behind. They were star travelers, but they didn't use ships. They flew on membranous wings that acted as solar sails. Like spores cast on the wind, they lived in a dormant state, sailing into the void. When a place suitable for life was found, one of these travelers would found a new colony.

Such a colony had existed on Earth before there was any other life. A colony of Old Ones, as the first discoverer of their city called them. And the truth that shattered mankind's sanity was that we were the evolved byproduct of the Old Ones' biological technology. We were an accident.

Humanity wasn't even created by the Old Ones for the purpose of serving them. We evolved from their scrap heaps, the bits of experiments that they threw away. They did have servants, however. Servants who eventually turned on their masters and destroyed them.

When the shoggoths, the shape–changing former servants of the Old Ones, erupted out of Antarctica, they tried to destroy humanity as well. The Shoggoth Wars raged for twelve years, and left three continents as radioactive wastelands.

After the wars, humans wanted nothing but to leave the shattered Earth. The star drive technology was refined and made practical. Groups of humans took off for the stars. Most of those groups rejected the truth of the Old Ones, and vowed to renew their mythologies in their new homes. We don't have a record of where most of them went. We don't know how many survived. There could be hundreds of planets with humans on them, or just a dozen.

One of the most ancient of human beliefs, carried on in secret by small cults in secret places on Earth, was that a god or gods slept under the ocean and would return someday. Scientists wouldn't have given this idea any credence at all, except that the records of the Old Ones mentioned another alien species which they fought long before mankind existed. The Old Ones barely won this war, and managed to contain the other species in a sunken city in the deepest oceans of the planet. This belief system wouldn't have mattered at all after the Shoggoth Wars, with humans already leaving in their star ships, if some of the believers hadn't found and revived their gods.

The last few ships that left the Earth were lucky to get out. If any humans still live on Earth they are slaves, or food, for what arose from the deep. The founders of our society here on Alpha Nine were on one of the last ships. They refused to enter into the historical record what Earth was like in those last days.

One thing is certain. Humankind can no longer be destroyed if one planet meets its doom. With many planets to live on, humans will exist in the galaxy for a very long time. Here on Alpha Nine, where reason and scientific inquiry still have a place, we have come to terms with the truth of the Old Ones. They were living beings, seekers like ourselves. They made a mistake in creating the shoggoths, but that just shows that they were not omnipotent. I would someday like to meet one and shake its tentacle.

—Dr. Elias Poole, in the introduction to his book, "Secrets of the Old Ones", published by Alpha Nine University Press.

"What would we learn if we could meet the Old Ones?" Alan Thurston once asked me. Looking at his frozen corpse, I wondered if he had learned anything.

*   *   *

Alan's official mission as captain of the refurbished *Albert Einstein* was to find other human colonies and begin to build contacts with them. When our great grandparents first arrived on Alpha Nine, having escaped Earth in its last chaotic days, they had no knowledge of where other ships might have ended up. They also had a lot more important things to think about, while building a new colony. The *Einstein* had orbited, abandoned, for many years, before we got to the point where we could consider star travel again.

As part of the bicentennial of the founding, parliament authorized refurbishing the ship and trying to find other human worlds. Alan Thurston was the logical choice as its captain. He had a scientific mind, experience piloting every kind of aircraft, and a boundless thirst for adventure.

Unknown to the general public who saw him on their view screens preparing for this new, bold venture, Alan was fascinated by the Old Ones. He had read the scant records from Earth over and over again. He complained to me several times that there wasn't enough information. "We only have a few shards of their sculpture left." he said, sipping tea on the balcony of my quarters overlooking the city. "The rest was destroyed in the wars. We know what they looked like but little else."

"You're going to have trouble enough finding other humans." I told him, "much less the Old Ones."

"They have to be out there," Alan said. "The Earth can't be the only place in this stellar vicinity that they settled. There might be thriving cities of them on any number of nearby planets."

"Or they might all be gone, like the ones on Earth."

"If that first account is right, some of them were alive when the expedition found them."

"No living Old Ones, or even intact corpses, were found during the Shoggoth Wars," I said.

Alan put down his teacup and stared at sunset sky. "I will find them, if they are there," he said. I believed him. I believed that he would look for any clue to the Old Ones, and probably never succeed. He would fulfill his stated mission of finding human colonies, but he would never consider his life a success until he had personally met one of the star-headed aliens and discussed philosophy with it.

Alan's first mission was a brilliant success. He found a human colony at the third planet he tried. They were a group of Mennonites barely surviving as farmers. Their planet had a narrow equatorial zone with temperatures warm enough to support human life, but even then the winters were harsh. They were happy there, though, and turned down an offer to transport them back to Alpha Nine. They said their God had led them to their new home, so that's where they were meant to be. They had taken apart their ship long before and used its metals for tools. They believed in living a simple life, but were welcoming and friendly to Alan's crew and did not turn down the possibility of future trade with us.

Alan returned a hero. His broad, dark face was all over the view screens for weeks. He was interviewed, paraded, and given a medal. Then one night, very late, I was awakened by my doorbell.

"Sorry it's so late," Alan said after he settled into one of my comfortable chairs. He rested his hand on the mysterious cloth wrapped package that he had brought with him, which sat on the small table next to his chair.

"It's all right," I said, "Always glad to see you. So you found something interesting at the Mennonite colony?" I indicated the package.

"All I found there were boring people clinging to outmoded religion. I found this on the first planet I visited, a place of stone and hot gas vents where no colony could have survived. At least, no colony of humans."

He started to unwrap the package, and my heart lurched at the familiar shapes that were revealed.

"Is that?" I asked.

"It most certainly is." Alan grinned. "It's just a small piece, but I think it's significant."

It was unmistakably a piece of sculpture created by the Old Ones, the kind they used to record their history. It was similar to the ones that were found on Earth, but different in subtle ways.

"Do you think there was a colony on that planet?" I asked.

"Possibly, but the place is so torn up now it would take years to search for any more pieces. Besides, I think this one is all I need."

The piece had once been part of a row along a wall, just as in the Antarctic city on Earth. It was a tiny piece of a long history, a shard of time sculpted in stone. It showed an Old One, with the familiar star shaped head, looking up at some dots in the sky.

"It's a star map, I think showing the last place they came from," Alan said. "I compared it to the sky view from that planet and I think I know where it leads to."

"It could be millions of years old. The sky could have changed," I told Alan. "And it could just be part of an astronomy lesson, not their old home."

"It's worth checking out." Alan started to rewrap the sculpture.

"Parliament isn't going to authorize any wild goose chases for ancient aliens," I said.

"Well, sometimes a captain has to make a decision to change the mission, just a little. Go on a little detour." Alan was grinning even more than before, and I could see in his eyes that he had already made the decision to chase his vision, perhaps had already gone past sanity into the unknown abyss between the stars.

∗ ∗ ∗

"Dr. Poole," someone said on the radio of my space suit. I tore my sight away from the frozen thing that had been my friend, and saw a person approaching, using handholds in the weightless and silent ship. I couldn't make out who it was until she got close to me and I could see into the helmet of her suit. It was a young ensign on the crew that had brought me up to the *Einstein*. She held a data disk in her gloved hand. "This is a message to you from Captain Thurston."

On the shuttle from orbit I thought about the last time I had seen Alan. It was just before he left on his second mission. He left in a blaze of glory, the hero going out again to seek other human beings in the cosmos. Only I knew what he considered to be his real mission. He and his crew stopped at the shuttle hatch and waved. Fourteen other brave explorers accompanied Alan, not knowing their captain's obsession. Now they too were frozen corpses on the ghost ship that had returned.

Should I have done something? Warned the authorities that Alan was so obsessed? Could I have saved the crew? I certainly didn't think to do anything at the time. I suspect the government wouldn't have listened to me if I had.

The *Einstein* had headed out on that second mission, and was gone for almost five years. The first mission had taken less than two years. The government issued increasingly less hopeful news releases, and speculation in the press ran wild. If the ship had run into trouble and sent back a radio message about its situation, we wouldn't receive the message for many years. Only the *Einstein* itself could transcend the speed of light and return to us any faster, and if it was destroyed, many of us would have died of old age before the news could reach us.

Then one day we started to pick up a beacon from the *Einstein*. As it got closer and we were sure that the lost ship had returned, a wave of joy spread throughout the planet. Shortly the joy turned to sorrow. There were no messages from the crew, no faces of the explorers on our view screens, describing their ordeal. There was just the automated beacon, saying that the ship was programmed to return and put itself into orbit.

A shuttle met the *Einstein* in orbit and it was confirmed that the crew was dead. The life support system had run out of air long before, and the ship had become a faster than light tomb, hurtling through space with no human at the helm.

I was invited to see the inside of the ship because I knew Alan, and I was considered an expert on space matters. That's when I received the message that Alan had left me.

After returning home, I went to my study and slipped the data disk into my terminal. The picture formed itself into Alan Thurston's familiar features, but he was haggard and thin, with bags under his eyes. Not the hale and hearty man I knew. This following is what he had to say. I have now turned the message over to the government, and what they will do about it, or whether they will even believe it, I do not know. I have had many sleepless nights since I saw the message. I have spent hours at the University telescope, trying to see if the sky has changed, though I know it is too soon.

This is Alan's message:

Elias, I am addressing this message to you, and I will let you decide whether to pass it on to the proper authorities or just keep it to yourself. The government will try do something if they know, but nothing they do will make a difference in the long run. The last time I saw you I showed you the sample of sculpture that I found. It gave a clue where to look for the Old Ones. Shortly after we left on our second voyage, I told the crew that I was changing the mission. There was some resistance, but I am the captain and I am in command. I do regret now that they have to share my fate.

It took us more than two years to arrive at the coordinates that I had decided were represented by the Old Ones' sculpture. When we arrived, we were nearly at the half-way point in terms of food, air, and fuel, including all emergency supplies. If we had stayed a short time and started back to Alpha Nine from there, we would have made it alive, though we would have had to ration the food.

We were in an ordinary solar system with three planets, two of them gas giants. The third was a rock that was smaller than Alpha Nine. It had no atmosphere to speak of, but our instruments did detect water ice below the surface. We passed through an asteroid belt and orbited the smaller planet. I was getting ready to take a team down when my second said she was getting some strange energy readings.

Something was causing all the sensors to go wild. We couldn't see any cause for it at first. Then we noticed something happening on a screen that showed a view of the system's sun. It was like an eclipse, but that didn't make sense. The sun was occluded by something that was jet black and yet had streaks of color in it, something big. Bigger than the sun itself.

We tried our best to get readings on the thing, but it was both energy and

The Thing Beyond the Stars

matter, and yet was neither energy nor matter. It was just a blackness, darker than the black of space, with wild colors racing through it. The colors didn't shine brightly, they were visible only in contrast to the ultimate darkness of the rest of the thing.

Soon the sun was completely covered by this blackness, and then it was gone. The darkness receded away from us and the system of planets was thrown into chaos. The star at its center, the sun, was no longer there. The star's gravity no longer kept the planets in orbit. The asteroids we had passed through no longer were guided in the paths they had followed for millions of years. Our ship was in danger of being struck by them.

We fought clear of immediate danger, then I ordered that the ship should investigate the cause of the sun's disappearance. We found the strange blackness on our instruments. It was retreating from our position, so I decided to follow it. The *Einstein* was much faster than the speed of the thing, so we caught up to it and then established a speed that would keep us near it.

The blackness became dubbed the "Star Eater" by the crew. We studied it and took every bit of data from it that we could. I have included all that data in this message. I'm sure you will review it and apply your fine scientific mind to the problem. You will come to the conclusion that we did, that the thing is impossible.

We followed it for nearly two months. I was determined beyond all reason to find out what it was. The crew started telling me that we would never make it back to Alpha Nine if we went any farther. I didn't care. I have always believed that a rational mind can solve any problem if it was given enough data. I pored over the information we had. I didn't sleep for days at a time.

We would have known what we were approaching if it followed the normal laws of physics. Something that big should have had a gravity field that would pull on us like a black hole. We had noticed that the piece of blackness we were following was oblong, not a sphere as we originally thought. It extended so far into the distance that we had not been able to measure its length. Eventually, we increased our speed and traveled along its length, trying to find the end.

There was no end. We came upon the bulk of the thing and almost flew right into it. The star eater was just an extrusion, or tentacle, of a thing so large it blotted out all view of the stars. It had reached its hand out to take the star like you or I picking a marble from a table top.

It had many more such tentacles. Many more stars were being consumed by the appetite of something that is vast beyond comprehension.

We measured and catalogued and took all the data we could. All we knew is what we learned when we first encountered the tentacle. It was a blackness with dim colors flickering in its depths. For all our scientific knowledge and reason, that was all we could say for sure.

We did decide that it was moving. All in its own good time, not hurrying. It will be a good two hundred years before it approaches Alpha Nine. For all of that two hundred years our civilization will exist in the shadow of a thing that cannot be understood, and cannot be stopped. You don't even see it yet, because light takes a long time to travel the distances of space. There are many stars you can see in your telescope every night that have already been consumed, but their light continues to shine.

In your book, Elias, you say that humanity cannot be destroyed by one planet's extinction now that we live on many planets. We now face the destruction of all those planets. The unmeasurable thing that approaches is not a star eater. It is a galaxy eater. It blindly gropes through the universe, plucking and eating the stars like ripe fruit.

All the human colonies, whether they follow science or a god they took with them from Earth, will be swept away when their suns are eaten. If the Old Ones are out there, they may be able to send out seeds of themselves, but there may be no place for the seeds to take root.

You could build ships and flee, but each time you found a new home you would still be in the galaxy eater's path, and would have to flee again in a hundred years. As for fleeing the galaxy entirely, I don't believe our technology is capable of the trip. The closest galaxies are further than we could possibly go.

I have programmed the *Einstein* to return to Alpha Nine as fast as it can, and I have diverted all resources to that flight, including life support. The crew has agreed that the information about what we found has to be returned as fast as possible. We do not have enough food for the return journey anyway.

I am giving you the option whether to turn over this information to the government. Perhaps it is best to leave the next generation or two in ignorance.

Good luck, my friend.

✳　　　✳　　　✳

There the message ended. It has been a month since I viewed it, and I did decide to pass it on to the government. All they have done so far is debate endlessly in parliament. I can think of nothing to do but enjoy my life. I will be long dead before the galaxy eater approaches. Occasionally I focus the university telescope in its direction, and wonder which star will be the first to disappear from the sky.

MEHITOBEL WILSON has been publishing horror fiction since 1999. She has been a Bram Stoker Award nominee 1.5 times, and many of her short stories have been granted Honorable Mentions in *The Year's Best Fantasy and Horror* series. She lives in Georgia with two German Shepherds, two cats, one cockatiel, one ferret, four video game consoles, an army of action figures and Asian ball-jointed dolls, and one alleged human. "Fire Breathing" received an Honorable Mention in the 16th Edition of *The Year's Best Fantasy and Horror*, edited by Datlow and Windling.

Fire Breathing

by Mehitobel Wilson

Eric lay on his back, clutched the grass, and screamed at the sky. The lights that writhed across the star field were so dense that he thought he could taste them. "Go outside, look up," the anonymous caller had said, and Eric had checked his watch, marked it just past 2 a.m., and cued up a Fugazi album. He'd murmured something about a set into the mic and let "Burning Too" begin with a hard start, no time for a fade.

He had glimpsed the Northern Lights just once before during a Greyhound trip mid–fall through Minnesota. This, though, was far more than a glimpse, these lights were cobalt whips and crimson gashes, pennants of searing magnesium. They were not supposed to be chasing one another in the August skies of coastal Georgia. Yet there they were, and he was beyond himself with the rapture of it, and screamed to them.

A palmetto bug scattered feet across his cheek and lips. He shook his head and blew a raspberry, closed his eyes. When he opened them an instant later he saw indigo tongue across the sky and then wink out so suddenly that it left the illusion of a rent in the heavens, a slit blacker than the night. His eyes fed the smear of blackness after images of the lights, and for an instant, faint pale tendrils crawled within the wound.

Then it was over.

Eric lay on the grass for a long moment, spent. The lights were gone. Dazed, grinning, he returned to the station and discovered that his hands were shaking too hard to cue up another album, so he ran a PSA about the dangers of smoldering upholstery and let it play twice. Hands now steady, he cued the disc to his signature closing track, MC 900 Ft Jesus, "While the City Sleeps." Then he took the mic and opened the channel. Still smiling (the audience can hear a smile), he said, "Three o'clock in the ay–em and time for me to let it sleep. Don't burn it down, kids. I'd like to thank the gentleman who called and gave me the fire in the sky. Tomorrow my guest will be Cliff Wheeler, and we will discuss religions spawned by media. That's midnight to two and music 'til three. That's it for DJ Heat on WRYY. Burn on."

He dropped the mic channel and cranked the MC. DJ Mister Bitterness hovered outside the plexiglass booth, his arms laden with albums, chamois mixing glove draped over his sharp shoulder. Eric beckoned the next host into the booth, grabbed his satchel, and left the airwaves for another night.

The beach was empty when Eric arrived, and so were the skies. He smoked a few cigarettes and wished that the lights would return. Florida was burning again, as it did every summer. Some days Savannah's breeze carried the sting of doused flames, and the humidity held tight to the odor of distant carbon and chemicals.

The lights in the sky might not have been actual aurora. Bands of Florida's ash high in the atmosphere might have reflected some stray cosmic light. If that were the case, Eric thought, let Florida burn, let Georgia burn, let it all burn, and let their ashes fling paint across the skies while he screamed.

*   *   *

Fire: *when Eric was a boy, his mother, Mrs. Alastair Fordbin, torched her home and her husband with it. She received a large amount of money.*

"You burned him up," said Eric.

"Watch your mouth," said the Widow Fordbin, "that's not true, but just saying it could ruin me." She washed Eric's mouth out with soap. Her grip on his jaw, fierce with rage and slickery with suds, left bruises.

His cheeks still ached when he said to the police sergeant, "She burned him up." Eric received a new home and a small amount of money, which was a slight degree larger by the time he turned eighteen. It was enough money to buy records and bus tickets.

*   *   *

Eric locked his front door, dropped his knapsack on the floor, let the Mighty Dog bump his heavy yellow head against his hip a few times, and then went to the refrigerator.

The apartment in which he lived consisted of a single large room. The rental agent liked to call it a studio, but it was a room.

The mini–fridge, a ratty loveseat, a vast pallet of blankets, and crates of records were the only things in the living room. Eric had painted the window glass opaque and nailed the frames shut. His elderly television, which showed all images in rowdy green hues, sat atop the fridge.

It was 3:30am. Eric pulled a Pabst from his dwindling supply and retrieved his last few Krystal burgers. He tossed one of the burgers to the Mighty Dog, who let it bounce off his cheek and hit the floor before he realized it was edible.

The all–night news channel staff was thrilled to their green gills with the extent of the Florida fires. Experts charted smoke density. Weathermen discussed the impact of smoke and rising heat on storm systems, and threatened fiery tornadoes and ash–laden hurricanes. Anchors nodded their heads beside graphics of filthy forest firemen. Pilots shook their heads and ignored the ques-

Fire Breathing

tions of reporters. Tourists, travel agents, and theme–park operators gave interview after interview. Homeowners were conspicuously absent. Residents don't bring a city money, only visitors do.

Eric looked around his apartment, smirked, and thought the reporters might be right to ignore the common man. He lived like a garage boarder, blowing his cash on beer and obscure vinyl, records he could never play at the station.

His radio gig was a scam: WRYY was a college station. Not only was Eric not enrolled in the Communications major, he was also not enrolled in the college. Never had been.

His dime would never go for education, no sir. He spent his money on beer and records, and sometimes on cross–country bus tickets.

He made that money a little at a time, bringing home a bill or two a day, sometimes just twenties, sometimes hundreds. He made his living with his voice.

Eric was a professional snitch. A rat. He was the word on the street. He was a stoolie. He burned 'em, turned 'em, and earned 'em. He was a finger man throughout the Low country, and his finger was indiscriminate.

It was an easy gig. Find the shoddiest bar in town, the kind of bar where men are face–down on the bar by lunchtime, the kind of bar where there are more teeth in the ashtrays than there are in the patrons' heads. Order a draft, tell the bartender you're a college student and on vacation in their fine town, and that you plan to hit every bar within a twenty mile radius. The bartender will always say, "You ought to just stick around here, kid, we've got dollar Bud and pretzels—but if you insist on hopping all over, that's your call. Word of warning, though: don't go into this joint," and then they would name the bar that scared everyone, the kind of bar that never had a name, never had a front door. That was the bar where Eric could find his pigeons.

If he hit the first bar at the right time, though, he often saved himself the trip. Right about four in the afternoon, all the docks and railyards whistled their workers homeward, and a good number of those workers went drinking. The homeless, the whores, and the layabouts knew this, too, and came out to meet the workers, maybe hustle them for a beer or four, maybe offer quitting–time head in the alley.

Every one of those folks, once they got warmed up, had stories about folks at the town's scariest bar. All Eric had to do was play fortune–teller, gather names and a detail or two, and come up with a feasible story. Sometimes he'd come up with a true story, but that didn't matter. If all else failed, he'd wait until someone left the bar, and then call in a DUI complaint. The only thing that counted was a good tip.

Then he sold the story to the cops.

It was a fine art, Eric believed. He said a few things, got a few bucks, maybe sent some asshole to jail. At the very least he entertained the cops, gave them a little bit of purpose.

His very favorite moments on the job were those when, as he walked out the door, he heard an officer repeating Eric's words over his radio.

*   *   *

Partial Transcript of WRYY 90.2, Savannah, Georgia, USA
Broadcast [FCC Air Verify] b2359.09.08.2001 e0300.10.08.2001
Eric Fordbin hosting Clifford Wheeler

Host: Well, I'm back, but—oh, he came back too, speak of the devil!

Wheeler: My ears are burning, are they, Mr. Fordbin?

Host: That's my job. Cliff, my intention was to discuss a variety of groups who incorporated stuff from movies and books into their own lives as religion. I'm sure your own beliefs are [pause] important to you, but let's talk about something a little less Cliff-centric. Let's talk about—

Wheeler: You have it backwards. The Necronomicon—

Host: The Necronomicon is fiction. My guest today is Cliff Wheeler, who won't quit talking about The Necronomicon. We were going to talk about people who worship superheroes, people who watch George Lucas films and construct religious creeds and figures, but it looks like we're just going to talk about the Mad Arab. The fictional Mad Arab.

Wheeler: Look, you asked me here to discuss this. You aren't discussing anything. You are attacking me. The Necronomicon is fictional to some extent, but what you don't understand is that it is based on fact. On fact! Terms have been changed, invocations have been changed, histories and descriptions have been changed, but the genesis is fact. Look at Greek myth, for instance. The Kraken. Think about the Kraken. Spawn of an Elder god. Look at Hebrew lore: the cherubim. These are many–limbed fire beings from another dimension. Have you heard of Lilith? Or Lilith's daughter, a column of flame from the waist down? Look at Kali.

Host: All of those examples are folklore! Myth! Legend! Religious figures whose descriptions are metaphors! You can't possibly claim that a work of sensationalist pulp fiction must be based on fact because it contains elements that also appeared in ancient fiction.

Wheeler: I can claim that, yes.

Host: You're listening to the Burning Man on WRYY 90.2, and my guest is

Fire Breathing

Cliff Wheeler, who uses a distinctly circular logic to support his worship of wiggly imaginary beasties.

Wheeler: [expletive] you.

Host: Oh, nice. Real nice. The delay is down, folks, and I do apologize, and dear, dear, beloved FCC, please don't fine us.

Wheeler: [Unintelligible.]

Host: Shut up, Cliff. I'm serious, you nutball, cut that out or I'm going to pull your mic.

Wheeler: [Unintelligible.]

Host: All right, gang, our guest has proven beyond a shadow of a doubt that he's either totally bonkers, or a juvenile pain in the ass.

Off Mic, Wheeler: [Unintelligible. Pause. Expletive. Pause. Laughter. Unintelligible, approx. 6 seconds. Laughter.]

Off Mic, Host: Shut up!

Host: We're gonna pause now for station ID and some commercials and music while I sedate our guest and see him out.

✳ ✳ ✳

Eric stared at Wheeler for a long moment, hypnotized by the cadences of his guttural, somewhat moist incantations. Wheeler finished, then, closing his final alien syllable by swallowing it with a glottal click. Eric began to giggle.

"Nice job, man. You sounded like a complete loony. I didn't get it at first. Thought you were serious."

"Think," said Wheeler, "where radio goes. Think about your voice, the words you say, the songs you play. My voice. On the air. Through the airwaves. This is vibratory energy, invisible but effective. Sound travels invisibly but the waves can touch you. They can make you sick, you've felt deep bass pressing against your organs, right? They can make you bleed, make you cry. Give you orgasms. They touch flesh and influence it. Imagine, then, what they do to ether. Imagine what sound waves can do to things that are themselves intangible but influential."

Eric glanced behind him to make absolutely sure that the On Air sign was not lit.

Wheeler pulled a cigarette lighter from his pocket. "Here. Light this. Can

you raise the levels on the booth monitors without redlining the board?"
Eric nodded.

"Okay. This song, what is this, 'Firestarter?' It's got good bass. Hold the lighter in front of the monitor's subwoofer—which one do I slide? Got it," said Wheeler, answering himself though his voice was lost in the sudden increase of volume. He looked pointedly at Eric's hand and Eric watched too as the bass snuffed out the little orange flame. He felt the sound moving the hairs on his hand as if the song were exhaling across his skin.

"So," said Wheeler, lowering the monitors to normal levels again, "do you know what fire is? What flame itself is? It's not solid, either. It's energy and the expenditure of energy, both a cause and a result, real and unreal. It's intangible but visible. The effects of sound can be visible, as you can see. Sounds themselves must be tangible to be heard, and that result can be applied to other energies, with noticeable results."

Eric rolled his eyes and stood up, tossing the lighter into Wheeler's lap. "Yeah, energy. Science. I'll play some Dolby for you, pally. You can listen in your car. Thanks for stopping by, yadda yadda, get on out."

Wheeler's smile was broad and relaxed. He pocketed the lighter, slapped his knees, and rose. "Mr. Fordbin, I thank you again for having me on your broadcast. Enjoy your evening. I'll see myself out."

The call light strobed, silently notifying Eric that he had a phone call. He answered as the door fell shut behind Wheeler.

"I heard you howl last night," said the caller. "The sky crawls again. Enjoy." The soft-voiced man hung up.

Eric set the phone back in the cradle, his smile wry. *Goofballs*, he thought. *All of 'em. That's my audience. Hurray.*

He cued up a Taiko disk and grabbed his cigarettes and his radio. He plugged the earbud into his ear and listened to the drums as he crossed the street to Forsyth Park, empty at this hour. One of the houses at the perimeter contained, he assumed, the man who had called him. Savannah is a compact city.

The lights unfurled above him, green spun glass. Eric stared up at them, jogged through the grassy parade grounds, and, in the center, collapsed to sprawl and fill his eyes with the sky.

He pounded the heels of his hands against the earth in time with the drumming. He writhed his hips, following the undulations of the dragon lights. He gasped as he found a rhythm in their twining and untwining, and by a trick of imagined perspective, they appeared at times to be ascending, rocketing worms, rather than banners across the sky. Then they would curl and heave like the tentacles of a swimming jellyfish. He shouted at them, once, and he was stunned to see them all twitch, as if he'd startled them. He thought about the frequencies of light and of sound. Could one affect the other? Were the lights dancing to the war drums he had sent out?

Of course not, thought Eric, and the drumming stopped.

Fire Breathing

Dead air.

Then the lights came down.

They darkened as they fell, from green to cobalt to a sickening swamp brown. Eric lay spread–eagled on the grass, so awed that he could not move, could not scramble away as he thought he should, so he lay as if he had been sketched onto the earth in flesh.

One of the muddy, luminous streaks lashed him from sternum to skull. Another fell like a guillotine across his throat, chilling his chin. A third, fat and foul, lit his tongue with tangible, lumpen irradiance. Bulbous and sharp, the third corkscrewed against his palate and siphoned his screams. Then, elastic, it withdrew with the others, darkening to void–black as the mass ascended and disappeared.

Eric was unable to differentiate between rapture and agony. The light had wrung him, turned him inside–out. He felt pressure in his skull as if his brain were steaming. When he managed to draw a breath, the air pulled across his vocal cords in ragged harmonics, a multiple hum in the thick of his throat, vibratory and ticklish. He felt as if his throat were gilled, his larynx ruffled like the fungal fringes of a mushroom's cap.

He barked out part of a sob, the afterbirth of his silent scream, and the sound made his eardrums itch. The noise had its own discordant attendant sounds, little minor hums and a foul undertone, like that of a Scottish chanter, but more grating. The sound Eric made had satellites and echoes, and he caught his throat in his hands, his fingers tangling in the headphone cords, and gripped himself to stifle any further moans.

Eric lay on the grass and scanned the star field. *To hell with dead air*, he thought.

The air was not entirely dead.

The tower had picked up another station's signal and was, faintly, rebroadcasting it. Eric focused on the distant sound, imagining that he reached into the headphones to retrieve these vague frequencies from deep space, and hoped that he could fix his attention on the song well enough to distract himself from the fluttering multiplicity of each breath.

He strained to hear, and then to identify the song. He heard thuds and squeals, perhaps drums and flutes. Ignoring his own breath, he tried to pick out the rhythm in the music, struggled to sort the maddening beats into some recognizable pace. Beneath the twisted etch of the sour–toned flutes, the drum beats faltered, accelerated, one moment almost tripping, another approaching ponderous—but never quite achieving anything. This was a song of fibrillation and idiot wheedling cries, halfhearted squalls and diseased percussion. It was no song at all, this minor threat of deep–space noise. Eric thought of water torture and spastic ventricles, of soggy bagpipes dropped and lungs punctured.

The voice that came through the headphones then scared Eric so badly that his own heart banged and stuttered in his chest.

"Dead air—heavy, isn't it? So vast. Can air truly be dead? Or is it just *deep* air?"

DJ Mister Bitterness thrust his voice into Eric's head, superceding the distant anti–song. Bitterness, in a particularly obnoxious mood—pissed that Eric had walked out on his shift, likely—spindled an Arab on Radar album; for one confused moment, Eric thought that he could finally clearly hear the earlier sounds.

Imagination, Eric thought. *Sensory deprivation after the overload of that fucking light show. Sound of my own breath, my own heartbeat. My own breath*—he inhaled, exhaled, and still felt the odd hall of mirrors in his throat, still heard the extra rancid harmonics.

Asthma, he thought. *Taxing my voice on the radio, inhaling some shit in the air from the Florida fires. Just great, just great.*

Eric pressed his palms into the loam, shoved himself upright, and went home for the night.

✳   ✳   ✳

"I can't do the show, Jake," Eric said. "I don't know how many times I have to tell you this. Can't you hear my voice? My throat's ripped to hell. Damn wildfires ate me alive. I sound like a goddamn kazoo."

"You sound fine to me. This is all in your head. I need you in here in twenty minutes." Jake hung up the phone as Eric protested in at least three tones of voice.

✳   ✳   ✳

Eric started his set, as usual, with "Time to Burn" by Pennywise. He spun as much as he could without speaking, and even ran the old cart machine, slotting Smokey the Bear carts one after the other.

He had spent the day wrecking his throat as he tried to clear it. He had gargled with Jack Daniels. He had forced himself to cough until he thought he'd sprained something in his throat. Eric had hawked and retched, swallowed warm salt water, and throttled himself. He had stood before his mirror, aimed his flashlight down his throat, and peered between his own jaws, hoping to see something that would explain the feeling, and the sounds. He had smoked cigarettes and let the smoke find its own way up from his lungs, let it seep out and hang in the air, while he inspected the smoke for patterns. Eric had gagged himself with his toothbrush. He had screamed into his pillow. He had, by the end of the afternoon, made himself very tired and very sore, and his voice—most of it—rasped slightly. But when he spoke, there were some extra tones, ticklish eddies of sound, that rang clear.

At the station, while playing "Burn it to the Ground" by the Candy Snatchers, he checked the internet. Yes, the smoke from the Florida fires could exacerbate allergies and asthma. No, such things did not seem to cause fractured voices. He did find information about harmonic–overtone singing, multi–tonal voice manipulation used in meditation by Tibetan monks.

Eric raced to the WRYY catalogue room and thumbed first through the World Music section, then the New Age section, until he found the disc he sought: chants performed by the Gyuto monks.

He slotted the disc into the cue unit and listened.

The monks' chanting was thick and chilling; it raised the hairs on Eric's wrists. But their voices sounded as if they were speaking through long cardboard tubes. Eric's voice sounded as if his throat were the tube through which many sounds came at once: the residual twang of a taut wire just snapped, the burr of heavy wood dragged across asphalt, the sub–bass hum of an overloaded transformer, the hollow supplication of a beggar's crushed Pan flute.

The strobes flashed in the booth. The phone was ringing.

Eric was unsure, after the telephone conversation with Jake, whether or not his voices could be heard by a caller, but the fucking Northern Lights or Florida smoke–bands seemed responsible, and he'd been sent outside by a telephone call.

The strobes flashed again. Eric could hear that each flash was accompanied by a short, very high–pitched tweak of sound. He was getting more sensitive. That, at least, will come in handy, he thought.

"Hello," he said, and fought not to gag on his voice. The depths of his throat still felt frilled.

"The skies," said the caller, "are acrawl."

Eric gripped the phone and leaned into the handset. "Who are you? What do you know about the lights?"

"You were very quiet last night, in the grass."

"Why are you watching me?"

"Beautiful, aren't they?" The caller chuckled.

"I was choking! Quit playing around and tell me what's going on. My voice is screwy now, can't you hear that?"

"You speak. Your words have influence. You are on the radio now. Your voice can reach," the caller paused, and to Eric he sounded as if he might be masturbating, or thinking of something dirty, at least—"over the radio, your voice can reach *the center of the universe.*"

"Wait a minute, pal—are you one of Cliff Wheeler's friends? Hello?" Dial tone.

The lights were in the sky again, as the caller had said. Eric could feel them; he didn't need to see them to know they were there.

The sudden dread that overcame Eric sickened him. The strange caller, the throat infection, the resultant voice—these things were only the vaguest of annoyances to him, then. The lights, the lights were the thing to fear. The lights were out there, shifting and rallying, reflections with mass, and he could sense them. He could almost hear the arrhythmic drumming and splintered piping; at first, for a second, he strained to hear it. Then he shook himself and strained not to. Eric knew for sure and for certain that whatever infested the skies, they sure as hell were not Aurora or skeins of Florida ash. No sir, they were not. They were as insubstantial as air, but as inattentively devastating as a tornado.

Eric found that he was cowering. He didn't care one bit—in fact, he was a bit fascinated that his body had gone animal without his agreement. He was proud of his flesh for knowing enough to hide. He wheezed, and a score of feeble half-tones tagged along with each ragged breath.

Then, relief, a dispersal of pressure, instant and overwhelming. Eric staggered on gelatinous legs to the booth chair, and collapsed into it. The casters shrieked in vibrato as he quaked in the chair.

He made a jerky transition into PIL's "The Order of Death" and all his voices chanted along with the song for a moment, *this is what you want, this is what you get*—and then he dialed Cliff Wheeler's number, and when Wheeler, wide awake at quarter of three in the morning, answered, Eric said, "I think I may need your help."

* * *

Breath: *"Man goes by the name of Ruckus. You had a knifing on the riverfront last week. Ruckus tossed the weapon—it was a box cutter. Is that enough?"*

"I hear you're looking for the key man at the crack house on Waters. Talk to the albino that hangs out at the QuikStop on the next block."

"Twenty past each hour the cook at Hijinks sucks off anybody who hands him ten bucks. He also jerks off into the jello shots and Irish coffees. Yeah, black guy. He's only got one arm but that's all he needs."

"That ATM that got jacked on Lakeside South? Kid named Micah, goes to the high school over there. Wears an old letter sweater, that's his trademark. You can get him for carrying, too—kid's got heat and rock both. He popped the teller for seed money. Venture capital, like. He'll be eighteen in three days—I don't want to tell you how to do your job, sir, but if you hold off, you can get him as an adult."

"Yeah, forty bucks is great, thanks. I do what I can. Word on the street is..."

* * *

They met at a bar, one of Eric's dives. Wheeler had agreed that the likelihood that all the other patrons would be too drunk to eavesdrop made for an ideal setting. Even the bartender, Mama Su, muttered in gravelly Vietnamese and had trouble keeping both of her eyes pointed in the same direction. Eric ordered a pitcher of watery draft and Wheeler ignored it.

"Saw them, did you?" Wheeler leaned back on his side of the booth and smiled indulgently.

"They fucking touched me," Eric said. "Can't you hear it? My voice is fucked."

"Oh, yes, fucked is true."

"So you know about them, I knew you would, I knew it. What are they? Did you conjure them with that fucking nonsense on air the other night?"

Wheeler snorted and waved his slender semolina fingers in the air. "Conjure them? You can't conjure dust, or time, or space. To conjure, you must cause. I could manifest cash, brew you some agony, or bring forth a salamander, sure—but there is no cause for *them*." The occultist thumbed his chin and cast wry eyes on Eric. "I might have said hello to them, though."

"What would that do? Did that do this to me? Did you tell them to chew up my throat, to play that fucking music?"

"You heard the music? My, my. Fucked is true, boyo. Screwed as can be. I'd like to sit in on your next few radio shows, if you'd let me. I'd be very interested to see what may happen."

"What do you think is going to happen?"

"No way of knowing, kid. You can't—"

"Yeah," Eric said, "I know, you can't know about space–dust, whatever. Quit playing with me and tell me what's happened to my fucking voice."

"Your voice has been restrung, it seems. Tuned. The music of the spheres is, they say, mellifluous. As well it should be, this celestial song; the spheres wheel in a measured minuet. But the center of the universe has no path, no steps to follow: it is the crux, an urgent point of stillness. The center of the universe has its own attendant cacophony, you see. And as I understand it, or rather as I've heard it said, only the musicians and their instruments—the players and the played—can hear the song. I also have heard it said that the song is rather unpleasant. Is it? I've never met an instrument before, only read of them." Wheeler leaned forward, crossing his elbows on the formica tabletop, sopping his tweed pseudo–professorial jacket in ash–clotted beer rings.

"You make me sound like an inanimate object," Eric said, scowling.

"As inanimate as a drum or a pipe, yes. You mean nothing to the center of the universe."

"That's nice."

"There's no nice or not–nice about it. You're the one who presented your voice to them, I bet."

"Your crony, the guy who sent me out there in the first place, to see the lights—he said he heard me scream, the first time. If it was a bad thing to do, he should have told me. You assholes knew all along that something bad could happen to me."

Wheeler's bramble–thicket eyebrows rose, and his eyes twinkled. "You were sent to see them? Curiouser and curiouser. I had no idea there might be someone else nearby with any knowledge. Most people who have seen them think they are a byproduct of the fires."

"That's what I thought. Fuck, can you hear my voice? It's in pieces. It's got extras. Do you think all this comes across over the radio? I don't want to sound like a freak."

"Boyo, it absolutely comes across over the radio. Your voice will reach the center of the universe, all right. Don't consider it bad, by any means. Consider it fun. Consider it...air play."

Wheeler placed his palms on the table and shoved himself up. Eric half-rose in protest. "You can't leave like that, you can't just go," he said. Wheeler grinned and kept walking.

"I know," he said. "You want me to pay the tab. Don't worry about it. Remember what I said about conjuring." He waved his flaccid hand around, a little bit at Eric, a little at the barkeep, a little at the bar in general, and walked out of the door.

The jukebox, dead all night, awoke then with "Ring of Fire."

Eric glowered. Son of a bitch had manifested Cash.

* * *

Eric called in sick for his next two shifts. Nights, he felt the lights come, and he cringed on his makeshift pallet while the Mighty Dog whimpered beside him. The Mighty Dog had taken to answering Eric's sounds, woofing and whining even at the odd harmonics of his breath.

When Eric felt the lights, he almost heard the drumming, and could truly not say whether it was his heart, or the darkness.

* * *

On the third day, Thursday, he returned to work. When the phone line strobed, he jumped for the receiver and said, "Yes."

"You aren't speaking," the voice said. "You are just playing music. You have your own music now, and yet you waste it."

"Who are you?" Eric could not yet feel the lights, but knew they would descend at any moment.

"I am a stranger to you."

"Why did you send me outside? Why did you let this happen to me?"

"No reason."

"There has to be a reason," Eric said, his voices wild. He hunched his shoulders and cupped his hands around the mouthpiece. "Did I—were you one of the people—did I give a tip about you?"

"A tip? Like the one I gave to you, the one that put you in their path?" The caller's laugh was harsh.

"Fuck, I did, didn't I. What did I say you did?"

"You're the center of your own universe, it seems. Fitting, you sing your own song. Isn't that what they call people like you, songbirds? Your first concern is what *you* may have said. Enamored with the sound of your own voice, aren't you. You are a perfect instrument: you might keep quiet now, but not for long. You can't hold your tongue."

"I can if I have to," Eric said.

"You don't even pause to apologize for what you *might* have said about me. You don't even ask what I did, you ask what you *told them* I did." The caller's usual urbane pretension was cracking under the heat of his scorn. "I will tell you three things, songbird. The first thing: you've done nothing to me. You never turned me in or fingered me. We don't know one another. Any fear of retribution you feel is your own problem. The second thing: I sent you out there simply to see what would happen. I bear you no malice. You will never believe that, but believe this: they can't be commanded. They can't even be addressed."

Eric readied a complaint but the caller continued, heedless of Eric's audibly-drawn breath. "The third thing: even if you never speak another word again, your very breath, the air you draw, is a broadcast to them. One day," he said, and his voice took on that fevered, hot-and-bothered tone he'd used once before, "one day your breath will bring the servitors of the Center of the Universe, led by Nyarlathotep, to the dance. One day, your breath will bring them, and the world will burn."

"Florida—did I do that?"

"A cigarette did that. Your breath will kindle the fires of Tophet, and none shall hear their own screams or the gnashing of their baking teeth, for the drums will overwhelm all. This world will be devoured by the worm that never died, and consumed by unquenchable fire. You think I'm mad, DJ Heat? Just breathe, my boy, just breathe. Breathe."

The line went dead, and Eric listened to himself breathe, and when the lights rallied a moment later, his voice sang to them as he wept.

✳   ✳   ✳

Eric's breath hummed and the Mighty Dog growled at him. He had called Wheeler and related what he could of the caller's words. Wheeler had chuckled and scoffed.

"He's playing off your ego, boyo. They come, they go. If they come here, they come here. If they leave fire in their wake, so be it."

"But you said I was an instrument. If that's true, can't they listen? Wouldn't I be, like, a beacon?"

Wheeler sighed and was quiet for a moment. Then he said, "I'll have to tell you the truth, boyo: your jester friend and I both, we're just guessing. We could each be right, we could each be wrong. There's simply no knowing the unknowable. But don't let it get to you. Don't let it worry you. No matter what, there is a bright side: we should all be mindful of our every breath, and all attend to our words."

✳   ✳   ✳

Shame: this was a new burn, and Eric turned his tongue against himself.

Lies, truth, ego, he thought. Words may reach the center of the universe, but they hadn't struck him yet. If the center was a mindless monster, what, then, was Eric himself?

Eric pitied himself, loathed himself and screamed for all to hear it, but mostly so he could hear his own anguish. And when he heard the clotted howls and hair-raising basso hums that rode his scream, he yelled to expel them, and thought he must be breathing fire.

* * *

"Not pretty," said the blonde man. "We did a full tox scan three times and came up dry—I've seen stuff like this with meth, but never clean. Flip side of that is that there was no trace of psych dosage, either, which might explain it. Family history is riddled with mental illness. A good number of them were institutionalized."

"What did he do to himself? My god." The intern strove to walk a fine line between professional and available.

"Wrecked his throat. Stabbed himself straight-on with scissors, then opened them and tried to stir the insides. He managed to clip his esophagus and do pretty severe damage to his carotid. Brain went hungry for some time. We patched him up, but we didn't get to him in time. Kid's in a vegetative state as it stands, and I anticipate that we'll list him as persistent eventually. Autonomic functions are regular and secure, but he does run a hot fever every night. Get used to him; he'll be here for a long, long time."

"No living will, nothing like that?" the intern asked.

"His only living relative is unfit to make such decisions. She's been in a ward for fifteen years now. We're stuck with him. If we'd gotten to him ten minutes earlier, we might have gotten him to wake up someday. Ten minutes later, and we could have harvested his organs."

"So he'll just lay here, then?"

"He'll lay here now, he'll lay here then, and he'll lay here long past then. All we'll ever do is change his drip and keep him breathing."

"He sounds a little weird. Scarring of the larynx?"

"You'll get used to it."

"Poor kid," said the intern. "Burned down to nothing but breath and a heartbeat, no mind at all."

"Ever the optimist, aren't you, kitten," said the doctor, and the intern flashed him a smile. "Your shift ends soon, right?"

"Three, yes. Come with me, we can watch the light show," said the intern.

They murmured to one another and wandered from the ICU.

In the dark room, the instrument that was Eric breathed, his heart pounded, and as the lights wormed across the night, his fever burned.

The *Oxford Companion to English Literature* describes RAMSEY CAMPBELL as "Britain's most respected living horror writer". He has been given more awards than any other writer in the field, including the Grand Master Award of the World Horror Convention, the Lifetime Achievement Award of the Horror Writers Association and the Living Legend Award of the International Horror Guild. Among his novels are *The Face That Must Die*, *Incarnate*, *Midnight Sun*, *The Count of Eleven*, *Silent Children*, *The Darkest Part of the Woods*, *The Overnight*, *Secret Story*, *The Grin of the Dark* and *Thieving Fear*. Forthcoming are *Creatures of the Pool* and *The Seven Days of Cain*. His collections include *Waking Nightmares*, *Alone with the Horrors*, *Ghosts and Grisly Things* and *Told by the Dead*, and his non-fiction is collected as *Ramsey Campbell, Probably*. His novels *The Nameless* and *Pact of the Fathers* have been filmed in Spain. His regular columns appear in *Prism*, *All Hallows*, *Dead Reckonings* and *Video Watchdog*. He is the President of the British Fantasy Society and of the Society of Fantastic Films.

Ramsey Campbell lives on Merseyside with his wife Jenny. His pleasures include classical music, good food and wine, and whatever's in that pipe. His web site is at www.ramseycampbell.com.

The Other Names

by Ramsey Campbell

They were past the top of Brichester and nearly at the twisted house when Arnold started. "What's the sign say, Sylly? What's it say?"

"It says BEWARE OF KILLER DOG," Bruce suggested, raising his fists as he did whenever he spoke.

"No, it says TRESPASSERS. WILL. BE. CASTARATED," Denzil said, pointing the fattest finger of his right hand at each bunch of marks on the signboard.

"Shut up, you. And you and all. I'll tell you what it says," Arnold said, and rubbed his scalp as if to conjure hair out of the grey shaved skin. "It says SYLLY'S TURN NOW WE'VE ALL BEEN IN OR HE'S A WIMP."

"Don't call me that," Sylvester told him. "It doesn't, either."

"Go on then." Arnold shoved his blotchy face and broken eleven-year-old nose at him. "You say what it says."

A wind blustered down from the dark Cotswold hills and tried to find its way under Sylvester's leather jacket. While he didn't shiver, everything around the abandoned house did: the tall scrawny trees like charred bones hanging from the black sky, the knee-high grass and shrivelled weeds that sprawled over the cracked mossy path beyond the fallen gate, the segments of rotted fence leaning away from one another on top of the crumbling wall. Even the board shook as though impatient, but the marks on it conveyed no more to him. "It says JUST AN OLD HOUSE WITH NOTHING IN," he muttered.

If that was true, it hadn't been. He remembered the items the others had brought back to show they'd gone all the way in. Bruce had run out carrying a mask that couldn't have been meant to be worn, since it had only one eye-hole and far too big a grinning face—he'd run so fast that he'd dropped it to smash on the path. Denzil had found a bowl that seemed to have been used to grow fungus in, but when he'd felt underneath it he'd thought it was somebody's skull cut in half down the middle and had thrown it over the fence. And Arnold had returned with a screw-topped jar so grimy it had been impossible to tell whether its contents were a little hand or a spider with not enough legs, particularly once he'd tipped it out and they had all trampled on it when it had appeared to try to crawl away. Perhaps Arnold was recalling this as he said into

Sylvester's face "If there's nothing in it, why aren't you going?"

"Give us the light and I will."

Arnold handed him the club of a flashlight so readily that Sylvester demanded "Have you messed with it?"

"You'll find out," Arnold said in a tone that left him no other choice.

Sylvester poked the beam of Bruce's stolen flashlight through the gateway with dried-up rasping weeds for gates. The light found the mouldering front of the house, but that was as far as it reached. Six windows showed him darkness which appeared to go back farther than it should. The way the pairs of windows shrank as they went higher was not the only reason why he saw the house tilting backwards, tipping the unhinged front door into the dark. As he and the others had swaggered along the lane with no other houses in it he'd seen how the rear of the building was at least a foot lower than the front, and twisted to the left as though it was trying to drag the rest of the house with it. Now that the wind was holding its breath he saw that all the grass and weeds leaned towards the house, suggesting that it was stronger than sunlight. He fancied that the path was sloping downwards underfoot, though his eyes told him otherwise. He slashed at weeds with the flashlight and wished he could feel like an explorer in the jungle as the dark beyond the windows lurched at him.

It was only a house that was falling down, and it wasn't going to fall on him. The owner who'd died in it while it was starting to collapse had just been a crazy old man who used to shout and sing at night in a language nobody could understand. No wonder the people who lived nearest had told stories about him when he'd kept wakening them at all hours—how on the night he died they'd heard a voice joining in with his, and then the old man trying to shout it down, maybe because it had been much bigger than his and had seemed not to need to breathe, until his voice had come apart as if the other one had been tearing him open. Could his mouth really have been wider than the hands with which he'd tried to shut it? Only the police who had found him would know. Sylvester was a very few steps from the house now, yet the flashlight was making no appreciable difference to the dark beyond the fallen door. "Don't come out till you've got something," Arnold called along the path, so that Sylvester couldn't hesitate for being watched, even though the doorstep seemed to tilt slyly inwards as he trod on it and aimed the flashlight beam into the house.

At first the light slid over the darkness, which only gradually admitted to containing walls and bare floorboards and, when he raised the beam, the lofty ceiling of a hall. Every surface was as black as the sky between the stars. Although doors were open in both walls, the darkness of the openings was virtually indistinguishable from the walls themselves. "There's nothing left down there," Bruce advised from the safety of the pavement. "You'll have to go up."

Sylvester showed him a vicious finger and stepped over the skewed door, and felt himself being tilted down into the house. Perhaps it was the way the light seemed unable to keep hold of the surfaces of the interior—crept over

The Other Names

them even when he gripped the flashlight with both hands—that made him feel in danger of sliding all the way down the hall, past a fallen chandelier like a translucent stranded deep-sea creature, to the point where the house was most warped. A spasm of panic sent him onto the stairs which the darkness to his left had abruptly produced. At least their angles caught more of the light than the hall did. He'd go as far as the first window from which he would be visible, and then the others would have to admit he'd ventured farther than they had.

The creak of each stair echoed into the distance, enlarging the darkness and sounding as though the house was continuing to warp. He had to believe that the black underside of the roof was coming closer only because he was climbing towards it, not lowering itself, but he was beginning to feel as though he was being trapped under a stone with whatever might live there unseen. He was wishing he'd hidden some object in a pocket before leaving home so that he could say he'd found it in the house when all at once there were no more stairs between him and the middle floor.

At least he was able to see outside the house. Beyond a doorway to his left the hole of a window showed him the highest streetlamps of Mercy Hill leading down into Brichester. He took a step towards the room, and was unable to halt. Whatever had taken place in the house had warped this corridor even more steeply than the ground floor, and he seemed to have no option other than to stagger into the room, flailing the air with his fists and the cone of light, unless he wanted to be carried helplessly deeper into the house.

The room was almost bare. A bedstead off which a mattress lolled had been dragged away from the window, leaving deep scratches in the floorboards. The mattress had been torn open, and its dangling innards were unpleasantly suggestive of withered dusty entrails. Protruding from beneath the heap of them as though it had been concealed within the mattress was a book whose covers were as black as the inside of the house. His sense of how useless a book would be to him was so overwhelming that he almost forgot he could take it to show. He ran across the room, pursued by footsteps that must be his, and grabbing the book by a corner, snatched it out of the clinging mass. The cover fell open, and he saw the first page.

Except the book, which was bound like a real one but had lines ruled on its pages, didn't just fall open. It twisted in his hand, and he had an impression of its warping exactly as the house had, a notion which overwhelmed him so powerfully he thought he felt his mind change shape. Before he could grasp the impression it vanished, and the book was straightened out. It was just a book, yet he couldn't take his eyes off it, and nothing else mattered. He could read the page.

Charles Horus, his book so long as he shall live. Copied under the protection of Nyarlathotep, Stalker in the Shadows. Written from memory of the Necronomicon, British Museum, 1985-1995...

Each shakily handwritten word in the midst of the shrinking island of light seemed to be forming itself especially for him. He squatted to turn the page, then considered perching on the edge of the bedstead, at which point his awareness of his surroundings returned to him. That didn't cow him, not when he suddenly had so much more of a mind. He ran to the window and saw the three boys throwing chunks of the wall at streetlamps, having lost interest in watching for him. He'd show them a prize that was worth all of theirs, one they wouldn't believe until he proved it. Hugging the book with both arms, he bore it from the room.

The tilted corridor didn't bother him. He only had to walk uphill to the stairs, and he did. The stairs themselves were worse—as he clattered down them he had a sense of climbing towards the secretive darkness beneath the roof, and grabbing the banister was like trying to hold onto a dead eel—but by telling himself he was on his way out he managed to keep going. His heels struck the canted floor of the hall at last. Three upward strides took him past the torn–off door and onto the path, whose roughness prevented him from sliding back. He was almost at the gateway before the others saw him.

Denzil pointed so wildly that Sylvester thought there was something at his back until he realised the subject of the gesture was himself. "Look at him," Denzil scoffed, and when he'd finished laughing at that: "Look what he's got."

Bruce told the joke a different way. "Sylly's got a book."

"Let's see it," Arnold demanded as if the sight of it wasn't convincing enough.

Sylvester thrust the flashlight into his hand before opening the middle of the book. "It's only wrote in," Bruce complained.

Denzil gave the pages twice as much of a look while he dragged his finger along the air in front of them. "Isn't even a diary," he decided as soon as he could.

"Give us a look, I said." Arnold shoved the flashlight under his arm and slammed his hands on top of Sylvester's on the edges of the book. When Sylvester refused to let go, Arnold wrested the book towards the light of a surviving streetlamp. "Thought so," he said. "It's just mad stuff. Let's tear it up."

"Don't." Sylvester backed away, taking the book with him, and could have imagined he felt it helping him, nudging its edges into his grip like a creature settling into its lair. "I found it. I want to keep it. It's mine."

"Reckon he's going to try and make out he can read."

"Bet his dad'll give him a kicking if he does," Bruce exulted.

"Couldn't even read that sign," said Denzil.

Sylvester closed the book and clutched it to himself, and looked at the signboard above the fence. "Well, I can," he said as the letters instantly fitted themselves to his mind. "It says BUILDING PLOT FOR SALE."

"He's guessing," said Arnold, then glared at the others. "Or somebody told him."

"I never," Bruce said, shaking his fists at the idea.

"Wasn't me," protested Denzil.

Sylvester wished he hadn't revealed his new ability until he'd seen what he could do by hiding it. "Wasn't any of you," he said, "but I'm not saying who."

"See, I told you someone did," said Arnold, and considered punching him in the face, but contented himself with leading a fresh bout of derision. "Let's do something down the hill," he said at last and strutted off, pausing only to shatter the undamaged lamp.

Sylvester looked back from the slope. The twisted house was sinking out of view beyond the crest of the hill, as if it was collapsing for want of a support he'd taken away with him. He had little time to reflect on this, because once they'd marched down the steeply terraced street he was too busy trying to outdo the others in causing a row outside the hospital, playing the railings with a bit of someone's fence and yelling the worst words he knew. He couldn't let on that he knew the sign said PLEASE BE QUIET NEAR HOSPITAL. Soon a guard with a truncheon that whooped through the air chased the boys down past the graveyard, and Sylvester glimpsed a few of the inscriptions on the stones. He would have liked to read more until he grasped how the reduction of lives to hyphenated dates affected him. Shortly, however, he and his companions were in central Brichester, and there was much to read.

The pedestrianised streets were plates of neon, and the night crowds were out—children sharing bottles they'd persuaded someone to buy or to sell them, young couples pretending they could afford everything they wanted, people buying commodities in doorways, gangs in search of a pub and a fight—but all Sylvester could see were signs. LATEST FASHIONS. 20 KING SIZE. INSTANT PRIZES. SHOPLIFTERS WILL BE PROSECUTED. BEER OF THE MONTH. ALL DAMAGE MUST BE PAID FOR. EVERYTHING HALF PRICE OR LESS. 24 HOUR SECURITY. ADULT BOOKS...In particular his understanding that the sign he'd always thought said SHOP in nearly every window was SALE came as a revelation, yet the more he deciphered, the more he seemed to sense the yearning of the book in his embrace to be read. When his companions began looking for burglar alarms to set off or better still, that were already triggered so that the boys could break in, he said "I have to go now."

"He's going home to read," shouted Denzil, jabbing the book with his favourite finger.

"Going to show his book to his dad," Bruce crowed between his fists.

"Hide it from him, more like," Arnold said, and lowered his head in case it was required for butting.

Sylvester hurried to the bus station full of sleeping people being woken up by guards. A bus not much larger than his father's van was about to leave for Lower Brichester. It smelled at the very least of booze and tobacco, but he hardly noticed once he turned to the book. Perhaps it was the lurch of the bus as it raced to overtake one from a different company which made the book open itself.

Daoloth is truth. Before the eyes and minds of men shrank from all about them and within themselves was Daoloth. Daoloth knows all names and is all names, and all names are Its name. All things within the universe, and all which are beyond and so are part thereof, must yield their true names to the power of

Daoloth. He who utters the name of Daoloth shall hear Its voice in all things and so learn their names. As those names are called in Its name, so must those called shed the cloak which men have draped about them and reveal their veritable aspect in Daoloth...

Though Sylvester couldn't have paraphrased any of this, he felt it settling into the depths of himself. He seemed hardly to have started reading when he grew aware that he was about to be carried past his stop. Ordinarily he would have seen how far he could travel beyond his fare before he was thrown off, but now he wanted to give himself up to the miracle of reading. He depressed the bell until the infuriated driver stopped the bus and came for him, at which point Sylvester dodged around him to haul on the lever that released the doors and sprint into the nearest back alley which led home.

His father's van, which he saw at last said BENNY BENTLEY BUILDER, was parked mostly on the pavement in front of the house, and casting its shadow across the sliver of a garden as though to cover up some of the work his father had done—the yellow paint outlines too large for the windows, the plastic gutter sagging from the roof, the cracked pebbledash. The bespectacled old woman who always complained about any children in sight was dragging her wheezing tartan–lagged dog out of the house opposite. "Don't you be looking at me, Sylvester Bentley," she said at once, "or I'll set him on you."

Sylvester turned away without speaking, which gave her a reason to start an extended complaint, and let himself into the house. He was hoping to sneak upstairs now that the front door didn't stick, since his father had been at too much of it with a plane. Besides, in the front room he could hear a video making the kinds of noises his parents sometimes emitted when they thought he was asleep. He was halfway up the stairs, and just had time to sit on the book, when his father came out glowering and stuffing his shirt into his jeans. "Where've you been? How long have you been hanging round there?"

"He's not been pinching," Sylvester's mother called or groaned.

"You heard your ma. Have you?"

"I've just been with Arn and them."

"I hope you didn't let them take advantage of you," his invisible mother said.

"You want to get yourself some decent mates." Having dealt with that, his father withdrew. "Don't come in here," he said, and slammed the door.

Sylvester might have listened outside if he hadn't been eager to return to his book. He ran up the stairs, above which the highest of a trio of plaster ducks had begun an inadvertent nose–dive, and into his room, where he set the book down on the bed while he leafed through his computer manual. Although he could read it at last, it told him nothing he hadn't been shown at school. He threw it on top of the bookcase stuffed with computer games and sat down with the book from the twisted house.

It skewed itself open at the page he'd read. He went through the sentences again and felt them slither between his thoughts. Perhaps he wouldn't understand them until he had obeyed them. He carried the book to the window and stared along the concertinaed terrace, and had an inkling of how long the book had occupied him when he saw the old woman already dragging her dog homeward from its lavatorial quest. "Miss Whittle," he whispered, and added what the book seemed to want him to say. "Day oh loth."

The dog insisted on halting at the streetlamp closest to home, and the old woman saw Sylvester. He almost flinched back as she raised her face into the white glare of the lamp, but she couldn't know what he'd done when he didn't know himself. Despite the promise of the book, he didn't quite hear a voice, unless that included the one in his head. It was more as though he glimpsed, or had a memory of glimpsing, shapes that were hidden by Miss Whittle and her dog—that were hiding either behind or within them or, somehow, both. However nearly indefinable it was, the glimpse suggested words to him, words that would help him see it.

"Old Bones That Crawl," he said like answering at school. "Day oh loth says."

The dog lowered its leg, and the old woman's spectacles aimed the glare at Sylvester's window as if her eyes had grown white and blind before she and the dog waddled up their path. It seemed to him that a bit of the world had twisted in the instant he'd ceased to speak. He wasn't sure that he wanted to see the outcome, but he watched while Miss Whittle appeared to have some trouble with wielding her key in her door. As the dog yanked her into the unlit house the door swung closed, so that Sylvester couldn't be certain whether he saw her fall or be pulled to all fours, and her spectacles fly off. Perhaps it was only the darkness that made her seem to shrink. He observed how the house remained dark, and listened until he began to nod, which put him in danger of dropping the book. He slid it under his quilt for safety while he prepared to join it in bed.

Sleep was unwilling to come near him. Whenever he drifted towards it he was pulled up short by a fear of talking in it, not that he was aware of ever having done so. The possibility that he might change things without knowing, or of dreaming he had only to find it was true, unnerved him. When at last he slept he dreamed of going to the window to shout "Old Bones That Crawl." He watched Miss Whittle's door falter open, and a crouched shape begin to grope into the light before he managed to awaken. He had to venture to the window to confirm her door was shut and her house dark, at which point he realised that he hadn't heard the wheezy yapping of the dog since they'd vanished into her house.

In bed again, he was awakened by his mother's morning screech. "What do you think you're up to, Sylvester?" He thought she'd found him out until she added "Never mind trying to be late for school." While he was in the bathroom she shouted upstairs three times that his breakfast was going cold, though he knew it wouldn't be on the table yet, and when he stumbled downstairs she kept telling him not to eat so fast or he would make himself ill. His father confined himself to saying to do as she said. No wonder Sylvester was glad to leave the house, though not for school. Nevertheless he headed for it, to confirm what he already knew.

The narrow streets lined with failed trees were full of second-hand cars and people to go with them, and puddles doubling both. All the activity around him was infinitely less meaningful than the words of the book in his bed. Opposite the school he hid in the bus shelter, or rather under it since its glass sides had been smashed. He saw some of his classmates being led into the schoolyard by their parents, and expelling the noises they were supposed to try not to make in class: Kevin sounding like a seal, Jimmy like a megaphone forgetting how to talk. Their special teacher was representing order in the yard, and greeted them in his tone of telling a joke at which nobody was expected to laugh. "And how are we this inclement day?" Mr Westle said, and Sylvester saw the joke was on the teacher—felt as though the words he had read in his book were sharing this secret with him. By including himself with the people he addressed Mr Westle meant to appear sympathetic, but in truth there wasn't much to choose between their minds and his, which was smaller than his head. Before Sylvester could be noticed he turned away from the school and all its Mr Westles for ever. He wanted to be where he could read as much as he liked without having to explain his ability.

The central library was one of the largest buildings in Brichester, and so heavy with books it needed six pillars to hold up its front. Once he'd climbed the wide steps and passed beyond the giant doors, he felt as he imagined you were supposed to feel in church. Everybody kept their voices down, yet the murmurs rose to have their own mysterious conversations under the dome where the sun was starting to appear. He walked beneath the echoes of his footsteps to the History section and pulled an armful of thick volumes off a shelf to set down gently on a table. At last he was going to learn what books had to offer.

Those he'd selected were histories of the world, and they didn't detain him for long. He had a go at the Religion shelves, then went to Science, his reading of which only affected him the same way. The more he read, the more he knew that the secret which the book from the twisted house had lodged in his brain rendered every other book untrue. Books were lies the world told about itself, he saw, and went to the window in case the spectacle beyond it might seem more real.

Groups of people were crossing the pedestrianised street from every direction. Their only function appeared to be to form meaningless patterns, just as the rain drying on the pavement had to. He watched until a librarian tapped him on the shoulder. "Shouldn't you be at school, son? If you don't want to read, you're distracting folk who are, and we'll have to ask you to make yourself scarce."

"I'm not doing anything," Sylvester said to her fat reflection infested by the herd.

"Then go and do your nothing somewhere else like a good boy before I have to call security."

She was trying to patronise him into insignificance, but he knew whom to call to demonstrate his power. "Daoloth says," he muttered, and trailed off before words for her had time to suggest themselves; he wasn't certain that he wanted all the readers to see what would happen then, especially if he got the blame. He shouldered his way through her heavy perfume, which he couldn't help thinking was meant to disguise her true nature that he had almost revealed, and let the clamour of his footsteps crowd him out. He was trying to escape the words he'd muttered, but they came with him.

They paced him as he wandered home. They lurked behind everyone he met and everything he passed, so that all this seemed to be trying to hold onto its appearance for fear that by completing his sentence he would change it into its true self. "Faces that slide over the earth…cells that store the night…hands that swarm…eyes worming in the earth…leaves that suck the dead…windows of the buried…rotting brains…" He had no idea where all this came from; he was afraid that simply thinking it might cause it to emerge from the concealment of itself. Once he was home he could read his book, which perhaps would calm his thoughts down. But as he returned to his street he couldn't avoid realising that he'd spent the day so far in staying clear of seeing what he might have done to the old woman.

He shut the front door and fled to his room. His father was out damaging somebody's property with a view to mending it, and his mother had gone to call Bingo for the afternoon, leaving a premonitory smell of her stew which never tasted as good as that promise. He could do what he wanted, but he discovered that wasn't reading the book while he didn't know how the old woman had lived up to his words. He stood at his window and gazed at her silent darkening house.

The sight focused his sense of a presence hidden by the world, and he no longer felt urged to finish his sentence; in her case, after all, he already had. He was prompting himself to call her when people began to appear in the street, mothers wheeling babies home or rather couples that looked like that and then, as the streetlamps produced their flutter, older children walking. Sylvester had become preoccupied with the gathering of darkness in the old woman's house when he saw his mother at the end of the street. He retreated and sat on the bed, clutching his book, but all too soon she and his father summoned him down for dinner. He hadn't taken a mouthful from the plate that had been laden to await him when the questions began with his father pointing a fork at him. "Good day at school?"

"Fair."

That was usually sufficient, and Sylvester tried to say it in his habitual manner, but his father persisted in staring at him. Sylvester would have been grateful to his mother for interrupting except for her question. "Have you seen Miss Whittle today?"

"Who," Sylvester blurted, "me?"

"Why, what's up with her?" his father said.

Sylvester fed himself a mouthful of stew while he braced himself for the reply. "That's what I want to know," his mother said, however. "She wasn't in her seat at the Bingo where she always is."

"Maybe the kids have scared her off the streets at last."

"So long as it wasn't you, Sylvester."

"It wouldn't be him, would it? He's not capable of anything."

That sounded as patronising as the librarian had, and Sylvester was keeping his mouth full so as to be unable to disprove the statement when his mother said "When we've finished I'll go over and see how she is."

Sylvester almost emptied the tasteless mouthful outward before he could swallow. "No," he spluttered. "I mean, she's gone away to stay. I heard."

"What did you hear?"

"Heard her saying to some friend of hers about going away for a week. When I was going to school. And," he gabbled once the necessity occurred to him, "taking her dog."

His mother gazed at him for so long he thought his haste had betrayed him. "Peculiar nobody at the Bingo said," she eventually revealed herself to have been thinking. "What's the matter, don't you like my stew any more? It's the same stew you've always had."

That aggravated his sudden fear of how the food might taste if he even thought of words for it. "I'm a bit sick," he wailed.

"Maybe he'd better go up and lie down," his father said.

"He can have it tomorrow if you don't finish it."

Sylvester didn't know which of them that was intended to threaten, but managed to stifle the idea of food as he hurried to his room—to his window. The house in the midst of the terrace opposite was unlit, and seemed to be holding itself still in anticipation of his voice. He eased the wobbly sash up and poked his head out to survey the deserted street, and drew a breath which tasted of the chilly night, and spoke. "Daoloth says you have to come out now, Old Bones That Crawl."

In the white glare of the streetlamp the door of the house resembled the entrance to a tomb—a marble entrance which he realised he was dreading to see opened from within. When it appeared to shift, he thought that was because his eyes were nervous. Then the glare slid off the door as it faltered ajar, revealing darkness and a dim shape that was hunched within it.

Just as he guessed that the door was moving awkwardly because its opener was, the tenant of the house sidled into the pitiless light, and Sylvester saw its difficulty in managing so many limbs. It raised its face, or more accurately the front of its head, towards him, and he ground his elbows against the windowsill as if the pain could anchor him in the world whose reality he used to take for granted. Then the misshapen figure robbed of flesh crouched even lower, veiling its head with the material that sprouted from it, and scuttled into the concealment of the garden wall. The hedge between the wall and the house quivered, and Sylvester understood that the thing had writhed through.

He wanted to see where it went and what it did. It couldn't touch him or come closer than he liked if he told it Daoloth said not to; in any case, it seemed anxious to conceal itself from view. He leaned on the sash to lower it and rubbed his bruised elbows; then, pausing only to hide the book in his bed and grab a jacket, he tiptoed quickly downstairs. He might as well not have bothered with stealth, since as he reached the hall his mother turned from pegging her rubber gloves above the gargling kitchen sink. "Where do you think you're going?"

"Out."

"I can see that all by myself. I thought you were meant to be ill."

"I'm better," Sylvester said, and felt it—no longer needing to eat, filled up and energised by the words from the book.

"Your mother still wants to know where you're going," his father said, draping a dish-towel next to the gloves.

"To see—" Sylvester was suddenly afraid that if he didn't escape at once he would give in to the temptation to release himself by using his secret on his parents, not least because their banality felt like a weight they were loading onto his head. "To see Arn and them," he blurted.

"Just you make sure you're back by ten. By half past nine." As Sylvester sprinted for freedom, having agreed to both of her stipulations, he heard her say rather defensively "Fresh air ought to do him good if anything will."

Sylvester dashed across the whitened glaring road and slammed the door of Miss Whittle's house before anyone could wonder why it was open. His haste was such that only then did he think to peer at the hedge, beneath which he made out a dim twisted shape. By straining his eyes he was able to distinguish that it was a tangle of roots and branches which looked not unlike the object he was searching for. He raised his eyes to the rest of the blocks of stained marble foliage dividing the cramped gardens, and saw the farthest hedge shudder as though with loathing of whatever had just crawled through it. "I see you," he cried, and ran to the corner.

Fewer houses were occupied in the cross street, which was even narrower than his. Some of the windows had been walled up, and quite a number of the cars parked on the pavement between the destroyed streetlamps looked abandoned. All the same, the street wasn't as deserted as Sylvester would have wished. He was watching hedges twitch and creak one after the other along the left side of the road when the three boys emerged jostling and yelling from Bruce's house on the right. They saw Sylvester, but not the surreptitious activity that had passed beyond them. "Look who it isn't," Denzil shouted.

"It isn't Sylly," Bruce agreed, and looked to Arnold to top his wit, which Arnold did: "It's Building Plot For Sale."

"Read us something if you're not Sylly," Bruce yelled, raising his fists while he scowled around him in search of an appropriate task for Sylvester.

"Read us that," said Denzil, jabbing a finger at the plaque on the wall at the alley entrance halfway down the street.

"You heard, let's see you read it," Arnold said and rubbed his scalp as if to increase its baldness.

Sylvester was tired of skulking inside himself and besides, he needed to distract them from the movements that had nearly reached the alley. "It says DOMESTIC ACCESS ONLY and NO CYCLING OR TIPPING."

"Does not," Denzil scoffed, then jerked his finger along the first line of the plaque across the street, and frowned hard. "Doesn't, does it?"

"If it does someone told him," Bruce said, readying his fists for the culprit.

"This time you just tell us who did," Arnold warned Sylvester, and led the advance towards him.

Sylvester glimpsed movement in the nearer of the gardens bordering the alley—a shape that clambered rapidly over the low wall between the garden and its neighbour and huddled in the shadows, awaiting its chance. "Nobody," he said. "I read it myself."

By the time the others had done jeering at him they were around him, so that he could smell their sweat and their breaths. Arnold took hold of his left upper arm and began to roll the flesh and muscles of it in his grip. "Thinks we're stupid."

"Stupid like him," said Denzil, and poked him in the chest.

"Must be stupid to think that," Bruce said, and was in the process of selecting which area of him to punch first when there was a clatter in the alley, and a dustbin fell out, spilling its meagre contents. "Hey," Bruce threatened, spinning round so fast that he almost punched Arnold.

"Cat," said Denzil, though his finger seemed less sure of it.

"Dog," Arnold said without looking, and intensified his treatment of Sylvester's arm.

Sylvester kept his gaze on the passage leading to the dark between the back yards. "Wasn't either."

"Who says?" Arnold demanded, and when that produced no response, pinched Sylvester's muscle. "What was it then, eh, Sylly?"

"Ow. Something you'd be scared of."

"Me, right." Arnold let go in order to rub his scalp, kindling the glower in his eyes. "Like you were scared to go in the house up the hill. You'll be dead before you see me scared."

"Go on then, go and look."

"Right, so you can get away." Arnold grabbed his arm again, but only while he said "You two hold him and I'll look. And tell him he'd better be scared of me when I come back."

"You'd better be scared," said Bruce, having seized Sylvester's bruised arm, and dug his knuckles into it. Denzil contented himself with digging Sylvester in various ribs. The boy succeeded in ignoring the discomfort, which after all would soon be over. He watched as Arnold stalked into the passage and stared both ways into the dark at the end. "Can't see a thing," Arnold declared.

It would try to hide from him unless it was called, Sylvester realised. "Daoloth says go to him, Old Bones That Crawl."

Denzil pointed violently at him. "What'd he say?"

"Sounded like he was telling something something," Bruce said, and shoved his face at Sylvester. Before he could enact the proffered butt, Arnold disappeared into the alley. "Hang on, there's..."

Sylvester couldn't quite contain a grin. Denzil stared at it, then at the entrance to the alley. "What's he done?" he muttered, and raised his voice. "Arn, wait. He—"

Arnold's response, or at least the noise he uttered, cut him off. It sounded as though Arnold was trying to scream while being sick. Deeply satisfying though Sylvester found it, he couldn't have it attracting attention. "Daoloth says you're not Arn now," he murmured. "Daoloth says you're Scalp For A Face."

He felt the world twist a little more, and his mind too. Arnold's noise ceased instantly as if a gag had been applied to its source. Denzil was at the mouth of the passage, having shouted to Arnold that he was coming. He wavered there and glanced back furiously at the other boys, and fished in the air for them with his finger as he dared another step. It was time, thought Sylvester, to continue what he'd started. "Daoloth says stop being Denzil, Worms For Bones."

He didn't see the result—he was busy dodging a punch Bruce threw at him—but Bruce did. His face clenched like a fist, then opened to release a howl as Bruce fled along the street, waving his splayed fingers to ward off everything around him. Sylvester let him almost reach the crossroads before addressing him. "Daoloth says goodbye to Bruce and hello to Living Inside Out."

He had to look away at once, and to turn his back as he heard the new thing flounder through the shadows of the walls to join its companions. The sounds they made in the alley, blundering and slithering and slopping about, were enough for now, in fact rather too much before long. "Daoloth says go to the house on the hill where the book was," he called. "Daoloth says not to let anyone see you and when you get there go under the floor."

He was able to bear the ungainly confusion of their retreat. Quite soon with distance they sounded more like insects than anything else remotely familiar, and then they were gone. He'd done enough for one night. Tomorrow he would go to the twisted house and call them out and have some fun. As he turned homeward, it occurred to him that he mightn't live there for much longer. Perhaps soon he would know, and call himself by, his name.

DAVID ANNANDALE did his MA on the Marquis de Sade at the University of Manitoba, and his PhD on horror fiction and film at the University of Alberta. His novels (published by Turnstone Press) are a thriller series featuring rogue warrior Jen Blaylock. They are *Crown Fire*, *Kornukopia* and (coming soon) *The Valedictorians*. His short stories have appeared in numerous anthologies of horror fiction, including *The Asylum, Volume 2: The Violent Ward*, and *Wild Things Live There: The Best of Northern Frights*. He teaches literature and film at the University of Manitoba, writes film reviews for Videoscope and upcomingdiscs.com, and is working on a book about video games. His life has been complete since *The Flesh Eaters* was released on DVD.

Final Draft

by David Annandale

The first sight of the cathedral was like a blow to the chest. Working his way through the twisting, confined streets of Archenburg, Stonefield hadn't caught more than a fragmented glimpse of the monster. Outside the town's deep valley, the church was invisible. Even as he descended into Archenburg's bowl, he never got the whole thing, never the full impact. But then he broke free of the labyrinth's embrace, stepped into the Domplatz, and the building, leviathan, reared up and pounced.

The size was crushing. Stonefield stumbled, dizzy. Black stone, twisted into a mass of needles and stalagmites, clawed for the sky, and very nearly reached it. Saints, gargoyles, angels and demons danced darkly or writhed, impaled. The stained glass window above the main door was fifty metres across. From outside it looked like an eye, dimmed by cataracts.

Stonefield walked across the square, feeling the shadow of the cathedral push him into the ground. It took a conscious effort to keep his neck muscles from tensing up. He trotted to one of the small side doors and shoved his way in.

Cold, damp dark pressed itself around him. He stopped and waited for his eyes to adjust. When he looked up, the ceiling was so far away it was almost invisible. How high were the vaults again? The priest's letter had said one hundred and thirteen metres, right? Right. Incredible. Ab–so–lute–ly incredible. Gothic architecture's best kept secret was also its biggest. You could have placed Notre–Dame inside and had room to spare.

"Professor Stonefield?"

Stonefield jumped. Eaten like a fly by the size of the cathedral, he hadn't seen or heard the priest approach. "Uh yes...Yes."

The other man smiled and held out his hand. "Dieter Neumann," he said. He was praying mantis thin. Stonefield placed him in his early sixties, but the skin was so tight on bones so narrow it was hard to tell.

"Pleased to meet you, Father." The handshake was dry as bundled twigs.

"The pleasure's mine." His English was impeccable, and he spoke with a flat, neutral accent that carried only a faint aftertaste of his mother tongue. "I greatly admired your book."

"Oh, you've read it, have you?" Stonefield asked, pleased.

Neumann nodded. "*Applications of the Thurston–Bellarian Test to Architecture* was on the curriculum of a course I attended in America last year."

"Really." He hadn't expected that. "And did you find it as boring to read as it was to write?"

Neumann laughed. "Hardly. I was particularly impressed by the foundation of the test. You pay a lot of attention to detail, and the amount of evidence you sifted through…Well, let me just say that that is the reason you were invited here. If anyone is qualified to date this cathedral, you are."

"I'm very flattered. I–"

Deep in the cathedral's interior, something clanged, cutting him off.

"Ah," said Neumann, smiling. "The other project. Come and see."

They started down the central aisle. An angel stood on the high base of each pillar, eyes blind, hands fearfully clutching sword. The rows of pews seemed to stretch for kilometres, hypnotizing Stonefield with patterns. An ornate altar stood at the transept crossing.

"This August, Archenburg celebrates its millennium," Neumann explained. "The city council, in its infinite generosity, no doubt enabled by some unexpected largesse at the national level, has provided some funds for a bit of sprucing up. And the diocese thought it would be nice to get the cathedral's date of…birth, if you will, straight once and for all."

They stopped at the altar. Stonefield felt himself being overwhelmed again by the cathedral's immensity. He was standing at the intersection of vastness, floating in space while stone was too high and too far away.

"Here's one of our problems," said Neumann. "Your department, Professor." He pointed down, at a large worn paving stone. MCCCXXVIII, it whispered.

Stonefield bent down to get a better look at it. Sounds about right, he thought. Well, that was easy. Short work, easy job. Nice trip, though. "I don't see that this is a problem," he said. "I wouldn't want to date construction too much earlier than that." He looked up at the priest, feeling a little disappointed. Maybe a touch annoyed? Maybe.

"We thought so too," said Neumann. "Unfortunately, that is a tombstone."

Stonefield stood up. "What?"

"We recently discovered that this marks where a bishop was buried in 1328, not the erection of the cathedral."

Stonefield grinned. This was *much* better. "Intriguing," he said.

"I'm glad you think so," said Neumann, and he moved on.

He stopped again in the rear chapel. Stonefield still couldn't get over the size of the place. The chapel was large enough to be a baroque church.

The priest pointed up. Scaffolding climbed to the half–dome of the chapel's ceiling, where workers swarmed over an immense painting. It showed God's right hand pointing to a configuration of stars. Below the stars, the divine left hand held the Earth (medieval version). The glittering spires of Paradise smiled in the bottom half of the painting, and, below this, silver letters praised God in the Highest in equally High Latin. The grime of centuries of candle smoke dirtied and hid the piece. It was drab in the dim light.

"Forecast of the Second Coming?" Stonefield asked.

"We believe so." Neumann turned around. "James Riley is the man in charge here." He pointed to a bear of a man working near the stars. "We're hoping to have this work restored, funds permitting. Or, at the very least, cleaned. It's this particular cathedral's showcase."

"A lot of work," Stonefield commented. It looked dangerous too. The scaffolding opened onto some very big drops.

"When do you think you can begin, Professor?" Neumann asked.

"Early tomorrow morning."

"Good. Can I show you the record vaults at that time? I have a service in a few minutes."

"Of course. Don't let me keep you."

"Thank you. I'll meet you in the vestry tomorrow, then."

Stonefield wandered back to the exit. Once outside, he realized that he'd been hunching over slightly all the time he'd been in the cathedral. He rotated his sore shoulders. Get used to this, he told himself. It's only a building.

At the other end of the square was a small newsagent's. It was just closing up. A rack of postcards stood on the sidewalk by the entrance. Stonefield stopped and spun the rack, looking at the cards. They had turned blue with age. Not much of a tourist trade. Which again struck Stonefield as odd. He'd have thought that something this big would have landed the town three stars in the Michelin guide. Yet he'd never heard of the place until the parish had contacted him. And that was another thing: why was the cathedral in the hands of a mere priest? Why did Archenburg seem to be an administrative island unto itself? It was as if the Church Fathers had quarantined the town. Even locating Archenburg on the map had been a challenge. It had taken him almost an hour of peering cross–eyed before he'd spotted the barely discernible *A'burg* smudged on a crease. And even then, even knowing where to drive, even knowing which unmarked turn–off to take, the town had been a surprise as sudden as a crater, a stark drop in the middle of the Black Forest.

He looked at the cathedral again. Even from across the square, he felt as though he were standing too close to a toppling mountain. He began to guess why the tourists had stayed away, why the town hid as though in shame. The cathedral was purely and simply *too* big. It looked down from on high, judged, and found you wanting. It condemned. It punished. It was not the sort of sensation one would seek out. The traveller did not like arriving at the far destination, only to be told to despair.

Stonefield shrugged. Relax. Yes, the place was a bit much. Yes, it was a bit oppressive. But he was still going to enjoy this. The challenge was worth it.

He turned his back on the cathedral (enough for one day) and wandered through the streets, looking for a restaurant that fit his budget. He wasn't sure he would find one, what with the strength of the deutschemark. And Archenburg's eating places were few and far between. But find one he did, and the food was good, and the service was friendly, and they understood his pig–German. He walked back to his hotel confident in the knowledge that God was in His Heaven, all was well with the world, and they just didn't make pastries like that in Toronto.

He let himself into his room around nine, and had only been there five minutes when one of the hotel employees banged on the door. It took a few moments before Stonefield understood that he was wanted on the phone. He almost knocked the teenager over as he ran downstairs to the front desk.

Rose, he thought, and when the manager smiled and handed him the phone he turned to look at a wall so the man couldn't see his face because

hisscracklepop "Alan?" *fizzzz*

yes it was

"Rose. Hi. God you can't imagine— I— It's good to hear you." How lame. Satellite delay. "It's good to hear you too. How are you doing?"

"Missing you. Where are you phoning from?"

"Sidney." The "s" sounded like radio static. "Airport. And don't ask me what time it is. I don't know anything anymore. I love jet lag, I really do."

"When are you getting to Easter Island?"

"The plane's leaving tomorrow morning, whenever that is. And our boat's waiting for us there."

"The seismometers still acting up?" he asked into a sudden burst of aural lightning.

"Sorry, what was that?"

He repeated.

"Last I checked, yeah. If this keeps up we're going to have to do some serious re–evaluating of plate tectonics. Listen, what's new at your end? The church interesting?"

"Rose, I wish you were here to see it. It's incredible. It's immense. It's way bigger than it has any right to be. And older too, looks like."

Another burst. Rose: "What?"

He tried again, but the static just got worse. What the hell was wrong with the lines? When the noise dropped for moment, Rose spoke quickly. "I'll call you! I'll write you! I miss you! I love you!"

"Me too!" he shouted, but the sound boomed and the line went dead. "Bye," he whispered to the receiver. The honeymoon not even a month in the past, the two of them at opposite ends of the Earth, and he really didn't think wanting the phones to work was asking too much. He sighed.

Stonefield turned and handed the phone back to the manager. The man was still smiling. Stonefield gave him a smile too, plastic and fake. Then he went upstairs to bed.

*   *   *

A clanging uproar greeted Stonefield as he stepped into the cathedral the next morning. Riley and crew at it with a vengeance. Sound bounced and ricocheted and turned itself inside out around him as he walked to the vestry. He had to knock on the office door twice before it was opened. Neumann nodded a greeting, friendly but deafened, and led him to the transept crossing. A stairway by the west side of the altar's dais led down to the crypt.

The muffling effect of the stone was so sudden that Stonefield's ears popped. He put his laptop down and rubbed at them. "Interesting acoustics you have here," he said.

The priest rolled his eyes. "I hope Mr. Riley's work won't always be this loud."

The crypt was small and cramped. Too small, just as everything else about the building was too big. It was maybe ten metres on a side, and the ceiling breathed against Stonefield's hair. Neumann had to stoop.

"I wanted to show you this," said Neumann. He moved to the north wall of the crypt and touched its centre. Stonefield came closer and saw that one of the stones had markings on it. He crouched and peered at the faded engraving. An unpleasant buzz spread from his fingers, up his arms, to the back of his neck.

"As you can imagine, we don't know quite what to make of this," said Neumann.

"*1023?!*" Stonefield exploded. He looked up at Neumann. "No. Unh–unh. Out of the question. St. Denis was the first gothic cathedral, and work on it didn't begin until 1140. This can't possibly mean what you think it does." He stood up.

"I understand your skepticism, Professor. We had our doubts too, believe me. We've had this examined very thoroughly, and we did find some papers that shed some light on this engraving. You're right. That year does not mark the construction of the cathedral." He spread his hands. "We wouldn't be needing your help if it did."

Stonefield said nothing, nodded, and waited for Neumann to go on.

"It marks this house's reconsecration."

Stonefield blinked, and the world was suddenly very slippery. The buzz started again, this time spreading over his entire body. He broke out in gooseflesh.

"It gives one pause," said Neumann.

Oh, it gives one pause all right. Good call on that one, Father. Just what I was going to say. Stonefield grunted, still trying to gather up his scattered words. This couldn't be right.

"I showed you this," said Neumann, "so that you would be prepared for some rather unexpected findings when you start your work."

"Bracing me, as it were."

"As it were."

Stonefield took a deep breath and held it until he felt sure that yes, reality was still there. He crouched back down and looked at the inscription again. He traced it with his fingers. For a moment he thought the stone was frozen, it was so cold. Then he realized that it was because of a faint, tiny breath of a frigid breeze that was coming from the wall. He looked for the source, and found that the date was not carved into the wall itself but was on what appeared to be a stone plaque. There was a hairline crack between the plaque and the wall. The draft came from there.

"Would you like to see the archives now?" Neumann asked.

"Yes, thanks." Yes, Stonefield thought he would like to see the archives. Get back to his specialty in all its dusty anality. This little mystery could wait until he had the rational and empirical gears well oiled and rolling again. Neumann floated back up the crypt stairs. Stonefield followed.

He was surprised, actually, that the archives weren't in the crypt. He got worried when he saw that Neumann was heading for the door leading to the east tower. And it was full-out dismay he felt when the priest stopped at the entrance and looked apologetic.

"Oh no," said Stonefield.

"Yes, I'm afraid so. There are two large storage spaces, one near the top of each tower. Not the most logical place, I admit."

No, Stonefield thought. Not logical at all. Though by the terms the cathedral seemed to be setting, he supposed he should have expected it. The building specialized in the absurd. "I don't suppose there's an elevator," he said.

Neumann shook his head. "No electricity at all beyond ground level." He produced a large flashlight from his robes. "You'll need this."

Stonefield took the flashlight and stared at it as if it could offer an easier way of going about this. It couldn't.

"Would it be all right if I left you to examine the archives on your own?" Neumann asked. "I try to avoid the climb as much as I can and..." His look was almost pleading.

"No, that's fine," Stonefield lied. "I'll manage."

"Thank you. Just take the stairs, and you'll reach the archives. You can't go wrong. I wish I could suggest which one to start with, but..." A shrug.

Stonefield nodded. Better get this over with. He opened the door and started up the stairs.

It was an hour and two rest periods before he reached the midpoint of the first tower. He had felt horribly claustrophobic as the stairs wound up

and wound up

and wound up

and wound up

forever and ever world without end amen in the cramped dark. Reaching the arched windows here felt like being born. He lay down on the cold floor and rested again. Then the second half, just as high but with half the energy, up up up, up past the frowning bells, up into the tapering spire, up up up, round round round.

Final Draft

When he finally reached the archive, nestled just below the roof, all he wanted to do was sleep. But here he was, and it was time to work. Even though the tower was at its narrowest here, the room was still huge. One little window was all there was for light, and that wasn't much. All it showed was the front line of stacks, taller than a man, and then it gave up. Stonefield glanced through the window, gazed down four hundred and fifteen metres of sheer stone at an Archenburg that was now a web of cracks and dots, and decided not to look again. He faced the papers, turned his flashlight on, and waded in.

The archaeology of paperwork. Nothing was simple, nothing was easy. It was fair to guess that the older manuscripts would be buried far from the entrance to the room, but there was no guarantee. Things got moved around during the centuries. And filing had clearly never been a concern here. Archaeology: dig, dust off, compare to known quantities, take a guess. Very little had been dated with posterity in mind. Stonefield had to examine the language, the state of the Latin, the style of writing, contemporary references (if any). When he found something he couldn't be sure about, he would feed the characteristics into his laptop. He had a multi–gigabyte database loaded up, which would search for a match with a confirmed item from elsewhere. Science, the wonders of. But it still took time. It was still difficult. And up here, in the dark, in the dust, it was that much harder. The further Stonefield dug down and back into the stacks, moving from paper to parchment, the more he felt he was burrowing into the earth, and that he would be buried alive by a toppling stack. No one would miss him, and he would lie here undisturbed until the next archaeologist came along. Perhaps he had a predecessor that he would find under the next pile.

He found no body, and no stack fell, and he made progress. Slow progress and small, but progress. By the end of the day, batteries going dim in both flashlight and computer, he had established beyond a shadow of a doubt that the cathedral was built before 1597. Now wasn't that grand? And then, of course, he had to go all the way back down those stairs.

In the swirling grey of the evening, Stonefield used his last spark of life to drag himself back to his room.

* * *

The second day, he did it again.

* * *

The third day, he did it *again*.

* * *

The fourth day, he did it AGAIN.

* * *

And so to the fifth day, where the pattern continued, and his body was screaming *no no no*, but his mind kept him going because he just couldn't believe how *old* this place was turning out to be. And that little prickle of nervousness was there, getting ever so slightly stronger.

It got worse in the afternoon. Stonefield spent the morning in the crypt with the computer. James Riley caught him after lunch, as he headed for the tower. "Got a minute?" Riley asked.

"Sure." Stonefield was surprised. It was the first Riley had spoken to him other than to toss off start–of–the–day, end–of–the–day greetings. The cathedral had segregated them as well as their tasks. Stonefield understood what he saw in Riley's gaze though. He saw the look of one outsider reaching out to the other. And deeper than that: he saw incomprehension sensing a fellow.

"Want to show you something." Riley led the way to the chapel.

"How's the restoration going?" Stonefield asked as they walked.

Riley shrugged. "That's what I want to show you. And your project?"

"Only just hitting the Middle Ages."

"No short cuts, I take it."

"I wish."

They reached the chapel. Stonefield noticed that the work seemed more subdued than usual. A lot of Riley's crew were looking at the painting but not touching it. The others were tentative in their movements. "Something wrong?" Stonefield asked.

"Come and see." Riley started up the scaffolding. Great, Stonefield thought, more climbing. He sighed, but followed. If his heart didn't give out, he was going wind up with legs you could smash bricks on. But not yet. His limbs howled with every step.

Once at the top, the painting lost almost all of its remaining colour. This close, it was a study in grime. One section, however, had already been cleaned. And it gleamed. Riley brought Stonefield over to it. It was part of the star configuration.

"Look at this," Riley whispered. "Just look at this."

The stars were not a painting. They were patterns in the very stone of the building. Black sky, white spheres, tiny details, but it was all rock, not paint. Stonefield glanced at the finger that pointed at the stars. To his relief, it was flaking. Still, though. He turned to Riley. "What the hell?"

Riley shook his head. "I don't know. I'm really bothered, though. Maybe I'm overreacting, but I can't help it. This is creepy."

"Yes," said Stonefield. The tingle was back.

And later that day, he found evidence that took the cathedral back to the tenth century.

* * *

Day thirteen, and the mail arrived. Little notes from Rose, kept until a supply plane came by and collected outgoing messages. Stonefield sat in the crypt, which, by virtue of having a light bulb, had become his office when he wasn't clambering about the heights.

The Twilight Zone
August 10
Dear Alan,
Hey hey, here we are, in Sunny Nowhere, south–southwest of Easter Island (wish you were here). And this is great, indeed it is. A thousand kilometres at least from the nearest fault line or tectonic ridge, and what's this? Why, it's enough seismic activity shake–rattle–and–rolling to wake the dead.
Your wife's excited, believe it.
I love it.
More tomorrow, no rest for the wicked.
XXOX
Rose
PS. That was fun the night before you left. Let's do it again.

Yes it was, Stonefield thought. Yes, let's. He put the letter down on the floor of the crypt and turned to the next. The discarded paper rasped slightly against the stone, pushed by the draft from the plaque.

The Outer Limits
August 11
Dear Alan,
Sorry these missives are so tiny, but things are really hopping around here.
OK, are you ready for the Big News? We've definitely got a new island coming up here. How does that grab ya? It's grabbed us but good. I was born too late to catch Surtsey but hot damn I'm making up for it now.
More tomorrow.
Love,
Rose

August 12
Dear Alan,
More Big News. Biggest yet.
This is not *a new island that's coming up.*
It's almost scary.
Oh hell. I'm having trouble with words here, so I'll let the Polaroid speak for itself. Keep an eye on the news!
Miss you,
Rose

He looked at the picture. The nasty, crawling buzzing he'd felt the first day in the crypt returned, and something cold grinned at his back. The Polaroid showed the upper bit of a tower rising from the ocean. It was black, slimed with green. It was intricately carved, but was too far away for any of the detail to show. There was no indication of scale. Even so, Stonefield knew that this thing was in the same league as the cathedral. The convolutions of the tower suggested the movement of worms, and he was glad that the photograph hadn't been taken from any closer.

After a moment, he realized that the cold he felt wasn't in his mind. He turned around and stared at the plaque. Even from here, halfway across the crypt, he could feel its breeze. His swallow was dry.

Upstairs, something crashed. Big and heavy and loud enough to be heard through the stone. Stonefield ran up from the crypt and raced to the entrance of the chapel, where he saw snow.

Black snow.

Or no, not snow, but a swarm of dead flies swirling and blowing and falling, obscuring everything, dancing on a wind that wasn't there. And again, no, not flies. (Men shouting and swearing, someone crying.) Ashes? No. Now blue and pink mixing in the black, the cyclone twirl of...paint? Paint.

With a tired sigh, it began to settle. Lethargic, splintered soot, it dropped to the floor. Two minutes, and the air was clear again. Stonefield stepped into the chapel.

Riley and his crew stood stunned, half-heartedly brushing the paint off. Those on the scaffolding were climbing down in slow, shaky movements. One man had fallen during the storm, and was lying at the base of some collapsed framework, moaning over his broken arm. Stonefield looked at Riley, then followed his horrified gaze up.

The original tableau, the vision in stone that the paint had concealed for so long, leered down at them. It was very similar in design to its camouflage, but in content it was nightmares away. The hand that pointed at the stars was clawed and dark green. The fist that gripped the Earth was squeezing the planet, making it bleed. The city that had cast down Paradise was a mass of twisted, writhing monuments and towers. Their angles were wrong. The geometry of the city was so warped that Stonefield's eyes jumped from it to the inscription. The writing was no longer Latin. That it was writing was the one thing Stonefield could say. That, and the fact that he didn't want to look at it.

He realized that he was still holding Rose's Polaroid. Caught in the undertow, he looked down at the picture, and then (thinking *no*, but lacking choice) back up at the ceiling. And yes, the building was there too. Now he couldn't turn away.

He was still looking up, watching the city in spite of the way its shapes hammered at his skull, watching in case it moved, or something with two tongues spoke the inscription, when someone grabbed him by the shoulder. He jumped. It was Riley.

"What?" Stonefield asked.

"We're clearing out," said Riley. "Are you coming?"

Stonefield looked around and saw that they were alone in the chapel. He could hear voices echo–fading into the distance. "Now? You're leaving now?"

"Yes. Now. We don't need this. Do you want a lift?"

Stonefield looked at the chaos of metal and paint about them, then back at Riley.

"Yes, we're leaving it as is. Neumann and friends can clean it up if they want to, but we're getting out."

Stonefield continued to stare at him.

Riley shrugged. "Okay. Right, I'm a coward. I'll admit it. I'm scared. And I'm not stupid. Now, are you coming?"

Stonefield shook his head. "I can't."

Riley's eyes bugged. "Why the hell not?"

"Because my wife…" The word, still a novelty in his mouth, now felt like a bereavement. "My wife is there." He held up the photograph.

Riley's face twitched when he saw the picture. He didn't say anything. He just turned and ran from the chapel, bumping into Neumann, who was standing by the entrance. The priest looked as though his world had been raped.

"Because your wife is there," Neumann repeated, stepping forward.

Stonefield nodded. "I have to make this place tell me what it knows."

"Can I help?"

Oh yes. He very likely could. "Help me dig," Stonefield said.

✳   ✳   ✳

Archaeology of the last resort. Climbing the towers, each trip longer than the last, each trip darker than the last, the sky lower, the stairs more unforgiving, and the cathedral older. Day fourteen, fifteen, sixteen, back and back and back through history, an immensity of architecture turning from an impossibility into an obscenity. Day seventeen, day eighteen, Stonefield and Neumann under the gun, a deadline looming, coming up from the seabed, and the cathedral still ageing. Stonefield no longer thinking of the building as a church. The centuries of Christendom shrinking away, and the cathedral's lifeline still stretching out, no end in sight, through time. And the presence of the building itself, its hostility, its knowledge, its gameplaying, more and more obvious, one disguise after another being shed.

And then day nineteen.

Premonition.

Sixth sense.

All aboard for the end of the line.

Stonefield knew that it was coming up, and if he wanted to know the secrets, it was now or never, and so he climbed, CLIMBED the towers as though they were only minor obstacles. Neumann seemed to sense the final ticks of the clock too, and needed no urging, though his health was clearly failing. Pouched eyes, sagging grey face, thinning, bluing lips, but he didn't appear to care. He was a man who knew that he was going to die, and asked only that he be told why.

Around ten in the evening, the cathedral's age finally crossed the border that separated anachronism from menace. And it did so in a great leap. In the east tower, still far from the back of the storage chamber, Stonefield found some animal hide. No writing on it, but drawings. More sophisticated than the Lascaux paintings, but not by much. One of the drawings was of the cathedral. No mistake and there we go. Christ not due on the scene for a few thousand years, but the gothic beast of prey already there, reading and waiting.

Cold and numb, bracing himself against something worse to come, Stonefield left the archive and started down the stairs. He had to find Neumann in the other tower and show what he had found. And so down the steps, his first time doing it at night. He felt as though he were climbing down the interior of a snake. He could feel the thicker density of the blackness. It smothered the old and frail beam of his flashlight. It lapped at his heels.

He made it to the gallery and started to cross to the west tower. He was cushioned by shock, moving on autopilot, but still feeling a thread of anger, still wanting to know more. He didn't need to know the cathedral's age now. He was sure that Christianity wasn't the only thing it predated. So what did he want?

He wanted the building's secrets. The ones darker than age.

But what more could the cathedral tell him?

It could tell him what was behind that plaque.

Then he made the mistake of looking at the night sky. And he saw a pattern of stars, directly above, a pattern he had never noticed before, a pattern that was the same as on the ceiling of the chapel. He stared, feeling the last grains of the hourglass drop away, and Neumann screamed.

The shriek sailed out of the west tower, and was swallowed by the smiles of the night. Stonefield dropped the animal hide and ran to the tower's entrance. "Neumann!" he called. He thought, for a moment, that he heard something on the staircase above, but whatever had made that noise was not the priest. He was about to step in and go up, try to help. But he didn't. A cold stone dropped into the pit of his stomach, and a tingling held him back. There would be no one left to help, of course, and the last thing any sane person would do was set foot in that tower.

The blackness of the doorway looked back at him. He turned around and stumbled back to the east tower. Overhead, the sky was too big.

And so he went *down* (he did, he did), he went DOWN (with the breath at his neck). He reached the nave, and the lights were dimming, but he had his torch, so it didn't matter. He ran (past exhaustion, past second wind, into the final stretch of desperation). He ran to the chapel, and dug through the tools left by Riley until he found a crowbar and a heavy mallet. He ran to the crypt, and as he did so, he noticed that the angel statues seemed to be hunching forward, as though stabbed in the back.

In the crypt, his papers were being rifled by the wind. The cold was intense. He went up to the plaque and attacked the crack with the crowbar.

"*Tell me!*" he screamed.

He smashed five times, and then he was able to fit the end of the bar through the crack. He worked at it, pried, and the plaque began to give. It wasn't as hard as he would have thought. The tablet left the wall quite willingly. Oh yes, no doubt it was willing. He banged with the mallet, strained with the crowbar, and the wind picked up to a howl. Stonefield felt the beginnings of frostbite.

Then *crash*, the plaque fell to the floor, and the wind leapt out and screamed at him, gale force, hurricane and beyond, and he fell over.

Defying the wind, he crawled to the hole and shone his flashlight in. Recessed half an arm's length away, ignoring the wind, was a small ceramic cylinder. He reached in and pulled it out. It seemed to be a scroll tube. He looked inside the hole again.

It carried on for several metres, and after that, he had the impression that it opened up into something vast. The black in there suddenly shifted. There was a hint of something that looked like light but wasn't. And then he was running out of the crypt because in another instant the thing in the dark, the thing that was the dark, might see him, and if it saw him, it would kill him.

In the nave, the angels were dead. Their statues lay on the ground, broken. There were new figures on the pedestals. They were all the same. Wings of dragon, head of octopus, and hands coated with the angels' blood. Stonefield, resignation slowing him down, looked more closely at the nearest statue. Yes, he thought, of course. The hands were the same as those on the chapel ceiling.

He closed his eyes for a moment, and when he opened them, all the lights but the one he held had gone out. He walked slowly to the exit. The door wouldn't let him out. He hadn't thought it would.

He sat down in the rearmost pew and smashed the tube open. The sheets of paper were modern. Fresh. He looked at the first one, and when he read "Dear Alan," he moaned.

He read quickly. Rose's handwriting, Rose's words, describing the stately emergence of the island. Her enthusiasm leaking away as the dates at the top of each page drew closer to the present, fear oozing out from between the lines, finally taking over.

The next–to–last letter was dated from the day before.

August 31
Dear Alan,
   I hope you're reading this, because if you are, that means we got some mail off,

which means we finally had some contact with the outside world, which means we got out of this okay.

We should have left sooner. We were so stupid. But we didn't leave and this morning the rest of the island came up so quickly that we're aground.

I hate this place. It shouldn't exist. For as far as I can see are buildings that are too big and whose angles are impossible.

We're staying on the boat. We're too scared to get out and explore.

I want to go home.

I love you. I love you. I love you.

Rose

Stonefield was crying now.

He heard something drip, and he turned his light on the walls. The stonework was melting away, flowing down from the heights to die, having been no more real than the painting in the chapel. The writhing pitch beneath was neither stone nor bone, but their bastard offspring.

He brought the light back to the letters and looked at the last page.

Alan, it said in a scrawl, and that was all.

"*Rose!*" he shrieked, but the echoes said *Rise*, *Rise*, *rise*.

And then something huge whisper–snarled, and what it said was *Strossssssss–k–k–k!* and there was a jerk, and violet light spewed in through windows that were stained, but no longer glass.

Stonefield heard the sound of waves. He stood up and turned around. The massive doors opened for him. He walked, sobbing, to stand on the porch, and know all at last.

Archenburg was gone, but there was snow.

Black snow.

And this time, that was exactly what it was: black snow streaming down from the purple sky. Halfway to the horizon, three long gashes had been torn in the firmament. Blood oozed from them, pouring down in a thick, sluggish cataract to mix with the snow on the heaving sea. The waves crashed against the steps of the church.

Then the god whose images had killed the angels, the god who had hurt the sky, rose up from the dead water, and he dwarfed the cathedral.

The end of the world spread his wings.

KEVIN ROSS has written for the Lovecraftian roleplaying game *Call of Cthulhu* for over two decades, and has been published in over thirty supplements for the game, including *Kingsport: The City in the Mists*, *Escape from Innsmouth*, *Sacraments of Evil*, and *The Dreaming Stone*. He has also published stories and articles in *Made in Goatswood*, *The Anthology With No Name Volume One: A Fist Full o' Dead Guys*, *The Asylum Volume One: The Psycho Ward*, *The Dragon*, *The Unspeakable Oath*, *Crypt of Cthulhu*, and *Cinescape Online*. *Dead But Dreaming* was his first attempt at assembling a fiction anthology, and he hopes it won't be the last.

Afterward
(yes, Afterward)

I'm writing this hoping that more people will actually get a chance to read the book this time. Back in 2002, when the first edition of Dead But Dreaming appeared, DarkTales Publications was in the process of closing its doors just as our poor little book was coming out. As a result, apparently only 75 or so copies of Dead But Dreaming were ever printed (though it seems to me I might have heard 90 copies mentioned at one point). Given that 15 copies were given to the contributors, and I bought a couple extras from the company, that doesn't leave much of a chance for anyone other than the authors of the book to be able to find a copy. Still, I know of quite a few people who bought theirs from Amazon, or Barnes & Noble, or wherever.

And the most gratifying part of assembling Dead But Dreaming -- in addition to working with such fine, gracious, and talented people, of course -- was the response from the few who did manage to snag a copy. We were lucky enough (or good enough) to be cited more than once as probably the best collection of Lovecraft-inspired fiction in the past decade. Given that the competition included books by better-known and more experienced editors, often with more established or well-known writers, I thought that was pretty damn cool. I just wished more people could have had a chance to see the bloody thing.

That situation should change with this new edition of Dead But Dreaming. Doc and I have wanted to reprint this thing for a long time now, but various things kept getting in the way -- mostly my incorrigible laziness. But with Doc running the show at Miskatonic River Press, this time we're gonna do it right.

As I said earlier, one of the best things about putting this book together in the first place was the opportunity to work with such great people. Unlike a lot of Lovecraftian anthologies being produced at the time, we didn't rely on name authors, or even authors known in Lovecraftian small press circles. Names didn't mean anything here -- what mattered was good stories. I'm ridiculously proud of the fact that some of the authors I chose for Dead But Dreaming were relative newcomers who've gone on to publish stories and novels for more prominent presses.

So now you don't have to come up with $200-$350 to get your mitts on a copy of this book. Yes, I've seen several copies go for that much on Ebay, including one just in the past week. Heck, there's some poor bugger on Amazon right now waiting to sell a copy for $300. Hopefully folks will be smart enough to spring for this new edition instead, since it's got some corrections, revised stories, and biographies of all the fine people who contributed. All for a fraction of the price!

I just wish I'd been smart enough to sell one or two of my copies at those crazy Ebay prices. Ah, maybe I'll just save 'em to sell in my dotage. Which I think is coming up in January or so...

Enjoy the tentacles!
Kevin Ross
desolation angel
July, 2008

Order by mail or via the web at:
www.miskatonicriverpress.com

Miskatonic River Press
944 Reynolds Road, Suite 188
Lakeland, Florida 33801

Coming December, 2008
For the Call of Cthulhu Roleplaying Game
Five Frightening Adventures in the World of H.P. Lovecraft

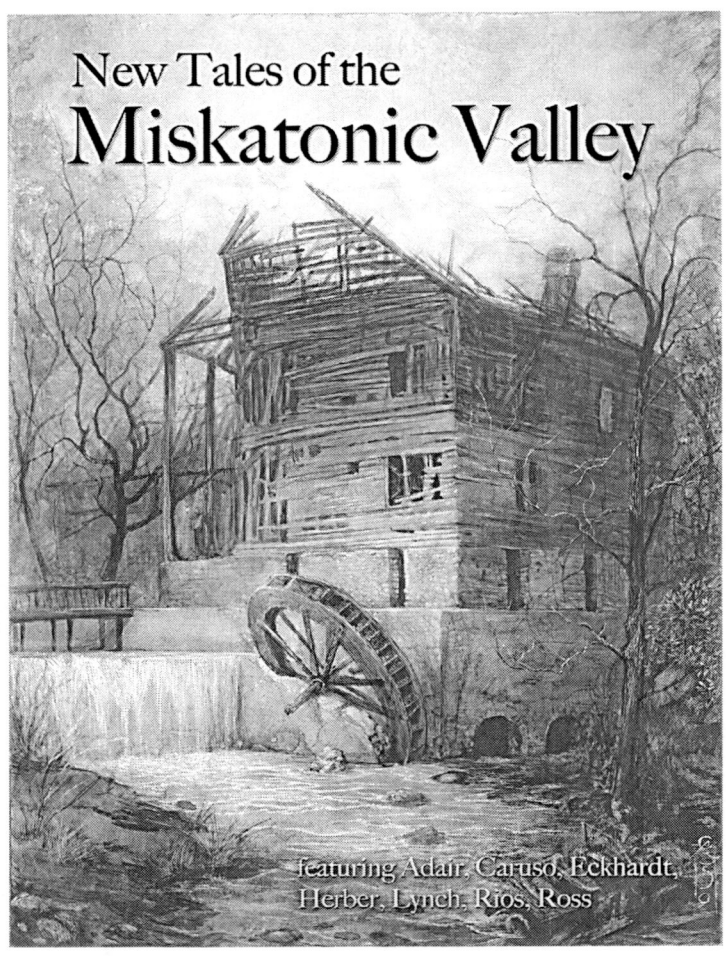

www.miskatonicriverpress.com
www.chaosium.com

Live the Adventure!
Learn More about the Call of Cthulhu roleplaying game at:

www.yog-sothoth.com

The Internet's Number One Site for Call of Cthulhu News and Information

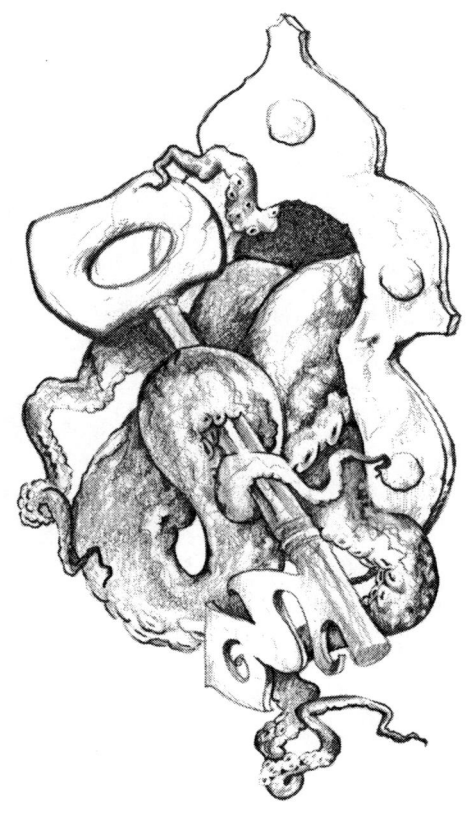

Ten Years of Terror!

Dead But Dreaming was initially printed by DarkTales Publications in April, 2002, using Garamond type on 60# offset white. The cover stock is 10 pt. stock with glossy finish. Cover art, typesetting, and book design by Keith Herber. Reprinted in September, 2008 by Miskatonic River Press.

CPSIA information can be obtained at www.ICGtesting.com
Printed in the USA
LVOW10s1826051113

360106LV00016B/870/P